STARGAZING

Kate Glanville

Published by Accent Press Ltd 2016

ISBN 9781783757398

To my wonderful parents Hugh and Biddy Glanville
who are a constant source of love, support and inspiration.

The black BMW moved slowly up the high street in the early-morning traffic. The driver had wound down the tinted windows so that it was easy to see that his sunglasses were expensive and his linen jacket well cut.

Seren didn't know why she turned to look at the car, or why she noticed the driver, but as she did so the little pot of lavender slipped from her hands and smashed onto the pavement. The car disappeared into the distance while Seren looked down at the earth and shards and broken flowers, and all the memories came flooding back.

Seren

Seren tried to concentrate on the day she'd been planning for months. She tried not to think about the car she'd seen the day before or its driver, and she tried especially hard not to wonder why he had come back after so many years.

She placed the last star on top of the cake – it had taken her a long time to cut them out of fondant with a tiny star-shaped cutter. Each one was brushed with edible gold so that they shimmered and glittered on top of the dark chocolate icing.

She turned the glass stand to check that the ganache was evenly spread and licked a smudge of chocolate from her finger. Finally she placed a single red rose beside the cake and stood back to admire her work.

Seren smiled. The boys at Tremond's Patisserie had offered to make the cake but she'd wanted to do it herself as an extra-special way of thanking her parents for everything they'd done. She took a picture with her phone and sent it to Trevor.

A text came back almost immediately:

Can see we have some serious competition – Edmond says, 'All hail the new sugar-craft queen!!!' xxx

Seren laughed and bent down to check the quiches in the oven. Her hair brushed against her face and she pushed back her wild red curls for the hundredth time that morning. She should have tied it back as she usually did, but at present her hair clip was a vital component in a tee-pee-style den that Griff and the cousins had built in the living room. If it kept them all quiet while she got ready for the party Seren didn't mind getting hair in her eyes.

She turned down the heat on the oven and stood up. Now all she needed were Ben and Suki to arrive with the present and the

1

champagne – then everything would be perfect. Even the sun had come out, chasing away the morning drizzle and giving them the first warm day of spring. She wished that Tom could have been there to enjoy it. He would have wanted to make the day special for her parents just as much as she did.

'I miss you, Tom,' Seren whispered. She thought about the driver of the car. 'I miss you very much.'

Through the open window Seren could see the little group beside the cherry tree, pink blossom forming a ridiculously beautiful backdrop. Anni, baby balanced on one hip, was pouring generous amounts of Chardonnay into the red goblets that Seren had bought specially from the antiques shop on the high street. Anni laughed as Daniel protested at the quantity of wine in his glass, then turned and said something to Nesta; and Nesta laughed and leaned forward to pat Daniel's knee. In the kitchen, Seren smiled.

It was rare to see her mother sitting down. Even though Nesta was leaning back in the canvas chair with a serene expression on her face, Seren knew that she was itching to get up and organise the party herself.

To appearances at least, Daniel looked a little less comfortable in the role of guest of honour. Seren noticed how her father ran his fingers around his shirt collar as though it were too tight, frequently crossing and uncrossing his legs.

Earlier that morning he'd appeared at The Wheat House kitchen door, his silver hair and short beard speckled with rain drops, a bowl of eggs in one hand, a fresh-baked loaf of Nesta's bread in the other. For a while he had leant against the doorframe watching silently as Seren arranged peonies in a vase.

'They look beautiful,' he'd said after a few minutes.

Seren had smiled at him. 'Wasn't it pink peonies that Mum had in her bouquet?'

Daniel didn't answer. Instead he stepped into the room and

said, 'I wish you weren't all making such a fuss.'

Taking the bread and eggs from his hands she'd reached up and kissed his cheek. 'Indulge us, Dad. It's not every day our parents get to celebrate their ruby wedding anniversary.'
Seren looked at the clock; Ben was late as usual. She arranged slices of her mother's bread in a basket and remembered that her father had started to say something else that morning, something he'd said was important. She'd interrupted him, shooing him back to The Windmill, teasing him that he'd better not be wearing his old denim shirt to the party. Now she wondered what it was he'd wanted to say.

'You're so dead, squirt!'

'Not if I kill you first.'

'I'll get you, dill brain.'

The shrill voices shattered the silence of the kitchen and suddenly it seemed as though dozens of children were marauding through the room with an armoury of assorted weapons. The den had obviously lost its appeal. Seren flattened herself against the cupboards to avoid being bulldozed by her three nephews and breathed a sigh of relief as they tumbled through the doorway into the garden and headed for The Windmill on the other side of the lawn.

'Mind Granny's flower beds,' she shouted after them. Too late. The pack leader had taken a short cut straight through an island of burgeoning foliage, flattening a path that the other two followed. Seren looked across at the group beside the cherry tree; Anni was stoically ignoring her boys, topping up the glasses, trying to distract Nesta by handing her the baby.

'Which way did they go, Mum?' the voice had a familiar wheeze.

'Hello gorgeous,' Seren ruffled her son's auburn curls with one hand, the other was already pulling open the dresser drawer and handing him the inhaler.

He took it gratefully and put it to his mouth. Seren looked

3

away, something about the quiet puff of air always pulled at her heart.

'Which way did they go?' he asked again, handing back the plastic pump, gazing up at her with eyes made bigger by thick glasses.

Seren pointed through the open door. 'I think they've gone to Granny and Grandad's house.' Griff immediately took off, through the door and across the grass, swerving to avoid the flowerbed.

'Don't run,' Seren called out after him. 'You'll bring on another attack.'

He slowed down to a swift stride: his thin legs like matchsticks beneath the baggy shorts he liked to wear all year round, his arms swinging, soldier-style, bright white against the lawn. He turned around and grinned at Seren, she gave a thumbs-up sign and pointed to where she could see his cousins disappearing through the front door of The Windmill. Anni's children seemed like another species compared to Griff; they looked so tall and strong, golden from the Australian sun.

Seren surveyed Nesta's lovely garden with its long herbaceous borders and neatly cut lawn. Beyond the mossy wall she could see the chickens pecking in the orchard and a row of white sheets flapping on the washing line between the trees.

In front of her The Windmill rose up like a giant red-brick pepperpot against the sky. Stone steps wound up the outside, ending at a wooden balcony that would once have provided access to the sails. For many years Daniel had debated whether to reinstate the great white sails but had finally decided they would interrupt the light flooding through the balcony doors that led to his and Nesta's bedroom. Instead he had installed a large brass telescope that perched like an elongated eagle on the balcony rail. He had bought it as a fortieth birthday present for Nesta, 'to indulge your bizarre obsession with looking at the stars', he had said as she unwrapped the enormous box.

Seren had taken her first breath in that circular bedroom at the top. She'd spent her childhood running up and down the spiral staircase inside, gazing out from the windows, running her little fingers around and around the curving walls, feeling safe and happy within them. Seren smiled. Despite all the teasing she'd had from Anni and Ben for never leaving home, this was the only place she'd ever really wanted to be. That was why Daniel and Nesta's wedding present to Seren and Tom had been so wonderful; the old barn at the end of their garden had been perfect for converting into a house and Tom had set about the design and building project with great enthusiasm. It was the first project he'd taken on single-handedly after joining Daniel's architectural practice. He had loved the challenge and Seren had loved being able to live so close to the house that Daniel had made from the dilapidated tower and the beautiful garden that Nesta had created around it.

In the afternoon sunlight the glass walls of Daniel's magnificent extension on the side of The Windmill reflected The Wheat House back at Seren. She could see the first wisteria flowers coming out around her door just like the ones that were already blooming on the south door of The Windmill. It was all she'd wanted, to have what they had – a beautiful home, a happy marriage, wisteria flowers around the door. A big tumbling family.

Seren glanced across to the cherry tree again and for a few seconds let herself imagine that Anni's chubby baby girl was hers. She closed her eyes at the memory of a tiny bundle in her arms, a soft pink cheek, delicate eyelashes, the faintest suggestion of red hair. Then she was thinking of another baby: the skin a soft olive, a smudge of black hair. With a start she opened her eyes, not wanting to remember. She thought about the car she'd seen the day before and hoped she'd been mistaken.

Anni had disappeared from the scene beside the cherry tree and

Nesta and Daniel were alone now, sitting side by side; Nesta had the baby on her knee, gently jigging her up and down on her lap, letting her play with the long beads around her neck. Daniel's face was turned to the sun, his fingers tapping on the arm of his chair in time to the jazz compilation that Seren had put on especially for him.

A light gust of breeze blew the tree so that blossom swirled around Daniel and Nesta like confetti.

'Hey, where's my little sister?' a clinking of bottles heralded the arrival of Ben. 'I'd give you a big squeeze but I'm laden with champagne.'

'You're late,' Seren tried to sound stern but as usual ended up grinning at her brother's handsome face. She ran a finger down his cheek. 'And you haven't even shaved!'

'Can't have Dad thinking I've got my act together just yet. He'll be wanting me to get a proper job and everything.'

'You have a proper job.'

'According to Dad, game design isn't a serious profession.' He furrowed his brow and put on a solemn voice. 'Not like architecture.' He winked at Seren who'd started to relieve him of his bottles; she tried not to laugh.

Once Ben had his arms free he wrapped them around Seren and hugged her. 'How are you doing?'

'I'm fine.' Seren's voice was muffled by his tight embrace.

He stopped hugging her, stepped back and looked intently at her face.

'Honestly?'

Seren shrugged. 'Oh you know – good days bad days. Today's a good day because I'm busy.'

'And Griff?'

'He doesn't say that much but I know he misses Tom. Dad's very good – he plays endless games of chess with him, listens to his trumpet practice. I don't know what either of us would do without Mum and Dad.'

There was a thudding noise and Seren turned to see a

6

gigantic red box trying to get through the kitchen door. The box began to move forward and then became wedged in the door frame.

'Help,' it said, and Ben stepped forward giving it a hefty tug. As though Ben had performed a magician's trick, the pretty face of Suki was revealed. Seren looked at Suki's short silk tunic and staggeringly high heels and felt immediately dowdy in her linen dress and ballet pumps. She knew she'd lost a lot of weight over the last year and Suki's petite curves made her aware how scrawny she must look.

'Thanks a bunch for waiting for me, Ben! I couldn't see a thing. I've been blindly walking into the brick wall feeling for the door like some kind of demented bee buzzing at a window. I felt like a right eejit.' Suki's Irish accent still took Seren by surprise. With her delicate features and glossy black hair, Suki looked as if she should have been brought up in some Imperial Ming palace rather than the back of a Chinese takeaway in Cork.

Suki directed a scowl at Ben and then grinned at Seren. 'I'm so sorry we're late, your brother is a great one for ignoring the concept of time, especially the concept of the time it takes to get out of London.' She cast another scowl in Ben's direction and looked Seren up and down. 'You look gorgeous. Love the dress, very Grace Kelly.' Seren felt better.

Ben put the box on the table. 'I don't know why you're blaming me for making us late, Suki. You were the one who missed the diversion sign by Putney Bridge so that I nearly drove into that trench for the water pipes.'

'I couldn't see any signs; in fact I couldn't see anything. I had an enormous box on my knee for two and a half hours; all I could see was that shiny wrapping paper, like some vision from hell. I am so not into red any more!' Suki made a face at the box and then turned to embrace Seren. 'How are you doing?'

Seren breathed in Suki's delicious perfume. 'I'm OK…'

Suki held her at arm's length. 'You know if you ever need to

7

talk I'm a great listener. It would make a change from listening to your brother going on forever about the challenge of getting through the eighth ring of Owldoor and how many high elves make up a skillet.'

'Hey!' Ben sounded indignant. 'I thought you were interested in my work and it's scrivet not skillet. Anyway I have to listen to you going on about lycra and high-cut legs.'

Suki laughed. 'You know you love it really, all those scantily clad women.' She turned back to Seren her face serious again. 'I'm just saying I'm there if you need me.'

'Thanks.' Seren started to whisk salad dressing in a little jug, her hair falling over her face. She didn't push it away this time, using it to shield her eyes so that Suki couldn't see her tears. She changed the subject, battling to make her voice sound normal. 'How is the world of swimwear?'

'Soggy! Or should I say water-logged! Our biggest client has just gone bust after I spent three months working on next year's Spring/Summer for them. I'm so pissed off, I'm thinking of going home to take over the business from Mum and Dad. They keep telling me they want to retire.'

'Oh no, you mustn't do that,' Seren looked anxiously at Ben, waiting for his protest but he was busy trying to find spaces for champagne amongst the bowls of salad and strawberries in the fridge. Of all the numerous girlfriends her brother had had Suki was Seren's favourite. So far they'd been together for three years and that was a record for Ben.

Ben's head emerged from the fridge. 'Are you not going to ask what's in the box?' he grinned.

'I thought we'd agreed we were only giving them the tickets,' said Seren.

Ben's grin broadened. Seren picked up the box with both hands – something inside the box thudded into the side. 'It doesn't feel like tickets. It's heavy.'

'Hey, careful! I forgot to get bubblewrap so go easy on the shaking.'

8

'What's in there?'

Ben tapped the side of his nose. 'Ah ha! Later, little sister. It's a surprise.'

Seren rolled her eyes and laughed. 'I've had your surprises before. The last one was a goldfish for Griff that was dead by bedtime.'

'The man in the shop swore it would live for years.'

'And the surprise before that was the box of dodgy fireworks that spontaneously combusted while we were having pumpkin soup in Mum and Dad's kitchen. We could have all been killed!'

Ben rearranged the red satin bow on the top of the parcel and smiled. 'Trust me, Seren, this is guaranteed to impress. Daniel and Nesta will just love it. Where's Anwen anyway?'

'Rounding up the boys, I think.'

'And hopefully tying them up for the duration of the party. I swear they get more feral every time she brings them over.'

'I heard that, Ben.'

Anni stood in the kitchen doorway, her arms folded across her chest.

'Sorry Anwen, I just…'

'Anni,' she crossed over to the table and pushed the box with one finger. 'Don't call me *Anwen*. What the hell is this? We said just the tickets to Rome. We agreed.'

Ben shrugged.

'You always have to do your own thing,' Anni leant down and pressed her ear to the box. 'My God, it's ticking.' She picked it up and gave it a shake. 'Is it a bomb?'

'Anwen, don't!'

'Call me *Anni*!' Anni tipped the box back and forth once more.

'OK *Anni*, just don't shake the box. It's very delicate,' Ben took the box from his older sister's hands and placed it gently down on the table. Seren touched Ben's arm.

'Would you move the chairs onto the terrace please? It's the

9

last thing that needs to be done before lunch.'

'Happy to help Star Girl. But first I must go and congratulate the happy couple – forty years together, I can't imagine what that must be like.'

As Ben disappeared into the garden, Anni let out a growl through gritted teeth and Suki laughed.

'Family dynamics – always a great spectator sport.'

'Sorry Suki,' Anni gave her a kiss. 'Maybe he does something for you but all I can say is thank God I live on the other side of the world.'

Lunch passed in a chaotic blur as serving bowls were passed back and forth, Anni's boys were prevented from throwing food at each other and the baby was passed along the table to stop her from howling. Daniel and Nesta sat side by side. Nesta smiled and chatted with her assembled family while Daniel, unusually silent, sat back in his seat. Seren noticed that he had hardly touched his food and wondered if the noisy presence of so many grandchildren had exhausted him; his face looked strained, the lines across his forehead deeper. She saw Nesta touch his arm and lip-read the words 'are you alright?' He nodded and, as Nesta turned away, Daniel reached into his jacket pocket and looked at something on his mobile phone.

After the main meal had been cleared away, Seren brought out a heart-shaped pavlova, studded with strawberries and white chocolate curls. Ben proposed a toast to Daniel and Nesta and they all raised their glasses and cheered. Anni's boys got carried away and whooped for far too long. Trying to copy them, Griff started to wheeze. Seren pushed back her chair to fetch his inhaler but stopped. *Give him a minute, let him recover by himself,* in her head she could hear Tom's calm voice. Seren counted thirty seconds. Griff's wheezing stopped and, within a few more seconds, he was laughing with his cousins again.

As the last mouthful of meringue disappeared the boys were released from the table like hounds being let out of a cage.

'Don't go near the pond,' Anni called after them half-heartedly; she was pinioned to the chair by a suckling baby, one hand cradling her child the other checking her phone. 'Or the staircase up to the balcony.'

'Come on,' Suki pulled Ben to his feet. 'Let's see if we can engage them in some activity that won't involve the air ambulance being summoned.'

'Why are you are always so good?' Ben sighed, reluctantly following Suki across the grass.

'There's a message here from Mike,' said Anni peering at her screen with difficulty in the bright afternoon sun. 'He sends his congratulations and wishes he could be with us today instead of getting ready for his conference in Perth.'

'Poor Mike,' Nesta smiled benignly. 'It's a shame he couldn't have come over.' Seren looked at her mother and tried to work out if Nesta really meant that. Anni's husband had never really fitted in; big and outspoken he had seemed to take up too much space in The Windmill and his opinions had always been at odds with those Daniel expressed.

Daniel suddenly stood up and began to gather up the empty plates and dishes.

'Leave that to me, Dad,' protested Seren. She leant across her father to pick up an empty bowl. Jazz music sounded from her father's pocket and with a sigh he fished out his phone.

'Work, I'm afraid,' he said, looking at the screen. He moved away from the table to stand beneath the cherry tree, his back turned away from his wife and daughters.

'Here, let me take those.' Nesta took the pile of bowls from Seren's hands. 'I can't sit here twiddling my thumbs. I'll go mad by tea-time if you don't let me do something to help.'

In the kitchen Seren and Nesta put tin-foil over leftovers, loaded the dishwasher and washed the larger serving bowls in the sink.

'Lovely peonies,' Nesta lightly touched the pale pink flowers in the jug. 'Are they from the shop?'

Seren nodded, 'I wanted to use the flowers you had in your wedding bouquet.'

Nesta laughed, 'Oh Seren, you are so sweet. Only you would remember that.'

Nesta picked up a cloth from the sink and began wiping the table.

'It must be coming up to wedding season now at work. Will you be needing my help as usual?'

'Yes please,' Seren said. It's gone mad since Ben set up the website for Stems. Six orders this week and loads of enquiries.'

Nesta smiled, 'That'll keep your mind off things.' Seren bit her lip and Nesta squeezed her shoulder. 'You're doing really well.'

'Don't start me off, Mum.' Seren warned. 'Let's not talk about Tom today.'

'OK darling,' Nesta said. She leant against the doorway and nodded towards Daniel. He was still standing under the tree, engaged in what looked like an intense discussion on his phone.

'How is your father ever going to be able to retire? He'll hate not working.'

Seren hung a damp tea towel over the Rayburn and went to stand beside her mother. 'You and Dad will have a lovely time together, gallivanting around the country, days out, trips to London: galleries, the theatre. You could go to Australia and visit Anni and the children.'

Nesta arched one eyebrow and Seren laughed. 'Well, maybe give that trip a miss until the boys are slightly less crazy.'

'You think that's going to happen any time soon? My mother would have called them *bechgyn gwyllt,* wild boys; she would probably have taken her willow whip to them given half a chance.'

Seren remembered her solid, sharp-tongued grandmother, holding court in the kitchen of her Welsh farmhouse; dark eyes flashing, scolding her grandchildren in a language that Seren couldn't understand, berating her son-in-law for taking Nesta away to live in England. Daniel used to say that at least he had saved Nesta from the rain and his mother-in-law would swipe him with her chequered tea towel and then he would laugh and pretend to let her chase him around the big oak table in the middle of the room.

As a child Seren never tired of the story of how Nesta and Daniel had met. She would get her parents to tell it to her separately so that she could hear both sides. On her ninth birthday Daniel and Nesta took her on a trip to London and, rather than visiting Hamleys or Madame Tussauds, Seren had asked to be taken to the place where her parents had first laid eyes on each other. They stood on the steps of the V&A while Nesta explained that she had been going up the steps, 'Three days out of Wales, eager to experience all that London had to offer,' and Daniel had demonstrated how he had been walking out of the revolving doors, his head full of the William Morris furniture he was studying for his thesis.

'And suddenly, there she was – a vision in purple.'

'I thought he looked like Robert Redford and Paul Newman all rolled into one,' said Nesta climbing up a step towards him.

'She had long golden hair, like a shimmering field of wheat.'

'He wore a pink paisley shirt, velvet trousers and hair that my mother would have called disgraceful.'

'She had a tiny suede skirt that showed off her wonderful legs.'

'We certainly didn't have men like him in Llangadog.'

'She had the most beautiful face I'd ever seen, eyes like sapphires, skin like cream.'

'He looked at me and that was it.'

And standing on the steps their youngest daughter had beamed up at them with joy.

Now, Seren studied her mother in the doorway, still beautiful, still sapphire-eyed with skin like cream though her

13

hair was grey and cut into a neat bob. Despite three children she had retained her girlish figure; straight backed and elegant in a long silk tunic and wide linen trousers.

Daniel appeared beside her. Petals from the cherry blossom scattered over his head.

'Very pretty,' Nesta said. He looked confused. 'Your hair.' She picked off a petal and showed it to him. 'The pink goes so beautifully with the grey.'

Daniel brushed his hair ineffectually.

'Let me,' said Nesta. He bowed his head and she carefully removed the flowers. When she'd finished she kissed his cheek. Seren smiled at them. They were still such a handsome couple.

A burst of Thelonious Monk suddenly filled the room.

'Your phone again, Daniel!' Nesta exclaimed. Daniel slipped his hand into the pocket of his jacket and the music stopped.

After a moment's pause, he sighed. 'It's Odette. She can't find the plans for the new tourist information building and the meeting with the town council is tomorrow.'

'She must know we're in the middle of a family party?' Nesta still had the petals held delicately in her cupped hand. 'What's she doing in the office on a Sunday anyway? She's as obsessed with work as you are.'

'Are we having that cake or not?' Anni's face appeared at the open window, the baby fast asleep against her shoulder.

Jazz erupted from Daniel's pocket again.

'Tell Odette to wait until the morning.' Nesta was smiling but her voice had a tightness that Seren recognised as irritation. She scrunched up the petals and threw them into the bowl of compost scraps. 'Or are you as frightened of your PA as everyone else is?'

The ring tone stopped.

'I'm not frightened of Odette, she's just a bit...' Daniel started to protest but stopped mid-sentence as the phone started up again.

Seren watched her mother's face flush pink. 'For God's sake, Daniel, turn it off.'

Daniel took the phone out of his pocket but instead of turning it off he stared at it as though mesmerised by the screen. It stopped and the only sound came from a fly buzzing over the bowl of scraps until it found a strawberry to settle on.

'OK. Let's have cake!' Seren tried her best to sound cheerful.

Nesta started fetching crockery from the cupboard. She didn't look at Daniel as she stepped out into the garden with a pile of plates.

'I'll call the children,' Anni said and she and the baby disappeared in the direction of The Windmill.

After a brief hesitation Daniel started for the door but stopped at the threshold. He paused and turned around. 'Seren?'

'Yes?'

'There's something I think you ought to know.'

'Yes?'

'I…' he began, but his voice was cut off by a cacophony of shrieks erupting from the other side of the garden. A hoard of figures, including Ben and Suki (high heels discarded), charged over the lawn towards them.

'Sorry Dad?' shouted Seren above the noise. 'I can't hear you.'

Daniel shook his head, 'It doesn't matter. Here, let me give you a hand with the drinks.'

Seren put two bottles of champagne on the work surface and Daniel started to ease the cork from the top of one of them.

'Are you OK, Dad?' Seren said, as she arranged the champagne flutes on a tray. 'You seem a bit distracted.'

Daniel smiled. 'I'm fine, darling.' The cork came out of the bottle with a dull pop. 'A bit busy trying to tie up all the loose ends at work before I finish.' As the champagne mist cleared he started to fill the glasses. Seren noticed that his hands were shaking.

15

'Don't wear yourself out. Mum and I have just been talking about all the fun you'll have together when you retire.' The champagne frothed in a glass and began to overflow.

'Damn!' Daniel turned his back to fetch a cloth.

'Aren't you going to give a speech, Dad?' asked Ben as Seren lifted the knife, poised to cut the cake.

'I'm a nursing mother, you know,' Anni stared pointedly at the cake. 'Low blood sugar is always a risk.'

'Grandad always gives a speech at parties,' said Griff. It was true that an occasion never went by without one of Daniel's witty speeches; they were often the highlight of the whole event.

Everyone looked at Daniel. He shook his head, unsmiling, and Seren noticed his face looked very pale. She wondered if he was ill.

She quickly lifted up her glass. 'Congratulations to Mum and Dad. May you have many more happy years together.'

'Hear, hear,' said Ben.

The adults took a sip of champagne and the children drank their elderflower pressé and jostled for spaces as near to the cake as possible. Daniel downed his drink in one.

'And now it's time to give you this.' Ben bent down, produced the huge gift-wrapped box from under the table and placed it in front of Daniel and Nesta. All the children shunted up the table towards the present.

'For God's sake, Ben, can't we have a bit of cake first?' protested Anni but Nesta was already on her feet and starting to untie the red ribbon, exclaiming over the size of the box, trying to bat the boys' small hands away.

'Come on, darling,' she smiled down at Daniel. 'You open the end nearest to you. Whoever wrapped this certainly did a thorough job.'

'That was me,' Ben sounded very pleased with himself. 'Here, Anwen, pass them that cake knife to cut through the

16

sellotape.'

Anni scowled at her brother.

Nesta slit through the wrapping to reveal an envelope on top of a brown cardboard box.

'I'd just like to say,' said Anni. 'The contents of the envelope is your main gift. Seren and I have no idea what's in that box. Whatever it is it's *totally* from Ben.'

'I'm sure it will be lovely,' said Nesta smiling at her son. 'You always find the most interesting presents.'

Anni rolled her eyes.

Nesta picked up the envelope and offered it to Daniel. 'Do you want to open this, dear?' Daniel seemed to recoil as he shook his head. Nesta's mouth tightened briefly before she smiled again, opening the envelope, looking at them all with an exaggerated look of expectation. She slid out the printed sheet inside and let out a delighted cry. 'Rome! Oh, how wonderful. Look Daniel, a week's holiday in Rome, flying first class and staying at the Plaza del Majestic where we had our honeymoon. We always said we'd go back one day.' She looked around the table at her assembled family. 'You are all very naughty. This must have cost a fortune.'

'It's not till July,' Seren said. 'So it's a retirement present for Dad as well.' She waited for her father to say something but he was still sitting back in his chair, his expression unreadable. A light breeze blew more blossom from the tree and Seren shivered.

'Come on, look in the box.' Ben was jumping up and down on his seat like a child.

'Give your mother a chance,' Suki said, putting her hand on his arm.

Nesta peered into the box and lifted out the mystery object.

'Oh my God!' Anni's mouth dropped open.

'Wow, mega cool,' Anni's boys were crowding round.

'Well, well,' Nesta's Welsh accent seemed more pronounced as she held the astonishing object in front of her. 'I don't know what to say.'

'I do,' began Anni. 'It's…'

'I found it on a stall at the Portobello market,' Ben interrupted his sister. 'I thought it would be perfect for your anniversary present.'

Suki raised one plucked eyebrow. 'I was slightly worried that it might not quite fit in with the decor in The Windmill.'

'I'm sure we'll find somewhere for it,' Nesta looked dubious as she stared at the large model of the Colosseum in her hands. The walls were modelled crudely in plaster; at its base sat a little scooter with a couple riding on it; and a bright red enamel clock face was embedded in the walls.

'It's Gregory Peck and Audrey Hepburn,' explained Ben, reaching over to point at the scooter. 'You know, from the film *Roman Holiday*. Wait and see what happens every hour. You'll love it.'

Seren exchanged a glance with Nesta and tried not to laugh.

'I thought it might look good on Granny's old dresser,' Ben's enthusiasm wasn't dampened by his mother's expression.

'Maybe,' Nesta nodded slowly. She turned to her husband. 'What do you think Daniel?' Daniel didn't look at Nesta or the clock. He was staring at the plate in front of him. 'Daniel? Is there something wrong?'

He took the Colosseum clock from Nesta's hands and appeared to study it for a few moments before gently putting it down in front of him and staring at his wife. 'I can't do this anymore,' his voice sounded as though his throat were being constrained somehow. He stood up.

'Can't do what?' Nesta placed her hand on his arm, her eyes on his face, full of concern.

'This, all of this,' Daniel gestured around the table. 'The cake. The champagne. The presents. The celebration. I can't go on pretending any more.'

'What do you mean?' Nesta's arm had dropped down to her side.

18

'I mean,' Daniel took a deep breath. 'I mean that I have something difficult to tell you.' He gestured around the silent table again. 'In fact, I have something difficult to tell you all.'

Cancer, the word sprang into Seren's mind like a knife cutting into flesh; it hurt. She should have known, she should have realised; the way he'd been acting, the way he'd been looking. In her mind she reached for Tom's hand, wishing so hard that he was really there beside her.

'Go and play, boys,' Anni's voice contained a tone of authority that it usually lacked with her children. 'Have a race around the garden, check out the chickens, sniff some flowers. You too, Griff.'

Seren was relieved to see Griff follow his cousins across the lawn. She tried to imagine what it was going to be like to tell her son that his grandfather was seriously ill but she couldn't imagine it and her whole body seemed to be filling with ice. She didn't think she or Griff had the strength to face death again so soon. Suddenly she realised that Nesta was speaking, spitting out a sentence that didn't seem suitable at all.

'What's her name?' Nesta's blue eyes bore into her husband's face. Daniel turned away, addressing the garden rather than his wife.

'This isn't about someone else, Nesta. This is about me and what I need to do for myself.'

'What's her name?' Nesta repeated. Seren saw that her mother was clutching the edge of the chair with one hand, her knuckles white.

'Nesta, please, does it really matter?'

'A name? Don't I deserve that?'

Seren looked from one parent to the other, trying to make sense of what they were saying. She turned to Ben but he was staring intently at the table in front of him.

Daniel was still looking out across the lawn.

'Why?' Nesta's voice wavered. Anni passed the baby to Suki and went to stand beside her mother. 'Why?' Nesta

19

repeated. 'Why are you doing this?' Seren couldn't take her eyes off her father.

'I don't want…' Daniel began and then he paused. He turned to Nesta and looked intently at her face. 'I think we need some time apart.' Nesta stared back at him, he touched her cheek and didn't take his hand away, Nesta kept on looking at him, her eyes locked onto his. They seemed to stand like that for ages. 'You know I love you, don't you?' he said. 'But I need to be true to myself.' Time passed, maybe minutes, maybe seconds. The whole world seemed to hold its breath.

Nesta's voice was quiet, just a whisper, but Seren heard it. 'Bullshit.' Nesta never swore or cursed. She pushed his hand away from her face. 'You're full of bullshit just like my mother always said you were.'

Seren glanced at Ben again; he had picked up the ribbon from his parcel and was winding it very slowly into a coil, concentrating very hard. Beside him Suki rhythmically rocked the baby, her eyes averted from the scene in front of her. The silence seemed as thick as fog. Seren wanted to speak, tried to speak. She longed to find the words to make everything all right again. She couldn't.

A chime like gunshot rang out. Everyone looked towards its source; three more chimes emitted from the clock as the little scooter began to zoom faster and faster around the foot of the Colosseum as the theme music from *Roman Holiday* played a little too slowly and slightly out of tune.

'Shit!' Ben reached for the clock and desperately tried to make it stop.

'Well done, Ben!' Anni tried to snatch the clock from him but Ben stuffed it under the table where the sound was muffled but continued for at least another minute.

Daniel cleared his throat, seemingly oblivious to the tune, 'I hope you'll all begin to understand, it's just that I no longer feel…'

'Best go now,' Nesta interrupted him. 'No point hanging

about. I expect she'll be waiting for you, waiting to hear if you actually managed to do it.'

Daniel put his hand on Nesta's arm. 'I've been trying to talk to you for weeks but I didn't know how to start and then I thought this might be the best time, with all the children here to look after you.'

'I don't want to be looked after.' Nesta shrugged Daniel's hand away from her arm. 'A name, Daniel. That's all I want.'

There was another long pause before Daniel spoke again. 'Frankie.' Nesta's eyebrows shot up in surprise.

'Francesca,' Daniel hastily added. 'Frankie is her nickname.'

Nesta gave a brief, tight smile.

'How long?'

'Pardon?'

'How long have you and this Frankie been…' her voice trailed off.

Daniel sighed. 'Does it matter?'

'Yes.'

'I've known her for two years but…'

'Thank you, Daniel.' Nesta cleared her throat and turned to Seren. 'Now. I think we'd better have some of your delicious-looking cake. It will melt if we leave it out here any longer.'

'Nesta,' Daniel's voice wavered.

'Just go.' Nesta sat down and pulled the cake stand towards her. 'What beautiful decorations, Seren. It must have taken you ages.'

'Nesta,' Daniel said again. 'We'll need to discuss things, the house, our finances.' Nesta picked up the knife that lay beside her.

'Who's going to have a piece?' She started slicing vigorously through ganache and sponge and golden stars and rose petals. Daniel picked up his jacket and walked towards The Windmill. Nesta shovelled slices onto the plates.

'Aren't you going to go after him, Mum?'

'Sit down and eat your cake, Anwen.'

21

Anni didn't sit down. 'Go and tell him not to be so stupid.'

'Sit down.'

'If you're not going to go after him I will.' Anni set off across the lawn, her blonde ponytail swinging purposefully against her broad back. She stopped at the sound of a car engine starting up and the crunch of wheels on gravel. From that part of the garden none of them could see the drive, but they all knew it was Daniel's Jaguar that was heading for the gate and turning onto the main road. Anni marched back to the table. 'I don't believe it! He's gone!'

'He probably had a bag packed, waiting to go as soon as he could,' said Nesta.

'You sound as if you might have been expecting this,' Suki's voice was gentle, her eyes soft with concern for Nesta.

Nesta picked up a fork and took a mouthful of cake directly from the cake stand in front of her, chewing slowly, staring blankly into the distance while the rest of the table watched, completely at a loss for what to say. Nesta swallowed finally and wiped the corners of her mouth with the heart-printed napkins that Seren had bought especially from the new gift shop on the high street. She turned to Suki.

'No, I didn't expect him to do this today, not on our wedding anniversary, not in front of all of you.' She paused and looked into the distance again. 'But if I'm being honest I've been expecting this for years.' Then she stood up, pushed her chair away and started to walk towards The Windmill.

Nesta

Nesta headed for The Windmill. She felt sick. The chocolate cake had tasted horribly sweet in her mouth. She longed for a drink to wash it all away; as soon as she was in her kitchen she'd pour herself a long, cool glass of water – use one of the blue glasses engraved with little birds they'd bought on holiday in India. *How long ago was that? Twelve years? Thirteen?*

One foot in front of the other, over the grass, over the daisies. She noticed the moss and made a mental note to remember to ask Daniel to rake it over and then another mental note to remember that Daniel wouldn't be around to ask.

Behind her she could hear Anni telling Seren to sit down. *I'll go, the last thing she needs is a crowd.* Nesta's heart ached for Seren, she wondered what must be going through her mind. Anni would soon be back with Mike on the other side of the world – running in circles after her wild boys and baby. And Ben would be back in London – building his computer fantasies, oblivious to real-life games and dramas. It was Seren who would be left at home, still so raw from Tom's death, trying to make it all make sense.

Anwen was at her side. Nesta knew she was talking but she couldn't decipher the words. She found herself distracted by the wide herbaceous borders on either side of her; everything was growing so fast, lush and green and full of life. Aquilegias swayed in the breeze and a patch of giant alliums seemed to hover in mid-air. The geraniums were almost out already and a dark red peony pushed through the thick foliage at the back. Nesta thought she might bring it forward for next year. *Next year?*

On and on, the drone of Anwen's voice hurt her head. She wondered where the children were, and hoped they were leaving the chickens alone. She took a deep breath and the ground tipped up in front of her, the whole world suddenly lurching on its axis; the nausea increased, her head spun and her chest hurt. She needed water more than anything else. One foot in front of the other, she forced herself to keep going forward. It would be too easy to stop, to collapse and die in front of Daniel's tower; that would make it much too simple.

Anwen's words broke through, 'He'll be back by tomorrow, you'll see, Mum. He doesn't know what he's doing. It's probably a mid-life crisis. I thought that when he bought the car. And you know how men panic about retiring. He's always been obsessed with work.'

Anwen, please. Nesta wasn't sure if her words were audible. *Please stop, I can't listen to this...*

'It'll be some silly infatuation. A woman he thinks will make him feel young again. He'll soon realise how much he needs you. You've always been the only one for him.'

Not now...

'Mike's dad left his mum a few years ago, said he needed space to find himself. He was back by supper time – he couldn't even find a shop selling a pizza, let alone himself.'

Anwen...

'And my friend from baby club's husband thought he'd fallen in love with some waitress in Sydney...'

Anwen, just shut up!

Frankie

It was the tenth cup of coffee she'd let go cold that day. Standing in the bay window, Frankie put down the cup and pressed her forehead against the glass. The first star had appeared in the darkening sky. Where was he? She'd heard nothing since the phone call she'd made hours ago. He'd told her they had just finished lunch and that he was definitely going to tell Nesta that afternoon. She'd panicked then and tried to phone him back to say, 'Don't do it, it would be too painful for them all.' He hadn't answered.

She counted to ten as slowly as she could and searched the street again. She checked her phone and held her arm up in the corner where the signal was stronger, just in case.

He sometimes came round after work. An hour when he'd tell Nesta that he was still at a site meeting. He'd arrive with pastries and cappuccinos and join her in her single bed until he had to tear himself away and go home.

The cat jumped up onto the table and pushed his oriental nose into the small of her back. Frankie picked him up and buried her face in his fur; he vibrated with pleasure.

'Maybe it's just going to be you and me forever, Dante.' Putting him down, she stroked his back while her eyes scoured the street again. A car pulled away from in front of the house and left a perfect parking place for the Jaguar. 'We were alright on our own before,' she said to Dante. 'I'm sure we'll be alright on our own again.' She wished she believed this. Once she had longed to be on her own, and never imagined sharing her life again. But ever since she'd found herself sitting beside Daniel Saunders on the 17:35 from St Pancras, she had found it very hard to be alone.

25

Seren

Seren sat on the edge of the bed undoing the buttons on her dress. Her fingers stopped half way down. 'You knew, didn't you?' The words had been in her mind all evening. She twisted round to face imaginary Tom. He was reading a book, propped up by pillows, his T-shirt illuminated by the lamp, very white. 'Two years, Dad said. I think you knew he was seeing someone behind Mum's back and you didn't tell me.' Imaginary Tom remained immersed in his book. 'My God, Tom – two years! How could he do that to Mum!'

Seren continued to undo the buttons and once more stopped. She remembered the coroner trying to explain the accident at the inquest, *a momentary lapse of concentration*. Seren had wondered and wondered what had been in Tom's mind that day. Had he been distracted by a bird? By a sudden noise? Now she wondered if he had been distracted by something else? A secret he had discovered, a promise he had made? Had he been feeling worried, guilty, anxious? Had he found himself unwittingly duplicitous in his father-in-law's affair?

'You were always so loyal to Dad,' Seren glared at the bed. 'But what about Nesta, you were so fond of her. What about me!'

In her head she could hear his level reply. *It wasn't any of my business.*

Seren stood up, went to the window and pulled aside the curtains. She could see a light illuminating the top floor of The Windmill. Her mother must have woken up. She'd been asleep when Seren had peeped through her door half an hour before.

Seren wondered if she should go to her but thought better of it. Anni and her gang were sleeping on the floor below Nesta. If Seren walked in one of the children would be bound to wake up and all Hell would break lose.

'Just leave her, let her be on her own tonight,' said Tom.

'Supposing she does something terrible.'

'She's Nesta! She's far too pragmatic for that.'

Seren closed the curtains again and undid the rest of her buttons. The dress slipped down from her shoulders and she stepped out of it, wishing the events of the day could be shrugged off so easily.

She tugged her nightdress over her head. The cool cotton temporarily soothed her racing mind but soon her doubts and fears were back. Picking up her hairbrush she tried to brush away the day. But she pulled too hard so that the bristles tangled in her curls. The more she tried to release the brush the more it caught. Imaginary Tom got out of bed and watched her in the mirror for a few moments. Then he gently took the brush from her hands and carefully disentangled it strand by strand. When he had finished he put the brush down on the table, took Seren in his arms and held her tightly as she began to cry.

Nesta

The moon was big and white, slowly rising above the horizon. A milk moon, a hare moon; the full moon in May was a symbol of life and growth and optimism. Nesta swung the telescope away, she didn't want to see its hopeful face beaming down at her with its promise of everything she didn't have.

Nesta scanned the sky. Sometimes there were meteor showers in the spring. Last year there had been three nights in a row when Nesta had watched shooting stars crisscrossing the sky for hours. Daniel had grumbled that she was keeping him awake. *For God's sake, leave the heavens alone and get into bed.* Nesta couldn't stop watching, feeling a childish thrill every time one zoomed across the telescope lens. At first she'd wished on them but pretty soon she'd run right out of things she wanted. Life had been too good.

Now the sky was very still. She was weighed down with wishes but not even a plane or satellite moved through the constellations.

Nesta wondered where Daniel was. She doubted he was looking at the stars.

She tried to banish him from her thoughts, concentrating instead on the dark sky. She found Mercury, Jupiter and Capella, Procyon and Polaris and to her left the pale river of the Milky Way. Her eyes settled on the belt of Hercules, from there she tracked downwards to the constellation of Virgo and Libra and finally to Leo.

'Leo,' she said the word out loud. Leo had taught her everything she knew about the stars. She took her eye away from the telescope and leant against the balcony rail, looking down at the spot where his caravan had once stood and where she had made her pond. The moon and stars were reflected in it

28

now, a mirror image of the sky. Nesta longed to dive in and let the inky, starry water wash away her misery.

Seren

Seren was sure that she had hardly slept at all. When she heard the birds begin to sing she decided to get up and get a cup of tea but suddenly she was opening her eyes to find it was half past eight, the sun flooding through the gap in the curtains. She briefly touched the pillow where Tom's head should have been and climbed out of bed.

Opening the curtains she saw Suki walking over the lawn dressed in cropped jeans, satin slippers and the T-shirt Ben had been wearing the day before; she looked effortlessly gorgeous. She carried a steaming mug in her hand and, as she stopped beside a flowerbed, Seren noticed her mother kneeling, trowel in hand, somehow so much smaller than she'd ever seemed before. Her mother took off her gardening gloves and Suki handed her the mug. Nesta smiled and said something and Suki bent down to give Nesta a hug.

In the kitchen, the sight of a loaf of warm bread on the table and its comforting smell made Seren wonder if the previous day had just been a bad dream. She slipped her feet into Tom's old wellingtons and went out into the garden to join her mother and Suki. As Seren got nearer the solemn expression on Suki's face made it clear that it hadn't been a bad dream, something had really happened. Nesta stood up and held out her arms; Seren walked gratefully into them.

'Are you alright?' Nesta asked.

Seren pulled away from her mother's embrace so that she could see her face. 'Shouldn't I be asking you that? I can't believe you made bread!'

Nesta shrugged. 'I had to do something to stop myself from phoning your father and screaming profanities at him. It's very

30

hard to be abusive and knead.'

'Did you get much sleep?'

'A little. I got up at four. Anwen was awake with the baby so we chatted and drank tea and I made the bread and Anwen ate the rest of your cake.'

'Did she have any words of wisdom?'

Nesta sighed, 'She thinks your father will see sense and soon be home.'

'Is that what you think?'

Nesta shrugged again, bent down and with her trowel dug up a dandelion. She tutted as she straightened and dropped the leaves and ugly root into her trug. 'These things are everywhere at the moment, no sooner do I think I've got rid of them than I find there are twice as many in their place.'

Suki gently touched Nesta's arm. 'Is there anything I can do around the house today?'

'If you could just go and feed the chickens? I let them out at dawn but it seemed too early for their breakfast.'

'I'm on my way.' Suki headed for the orchard. Nesta watched her go and Seren noticed dark shadows beneath her mother's eyes.

'Such a lovely girl,' Nesta murmured.

Seren nodded. 'Where's Ben?'

'Asleep. He always was a terrible one for lying in. Not a bit like your father. He's always awake and full of energy as soon as dawn breaks.'

'Tom was the same,' sighed Seren. 'Do you remember how he was always up and out for a run or bike ride or busy getting ready to climb a mountain or disappear into some pot hole.'

'That's why they worked so well together. They used that energy within the business.' Nesta gave a small smile. 'They were a good team.'

The wind blew and Seren pulled her dressing-gown cord tight around her waist.

She paused, looked at her mother's tired face, tried to stop

31

herself and then she spoke. 'Do you think Tom could have known about Dad's affair?'

'Oh Seren,' Nesta tucked a strand of Seren's hair behind her ear like she used to do when she was little. 'Don't torture yourself with that.'

'He would have had ten months to know about it before he died.'

'Your father kept it from me, I'm sure he kept it from all of us, Tom included. It hardly matters now, though, anyway.'

'Oh Mum! Why are you being so reasonable?' She took Nesta by the shoulders and gave her a little shake. 'Isn't it about time you went inside and started ripping Dad's clothes into pieces and dragging scissors over his Miles Davis CDs?'

Nesta gave a dry laugh.

'Believe me, Seren, those things are on my to-do list for today!'

'Hello,' the two women were surprised to find Griff had crept up beside them. He held a bowl of Coco Pops in one hand and, with the other, he spooned a huge pile of cereal into his mouth. He grinned through chocolaty lips, cheeks bulging as he chewed. 'I woke up and thought it was a school day.'

'What have I said about talking with your mouth full,' Seren tapped his freckled nose.

Griff grinned again and swallowed, 'Then I remembered it was a bank holiday. It felt really good.'

Nesta laughed. 'I did that once when I was a little girl. I put my uniform on, plaited my hair, panicked because I hadn't learnt my French verbs. I can still feel the relief when I went downstairs to find my mother dressed for chapel. It didn't feel good for long though. My mother gave me a whipping for making us late because I had to go back upstairs to change.'

Griff gave a snort of laughter. 'Ouch! Where's Grandad? I want to ask him for a game of chess.'

'He's not here right now, sweetheart,' Seren ruffled his hair. How on earth was she going to explain where Daniel was?

'He's gone away for a while,' Nesta said with a reassuring smile. 'Gone to stay with a friend of his. You'll see him soon.'

'OK,' Griff shrugged, already distracted by his cousins charging towards him, armed once more with their plastic weapons. He handed his empty bowl to Seren and joined them as they rampaged past.

'You made that seem easy,' Seren looked admiringly at her mother.

'Keep it simple, keep it honest. It's something I always tried to do as a mother.' Nesta put her gardening gloves back on and crouched down beside the roots and branches of the lavender.

'I'll go and get dressed,' Seren picked up her mother's empty mug from the grass beside her. 'When Ben gets up we'll have some of that lovely looking bread with the strawberry jam you made last week. You will have some, won't you? You must eat, even if you don't feel like it.'

'Don't worry, darling. I'm sure I'll survive.'

Nesta

Keep it simple, keep it honest, Nesta sighed. How many complicated lies had she told her children when they were little? She half closed her eyes to make the world go fuzzy. She used to do this after her father died in the hope that if everything around her looked out of focus then it wasn't as bad as it seemed. Sixty years later and it still didn't work. Nesta's eyes ached. She opened them wide. Open or closed it all seemed pretty bad right now.

She thought Daniel might have phoned her – just to ask if she was alright – or at least phoned Seren. She always was his favourite – everyone could see that from the moment he'd first held her. Everyone apart from Anwen and Ben, who were too busy being jealous of each other to notice that their little sister was getting all the attention.

Nesta wondered if Daniel was at the office or on a site, despite the bank holiday. She could phone Odette but the thought of the fierce little French woman on the other end of the phone put her off. Odette had a particular way of making Nesta feel like the least important person in Daniel's world. Maybe she *was* the least important person. Nesta wondered how much Odette knew; had she played any part in taking down cryptic messages or rearranging Daniel's schedule so that he could steal a few hours with his mistress? After all, in France it seemed commonplace to have another woman on the side, even the French president had a lover.

Nesta pulled at a bit of bindweed twisting through a rose bush and tried to take a deep breath in the way her Pilates teacher encouraged her to do. *Feel it in your core, feel it in your powerhouse.* Nesta's core and powerhouse had disappeared. She tried another breath and smelled the lavender beside her.

34

When she was teaching she used to hang bunches of the flowers around the classroom. Her grandfather had used it on the farm to calm his horses, he hung it from the oak beams in the stable – swearing it made the young stallions he used for harness-racing easier to handle. Nesta had thought it worth a try on inner-city children. The other teachers raised their eyebrows but Nesta knew she wasn't the one shouting in every lesson and going home too exhausted to do anything else – though maybe that had been the effect of the lavender on herself rather than her unruly pupils.

Nesta had liked teaching; she'd wanted to go back after Ben was born but Daniel wouldn't hear of it. He had his architecture business to get off the ground, working long hours, chasing projects and doing what today would be called networking – what, to Nesta, seemed like having a jolly good time in restaurants and wine bars. She thought of all the nights she'd spent washing nappies and picking plasticine out of the swirly carpet, waiting for him to come home. They'd inherited the awful carpet when they moved into the garden flat in Putney – the first home they actually owned. The garden had been a concrete yard with a narrow flowerbed down its shady side. All it contained was a standard rose that never flowered and a desperately unhappy buddleia bush. In those days Nesta had seen the garden purely as a space to put the children while she did the housework. Now the garden was her sanctuary.

Her trowel automatically worked its way around an enormous dandelion plant. She gathered the dark green leaves in her gloved hand and pulled. The leaves tore away leaving the thick white root sneering up at her from the ground. She dug down again until she was able to get a grip on the root and tugged as hard as she could and then, squatting over it, tugged even harder, using both her hands and gritting her teeth as she heaved. Suddenly, after one almighty pull, the whole thing came away; Nesta gave a cry of triumph as she lost her balance

35

and tipped backwards onto her bottom.

She stayed where she had landed and wondered if Daniel's fancy woman was a gardener. Did she tug at dandelions and find herself robbed of all decorum sitting in the mud? Or was she too busy preparing her limbs with scented oils, smoothing satin sheets across her bed, slipping into floaty negligees and brushing her cascading hair? Daniel would probably be in those lubricated arms right now, sandwiched in between the satin, swathed in silken tresses. Nesta pulled up a nettle and heard her mother's scorn ringing in her ears, 'I told you so, you foolish girl.' She tossed the nettle in the trug. Maybe she was wrong about her mother, maybe she'd have wrapped her daughter up in her big leathery arms, wiped her eyes and said in her rich accent, 'Peidiwch a crio fy nghariad – don't cry my lovely girl.'

Nesta looked around her; the dandelions seemed to have multiplied since she'd been sitting there, the ground elder too. She pushed herself back up onto her haunches and pulled off her gardening gloves.

Her wedding ring glinted in the morning sun. 'Welsh gold for my Welsh wife,' Daniel had said when they'd admired it in the shop window in Tregaron. She slipped it off her finger, plunged the trowel deep into the soil to make a slit and dropped the ring into the muddy depths. In a flash she'd smoothed over the ground and it was gone.

Suki's tiny feet appeared beside her; satin slippers embroidered with blue swallows. Nesta wondered if she had seen her burying the ring and if she knew that she'd ruined her slippers on the grass.

Suki said something about coming inside for breakfast. Nesta stood up and put on a smile. She'd go and join them all around the kitchen table; drink the coffee, eat the bread and pretend that every mouthful didn't make her want to retch.

Frankie

The night had seemed like an eternity. Eventually Frankie had gone to bed but sleep was impossible. Now she was back at the window watching the street. If only he'd answer her texts or phone her, just to let her know what was happening.

Frankie thought about phoning the office, braving Odette, asking if Daniel had come in to work. But the thought of the immaculate little Frenchwoman with her severely pulled-back bun made Frankie keep the phone call as a last resort.

She tried to imagine a life without Daniel. How would it have been if their paths had never crossed, if she had got into another carriage that afternoon or sat in any other seat?

She had very nearly missed the train. She had run down the platform and jumped into the first carriage she could find. Damp from the summer rain, she had pushed along the crowded aisle and sat down in the only free seat she could see. As usual she looked around her, checking the faces – just in case.

An elderly woman sat opposite knitting an immense green jumper that was almost spilling into the lap of the man beside her. He was involved in a heated discussion about the price of petrol with a bald man with an East End accent wearing a kilt. The bald man was saying that he'd saved twenty-five pounds by travelling to his sister's wedding by train instead of driving.

'It's the third time she's got married. Our family's Scottish on our mother's grandfather's side and every time my sister insists that all the men wear a kilt! It's costing me a fortune in dress hire.'

Frankie heard the old woman and the other man laugh and she relaxed a little. Ripping open a packet of Maltesers she started looking through the postcards from the exhibition. She popped a Malteser into her mouth, sucking off the chocolate and letting the honeycomb melt against her tongue in the way she used to do as a child. She spread the postcards out in front of her: the colours were sumptuous, the women in the pictures ethereal. She wished she'd had enough money for the exhibition catalogue.

'I'm going to get a coffee.' The man in the kilt stood up and Frankie had to get out of her seat to let him squeeze past her. 'Can I get a drink for anyone else?' Frankie didn't reply. She saw the old woman shake her head and heard the other man say 'No thanks', and the bald man set off down the aisle, kilt swaying with the motion of the train. Frankie sat back down and glanced at the man opposite her.

'Miserable weather we're having.' He'd started talking to the elderly woman.

'Pardon? I'm a little deaf.'

He raised his voice. 'Miserable wet weather and it's so cold for the time of year.' He nodded to her pile of knitting. 'I'd be very grateful for a nice woolly jumper like that one.'

The woman smiled up at him. 'It's for my nephew, he works on an oil rig. I make him a jumper every year without fail.'

'He's a lucky man to have an aunt with such an eye for colour. That blue is just right with the green stripes.'

The old woman's cheeks turned pink with delight and she started to reply when her phone rang and, with one final smile at the man, she launched into a detailed description of how to make gooseberry jam with whoever was on the other end.

The man looked across at Frankie.

'I see you've been to see the Pre-Raphaelites too.'

Frankie realised she'd been staring at him and hurriedly looked back down at the postcards.

'Who do you favour, Rossetti or Millais?' the man asked.

Frankie looked up again. She noticed the deep laughter lines that extended from the man's blue eyes and the contrast between his mop of unruly silver hair and neat grey beard that gave him a slightly bohemian air.

Without waiting for an answer to his question, the man produced an exhibition catalogue from his briefcase. 'I splashed out and bought this for my wife to assuage my guilt. I should have taken her with me – but I only popped in on the spur of the moment, after a very long and tedious meeting.' He pushed the glossy book across the table. 'Would you like to have a look?'

Frankie hesitated before picking it up and beginning to leaf carefully through the pages. After a few moments she looked up at him and quietly nodded 'Thank you'.

The bald man returned from the buffet with his coffee and several packets of biscuits and the old woman finished her phone conversation. The bald man offered round the biscuits. Daniel said he had fond memories of British Rail fruit cake; the old woman said she could remember the days of dining cars; and the bald man told them that he was a steam train enthusiast involved with a group who were restoring an old locomotive in Shoreditch. This sparked off a discussion about disused railway lines being turned into cycle tracks, and then cycling in general, and the old woman turned out to have been a British road race champion in the 1950s. 'I still cycle at least ten miles every day.'

Frankie didn't join in but, as her eyes drifted across the jewel-like images in the catalogue, she listened to the conversation. The rhythm of their voices matched the sound of the train as she lost herself in the romance of the Victorian paintings.

The train lurched to a halt. Frankie looked around, anxious that she'd missed her stop, and relieved to see a familiar picket fence and petunia-filled hanging baskets.

'This is where I get off,' said the man with the silver hair, picking up his leather briefcase.

Frankie stood up, too, and handed him back the catalogue.

'It was kind of you to show it to me,' she said.

The man smiled. He waited to let her go down the aisle first.

Behind her she could hear him cheerfully saying goodbye to his travelling companions, and she wished she had that kind of confidence and easy manner.

It was still raining as Frankie stepped out of the station. She stopped to search for an umbrella in her bag. A basket of petunias above her dripped onto her head.

'You left these.' The silver-haired man was beside her, holding out the bundle of postcards. 'You left them on the table.' He handed them to her; raindrops glistened on his beard. 'I'm glad I caught up with you. I didn't think you'd want to lose them.'

'Thank you.' Frankie took the postcards and slipped them into her bag.

She found her umbrella, but as she pushed it open she remembered that it had torn in the wind the week before. Now half the fabric had detached from the frame leaving it lopsided and flapping. She sighed and the man laughed.

'Looks like that umbrella has been in the wars.' He looked up at the sky. 'This rain is relentless. Whatever happened to our summer?'

Frankie pulled up the collar of her coat. 'I think it's over.'

'Are you walking?'

Frankie nodded and set off, throwing the umbrella in the bin beside the notice board. Now the rain was dripping down her neck, cold as it trickled down her back.

'Let me give you a lift,' the man called after her.

Frankie hesitated, a second, a heart beat. She turned. 'OK.' The word slipped out before she could gather herself to tell him she'd be fine on the bus.

They crunched across the gravel car park avoiding tea-coloured puddles and the man told her his name was Daniel. 'Here we are,' he said getting out a bunch of keys.

'A 1971 E-type!' Again the words came out unbidden. Frankie bit her lip.

Daniel stopped. 'I'm impressed!'

40

'I had a younger brother.' She felt a stab of pain at the memory of Paul. 'When we were little he collected Dinky Toys. The Jaguars were his favourites.'

'He had good taste.' Daniel opened the door. She hesitated for a second and then slid onto the soft leather seat.

Daniel started the engine. 'I did a part exchange for a very sensible Volvo three years ago; a sixtieth birthday present to myself. My eldest daughter said it was a mid-life crisis.'

As the car negotiated the series of roundabouts on the edge of town Frankie felt panic mounting. What was she doing with this stranger: a married man, with daughters and a flashy car? Twenty-four years older than her if her maths was right. They passed a modern block of flats.

'This is where I live,' she said.

Daniel pulled over and she quickly thanked him, got out and walked around the back of the building, trying to look as if she knew exactly where she was going. She waited beside a line of green dustbins until she was sure his car had gone and then trudged through the rain for half a mile until she arrived at her Edwardian terraced house, much wetter than if she'd got a bus from the station.

Three weeks passed. Frankie immersed herself in her work. She didn't think of Daniel very often.

It was another rainy day, much like the day when Frankie had been to see the Pre-Raphaelite exhibition. She was already standing at the bus stop when she got a text to tell her that the art session had been cancelled due to a small fire in the day-centre kitchen. She sighed – there would be no pay that day – and set off back home laden with her carrier bags of paint and pastels and rolled-up sheets of sugar paper.

As she turned the corner into her street she spotted Dante sitting very upright on top of a gatepost like some wonderful Egyptian statue. In an instant he'd jumped down and was trotting towards her, tail upright, completely oblivious to the road between them.

The noises haunted Frankie for weeks: a dull thud, as though someone had kicked a heavy leather ball, and then the van accelerating very fast and a woman's scream – a scream that Frankie later realised had been her own. She didn't remember dropping the carrier bags till she found them the next day: soggy paper and pastels spilling like rainbows across the pavement.

When she reached Dante, he was lying in the gutter, rainwater gushing over him, streaked and mingling with his blood.

The first thing she could clearly remember was standing back at the bus stop with Dante in her arms, swaddled like a baby in a bath towel. Rain dripped from her hair into her eyes making it difficult to see if a bus was coming or not. Cars passed, drivers stared at her through their watery windscreens, passengers turned around to get a better look. No one stopped for the thin, blonde woman with the bloody bundle and desperate expression. Frankie looked down; so much blood. An image flashed into her mind of another blood-stained towel; she shut her eyes and when she opened them again she saw the pale blue Jaguar beside her and Daniel leaning across from the driver's seat, one hand beckoning her to get in.

Frankie bent down to peer into the open window.

'Your seats, they'll get blood on them.'

'Don't worry about my seats, just tell me where you need to take him – or her.'

Carefully she got in, trying not to let her bloody hands touch anything.

'It's a him. Dante.'

'I could tell you were a Rossetti kind of girl.'

Frankie didn't comment but pulled down the towel to examine the cat's face. She thought one eyelid moved but she couldn't be sure.

'Do you know the vet's practice on Rudge Street?'

Daniel nodded and edged back into the traffic. Frankie kept her eyes on Dante's face willing him to stay alive.

When they'd reached the vet's Daniel stopped at the entrance.

'Thank you,' Frankie said, her hand already on the door handle. 'You've been very kind.' And then she was out and up the stone steps and into the reception area before she even registered that Daniel had said, 'I'll just park the car.'

He appeared again just as the receptionist told her to take a seat and took the plastic chair next to hers.

Frankie kept her head down so Daniel couldn't see her tears.

They sat in silence until Dante's name was called.

'Would you like me to come in with you?'

Frankie nodded.

The schools were coming out as they drove back through the town; mothers in their 4x4s and Minis cluttered the roads and coaches heading for the comprehensive beeped their horns – their drivers gesticulating at the mothers. The relentless summer rain seemed to make everyone miserable. But inside the dry cocoon of the Jaguar Frankie felt happy. Dante was going to be alright.

'How many lives do you think he has left?' asked Daniel.

Frankie shrugged. 'A few more I hope. I can't bear to think of being without him.'

'Well, the vet did say he'd be good as new after the operation.' Daniel pulled up beside a grey four-storey building. 'Here you are, home sweet home.'

Frankie peered through the rain-washed windscreen. It took her a few seconds to work out why he had stopped beside a block of flats. The rain turned to pelting hail.

'Do you want to wait a for a while or make a run for it?' Daniel asked.

Frankie frantically tried to think what to say. Should she

43

speak the truth or carry on the deception?

'I have an umbrella you could borrow to get you to your door. I can pick it up from you another day.'

'Actually, I have a confession to make.'

Ten minutes later Daniel was sitting at the Formica table in Frankie's tiny kitchen. She sat down opposite him with two large mugs of tea.

'I see you've put up your paintings from the exhibition,' Daniel gestured to the postcards that Frankie had taped onto the front of the ugly boiler in the corner. They were additions to a whole gallery of postcards from exhibitions Frankie had visited.

'They cheer the place up a bit,' she looked around her. 'The landlord keeps promising to re-decorate but…'she shrugged.

'You could paint it yourself. Something bright like yellow, maybe a white wall opposite the window to reflect the light. If you were really ambitious you could extend the whole room into the garden, give yourself a bit more space.'

'I think my landlord might object to me knocking down the walls. He's not that keen on me even hanging pictures on them.'

Daniel laughed. 'Sorry, that's my architect's head taking over.' He looked at her. 'What do you do for a living? I'm guessing it might be something creative as you obviously appreciate art.'

'I used to paint,' she told him. 'I had my work in a few exhibitions after I left art college. I had a solo show too, with good reviews. I remember one journalist described me as a rising star on the British art scene. He said that I would be the next *big thing*. Frankie laughed and looked around the little kitchen. 'But as you can probably guess things didn't work out the way I'd hoped.'

She took down a dog-eared photograph from a shelf. 'This was from my degree show.' It showed three figures running up a hill, kites streaming behind them against an azure sky.

'I like it,' Daniel said, taking the photograph from her hand.

'Very expressive, very bold. Dynamic.'

'There were ten paintings in all; figures in motion, dancing, jumping, even flying. It was a sort of homage to my family; my childhood memories of them, lots of love and laughing and fun.'

'Do you have anything more recent?'

Frankie got up and fetched a picture from the mantelpiece in the living room. A girl, crouching in a dark space, body bent double, long dark hair hiding her expression. Daniel studied it.

'It's so much smaller. Tighter.' He looked closer. 'Sad.'

Frankie took it from his hand and laid it face down on the table.

'It was painted a while ago. I haven't really done anything since.'

For a few seconds Daniel stared at her and she was worried he would ask more. Instead he took a gulp of tea and asked her what she did to earn a living now. Frankie told him about the dementia group that she worked with, encouraging them to draw pictures of their favourite memories, and about the group of Down's Syndrome teenagers she'd been teaching to paint at Hawthorne House two mornings a week. Daniel asked her lots of questions and she found herself talking for ages about how much she enjoyed her work and the people who she helped learn to draw and paint.

'It makes up for not doing anything creative myself.'

Daniel picked up the photograph of her degree-show painting again.

'I really like this. Do your parents have the original?'

Frankie found her head full of memories of the chaotic cottage by the coast, the noisy kitchen, holidays in the beaten-up campervan, Paul always doing something clever with catapults or go-carts or the frogs that they had in abundance in the marshy fields around the cottage. Frankie realised she had been silent for a long time.

'They're dead.'

45

Daniel looked up from the picture.

'I'm sorry.'

Frankie stared at the little stars that covered the 1950s plastic tabletop.

'It was an accident. A car crash. My brother died too. He'd just got his GCSE results, ten A stars. They were going out to celebrate.' She tried not to think about the argument that had meant she stayed at home. She'd been watching *Friends* on the television when the police arrived.

'I miss them,' she said quietly.

'Was this before you went to college?' Daniel asked.

'Three weeks before I was due to start.'

'You were brave to take your place.'

'I had nowhere else to go.'

Frankie looked towards the kitchen window. The rain had stopped; shafts of evening sun struggled to push through a cracked, grey sky. Daniel followed her gaze.

'I ought to go,' he said.

'Sorry.' Frankie stood up and picked up the empty mugs. 'I'm sure you have better things to do than listen to me ramble on about my life.'

Daniel stood up and smiled. 'No. Not at all.' He handed her his business card. 'Let me know what time you need to collect Dante from the vets and I'll pick you up.'

'There really isn't any need – I'll get a taxi.'

'But I'd like to.'

Afterwards she spent agonizing hours re-living the conversation. Had she revealed too much – or not enough? She wondered if Daniel had noticed all the things she didn't talk about and had to remind herself that he wouldn't know, couldn't know.

That had been the whole point of all the changes she had made.

Frankie hadn't realised that she'd fallen asleep until she heard the key in the lock. Stiffly she struggled up from her position, curled up with Dante on the armchair. The cat jumped to the floor and Frankie stood up as Daniel walked through the door into the living room.

He looked terrible: dark shadows circled his eyes, his hair stuck up and his jacket was crumpled.

They stared at each other across the room. Frankie could feel the rough upholstery of the armchair against the back of her knees. The clock on the mantelpiece sounded too loud.

'I didn't know what was happening,' she said quietly.

Daniel sat down heavily on the sofa; Dante sprang up beside him.

He ran one hand over the cat's arched back and sighed. 'I told her.'

Frankie pursed her lips. They didn't look at each other.

'At least she has the children with her,' he continued. 'I left after the lunch.'

Frankie glanced at the clock: four fifteen. A whole day had passed. Her heart was beating too fast, maybe with fear at the enormity at what he had done or maybe because she realised it had taken him so long to come to her.

'I thought… I wanted…' He seemed to have read her mind. 'I needed to think, I couldn't come straight…' His words faded away as he gestured around the room. 'Sorry.'

'Did you spend the night at a hotel?'

'No. I had an urge to see the sea.'

'The sea? It's miles to the sea.'

Daniel shrugged. 'I drove a long way and sat and stared at the sea all night and then I started the engine, turned around and here I am.' He looked at her and his eyes seemed to be slowly coming back to life.

'Do you think you've done the right thing?' Frankie's voice was a whisper.

He gave a small smile. 'Yes.'

'Are you sure?'

He nodded and picked up the purring Dante to make more space on the sofa. 'Come and sit beside me and I'll tell you over and over again that nothing has ever felt so right in all my life.'

Seren

Clothes were strewn across the bed, skirts and dresses and jumpers, and Seren still couldn't decide what to wear. She pulled off her favourite cashmere cardigan, *much too hot*; a pearly button flew off across the room. She cursed out loud.

'Why aren't you bloody well here, Tom? You would know what I should wear for this.'

Sitting at the dressing table, she looked in the mirror. Her hair had been especially uncontrollable that morning, sticking out in all directions, *Having one of your crazy hair days*, Tom would have said. She brushed it fiercely, at the same time peering at her face. Her cheeks were flushed and her eyes were puffy. She looked away from her reflection and saw Nesta through the window, pruning the climbing rose that grew around The Windmill's walls. Even from a distance Seren could see that Nesta was more composed than she was herself.

Seren pulled on a pair of old jeans and a shirt she'd never thought especially suited her. She wasn't going to dress up for Daniel's family meeting. She manhandled her hair into her tortoiseshell clip, wound a silk scarf round her neck and wondered why he'd chosen the hotel restaurant to meet, so big and busy – it seemed a very public place.

'Are you ready yet?' Anni was knocking on her bedroom door. 'Ben's already waiting in the van.'

Seren scrabbled around in a drawer of the dressing table, finally finding a necklace of Venetian beads that Tom had bought for her one holiday. She took off the scarf and replaced it with the necklace.

'Come on,' Anni called. 'What's taking you so long?'

She was about to go when her eye was caught by the charm

49

bracelet, hanging from the frame of the mirror and glinting at her in the sun. Her father had bought it for her eighteenth birthday; a single star suspended from the silver chain. Every year he had given her another charm to add to it: the letter S, a daisy, a tea-cup, a bird and so on, until now it was so heavy with charms that Seren hardly ever wore it. She slipped it onto her wrist and it jingled cheerfully as if to tell her that everything would be OK.

'I hope Mum'll be alright.' In her rear-view mirror Seren watched her mother waving from The Windmill door, the baby on her hip, smiling as though waving her three children off on a cheerful day trip.

'She'll be fine.' Anni was squashed between Ben and Seren on the bench seat in the front of Seren's small green van. 'She wanted to look after them, didn't she? Said it helps to take her mind off things.'

This was true; as soon as Daniel had told her that he wanted to meet the three of them for lunch Seren had arranged for her friend to come and babysit but Nesta had protested. 'I've not turned into some sort of invalid, Seren. I'm sure I can still manage to spend a few hours with my grandchildren'.

'At least Griff's back at school,' continued Anni. 'That's one less for her to contend with.'

'But…' Seren wanted to say that Griff would hardly have been any trouble compared to Anni's boys, but she bit her lip and changed the subject. 'I wonder if Suki's back in London yet?'

'I should think so,' said Ben. 'She left at half nine and she drives like a maniac, especially in my car.'

'She's been wonderful this weekend, she seemed to know just the right things to say to Mum.' Seren paused as she negotiated the roundabout on the edge of town. 'She's really special, Ben. You're lucky to have found her.' Seren turned onto the high street.

Ben stared out of the window.

'I see the Fabulous Baker Boys have survived the recession,' he suddenly said, as they stopped alongside a mullioned bow window to let a delivery lorry manoeuvre into a parking space. The window was piled high with pyramids of meringues and chocolate brownies and multi-coloured macaroons. A painted sign swung from a cast-iron bracket, Patisserie Tremond. The name was an amalgamation of Trevor and Edmond, the two men who owned the shop.

'People will always want cake,' said Anni, leaning forward to get a better look.

'You mean you will always want cake,' Ben said, grinning. 'As much cake as possible.'

Anni punched him. 'Shut up, Ben.'

Ben hit her back.

'And we are now passing Stems.' Seren affected a tour-guide tone of voice to distract her siblings. 'As featured in last month's *County Brides* magazine! Unfortunately due to an unforeseen family crisis the shop is closed today.'

Flowers filled the tiny window of Seren's shop, bursting out of oversized vases, cascading from baskets and vintage kettles and jugs. When the shop was open, enamel buckets of flowers were arranged outside, alongside olive trees and lavender bushes planted in weather-beaten wooden crates and antique terracotta pots.

Anni had stopped hitting Ben. 'Looks like you've got some disappointed customers.'

Seren glanced at the shop as they passed. A man in a linen jacket was peering through the window, a little girl beside him, stretching up on tiptoes to look inside as well. He took the girl's hand and turned and Seren felt herself turn cold. She recognised the smooth hot-chocolate skin, the tight dark curls and, as he looked down at the child, his smile.

'Watch out!' Anni's voice shrieked in her ear. Seren turned her head back to the road just in time to see an elderly couple

51

metres from the bonnet of the van. She hit the brake as hard as she could and Anni and Ben had to hold onto the dashboard as they lurched forwards. With a horrible screech the van came to a halt.

'Bloody Hell!' said Ben. 'No wonder it took you five tries before you passed your test.'

'I could sue you for whiplash,' Anni rubbed her neck. 'Have you never noticed there's a zebra crossing here?'

Seren watched the couple shuffle to the opposite side of the street; they turned and waved at her, apparently oblivious to the near miss they'd had. She took a deep breath, her heart hammering in her chest, and started the engine again. As she drove slowly up the street she checked her rear-view mirror. The pavement outside her shop was empty. Maybe she'd been wrong. Maybe she'd imagined it had been him looking in the window. Maybe she'd imagined it had been him driving the car three days before. She looked down at the charm bracelet on her wrist. He'd been with her when her father had given it to her.

Seren parked the car in the car park and the three siblings headed for the grand colonnaded entrance of the hotel. Seren couldn't stop her eyes from scanning the street, searching for the man and the little girl.

Anni linked her arm through Seren's.

'I'm absolutely ravenous. I hope the hotel is as good as it used to be.'

'I'd have settled for a bag of chips in the park,' said Ben. 'Do you remember Dad used to do that with us after swimming sometimes?'

'No,' Anni shook her head, her blonde hair swinging around her shoulders.

'I remember,' said Seren. 'Sunday mornings; he taught me how to swim before I had even started school.'

Anni made a disgruntled noise, 'I expect it was while Mum was busy talking to Granny on the phone. Every Sunday morning – Mum sitting on the bottom step in the kitchen, gabbling away in Welsh on that two-tone grey phone they had, and Dad trying to butt in, asking what they were going on about. I think it made him feel excluded.'

'I don't remember them having a phone like that.' Seren's expression was puzzled.

'It was the one before the scarlet-trim phone in the living room,' said Ben.

'I don't remember that one either.'

'I forget how much younger than us you are,' Ben patted her head.

'That was it,' Anni's face suddenly took on the satisfied expression of having solved a mystery. 'I was probably too old to come swimming with you. I'd have been busy doing my homework or revising for my GCSEs.'

'Or busy snogging your way through the town's Boy Scout troop in the back pew of the church.' Ben grinned at his older sister.

'Holding hands with Samuel Pond at the Remembrance Day service is not the same as snogging an entire Scout troop!'

'I remember how you were drummed out of the Girl Guide movement in disgrace,' Ben continued. 'Stripped of your funny little red tie, never allowed to swear allegiance to the Queen again.'

'I left because it clashed with jazz aerobics in the Civic Hall.'

Seren smiled at their bickering and began to feel a little better. Maybe it hadn't been him outside the shop and maybe her father wanted to tell them he was coming home.

As they walked into the hotel foyer they were laughing; at the sight of their father they all stopped. Daniel looked ghost-like in a leather armchair by the fire. He stood up, not quite able to look them in the eye.

'Thank you for meeting me.'

53

He repeated it three times, and as the waiter showed them to a window table, Seren knew he wasn't going to tell them he was coming home.

Nesta

Nesta's arms ached from hacking and sawing and wrenching the rose bush from the wall. The baby was sleeping and the boys were glued to *Scooby Doo*, stuffing their faces with flapjack and popcorn.

As Nesta pulled at a thorny branch she wondered how they were getting on in the hotel. She hadn't been there for years – though they used to go all the time for birthdays or evenings out with friends. Sometimes the firm had held their Christmas meal in the elegant dining room and once they went to a New Year's dinner dance, and she and Daniel had got drunk on White Russians. They had giggled like teenagers all the way home in the back of the taxi.

She was nearly finished, just the last bit of stem and that would be the end of it. Later she would pour a bit of Round-Up on the stump just to be sure.

Daniel had given her the rose on their seventh wedding anniversary and had told her where to plant it – even dug the hole himself. He explained how the delicate apricot flowers would perfectly complement the terracotta bricks – as though she had no idea of colour or design.

They'd just moved in. One year living in a rented flat with two small children and thirty packing cases had nearly driven Nesta insane. She'd said she wanted to go back to London, to the tiny garden flat. She even missed the swirly carpet. Deep down, she wanted to go back to Wales. But Daniel had finally finished his tower – his labour of love, that's what he called it. He'd said it was for her.

Nesta had never asked him to go out and find an old windmill to turn into a family house. All she'd wanted was a little bit of his time, for it to be like it had been in the beginning, when all his energy had been for her rather than for bricks and slates and timber.

Seven years since the wedding, six and a half years since Anwen, five since Ben, two since he'd stopped telling her she was beautiful – standing in a broken yard full of brambles, watching him digging a hole and wondering how one rose bush would make it seem any better.

It was three more months before she found out about Lillian. She'd often wondered if Lillian had helped him choose the rose. 'Compassion' it was called – that was a joke! To think, he'd asked *her* to design the garden. She would have had free rein if Anwen hadn't spotted them outside the supermarket. 'Look Mummy, Daddy's kissing a lady in that car.' Nesta looked, then looked away, and continued loading the shopping bags into the boot of her Austin Princess. The bags included the ingredients for the supper party they were having with Lillian and her husband Gerald the next day – salmon en croute, Black Forest gateau for dessert – Nesta had been planning it for weeks. On the way home she stopped at the public library and took out every horticulture book they had. If she couldn't control her husband maybe there was something else she could.

She sat in bed that night with *The RHS Encyclopaedia* lying on her lap, *A Common Sense Guide to Beautiful Flowers* and *The Easy Path to Gardening* on the bedside table. She didn't look up from her book when Daniel finally came home. She turned a page and told him she needed a wheelbarrow and a man to help her smash up the concrete.

Daniel had started to protest but Nesta turned another page and quietly mentioned the phone call she had made to Lillian cancelling the supper party. 'She was out with a friend but Gerald and I had a lovely chat.'

And here she was thirty-three years later, with her back to her wonderful garden, pouring weedkiller onto her husband's favourite climbing rose. Nesta hated killing plants but at least she would never have to look at those insipid orange flowers and wonder again whether Lillian had chosen them.

She looked at her watch. The children would be back soon. What would he have said? Begged for understanding? Forgiveness? Explained how things hadn't been right between them for years? That it was all Nesta's fault?

'But we were happy here,' Nesta whispered at the wall. 'In the end.'

After Seren had been born they'd been very happy. Daniel had his business, Nesta had her garden. They'd put the rocky, early years behind them. If there was anyone else for him Nesta didn't want to know. He never asked if there was anybody else for her.

Tomorrow, thought Nesta, *I'll go out and buy a clematis – something big and blousy, pink or purple – just to see the look on his face.*

Frankie

Frankie was immersed in watery silence. The distorted echoes of the swimming pool had vanished as soon as she dived in and now all she could hear was the rush of her own thoughts. Would he change his mind? Would *they* change it for him? Would he come back at all? Frankie's head broke the surface and the noise came back, temporarily shattering her anxiety. She swam down into the silence again, pushing her body deeper so that she was swimming underneath the other swimmers, so deep that she could feel the weight of the water on her body.

Images floated through her mind; a sparkling clear blue sea, white sand between her toes, a beautiful view from a hotel window, laughing faces on the beach below – and then suddenly someone shouting in her face, spitting out words, twisting the belt of her dressing gown around her wrists until she couldn't move her arms.

She came up quickly, gasping for breath as she clung onto the edge of the pool. She would tell Daniel everything. No, she wouldn't. She would tell him to go back to Nesta and forget her. It had all been a terrible mistake.

She heaved herself out of the water, heavy with guilt; dripping.

In the confines of the cubicle she roughly rubbed the towel over her cropped hair and tried to remember how she had allowed herself to get so entangled with Daniel. She hadn't been looking for a lover, she hadn't even been looking for a friend.

Daniel had come with her to pick up Dante from the vet's. Back at the house, they laid the sedated cat on a blanket in front of the gas fire in Frankie's living room and Frankie knelt beside

Dante until he came round. When he began to purr Daniel went out to the corner shop and returned with crumpets and Cava. She thought that had been the start: sitting beside him on the sofa, butter dripping on her fingers, Cava in the pale pink tumbler she'd bought from Oxfam. For the first time in years she had let another person in.

After that there were more visits from Daniel to check up on Dante's progress, a trip to see a special showing of *La Dolce Vita* at the cinema, lunch at a riverside pub on a blazing hot August day, numerous cups of tea at Frankie's kitchen table, many walks. Daniel took her to see a house he was building for a client. He gave her a hard hat to wear and together they climbed up a ladder and looked out of the empty windows at the setting sun. And they talked; they talked for weeks; they talked for months. Looking back Frankie couldn't say what they had talked about but she knew that she had been careful. Neither of them talked too much about the past.

Daniel often talked about Nesta, her busy life, her garden, her chickens, and about Seren and Griff.

'She has little time left for me,' he'd said, but then he'd laughed. 'Sorry, I don't want to be one of those men who go round saying my wife doesn't understand me. It's just we seem to have grown apart.'

To Frankie it seemed that Daniel was in need of a friend – just a friend, nothing else. They had a year of friendship, and then Tom died. Frankie didn't see Daniel for weeks. She missed him.

One hot night in early June he had appeared on her doorstep. The roses had just started to bloom on the dilapidated trellis around the front door.

'I can't pretend any more,' he'd said. 'Tom's death has made me realise life is too short.'

Frankie had asked him to come in but Daniel kept standing on the doorstep, scarlet roses arching over his head, their scent thick and sweet in the warm air.

'I love you, Frankie.'

They had stared at each other for a long time.

'I think I love you too,' she'd finally said.

Of course there had been guilt – huge guilt. There had been weeks when they tried not to see each other, tried to put a stop to it. Weeks when Frankie said it felt all wrong; weeks when Daniel said it wasn't right; weeks when both of them agreed to part.

'Will you wait?' Daniel asked as they walked hand in hand across a field at dawn. 'Wait until Seren has recovered from Tom's death a little. Wait till Griff has settled down at school again. Wait until Nesta is strong enough. Wait until the spring comes, when Nesta's garden is in bloom.'

They stopped walking, their breath coming out as small puffs of smoke in the early morning air.

'I'll wait,' Frankie whispered. And Daniel held her tightly and told her that everything would work out for the best.

Daniel had told Frankie about the other woman in his past. Lillian. A mistake, he called her.

Lillian, the name rolled round Frankie's head. She turned to face him in her narrow bed, her back cold against the wall behind. 'And me? Am I a mistake?'

Daniel took her in his arms and kissed her. 'No, this is something very different.'

Frankie squinted against the bright sunlight as she stepped out through the leisure centre's sliding doors. She didn't turn left to take the shortcut through the park like she usually did, instead she found herself turning right, crossing the footbridge over the railway track and following the narrow path that led to the high street. She'd convinced herself she needed milk and onions from Tesco's but five minutes later she walked past the supermarket, milk and onions long forgotten.

As she approached the hotel her footsteps slowed and she

began to envision Daniel with his children. She briefly imagined going inside. She would apologise, promise that she'd have no more to do with Daniel. His children could take him home immediately, and that would be the end of it.

She almost walked into the man. Frankie stopped abruptly, dropping her basket of swimming things at his feet. Her wet towel fell out onto the pavement narrowly missing his expensive-looking shoes.

Apologising, Frankie shoved it back into the basket. The man still hadn't seemed to notice her. His face looked familiar. A little girl had hold of his hand and was pulling on his arm, 'Come on, Daddy, let's go, please.' Frankie followed his gaze and realised he was staring into the hotel or, more specifically, staring at a group of people gathered behind the glass at a large bay window. Two women, one big and blonde, one smaller and fiery-haired, and two men. The younger man, dressed in a faded T-shirt and jeans, was slouching in his chair while the other, older, smarter, grim faced, was sitting forward, gesticulating with his hands as though trying to emphasise a point.

Frankie knew she should walk away – she had no right to be there, invisibly intruding – but she couldn't move, couldn't stop watching, like it was some awful television drama you can't switch off. Frankie knew the names of all the characters. Daniel had told her enough about his children to enable her to identify Seren, Anni and Ben.

Seren began to get to her feet; Daniel reached out and touched her arm. She sat down again and, as though for the sake of having something to do with her hands, loosened her hair, letting it fall around her shoulders in a waterfall of wild red curls. Quickly she pulled it back again, twisting it into a tight coil behind her head and fastening it with a clip. All the while her mouth was moving – a deluge of silent words pouring out. Daniel shook his head and Frankie knew that Seren wasn't giving him her blessing.

'You said we'd have a cupcake. You promised.'

61

Frankie remembered the man and the little girl; he seemed as transfixed by the scene in the window as she was.

'Daddy, I need a wee! Quickly. I think I'm going to wet my pants.'

That broke the spell. He looked down at the little girl and noticed Frankie.

'Sorry, do you want an autograph?'

'Pardon?'

'I would usually give you an autograph, it's just…' He indicated his daughter. 'I think we have an urgent situation on our hands. Do you know if there are any public toilets round here?'

Frankie said she thought there were some by the car park and he thanked her and hurried away. When Frankie looked back at the window Seren was staring straight back at her, her hand at her mouth, her expression horrified.

Frankie quickly walked away. She should never have gone to the hotel. Now Seren had seen her, she'd tell Daniel and he'd think that she was weird or mad or both. He'd be disappointed – maybe he'd be angry, she couldn't bear that. She began to run, pushing her way through the afternoon shoppers, desperate to get away. This was definitely it, she'd tell Daniel it was over as soon as he came home. She'd pack his things up and have them waiting in the hallway. Let him resume his life with Nesta, let her resume whatever she had had before. She knew she'd have to move away, of course, start again, but she was used to that.

Her head was throbbing as she pushed the key into the front door. Dante was at her feet, coiling his long body around her ankles but Frankie didn't have the strength to bend down to stroke him as she usually did.

The signs were familiar – soon she would be sick, the throbbing would get worse and then her vision would start to distort until everything became segmented, as though she were a fly observing the world through many lenses. It was too late

62

for painkillers to bring any relief; only a darkened room and sleep would ease the misery. She threw down her basket in the hallway and stumbled up the stairs cursing the oncoming pain for disabling her determination to pack Daniel's bags.

The new bed had arrived the week before, a king-size symbol of Daniel's commitment to their future. It looked like a giant raft in the small blue bedroom and Frankie collapsed onto it as though it were the only thing that could save her.

She opened one eye and saw at least ten disjointed Daniels; she opened the other eye and the Daniels converged into one. He was crouched down beside her, his hand on her forehead; it felt good.

'Are you OK?' he asked.

Frankie tried to nod but her head hurt too much.

'Are you ill? Do you have a fever?'

'Headache,' she whispered.

'Maybe you have flu?'

Frankie tried to shake her head but the slight movement brought on a wave of intense pain and she closed her eyes again. She wanted to tell him it was just a migraine, that she'd suffered from them since she fell down the stairs. The doctors had told her there was nothing they could do. She wanted to tell him that the headaches took hold of her at times when she was trying to make her most important decisions, punishing her for trying to make any kind of plan. Most of all she wanted to ask what Seren had said after she saw her staring through the window, but instead she felt herself slipping into sleep again and when she next woke up, she smelt toast and through the curtains she could see the street lights had come on.

Frankie lay very still, hardly daring to hope that the pain had gone. She took a deep breath and shifted her head on the pillow; it didn't hurt. She could hear jazz playing downstairs and every so often Daniel's voice, 'No, this is not for you. I've given you your supper... OK, have a little bit... I said a little bit, you greedy boy.' Hearing him talk to Dante made her smile. It was nice to know she wasn't on her own.

Slowly memories of the day swam up to the surface and a feeling of dread rose from the depths of her stomach until all she could see was Seren's face through the long glass window. Frankie pressed her fingers to her eyes. What must Seren think? It was only then that she began to feel her brain sliding the pieces into place – a Christmas-cracker puzzle where you move each plastic square to make a picture. Seren hadn't been staring, wide-eyed and aghast, at her at all. As far as Frankie knew, Seren didn't even know what she looked like. To Seren she would have been just a solitary woman looking through a hotel-restaurant window, peering in to see the decor, or looking for a friend inside. Frankie sat up, switched on the bedside light and drew her fingers through her tousled hair. Seren's horrified expression hadn't been for her at all, it had been for the man standing next to her. Then Frankie remembered where she'd seen him before.

Seren

'Mum. Mum. Mum!'

Seren was transfixed by the tiny drop of blood. She hadn't even realised she'd been picking at the skin around her nail but already the skin looked raw, a scarlet pearl glistening in the middle of the wound. She put her finger in her mouth; it tasted metallic.

'Mummy, are you listening?'

Seren forced herself to smile, 'Yes darling, you're doing really well. Fantastic reading.'

Griff closed *Horrid Henry* and slid it into the green school folder on his bedside table. 'No it wasn't. I got stuck on loads of words and you didn't even notice.'

'Sorry. I'm a bit tired tonight.'

Griff took off his glasses and shuffled down under the covers until only his mop of curls and half his freckly face were visible above the duvet. 'You don't need to read to me if you don't want to.'

'Of course I want to.'

Seren picked up the battered copy of *The Hobbit* and opened it at the page marked by a leather bookmark embossed with gold. The book had once been Daniel's. The bookmark had been hers, bought on a school history trip to London on September 11th 2001.

She held the bookmark in her hand; it felt soft. She could clearly remember that bright afternoon, queuing up to pay for a souvenir she didn't even want in the Tower of London shop. She remembered the boys in front of her messing around with a display of plastic swords and Mr Campbell marching Neil Wilson outside for trying to steal a Beefeater tea towel. 'It's for my mum sir, it's her birthday.' Seren remembered flicking back her painstakingly straightened hair as she chatted to her best friend Mandy Trump, only too aware that Arlow Lavern was standing right behind her.

Arlow Lavern, Arlow Lavern – she'd done it now, she'd let the name into her head after years of trying to pretend he'd never existed, even when billboards at bus stops and the covers of TV-listing magazines tormented her with images of DCI Zac Jones to herald yet another series of *Island Beat*. But it wasn't a poster or a cover of a magazine in the supermarket that she'd seen that afternoon – it was him, living, breathing and standing on the high street looking like he'd seen a ghost.

Why? Of all the days, of all the hours, of all the minutes; just when she had thought she was finally getting through to her father, just when she felt he had begun to understand that leaving Nesta would be the worst mistake he'd ever made. At the very moment that Daniel's determined expression had wavered, when he'd run his hand over his beard and sighed and asked if she really believed that Nesta would forgive him, Seren had looked through the window and the sight of Arlow's face had hit her like a bomb going off. After that the meeting with her father became a blur and by the time they got back into her little green van she found that instead of persuading her father to come home, she'd agreed to go with Anni the next day to meet his other woman in her house; the house her father twice referred to as 'our home'.

Anni had insisted that she wanted to meet Frankie before she went back to Australia. 'It would be good to put a face to the name.' Seren thought her sister had gone quite mad. Daniel had agreed, promising cakes and biscuits as though she and Anni were still children, and Seren had just nodded and said, 'That would be nice.'

Seren shook her head and tried to focus on the book in front of her.

'Where had we got to?' Griff didn't answer. Seren looked up

and saw that he was fast asleep. She didn't move. After a while she put the bookmark to her face and sniffed the leather.

Instantly she was sitting on a stuffy coach heading back to school, staring at the close-cropped fields that lined the motorway. The driver had his radio on and Mr Campbell sat forward on his seat at the front, straining to hear the news report above the roar of thirty sixteen-year-olds. Seren caught the occasional sentence from the radio and felt frightened. She wanted to be at home, sitting at the kitchen table eating her mother's shortbread and listening to her father's jazz. She wanted to be safe inside The Windmill, hearing her parents tell her that everything would be alright.

'Oy Seren!' Neil Wilson's words sent more shivers of fear down her back.

'Ignore him.' Mandy Trump got a copy of *Elle* out of her bag and handed it to Seren. 'There's an interview in there with Johnny Depp. Lovely picture.'

'Seren!'

Seren tried to concentrate on Johnny Depp's dark eyes, though the radio appeared to be saying that planes were flying into buildings and towers were collapsing, while behind her Neil Wilson's jeers were getting louder.

'What sort of a name is Seren?' He'd moved forward, pushing two girls out from behind so that he could sprawl across the seats himself. 'Why didn't they call you Ginger?' He reached through the headrests and flicked her head. 'Is your hair that colour all over your body?' He sniggered and began to kick the back of the seat. Seren tried to imagine that she and Johnny Depp were sitting on a beach together. 'I'll meet you down the park later and you can show me.' Johnny was telling her he'd love her forever. 'In that hut behind the swings.'

'Shall I get Mr Campbell?' said Mandy.

'It's alright,' said Seren.

'Why'd they call you Seren, anyway? Was it some weirdo hippy name your mum and dad thought up 'cos they couldn't think of anything else?' He kicked harder. Seren had to bite her lip to stop herself from giving him the satisfaction of hearing her cry out.

'It means star.' Seren turned around and saw Arlow Laverne standing in the aisle next to Neil Wilson, glaring down at the class bully with narrowed eyes. 'It's Welsh.'

'What? Is her dad a sheep-shagger or something?' Neil sneered, but he stopped kicking the seat.

'Shut up,' Arlow didn't raise his voice. 'I think her name is cool.' Mandy Trump nudged Seren in the ribs and Seren buried her flushing face in Johnny Depp's, though inside a little bubble of happiness began to grow. The most gorgeous boy in the school was standing up for her; the new boy who'd already impressed them all with his reading of Hamlet's soliloquy in her English class the week before.

'Sit down, Laverne!' Mr Campbell bellowed down the aisle. Arlow went back to his seat.

'Arlow's a fucking weird name, too,' Neil Wilson muttered, but he kept himself to himself for the rest of the journey.

'How did you know my name meant star?' Seren asked Arlow as they walked away from the school gates.

'I looked it up,' he said. Seren watched a grin spread across his smooth, brown face and wondered what it would be like to reach up and kiss his cheek. 'In the library.'

Fourteen years later, despite everything that had happened, the thought of Arlow with his box-fresh trainers and hooded top sitting in the small town public library searching through a book of names still made Seren smile.

'There you are.' Anni was opening a bottle of wine in The Wheat House kitchen when Seren walked in. 'I thought we might be in need of a little medication.'

Seren smiled. 'Did Ben get the train?'

'Yes, Mum and I waved him off; he should be halfway back

to London by now. He took that monstrosity of a clock back with him, even though Mum kept on telling him she'd like to keep it.'

'Is Mum alright?' Seren got out two glasses.

'She's insisted on doing the bedtime circus with the kids. Says it will be a welcome distraction. I thought it would be a welcome distraction to have a glass of this with you.'

Seren smiled at her sister as she watched her pour the wine. She seemed more relaxed now that Ben had gone.

'You OK?' Anni asked.

Seren shrugged.

'I know it must be rough. How long is it now since Tom…?' Anni took a sip of wine, unable to quite get the last word out.

'A year next month.'

'I wonder what he would have made of what is happening with Mum and Dad. He was always so level-headed. So measured in everything he did and said.'

Seren laughed. 'Are you trying to say he was boring?'

'Of course not! If you want a boring man look no further than my Mike. On and on he drones, about work, about football, about the bloody filter on the swimming pool.' Anni took another sip of wine. 'Tom wasn't like that. I think "sensible" is more the word.'

Anni's mobile phone started to ring. She looked at the screen. 'Mum.' A brief conversation followed and Seren gathered that the bedtime circus in The Windmill was getting rather out of hand.

'I'd better go and rescue her,' Anni downed her glass of wine in one gulp. 'I'll be back for more but I may be some time!'

Seren watched her go out of the door, striding across the garden towards The Windmill. Outside it was still light; the sky a pale pink gauze with wisps of purple cloud.

She stared at the sky and considered the word 'boring'.

Maybe Tom had been boring. Eight years older than Seren, he'd always seemed wise and steady, not given to huge displays of emotion. She had thought of him like a rock and clung to him. He had saved her from drowning. She had been grateful.

She took a gulp of wine and tentatively allowed herself to think of Arlow; he could never have been described as 'boring'.

Arlow Laverne. Seren had hardly been aware of opening the laptop on the dresser and typing his name into Google. There were lots of sites referring to him; she skimmed the list. Most seemed to be about the axing of *Island Beat* earlier that year. Seren clicked onto the Wikipedia entry.

'The only son of a Scottish hairdresser and a West African doctor, Arlow Laverne was born in Ealing and brought up in the South of England by his mother before attending the Central School of Speech and Drama, followed by two years with the Camden Theatre Company.'

There then followed a list of theatre and small TV credits before a long entry about his lead role in *Island Beat*, a Sunday night TV series about a black police detective sent to work in a remote yet crime-riddled group of islands in the Outer Hebrides.

'Personal Life – He is married to fellow actor Angellica Chadwick and they have one daughter.'

Seren quickly shut the laptop lid and took another gulp of wine. Leaning against the dresser she willed herself to wipe away the memories. There were more important things to deal with – a real crisis in the present – she didn't need to dredge up crises from the past.

Opening the laptop lid again, she resisted the urge to type in Angellica Chadwick and instead typed in Frankie Hyde. This revealed an organic butcher from West Wales, a Cornishman who had recently celebrated his hundredth birthday and an under-sixteen lightweight boxing champion. She tried Francesca Hyde and found a high-school girl from Ohio, a trans-gender hat designer in Skegness and a reference to one of the Edwardian suffragettes. None of them seemed likely to be the woman her father said he had fallen in love with.

Frankie

'They're coming here?'

'Yes,' said Daniel.

'Today?'

'Yes,' Daniel handed her a cup of tea. 'I couldn't tell you last night, you were too ill.'

Frankie ran a hand through her dishevelled hair. She looked around the kitchen, desperate to think of an excuse. 'But I need to tidy up. The house is a mess.'

It was true. Daniel's dishes from the night before were piled in the sink, Dante's muddy paw prints were everywhere, a pile of opened bills and circulars were strewn across the table and from where she stood she could see her swimming things still spilling from her basket across the hallway floor.

'Don't worry,' Daniel began rolling up his shirtsleeves. 'I'll start with the washing up. You have a bath and try to relax.'

'But I'm not ready.'

'They're not coming till this afternoon.'

'I mean I think I need more time before I meet them. I never expected you to invite them here.'

Daniel put his hands on her shoulders, looking down at her face with soft blue eyes.

'They want to meet you. Anni's going back to Australia soon; she's especially keen to get to know you. And I want them both to see how special you are. So that they understand why I want to be with you.'

Frankie still didn't understand why Daniel wanted to be with her, so she doubted very much that his daughters would.

'But why bring them to the house? It feels so... so...' The word invasive popped into her head but she knew she couldn't say that. 'So soon,' she said instead.

'It's my home now. I want the girls to know where I live.' Daniel gathered her into his arms and hugged her. 'Until we get somewhere better, of course,' he added.

'But they'll think it's so small and shabby. And they won't want to get to know me.' Frankie's words were coming out in short breathless bursts as panic mounted. 'All they'll see is someone who's stolen their father and hurt their mother.' She thought but didn't mention that they would also realise how big the age difference between her and Daniel was – she wasn't much older than Anni. 'They'll try even harder to make you change your mind. They'll hate me at first sight.'

Daniel kissed her. 'How could anyone possibly hate you? Now go and run that bath.'

They hate me. Water exploded out of the spout of the kettle, spattering Frankie's cotton blouse. Frankie turned off the tap and emptied some of the excess water from the kettle into the sink. *They really hate me.*

She could hear the awkward conversation coming from the living room.

'Frankie is an artist.' Frankie cringed at Daniel's words. 'Figurative mainly. Very talented.'

She couldn't hear the next sentence, but she thought she caught a slight Antipodean accent, so presumed it was Anni.

'Yes, that's one of hers on the mantelpiece.' Again Daniel's words made Frankie want to curl into a ball.

'Let me see,' Seren's voice sounded clear and confident. Frankie looked at the back door – she could climb over the fence, cross her neighbour's lawn, scale the high brick wall, run across the cemetery and be out into the open countryside within minutes. She knew the escape route – she'd had it planned since she first moved in.

'Is it a self-portrait?' Anni was asking.

'The girl looks frightened,' said Seren.

Please go away, thought Frankie as the noise from the

73

boiling kettle drowned out Daniel's reply.

'Let me take that,' Daniel took the tray from Frankie's hands. Frankie hoped that no-one noticed how much her hands were shaking.

'What about the cakes?' asked Daniel. 'I got them from Tremond's.' He smiled at his daughters, who sat perched on the edge of the couch. Both wore black; Frankie could see the cat hair clinging to them. 'I went out specially to get them this morning.' His tone was more appropriate for children than for two women in their thirties. 'Trevor picked out the selection for me. He told me it includes your favourite, Seren, raspberry crumble slices.'

'Sorry,' Frankie mumbled turning back to the kitchen. 'I've left the box on the dresser.'

Daniel stopped her. 'Don't worry, darling. I'll go and put them on a plate. You sit down and have a chat.'

As Frankie tentatively sat down on the armchair she caught Seren and Anni exchanging glances.

Frankie looked down at her hands, noticing her bitten nails, and wished she was somewhere else.

'So, Frankie,' Anni's tone was overly cheerful. 'Dad says you're an artist.'

Frankie looked up to see both women staring at her. Anni smiled fixedly. Seren appeared to be studying the carpet.

'Well, I haven't done any painting for a while,' Frankie said carefully, hoping that Seren wouldn't notice the large red-wine stain made by a previous tenant.

'Do you have a job at present?' Frankie felt as though Anni were interviewing her for a position.

'I teach art classes. Mainly to people with learning difficulties and older people with dementia.'

'You're not a school teacher then?' asked Anni.

'No.'

The room fell silent. Seren's eyes had left the carpet and

were darting everywhere. Frankie was painfully aware of the poky little room with its over-sized furniture and out-dated wallpaper.

'Can I use the oval dish on the shelf?' Daniel called out from the kitchen.

'OK,' Frankie called back. She hoped he'd wipe the dust off. She'd bought it from a charity shop and had never used it for anything other than display.

'Our mum used to be a teacher,' Anni said. 'In London. Before she had children.'

'Oh.'

'An inner-city primary.'

'That must have been challenging.' Frankie tried to smile. She wondered what Nesta looked like, big and blonde like Anni or slim and auburn haired like Seren? She'd always been so careful not to ask.

'You don't have children, do you?' It was the first time that Seren had spoken since Daniel left the room.

Frankie shook her head. Another awkward silence fell. Frankie cleared her throat.

'Daniel tells me you have a son, Seren.'

'Yes.'

'I look forward to meeting him.'

Seren's eyes flashed. Frankie immediately knew she'd stepped on a landmine.

'No!' Seren stood up.

'Seren!' Daniel stood in the doorway with the plate piled high with cakes.

'Calm down, Seren,' Anni stood up too.

Seren turned to face Frankie; her words delivered fast, like bullets. 'You'll never get to meet my son.' The words were tripping over themselves in their hurry to get out. 'My dad will be back with my mother as soon as he realises what a mistake he's making.'

Daniel looked as though someone had unexpectedly punched

him. A raspberry crumble slice slid onto the floor.

'I'll take her home,' Anni put her hand on Seren's arm. Seren shrugged her off and walked out of the room. The sound of the front door slamming shook the whole house and probably half the terrace too.

Anni looked at her father, then at Frankie. 'Sorry. She's very upset.'

'I don't understand,' said Daniel.

Anni shrugged. 'Seren's jealous.' She turned to Frankie. 'She's always been her daddy's favourite.'

'Anni, that's not true.' Daniel sounded hurt.

Anni laughed. 'It's alright, Dad – I've had years of counselling.' She took a chocolate éclair from the plate, still in her father's hands. 'I'm reconciled to it.'

Seren

Seren ran through the terraced streets, her heart beating hard. For a few minutes she thought she was lost amongst a maze of newly built houses, but then she saw the spire of St Stephen's poking above the roof tops and she knew where she was going. Her angry words were still banging round her head; she wished she hadn't sounded so hysterical. Stopping at the corner of the high street she leant against a wall.

It had been the thought of Griff. Poor Griff, trying to make sense of his world turned upside down. Seren looked up at the sky as a dark cloud moved across the sun. And something else had disturbed her in that tiny living room. The painting. Frankie's painting on the mantelpiece. The girl in it looked so lost, so scared and abandoned. Seren knew that girl, or at least knew how she felt. She hadn't liked being confronted with those feelings again.

She took a deep breath and walked onto the busy street, trying not to make eye contact with anyone she knew and trying not to think about the injured expression on her father's face. Her father, who had only done good things for her in her life. He had always been there when she needed him. She started to run again, swerving around pedestrians, barely looking as she crossed the little roads.

At last she reached her shop and unlocked the door, breathing in the familiar, comforting smells of foliage and flowers. Leaving the note on the door apologising for being closed, she sat down on the high stool behind the counter in the unlit shop to wait for her sister.

She couldn't understand what was taking Anni so long, she'd presumed that she'd be right behind her. The ticking of the big clock on the wall sounded louder than usual. After its hand had slowly moved around one half hour, then another, Seren started testing all the pens in a pot beside her, throwing away most of them. She tidied up the little rack of gift cards and checked the order book for flowers to be delivered the next day. She had just started to rearrange the rolls of ribbon when a figure burst through the door, setting the little bell attached to it jingling manically. It wasn't Anni.

'Tell me everything! Edmond and I have been desperate to know.'

'Hi Trevor,' she said, slowly winding up a reel of gingham ribbon that had unwound to the floor. 'We never ate the cakes.'

'Never mind about the cakes, sweetie, just tell me – what's she like?'

Trevor leaned over the counter and stared at Seren with large brown eyes, his hands cupping his perfectly chiselled jaw. 'Essex orange, plastic boobs? Leopard-print skirt? Rubber knickers?'

'Trevor! I don't want to think about her knickers, but if you're going to force me I'd say more of a M&S cotton brief – probably gone a bit discoloured in the wash.'

Trevor looked at her over his thick-framed glasses. 'Really!? *Fifty Shades of Grey: The Dowdy Years*?'

Seren laughed and started to feel better.

'Tell me exactly what she looks like.'

'Well…'Seren tried to remember; it all seemed a bit of a blur. 'She has big eyes and a kind of choppy crop. Sort of pretty, a bit thin, though.'

Trevor narrowed his eyes. 'I'm thinking Anne Hathaway in *Les Mis*.'

Seren nodded. 'Yes! But blonde – ash blonde I think you'd call it.'

'A L'Oréal home kit job?'

'Mmm, maybe.'

'What was she wearing?'

'A sort of tunic thing with a belt in the middle.'

78

'Shoes?'

'Um, I can't remember. I think they were slip-ons or lace ups – I wasn't really looking – something flat.'

Trevor looked Seren up and down 'What *is* that all over you? Is it bits of dog, or cat, or some kind of alpaca?'

Seren looked down at the cream hairs attached to her top and trousers.

'She has a cat.'

The bell jingled again and a large man with an elaborately waxed handlebar moustache and a completely bald head fell through the door, misjudging the small step down into the room.

'Sorry. I do that every time.' He found his balance and nearly toppled into a container of carnations. 'Sorry.' He pushed them back into position sloshing water down the red-and-white-striped apron that encircled his ample middle. After a few more apologies he made it to the counter.

'I couldn't bear the suspense. What's the news?'

'Edmond!' Trevor straightened up. 'What about the shop? It's a Tutti-frutti Cupcake Special Day – we might get a mad rush when the mothers pick the kids up from school.'

'I'm sorry, darling, but I can't possibly think about the tutti-frutti cupcakes with all this drama going on over the road.' Edmond looked at Seren imploringly. 'I've simply got to know – what's she like?'

'Well...' Seren began again before being instantly interrupted by Trevor.

'So far we've got a bottle-blonde, bug-eyed, scrawny, cat-loving spinster wearing a sack, comfortable shoes and ancient knickers.'

'What a relief!' Edmond clapped his hands. 'Sounds like Daniel will be home to the beautiful Nesta in no time.'

'Oh,' Seren sighed. 'I forgot to tell you one other thing about her.'

Trevor and Edmond looked at her eagerly.

'She's at least twenty years younger than my dad.'

The two men gasped at exactly the same time.

'Poor Nesta,' they said in unison.

'We should have realised when he got the car.' Trevor shook his head. 'The next step was bound to be a younger woman.'

Anni's face appeared at the window, peering through the buckets of flowers as she waved at the group inside. Trevor and Edmond beckoned her in.

'Where have you been?' Seren said as Anni came through the door.

'Trying to pick up the pieces. Dad was very upset. What on earth came over you?'

'Ooooo!' Trevor's eyes sparkled. 'Was there a scene? Seren, you haven't mentioned that.'

'Too bloody right there was a scene,' Anni folded her arms. 'I was trying my best to make polite conversation with Dad's girlfriend – admittedly not very well – I kept talking about Mum as though I was making some sort of point, but I really didn't mean to.'

'You didn't?' Seren looked surprised. 'I thought you mentioned Mum on purpose.'

Anni ignored her and continued addressing Trevor and Edmond.

'And then suddenly my little sister here decided throw a hissy fit – telling Frankie that she'd never get to meet Griff, that Dad was making a mistake, that he'd be back with Mum in no time!'

Trevor gave Seren an admiring look. 'Just say it like is, girl!'

'I think Frankie's alright,' Anni protested.

'But it's such a cliché,' Seren tried to make her voice sound calm. 'Older man runs off with younger woman.'

'So what? She must be at least forty anyway, and lots of men have younger girlfriends – I know I'd have a younger man if I had a chance!'

Seren sighed. 'I feel like Dad's been stolen.'

'He's not been stolen. He's made a choice.' Anni sounded exasperated. 'This is what happens in life, people change, they want different things. I don't think Mum and Dad have been happy for years. Maybe it's about time you accept that and grow up. For too long you've been…'

'Stop it!' Seren banged the table with her hand, sending rolls of ribbon bouncing into the air. Everybody, including Seren, jumped. She lowered her voice. 'Sorry. It's just I see them every day and I know that they're still very much in love.'

'Then why is he living with another woman?'

Seren said nothing and bent down to pick up the rolls of ribbon. She was determined not to show the tears that had begun to gather in her eyes. Too late –Trevor and Edmond, who had been watching the women's argument like spectators at a tennis match, both sprang round the counter to comfort her.

Edmond produced a Liberty-print handkerchief from his pocket. 'Don't worry, it's not been used. *Ever*.'

Trevor stroked her hair. 'Cheer up, sweetie. Shall I get you a raspberry crumble slice?' Seren shook her head and wiped her eyes with the handkerchief.

'Give me strength!' muttered Anni.

Seren looked up and glared at her sister. 'Don't you care about Mum?'

'Of course I do,' Anni said quietly. 'But there's not much we can do, is there?'

Silence fell. Seren twisted the handkerchief in her hand.

After a few minutes, Trevor said, 'Edmond, shall we tell the girls *our* exiting news.'

Edmond looked blank.

'The celebrity customer we had in this morning?' Trevor prompted.

'Oooo, yes, how could I forget? You'll never guess who came in and bought a tutti-frutti cupcake and a nutty nougat chocolate brownie!'

'Go on. Impress us,' said Anni with a sigh.

Trevor mimed his heart fluttering; Edmond mimed a swoon. They both said, in voices just above a whisper, 'Arlow Laverne.'

Anni looked at Seren.

'There's a blast from the past!'

Seren pretended nonchalance, though she was suddenly cold. 'I haven't thought about him for years.'

Anni snorted. 'Don't tell me you don't watch it?'

'What?'

'*Island Beat*. Even us lot down under get it. It's hard to get away from Arlow Laverne when each new series is on. His face is all over all the TV-listings magazines. I always think it must be weird for you.'

'I don't really notice.'

'I tell everyone, "He used to be my sister's boyfriend".'

Trevor and Edmond had turned back into tennis spectators; faces turning from one woman to the other as they lobbied back and forth, only this time they had open mouths.

'Is this…? Did he…? Seren's what?'

'It was a long time ago,' said Seren. 'Just a silly teenage thing.'

'Two years they were together,' Anni added. 'He was practically one of the family, always round at our house.'

Seren thought about the meal times round The Windmill kitchen table, eating Nesta's lovely food. Daniel and Arlow would talk about music together as they ate, tracing connections between jazz and contemporary black music; comparing Bebop with rap, Dixieland with hip-hop. Daniel would play Duke Ellington for Arlow on his ancient gramophone player and Arlow would make Daniel listen to Jay-Z on his CD player. Seren would listen, pleased that the two men in her life got on so well, but at the same time longing for the meal to end so that she could be alone with Arlow.

'Well, well.' Trevor stood back and looked Seren up and down. 'Aren't we the dark horse?'

82

Edmond whipped the hankie out of Seren's hand. 'Soaked in the tears of the ex-girlfriend of Arlow Laverne. I might get good money for that on eBay.'

'He's not that famous,' protested Seren, starting to wind a length of silver ribbon through her fingers. 'And *Island Beat* has been axed by the BBC, so I don't think he's doing very much at the moment apart from an appearance on *Top Gear* in January and *Celebrity Great British Bake Off* last month.'

Trevor arched one eyebrow. 'You seem very knowledgeable for someone who hasn't thought about him for years.'

'OK, OK,' Seren rolled her eyes. 'I Googled him – but only the once last night.'

Edmond tweaked the tips of his moustache and grinned at Seren. 'You must be desperate to know what he's doing back here.'

Seren avoided his eyes and, looking down, realised that her fingers had become completely tied up in the ribbon.

'There are far more important things to be thinking about than Arlow Laverne,' she said, trying to disentangle her fingers. She remembered being eighteen, lying on her bed, twisting the sleeve of her dressing gown so that the satin dug painfully into her wrist. Her father had sat down beside her and wiped away her tears. 'It's for the best,' he'd told her. 'Arlow wasn't right for you.'

Nesta

The afternoon sun filled the circular room with a soft yellow light. A warm breeze blew through the French windows and made the muslin curtains billow like ghostly dance partners. From her position on the edge of the bed, Nesta looked out across the balcony to the wide expanse of countryside below. Hills and fields and numerous wooded copses; tiny sheep and cows and the glittering thread of river running through it all. 'Like flying,' Seren used to say as a little girl.

Nesta reached behind and unhooked her bra.

Anni had taken the children to visit an old school friend and Seren was at work. Nesta had The Windmill to herself at last.

She stood up, pulled down her pants and swiftly stepped out of them, giving them a kick across the room. She threw her bra onto the chair with the rest of her clothes and, taking a deep breath, turned around and forced herself to look at her reflection in the full-length mirror. How long had it been since she'd seen her naked body, head to toe, completely exposed? How long had it been since anyone had seen it?

Daniel, of course, had seen it many times in the months that followed their first encounter on the museum steps. She used to lie on his rumpled sheets in Fulham, smoking Gauloises and drinking Cinzano. Nesta used to wonder what they'd say in chapel if they could see what she was doing.

She had been lovely then, so lovely. And she hadn't realised.

Nesta stared at the reflection in front of her. It had become a different body. Her stomach was soft like the dough she kneaded every morning; the stretch marks she had acquired in pregnancy were silver lines against her skin. Her breasts were still quite good, full and nicely shaped, but her ribs were much too prominent and her hips seemed to have expanded. She

84

reminded herself of the sacred cows that she and Daniel had seen wandering the streets in India. She stood sideways. At least her legs had always been long – colt's legs, her grandfather called them – indecently long, her mother used to say. Nesta turned around again and, looking over her shoulder, winced at the dimpled cellulite on her bottom. She held out an arm and poked the loose skin hanging down. She turned to face the mirror again and closed her eyes.

Why was she tormenting herself like this? Just because Daniel's lover was barely forty, it didn't mean her body was perfect. But Anni had told her that Frankie didn't have children, so that reduced the likelihood of stretch marks and droopy breasts. Seren said that Frankie was small and skinny. Nesta was five foot eleven; as tall as Daniel in the days when she had worn heels. And though she'd always been slim, no one had ever called her skinny. Maybe Daniel had always yearned for someone more petite.

Nesta took one last look at herself and got into bed, pulling the duvet high up under her chin. She would try to sleep; maybe, since she couldn't sleep at night, she could do it in the afternoon. Her eyes refused to close, scanning the room instead. It looked different in the day time – too bright, too big, too round.

She wondered why she lay so carefully on one side of the bed, as though Daniel was still taking up the other half. Tentatively she stretched an arm across. It felt flat and cold and empty. Her heart hurt. She still hadn't cried.

If Daniel had died there would be cards of condolence, phone calls, casseroles from caring neighbours, the vicar on his bicycle, a funeral, a wake.

But instead friends seemed to be avoiding her, as though a failed marriage might be catching. The vicar was nowhere to be seen and no casseroles were forthcoming. Instead of dying, Daniel had abandoned her for someone else, and there were no traditions or social niceties for that.

She pulled the duvet over her head and let out a long, low howl, repeating it over and over again, the pitch rising and falling. It was almost a song, a requiem, a lament – louder and louder until her throat hurt and her head ached. When she had finished, she lay very still and listened to the birds outside the window and the ticking of the bedside clock. The birdsong calmed her and her heartbeat seemed to slow in time with the clock.

After a while she felt stifled under the heavy covers and she threw back the duvet and lay, completely exposed, letting the dusty sunlight drench her skin. She stretched out her arms and legs like a star taking up as much room as possible on the bed, claiming it all for herself.

At last her eyes began slowly to close, her thoughts to surrender to unconsciousness. An image seeped into her mind, sepia and faded with age. She lay on a rough woollen blanket, her clothes discarded in pools on the grass. They watched as the stars came out one by one in the midsummer sky.

'*Rydych yn brydferth,*' the young man had said in Welsh. 'You are beautiful.' She had kissed him and tasted elderflower wine.

'Mum,' a voice outside the door. The image shattered. Nesta's eyes flew open as she grabbed the duvet and covered herself. 'Mum, are you in there?' asked Seren. There was the noise of the latch being lifted and the door opening slowly. 'Are you OK?'

Seren was holding a mug of tea in her hand. 'I didn't know where you were.' She was staring down at Nesta in the bed. 'Are you ill?'

Nesta clutched the duvet and pulled it back up to her chin.

'No, darling. I'm alright.'

Seren held out the mug to her and Nesta realised she'd have to sit up and reveal that she didn't have a top on. Seren glanced from her mother to the pile of discarded clothes on the chair.

'I felt hot,' Nesta tried to explain, wondering why, at sixty-three, she needed to justify what she did in her own bedroom to her daughter. 'And tired.'

Seren put the mug on the bedside table and sat down on the edge of the bed.

'Oh Mum, I can't bear to see you like this.'

Nesta took her hand. 'You can't spend forty years with someone and not be sad when they leave.'

Seren sighed. 'I think he must be having some sort of breakdown.'

'Maybe,' said Nesta. 'Or maybe he just fell in love with someone else.'

'No,' Seren shook her head. 'He can't be in love with her. Why would he fall in love with her? She's... she's...' She seemed to be struggling to find the words.

'Young?' Nesta said.

'Only youngish,' Seren said kindly. 'And she's not nearly as beautiful as you.'

Nesta lifted Seren's hand to her cheek. 'That's sweet of you to say, but look at me. My face is full of wrinkles, my hair is grey, my body is...' she paused, 'horrible.'

'Oh Mum, how can you say that? Frankie looks like nothing compared to you. She's so pale, so thin – and, it's a funny thing to say, but she almost seems invisible, like she doesn't want to be seen.'

'He always liked to help the waifs and strays of this world.'

Seren thought for a moment. 'Like Tom?'

Nesta shrugged. 'Yes, I suppose. I was thinking more of myself when we first met. I was so shy; fresh from the Welsh hills. I didn't have a clue about living in London. He loved showing me round, helping me to look for a job, getting me a room in his friend's sister's house. He couldn't do enough for me.'

Seren thought about Frankie's painting of the crouching girl. 'And now he's found someone else he thinks he can help.'

Nesta squeezed her hand. 'Maybe. He knows I can cope without him now.'

'But can you?' Seren's voice was almost a whisper.

'I'm not a hundred per cent sure but I'm going to give it a bloody good try.' Nesta laughed but Seren's mouth remained a grim straight line.

'What you had was perfect and now he wants to throw it all away.' She stared towards the French windows. Her hair was loose: a mass of curls, copper bright, glowing against her creamy skin.

Nesta longed to tell her about all the things she didn't know. She bit her lip; she could still taste that elderflower wine.

The sound of Griff's trumpet drifted into the room from the garden.

'He's playing to the chickens again,' Nesta smiled.

'He misses having his grandad to practise with,' said Seren.

'You'll soon have to explain to Griff what's happened.'

'But Dad will come back.'

Nesta squeezed her hand. 'I'm not so sure.'

Seren stood up and leaned down to kiss her mother's forehead. 'He will.'

Frankie

Frankie tried very hard to ignore the feeling of rejection that had pinched at her heart all day. It wasn't as though she really thought she had any right to accompany Daniel to say goodbye to Anni at the airport. And why would she have wanted to spend three hours in a hired people carrier with Daniel's hyperactive grandchildren and two daughters who clearly wouldn't have wanted her there?

Instead she had been for a long swim and tried to snap out of her melancholy mood.

Afterwards she wandered up the high street, unwilling to go back to the empty house. Once she would have longed for the solitude, lapped it up with relief. But now suddenly she didn't want to be alone.

Frankie undid the buttons of her jacket. Her wardrobe hadn't caught up with the early heatwave they seemed to be having. All around her people were in shorts and summer dresses – pale legs and arms resolutely exposed. Frankie wore black jeans and a T-shirt, a cardigan, a denim jacket and a long silk scarf. She felt conspicuous in her inappropriate layers and only slightly better when she had taken off her scarf and jacket.

She kept walking and found herself at the high street's upper end. Here the Tesco Extra, chain stores and the charity shops gave way to more genteel independent retailers who displayed their wares in the higgledy assortment of Georgian shop fronts. Tasteful boutiques, quirky gift shops and assorted speciality food shops jostled with cafés selling cupcakes and an art gallery showing landscapes by local watercolour artists.

This was alien territory. Frankie felt uncomfortable amongst the Boden-clad ladies clutching Cath Kidston shopping bags and the tourists taking pictures of each other beside the mullioned windows and hand-painted shop signs.

Frankie passed the WI market and nearly collided with a middle-aged woman with a wicker basket filled with vegetables. She wondered if it was Nesta and stood and watched as the woman strode away with her sensible hair, crisp shirt and beige slacks.

Frankie walked quickly on, past Daniel's architecture practice, past the gallery and the delicatessen and a gift shop called Ruby Retro. She noticed Arlow Laverne coming out of the delicatessen, tucking in to a rugged-looking sandwich. It made her think of lunch and she realised how hungry she was. Tremond's was just across the road, its window bursting with tempting cakes and pastries. Her mouth watered at the thought of something sticky and sweet and comforting.

As she waited at the crossing she gazed at the display of flowers in the window of the shop nearest her. The flowers seemed to fill up every available space inside and out. She didn't need to read the beautifully painted lettering on the swinging sign to know that it was Stems. Frankie was filled with curiosity. Seren would still be with Daniel making their way back from Heathrow – surely it wouldn't hurt to take a look inside. Cautiously Frankie stepped through the open door.

The tall woman with the sad expression behind the counter was too absorbed in arranging a bouquet of roses to notice Frankie. Frankie walked a little further into the shop, the wide floorboards creaked and the woman looked up with a start.

'My goodness, I didn't see you come in!'

'Sorry.'

The woman smiled. 'It was my fault. I was miles away. Let me know if you need any help.' Frankie noticed that her eyes were the colour of the bunches of cornflowers on the counter; they matched the denim apron that she wore over her loose-fitting linen tunic.

As the woman went back to the roses, Frankie slowly walked around the tiny shop marvelling at the billowing peonies, gigantic alliums, chrysanthemums, hydrangeas, lilies and irises of every shade. She wanted to sit down and paint it all.

She picked up a bunch of freesias and sniffed. The scent transported her back to her childhood kitchen; her mother arranging the flowers in a pale green jug – asking Frankie if she'd ever smelt anything so lovely before. Frankie walked up to the counter.

'I'll take these, please.'

'Are they a present?' the woman asked. 'Would you like them gift-wrapped?'

Frankie shook her head. 'They're just for me.'

The woman took a sheet of pink tissue paper from a drawer and laid it out in front of her. 'I'll gift-wrap them anyway – that way it's more special.'

'Thank you.' Frankie took her purse out of her bag. 'What a lovely shop.'

'Yes, isn't it. It belongs to my daughter. What colour ribbon would you like?'

Frankie heard a thud as her purse fell to the ground; coins spilling out of it, rolling across the floor. She felt her knees begin to give way and she was glad she had the excuse of bending down to scrabble for her change.

'Special delivery!' a deep voice filled the room. Frankie glanced up to see a large man with a bald head, an elaborate moustache and a cake box dramatically balanced on his fingertips. 'Seren tells me you're not eating enough so I bring you our best éclairs. Dark chocolate with Chantilly cream and strawberries – your favourite, I believe.'

'Edmond, you are very naughty,' Nesta laughed. 'You know I adore them. I'm sure you and Trevor put in a secret ingredient to make them so delicious.'

'Love is the secret ingredient, my darling. Every mouthful is filled with love.'

Frankie stayed crouching on the floor pretending to search

for more coins. She wondered if she would ever have the courage to straighten up.

'Are you alright down there?' Edmond was staring at her. She managed to stand.

'I'm fine.'

'The ribbon?' Nesta asked. 'What about yellow?'

'No. I mean, no thank you, I don't need a ribbon. Just tell me how much they are.'

'Four pounds fifty,' Nesta's face was concerned. 'Are you sure you're OK? You suddenly look very pale. Would you like me to bring the stool round so you can sit down? Would you like a glass of water? Maybe it's the heat.'

Frankie tried to speak but the words were jammed in her throat. All she could manage was to put a five-pound note down on the counter, turn around and walk out of the shop. Behind her she heard Edmond's voice.

'What was up with her? She didn't even wait for her change!'

She was gone before she could hear Nesta's reply.

Frankie hardly remembered the walk back home. Her head was full of Nesta. She had imagined someone more austere, more conventional, but instead she had been beautiful and kind.

At some point Frankie left the bunch of freesias on a wall. Someone else could have them. She'd never find any joy from their pretty colours or lovely scent.

Frankie couldn't make the woman in the shop into the woman she had spent so many months imagining from Daniel's descriptions. Daniel had talked about her as though she was cold and aloof. Frankie could see that she was capable and confident but the overriding impression she had given was one of warmth.

As soon as she stepped through the front door Frankie heard the voices. Daniel's calm and placatory, Seren's pleading and distressed.

'Surely there's no need.'

'I think it's best to get it sorted out as soon as possible.'

'But to sell The Windmill? It just seems so cruel.'

'Now sweetheart, it isn't good to be too sentimental about these things.'

'It's Frankie, isn't it?' Seren's voice was raised. 'It's Frankie that's making you do this?'

Frankie summoned up her courage and walked in.

'Darling, I didn't realise you'd come home.' Daniel came and put an arm around her shoulder. 'Seren and I are just discussing the future of The Windmill.'

Frankie thought of the expression on Nesta's face when she had first walked into the shop. It had been full of sadness, full of grief.

'She'll be heartbroken.' Seren's voice had fallen to a whisper.

Daniel looked into her eyes. 'Trust me, it's best to have a clean break. I've seen my solicitor, told him that I want Nesta to have as generous a share of the assets as possible.'

'But…' Seren began.

'I know you must have a lot of questions, so what do you say to a glass of wine?' Daniel smiled at his daughter. 'Then we can sit down and have a proper chat about it.' He turned to Frankie. 'We have that nice bottle of Chardonnay in the fridge, don't we?' He disappeared into kitchen and the two women were left alone.

Seren had turned to face the mantelpiece. Her red hair blazed in the sun that streamed through the bay window.

'I'm sorry,' Frankie said. 'I didn't know he wanted to sell The Windmill.'

Seren didn't respond; she was staring at the painting of the crouching girl. Frankie tried again.

'I think you imagine that I want to hurt your family. But I really don't.'

Seren suddenly turned around. 'I don't need to imagine it. I can see it. You have no idea of the pain you're causing. Especially to my mum.'

For the second time that day Frankie couldn't find the words to reply.

'I have to go and pick my son up from school.' Seren hurried past Frankie and left the house.

Frankie stayed rooted to the living room carpet until Daniel re-appeared balancing three glasses and a bottle on a tray.

'Oh!' He was surprised to find Frankie on her own.

She turned to him. 'Why didn't you tell me you were going to sell The Windmill?'

Daniel put the tray down on the coffee table. 'Well, we can't stay living here,' he gestured around the room. 'You've said yourself the landlord doesn't do anything to it and he won't let us improve it in any way. Besides we need a bigger place. You need a studio to start your painting again and we both need somewhere where we're not constantly falling over each other like we do now.' He shrugged. 'How else can we afford that? We need the capital from The Windmill to make a new start.'

'But Nesta…' Frankie began. Daniel walked across the room and put his arms around her.

'Nesta will be fine about it when she realises she's going to get a good divorce settlement. I'll make sure she gets enough to buy a nice little place of her own. She needs a new start as much as we do and the quicker we all get on with it the better.' He kissed Frankie on her forehead and gazed down at her. 'All I really want is for you to be happy.'

He stroked her hair and kissed her lips.

'Why don't we take the wine upstairs,' he murmured.

Frankie closed her eyes and nodded, but Nesta's sad and lovely face still swam in her mind.

Seren

Seren's eyes were fixed on the computer screen. She could hear the television in the living room and knew that she should be getting supper.

She heard Griff come in.

'Is Grandad back yet?' Seren still hadn't had the dreaded conversation with her son. 'I've been practising chess on the computer and I think I might actually be able to beat him now.'

'That's great,' Seren scrolled down the screen and decided to change the search term she was using.

'Can I have some chocolate, Mum?'

'It's nearly time to eat.'

Even without looking up she could tell that Griff was scanning the room for signs of a meal being prepared.

'What are we having?'

Seren tried to think. It would be too late for the spaghetti bolognaise she had planned.

'Baked beans on toast.'

Griff groaned. 'I hate baked beans.'

'Last week you said they were your favourite.'

'I don't like them now.'

Seren could hear the rustling of a wrapper and she looked around to find Griff about to take a bite out of a large bar of chocolate.

'Hey! I didn't say you could have that.'

'I'm starving.' Griff clutched the edge of a chair, his knees buckling dramatically. 'I might faint if I don't eat something now.'

Seren sighed. 'I'll do you a deal. We'll share it.'

Reluctantly Griff broke off three squares and handed them to Seren. She stuffed them all in her mouth at once. Griff laughed.

'You're such a greedy pig, Mum.'

'It's reverse-psychology parenting. I have to set a bad example so you know how not to behave,' Seren's voice was muffled by chocolate.

'I can't understand a word you're saying.' Griff's mouth was full of chocolate too. Seren leant back in her chair and made a grab for him, pulling him into her arms and hugging him around the waist. He pretended to protest and she squeezed him tighter. They were both laughing now.

He looked over her shoulder at the computer screen. 'What are you doing?'

'I'm just looking for something.' She had put 'Francesca Williams UK Artist' into Google. She clicked on the first listing, a link to an online arts magazine.

'Who's she?'

Seren saw the photograph and swallowed the chocolate too quickly. She began to cough.

'Who is she, Mum?'

'No one you know,' Seren said when she'd recovered. 'Have you done your homework?'

'Yes.'

Seren's heart was beating. 'Have you practised your trumpet?'

'Yes.'

'Then go and tell me if there's anything completely unsuitable we can watch on telly while we eat our beans.'

Griff disappeared out of the room, taking the rest of the chocolate bar with him. Seren didn't protest, instead she began to read the article. It had been posted over five years before.

Oliver Williams and his wife Francesca's joint exhibition at The Old Malt House Gallery has been heralded as a huge success.

Seren took a deep breath. As soon as she'd noticed the neatly sloping signature on Frankie's painting on the mantelpiece she'd been desperate to get home to put the name into the computer. Heart quickening, Seren read on.

Oliver Williams' powerful yet ethereal sculptures were complemented by Francesca's darkly thought-provoking paintings. Both use the human figure as inspiration, but while Francesca captures women with almost breathtaking realism, Oliver turns the female form into something quite unearthly. His life-sized bronze angels are suspended from the ceiling, watching their audience with blank eyes that convey a disconcerting mix of impassiveness and intimacy. In contrast Francesca's figures are earthbound; overly large eyes suggest fragility and unease and they twist and bend as though searching for an escape route from the canvas.

Seren quickly scanned the rest of the article, more artistic blurb about the exhibition and the suitability of the gallery space for the show, none of it seemed that relevant. She scrolled back up to the photograph. A man and woman: young, attractive, wine glasses in hand, obviously at a private view. The woman had long brown curly hair and stared into the camera with a slightly startled expression. Seren estimated she was at least a stone heavier but there was no mistaking who she was.

Seren phoned Ben. He answered on her third attempt. She knew he would still be at work. She imagined him in a dark room, dragging himself from the depths of some underworld, slaying a few demons as he did so, casting off his warrior armour as he emerged back into reality.

'Hey Sis, how's it going?'

'I've sent you a link to a website. Could you have a look at it?'

'Sure. I'll have a look after work.'

'Could you look right now?'

Ben must have sensed the anxiety in her voice. She heard tapping and waited for what seemed like hours.

'OK.' He spoke slowly, sounded confused. 'So this is about what?'

'Frankie Hyde.'

'Who?'

'Frankie. You know, Dad's…' Seren faltered as she tried to choose a name. '… woman.'

'OK.' Ben's voice was even slower now.

'She's not who she says she is. Her name's Francesca Williams and she's been married.'

'So?'

'And she looks completely different now. Her hair is short and blonde, she's very thin and she's changed her name.'

Ben sighed. 'So what? She's been married, got divorced, lost weight with the stress of it all, changed back to her maiden name – what's so weird about that? It happens all the time.'

'But her hair?'

'She probably got sick of it being long. Maybe she's always having different hairstyles, maybe she's wearing a wig in the picture, maybe she wears a wig now, maybe she's really completely bald.'

'You're not taking this seriously. Anyway why doesn't Dad know about her ex-husband?'

'Maybe he does.'

Seren was silent for a while.

'Do you know that Dad wants to sell The Windmill?'

There was a pause. 'I thought he might.'

'What about Mum?'

'It's a big house. She doesn't need all that space, all that garden. It's huge.'

'It's her life.'

Ben was silent. Seren could hear tapping and wondered if he was sinking back into his fantasy world. 'What are Griff and I supposed to do? Just sit here staring at the new people who'll move in? We practically live in the garden – how can we be forced to share it with strangers?'

The tapping stopped. 'You can build a wall.'

'A wall! I don't want to be stuck behind a wall.'

Seren looked back at the picture of Francesca Williams on the computer. She wanted to smash the screen.

'Seren?' Ben sounded suddenly very much back in the real world. 'Don't you ever think about living somewhere else? Starting again somewhere without all the memories.' He paused. 'I think it would do you good.'

Seren couldn't believe her brother was saying these things: Ben who was always on her side. Even as children he'd defended her against Anni's angry outbursts, let her hang out with his friends, helped her with her homework. It had been Ben who had taught her to ride a bike. He never argued with her.

Seren didn't want him to argue with her now. She changed the subject. 'How's Suki?'

There was another pause. It was a long time before Ben said, 'We've split up.'

Seren's mouth dropped open. 'Why?'

She could almost hear his shrug on the other end of the phone.

'Are you OK?' she asked.

'I'm cool with it.'

'And Suki?'

'She's gone back to Ireland for a while.'

'But why? What happened?'

'I just couldn't see the point any more. Relationships – they're messy.'

'Is this because of what's happened with Mum and Dad?'

'Look Seren, I've got to get back to work. I'm doing a late-nighter and I really need to get on.'

'OK.' Seren hung up.

She stared at the now blank computer screen. How could this be happening? How could this woman be changing so many people's lives for the worse?

There was a tightness in her chest that she recognised. The same tightness she had felt when she'd thought that she would be the one to destroy her parents' idyllic world. She closed her eyes as unwanted images battered at the doorway of her memory – the thin orange curtain around the bed, her grandmother's grim expression.

She couldn't bear to remember any more. Opening her eyes, she clicked on another link on Google. More pictures of the old Frankie appeared on the screen. Seren made a face at the pictures. *Just go away and leave us alone.*

'It's between *The One Show* and *Don't Tell the Bride*.' Griff was back.

Seren forced herself to smile. She suddenly had a desperate urge to be out of the house. 'Let's go into town and get a pizza. The beans can keep until another night.'

Nesta

The sugar sparkled in the late afternoon sun. For a long time Nesta stared at the glittery surface of the uneaten cake.

She wondered why she'd bothered making the Victoria sponge – using up the last jar of her homemade strawberry jam – and why she'd worn her favourite silk shirt, and washed her hair, and put on earrings.

'I'll come over for a cup of tea,' he'd said. 'I'd like to see you.'

Nesta's eyes shifted to the brown-striped mug they'd chosen together in a pottery in St Ives. She could see a tiny bee struggling in the untouched tea. She leant forward and with the corner of a napkin fished it out. It was the first time she had moved since he had left.

The sheaf of estate agent's details flapped a little in the breeze. Nesta closed her eyes and pretended they weren't there.

Daniel had arrived full of apologies, full of regrets; at one point he'd even cried. Sitting at the wrought-iron garden table he had reached across and held her hand.

'I can't tell you how awful I feel about this. It stops me sleeping. I'll always love you, Nesta. I miss you – we were soulmates you and I.'

For a few minutes Nesta thought he was going to ask to come home; her heart beat faster, with little pin pricks of relief. She started to compose a response; she wouldn't capitulate too easily. But suddenly he was talking about solicitors, alimony payments and an appointment that he'd made to have The Windmill valued. Nesta let him keep her hand in his. At least it stopped her from slapping him.

He had it all worked out. He'd even brought the name and number of a solicitor he thought she ought to use.

101

'It will be straightforward,' he'd said. 'No blame. A clean cut. No need to drag it out and add to the legal expenses. Don't you agree?'

Nesta opened her eyes and picked up the estate agent's particulars. Three houses. Daniel had told her they all had potential. Nesta peered at the first, she didn't have her glasses but she could see enough to make out the ugly redbrick bungalow and the tiny patch of scrubby grass surrounding it.

'You'll enjoy making a new garden.' Daniel had squeezed her hand. 'And it will be a challenge in a smaller space.'

Nesta glanced at the other two – a dingy cottage that she had passed many times on the by-pass and a modern house on the new estate in town. 'Badly designed, badly built,' Nesta distinctly remembered Daniel's damning words about the houses when they first went up.

Nesta let the papers drop onto the flagstones. The wind picked them up and blew them against the low box hedge that ran along the edge of the patio. They flapped like injured birds until another gust caught them and sent them tumbling across the lawn towards The Wheat House.

Nesta watched them and thought of Seren and Tom's wedding. Long tables had been set out on the lawn, billowing white tablecloths, hydrangeas, vintage china. Seren in lilac lace; still frail, still waking up with nightmares in the night. Nesta had hoped so much that Tom would help her get over whatever seemed to haunt her. Maybe Seren would be able to talk to her new husband about the things she refused to tell her mother.

Daniel had been in his element; greeting the guests, organising the party, showing off Tom's plans for The Wheat House, so proud that he had found his daughter such a perfect partner.

Nesta wondered what Daniel expected Seren to do now. She had asked him. That had been her only question. Maybe her only words all afternoon.

'It's all going to be fine,' he'd reassured her with his usual optimistic confidence

Nesta sighed. That was Daniel; Mr Don't Worry, Mr Fix-It. He had made a whole career out of it. *House too small? Don't worry, he'll convert your loft, design a garden room, extend your kitchen. A spare barn cluttering up your field? Let him transform it into a four-bed family home you can sell for thousands.*

Daniel had seemed so wonderful when they first met. He had found her somewhere to live, scoured the paper for teaching jobs when she had lost hope of ever finding one. He had bought her an outfit for her interview – always claiming that the brown suede wedges and matching handbag had swung the headmistress's decision in Nesta's favour.

Even their wedding had been planned by Daniel: a registry office ceremony with a handful of friends, followed by dinner in his favourite restaurant on the King's Road. Daniel had spotted the peasant-style dress that Nesta wore in the window of Biba; it just about concealed her swelling stomach. He had bought the bunch of peonies she had clutched so tightly as she said her vows and afterwards he had whisked her off to Rome as a honeymoon surprise.

Now he would organise their divorce with the same enthusiasm, getting the job done – a good result all round. What was it he had said? 'Let's make a positive future for you, Nesta; something that will make you as happy as you deserve to be.'

'Bastard,' Nesta said out loud.

'What did you say, Granny?'

Nesta turned her head to see Griff standing on the grass behind her. He handed her the crumpled estate agent's papers. She hoped he hadn't noticed what they were.

'Sorry, darling. I was talking to myself.'

'I saw Grandad's car when I came home from school. But Mum said I had to go to my swimming lesson and she wouldn't let me come and see him. Is he back from his holiday?'

Nesta hastily put the papers face down on the table. She held out her arms and Griff walked into them.

He smelled of a mix of chlorine and salt-and-vinegar crisps. Nesta squeezed him tightly.

'I miss him,' Griff whispered.

'I know. I miss him too.'

He stood back and looked at Nesta, eyes round behind the thick lenses.

'Barney Brown said he heard his mum tell his dad that Grandad was living with another lady.'

'What has Mummy told you?'

'That Grandad's gone away for a little while. But I don't think she's telling me the truth because she thinks I'm still a baby. Does Grandad not care about us any more?'

Nesta took his hand in hers. 'Of course he cares about us, you especially. But Grandad wants to live somewhere else.'

Griff pulled away and stared at Nesta. 'With another lady?'

'Yes.'

'Are you going to get divorced?'

'That's what Grandad wants.'

'But you're too old.'

Nesta laughed. 'Too old to get divorced?'

'Yes. I thought only mums and dads could do that, like Jake Vaughn's and Poppy Smythe's.'

'Well, it turns out you are never too old, my lovely boy.' She laughed again and Griff started to laugh too. Then he stopped.

'But will you be alright?'

Nesta glanced at the estate agent's details on the table and looked quickly back to Griff with a smile.

'Right as rain.'

Griff's eyes were on the tea things. 'Can I have some cake?'

Seren

Seren took a gulp of tea and dialled the number.

She felt slightly ridiculous, snooping around like some sort of latter-day Miss Marple, but she needed the evidence that Frankie was hiding something. Then her father would see the terrible mistake he was making.

Seren picked up a biro and began doodling little circles on the top sheet of the tissue paper she used to wrap up flowers.

The phone rang on and on. Seren imagined that the ringing would be echoing around an enormous workshop; tools and dust and gargantuan sculptures and somewhere in the middle of it all an artist too consumed with creativity to hear. But just as she was about to give up a voice answered.

'Oliver Williams speaking.' The internet photograph had shown a man in his late thirties or early forties, with unkempt hair, stubble and broad shoulders, no doubt well-developed muscles from chiselling heavy blocks of stone. The slightly crooked smile and bright eyes in the photograph had a friendliness that had made Seren feel he would be approachable. Now she wasn't so sure.

Seren took a deep breath, the little speech she had planned about being a long-lost relative rapidly evaporating. She found herself stumbling over her words.

'I'm sorry to disturb you.' Her pen made tighter and tighter circles. 'I just wondered if… I just thought that you might… I wanted to know…'

'Is this some sort of consumer survey?' His accent sounded vaguely northern. His website had said that he originally came from Leeds.

'No, it's not a survey.'

'PPI insurance? Solar panels? Insulation?'

'No, no,' Seren stammered. 'It's not any of that. I just…'

'Well, that just leaves double glazing.' He sounded amused.

'It's about Francesca Williams.'

There was a pause. Seren drew six circles before he replied, 'Francesca?'

'Yes.'

There was another pause.

'You've found Francesca?'

'Yes. I mean I think so. That's why…'

'Is this the police?'

This time it was Seren who paused.

'Is it bad news?' continued Oliver.

The panic in his voice made Seren wish she hadn't rung.

'No, no. I'm not from the police and she's OK.'

'Thank God.'

'In fact she's very much OK.' Seren took a deep breath. 'She's living with my father.' The shop bell jingled.

Seren looked up as she uttered the last sentence and found herself staring at the face of Arlow Laverne. She sat down hard on the high stool behind her and tried to focus on the telephone conversation; the pen in her hand had taken on a life of its own – round and round, the circles turned into spirals that overlapped each other across the thin tissue sheet.

'With your father?' Oliver sounded bemused.

'I'd like to ask you a few questions about Frankie, if you don't mind.' She felt her cheeks begin to flush, too aware that Arlow was listening.

'Of course.'

Seren glanced at Arlow. He smiled and she looked away. 'It's difficult to talk right now. Could I send an email or phone you at a time that suits you?'

'Why not come and see me at my studio and I'll take you out for a coffee? We can chat then.'

'When?'

'Friday? Eleven o'clock?'

Seren flicked through the diary in front of her. She'd have to ask Nesta to look after the shop and make the weekly flower arrangement for the GP's waiting room.

'OK. Friday morning is fine. Where is your studio?'

'South London. The details are on my website. I assume that's where you did your detective work to find my number.'

'Uh, yes.' Seren felt embarrassed. 'I hope it was OK to phone you.'

'Yes, I can't tell you what a relief it is to hear that Francesca is safe. I shall look forward to meeting you.' And then he was gone.

Arlow leaned against the counter. 'Do you need assistance from a policeman?'

Seren closed the diary. 'I thought you'd retired.' She was amazed that she could form a sentence.

'In the fictional world our characters go on working, but budget cuts and the endless quest for fresh talent mean that no one bothers filming us any more.'

'Really?' Seren picked up the diary and clutched it to her chest, her heart thudding against it.

'Oh yes. A part of me will be forever patrolling the shores of a Hebridean island, solving grisly murders and arresting serial smugglers.'

'And another part of you is back in town?' Seren tried not to look into the familiar eyes.

'You've noticed!'

'I've heard rumours.'

Arlow grinned. His teeth seemed straighter, whiter and shinier than they used to be.

The phone rang. Seren picked it up.

There was a shuffling sound before the line went dead. Seren put the phone back down. Arlow had moved away and seemed absorbed in a display of tulips. He picked out three bunches.

'I'll take these. Maybe they'll cheer up the cottage.'

A cottage sounded more modest accommodation than Seren

107

would have imagined for him, with his beautifuly cut shirt and designer jeans.

He seemed to have read her mind. 'I'm only living there till filming is over. We're shooting a supernatural thriller set in an old farmhouse. Three couples rent it for a Christmas with terrifying consequences.' He shivered dramatically and rolled his eyes. 'Most of the filming is done at night.'

Seren couldn't help the smile that twitched on her lips.

'I know. It's all a bit predictable. If I'd realised it was going to be so corny I probably wouldn't have agreed to do it.' Arlow shrugged. 'But when there's a mortgage to pay…'

Seren wrapped the tulips in tissue paper. An image of Angellica Chadwick's beautiful face sprang into her mind as she imagined her wandering around the no-doubt-lovely home she and Arlow shared. Angellica had started out as the youngest Bennet daughter in a TV adaptation of *Pride and Prejudice* – beguilingly doe-eyed and sweet.

'Do I pay extra for the original art work on the wrapping?' Arlow indicated the doodles that adorned the tissue paper around his flowers.'

'Oh sorry, I'll take that sheet off.'

Arlow shook his head. 'No, don't do that. I like it. I'll add it to my collection.' Arlow smiled and a tiny dimple appeared on his left cheek. Seren remembered how the tip of her little finger fitted perfectly into it. 'I still have that pencil sketch you did of me.'

Seren could feel herself blushing again at the memory of her attempt at drawing Arlow, naked on her bed.

Arlow handed her a twenty-pound note. 'You got cross because I wouldn't stay still. You threatened to send me home.'

Seren opened the till. She was completely incapable of working out the change. When she eventually handed over the pound coins she dropped one into her half-drunk cup of tea, making a splash that sent splatters across the top layer of tissue paper on the counter.

'Very Jackson Pollock,' said Arlow. 'I'll take that for my collection too.'

Seren crumpled it up and threw it in the bin under the counter.

'I was sorry to hear about your husband,' Arlow said.

'How did you know?'

Arlow pointed through the open door in the direction of Tremond's.

'They told me about your parents too.'

Seren handed him another pound coin from the till.

'They'll be back together soon. The woman Dad's gone off with isn't who he thinks she is.'

'Is that what the phone call was about?'

Seren didn't reply.

'None of my business?' Arlow laughed. 'But, as I said, I have experience. Seven years as a detective means I have a bit of insight. Do you remember the one about the woman who was masquerading as a doctor on the Isle of Lewis?'

'I've never watched *Island Beat*.'

Arlow looked surprised. 'Never?'

Seren shook her head. Arlow stared at her. Seren looked away.

'Well,' he said after a pause. 'If you need any help you can call me. I still have my police warrant card and gun. The crew gave them to me as a leaving present when I finished.' He laughed. 'I keep them in the glove box of my car just in case I feel the urge to make an arrest.' He picked up a pen and started to write down a mobile number on the edge of the tissue paper.

'I don't your need help.'

Arlow stopped writing and took a deep breath. Seren waited for him to say something but instead he turned around and walked out of the shop.

Seren sat down on the stool and stared at the bunch of tulips left lying on the counter. Two hours passed; Seren closed the shop and took the tulips home.

109

Nesta

Nesta leant against the balcony rail. She hadn't looked through the telescope for weeks. Somehow it made everything seem too close. Even the stars seemed overwhelming through its powerful lens. She stared down at the countryside below her. At night it looked like another world. The river became a shimmering ribbon of silver and the trees were lines of lace against the moonlit fields.

Nesta took a sip from her glass and coughed.

Picking up the whisky bottle from the floor beside her she peered at the label. Without her glasses she couldn't make out the name of the distillery. It had been the first one on the shelf. She was sure it must be good though it tasted foul to her. Daniel was a whisky connoisseur, subscribing to a mail order service from whom a different bottle was delivered every month. Nesta wondered if he'd had the delivery address changed, four weeks had passed and no new bottle had appeared.

She took another sip. Her throat burned. She hoped that it might work; the nights were getting worse – longer.

One more sip and the glass was empty, but Nesta still felt wide-awake. She filled the glass again. She'd never been a big drinker: a little wine with dinner; a bit of something fizzy for a celebration; those White Russians on New Year's Eve with Daniel.

When she closed her eyes her head began to spin. She opened them again and looked up at the myriad of stars in the velvet sky. She thought of Seren, *y seren mwyaf hyfryd yn yr awr,* the loveliest star in the sky. There had been stars that night long ago. She'd lain awake for hours staring through the caravan window, her head resting against the steady rhythm of his heart, gazing at the stars and wishing on them all.

Nesta drank some more and glanced down, hoping Seren couldn't see her in the dark. Seren wasn't talking to her anyway. Not deliberately not talking to her, but not engaging in the way she usually did. She had withdrawn, angry that Nesta had told Griff that Daniel had left.

'He didn't need to know about Dad. He will be back, I know he will.'

Nesta so wanted to comfort her, to tell her everything would work out in the end. The words of a lullaby her own mother used to sing drifted into her head.

Suogân, do not weep,
Suogân, go to sleep;
Suogân, mother's here,
Suogân, have no fear.

She could almost feel her face pressed into the coarse cotton of her mother's apron, arms tight around her, gentle kisses on her cheek. The memory surprised Nesta; she'd forgotten that her mother could be so tender.

While Seren seemed to never want to leave her childhood home, Nesta hadn't been able to get away from hers fast enough. As a teenager she longed to leave behind the cold farmhouse, the early morning milking, the chapel, her mother's scoldings and the stinging swipe of the willow whip. She poured another glass of whisky and smiled. Her mother always told her that drinking alcohol was nothing less than dancing with the devil. Nesta filled the glass to the brim.

An owl hooted.

'Cheers,' Nesta raised her glass in the direction of the sound, spilling whisky on her nightdress as she did so. 'To the future, whatever, wherever it is.'

She tilted back her head and let the amber liquid pour into her mouth. But, as she swallowed, she choked, spluttered and coughed until tears poured down her face.

With rising nausea she walked back into her bedroom. Sitting down on the bed, she tried to stop the tilting of the walls

111

and windows. A magazine still lay open on the quilt beside her. She picked it up and stared at the page.

Nesta didn't need her glasses; it didn't matter that the photograph and text shifted and blurred in front of her. She knew what the picture looked like and knew the words better than any lullaby she'd ever learned.

The man stood in a haze of lavender. The undulating terracotta roof of an ancient farmhouse was visible behind him, roses scrambling across the umber stone, pelargoniums cascading out of vast ceramic pots. 'Paradise Found, A Welsh Garden Nestled in the Italian Hills.'

He was smiling at the camera, his face older, more weatherworn and his hair much paler, but to Nesta he still looked just the same.

'*Y seren mwyaf hyfryd yn yr awr.*' He had said it to her as they planted roses in the newly dug borders. Hands muddy, heart singing, Nesta had turned to him. She was about to tell him that she loved him, but Daniel's car crunched up the drive and then Anwen and Ben were bursting out of it, running towards her with news of their visit to Daniel's mother, and Daniel was calling to Nesta to put the kettle on while he carried in the bags.

Nesta had left him standing in the flowerbed. When she came out half an hour later, he and his caravan had disappeared.

Years later Nesta broke a tooth eating an unripe pear from the orchard. In the dentist's waiting room she had picked up a dog-eared magazine from a pile of publications on the coffee table. She'd opened it at a random page and there he was: Leo smiling out at her from his Mediterranean dream.

Frankie

Frankie pushed the last few pieces of chicken around her plate. She couldn't get the image of the scratched paintwork out of her head.

'Come on,' said Daniel. 'I made it especially for you. It's an Ottolenghi recipe from the *Guardian*.'

Frankie reached across the table and touched his hand. 'It's delicious but I'm just not feeling very hungry at the moment.'

Daniel took her hand in his.

'Are you OK?' he asked. 'Do you have a headache?'

Frankie shook her head.

'Good,' Daniel smiled and poured more wine into their glasses.

'You're not upset about the car?' Frankie asked.

'It's just a scratch. Silly boys on their way home from school, I expect. The paint shop will make it disappear like magic.'

Frankie wished they'd make her anxiety disappear like magic too. Maybe it was just a silly boy, a dare, a prank, a neighbour with a grudge wanting the parking space the beautiful car was taking up. If it had been a careless line, a straight scratch, the thoughts would never have entered Frankie's head. It was the shape that had made her gasp when she saw it on the passenger door. Daniel said it was a circle. Frankie thought it looked more like an O.

'I've been thinking about Griff,' Daniel was saying. 'I miss him so much. I think it's time I tried to see him.'

Frankie nodded. 'That would be good.'

'I thought we could take him out somewhere.'

'We?'

'He must meet you as soon as possible.'

113

'I don't think Seren would be happy about that.'

'She'll come round. She's never been one to hold a grudge. She's a soft-natured girl at heart, you'll see.'

'Maybe you should spend time with Griff on your own first. He might feel resentful if I'm there too.'

'Nonsense. He'll love you.'

Frankie got up and started clearing the plates away. Dante wound himself around her legs and Frankie scraped her leftover chicken into his bowl.

'I thought a picnic in the park,' Daniel had it all worked out. 'He loves that treetops adventure walk and if I take my chess set we can play a few games at the chess tables they have there.'

'I still think it should be just you and Griff on your own.'

'But I want you to meet him. He's such a fantastic little chap.'

Frankie turned on the taps at the sink and began swirling washing up liquid into the sink. *O, O, O. It had definitely been an O.*

'You should hear him on his trumpet. He's a natural, and it does his damned asthma the world of good.'

Frankie slipped a plate into the bubbles. Dante had finished the chicken and stood crying at the back door. Daniel made a move to stand up.

'Don't worry, I'll let him out.' Frankie wiped her hands on a tea towel. She walked the few short steps to the door and opened it, letting in the scent of orange blossom and the sound of bees.

Dante scooted between her legs, and as he did so Frankie looked down.

Her heart stopped.

At her feet was a small glistening pool about the size of an egg yolk but instead of sunny yellow it was a deep, dark red. Frankie shut the door. Half a second later she was back at the sink, her hands submerged in the hot water to stop them shaking.

'What's the matter, darling?' Daniel got up and came to put his arms around her. 'You look like you've seen a ghost.'

She tried a smile but her mouth refused to move. Her heart seemed to be pumping at a rate of knots. She could hear it in her ears, feel it in her chest.

'Maybe you're right. I should spend a bit of time with Griff before he meets you. Though I know he'll like you very much.' Daniel held her to him now. The kindness of his voice somehow made it worse. Frankie wanted to push him away. *You don't know me – you think you do, but you have no idea who or what I am.* All Frankie could think about was blood on the kitchen floor in London. Pools of blood seeping into each other, joining together to form great tributaries along the tiles. The lemon slices she had dropped slowly turning orange as the blood reached them.

Dante was crying to be let in again. Daniel turned away from her to open the door.

'Don't,' her voice was too loud. He turned back, surprised.

'What's the matter?'

'You've done enough tonight. I'll let him in.'

Daniel laughed. 'I think I can manage to open a door.' His hand was on the handle.

'No, he likes me to let him in. He won't come to you.'

'Don't be silly, I've been letting him in for weeks.' He turned the handle and began to pull the door. Frankie stopped breathing. Daniel continued speaking. 'I've been thinking about fitting a cat flap for him.'

Dante scooted through the door leaving a singled bloody paw-print on the floor. Daniel looked down. 'Oh dear. There's blood all over the step.'

'Daniel, I've got to tell you something.'

Daniel was peering into the garden. 'Dante appears to have been massacring the local vermin.'

Frankie took a deep breath.

'Something I did.'

115

'Ah ha, here it is, poor little mite.'

'Something bad.'

'It looks more like a field mouse than a rat.'

Frankie stopped.

'Though it's hard to tell when it appears to have no head.' Daniel began gently to kick the remains of the body into the flowerbed. He came back through the door. I'll pour boiling water over the step. Get rid of the mess.' He started to fill the kettle. 'Sorry, Frankie. What were you saying?'

Beside him Frankie closed her eyes. 'Nothing.' She turned and kissed his cheek. 'Nothing important anyway.'

Seren

For some reason the thought of London had suggested heels. Now as Seren negotiated the fast-food boxes and empty cans that littered the uneven pavement she wished she'd worn flat shoes. She was already far too hot in the fitted dress and matching jacket she'd decided to wear. She realised she looked as though she was going for a job interview rather than a meeting with her father's lover's estranged husband.

She had Oliver's address written on a piece of paper, but she had to walk the length of the road three times before she saw the tiny door in the wooden frontage of an old warehouse. The number had been painted on it in black; the paint dripped from the figure five like oily tears.

Seren looked behind as a car stopped, disgorging hooded youths into a burger bar next door to the warehouse. The car boomed out loud music and as it sped away it engulfed her in a cloud of exhaust fumes.

Seren almost turned around and went home but the door suddenly opened and a man with dust in his hair and a wide smile was standing in front of her.

'I'd given up on you,' he said. She recognised the slight Yorkshire accent.

'I couldn't find the door.'

The man looked at the door as though seeing it for the first time. 'I really must get round to making a more salubrious-looking entrance. Come on inside.' He stood aside to let her pass.

Seren stepped over the threshold and found herself in an enormous, high-ceilinged space. Sunlight poured through a series of glass panels in the roof so that the room was almost celestially bright.

At first Seren could hardly make out what was around her but as her eyes gradually became accustomed to the glare she realised that she was surrounded by huge white figures, all female, all at least three times life size. Three were suspended from the ceiling by chains. Giant angels hovering above the ground. Others were poised on plinths or simply lying on the floor.

As Oliver closed the door the sounds of the busy street were replaced by silence. Seren was reminded of being in a church. A long, narrow table lined one wall like an altar. The tools of Oliver's trade hung in neat rows above it: hammers, saws, drills, mallets, knives. Large charcoal sketches of angels were pinned up on the opposite walls.

Oliver gestured to the sculptures around him, 'Don't expect much conversation from them. They're very shy.'

Seren found herself laughing. 'They're certainly...' She couldn't quite think what to say.

'Big?' Oliver suggested.

'Beautiful,' said Seren.

Oliver smiled. 'Thank you. The best ones will be cast in bronze.' He indicated one of the suspended forms. 'When she's cast she'll be off to Kensington. She's going to hang in the entrance hall of a millionaire music mogul's townhouse.'

Seren glanced at the naked, winged figure and took in the arched back and outstretched arms, head thrown back as though in ecstasy.

'Goodness.' She felt as though she sounded rather prim.

'Goodness indeed,' he laughed.

Seren shifted slightly from one foot to the other, aware that her shoes were pinching. 'I'm sorry to take up your time like this. I just wanted to ask you a few questions about your ex-wife.'

'Don't apologise. You're a welcome distraction today. I have an exhibition coming up and I've been in negotiation with the gallery about the catalogue all morning. Sitting at the

118

computer looking at layouts when I'd much rather be doing something else. Come and have a drink.'

Oliver set off and Seren followed him down the length of the vast studio into another smaller room.

'Sorry about the mess,' said Oliver.

Seren looked around her but she couldn't see any mess. Stainless steel kitchen units glinted along one wall, but apart from two sofas and a deerskin rug the room was practically bare.

It took Seren a few moments to see the cat lying on the rug, curled up, camouflaged against the deerskin. The cat opened one eye, looked at Seren and went back to sleep.

Everything was white and grey; the only colour came from the large pile of books neatly stacked up against one wall.

'Sit down and I'll get us a drink,' Oliver pointed to the sofa. 'Coffee? Or would you prefer tea or maybe a glass of wine. I have a bottle of white in the fridge.'

'Tea would be lovely.'

'Earl Grey?'

Seren nodded and sat down on a sofa. She noticed it was upholstered in pin-striped suiting: fine dove-grey wool that felt like silk to touch. Above the kitchen area Seren could see a mezzanine level accessed by a cast-iron spiral staircase in one corner. She could just make out the corner of a double bed.

Oliver spooned tea leaves into a yellow pot.

'It's lovely here,' said Seren, looking through the window into a gravel courtyard filled with more sculptures in various stages of evolution.

'Thank you,' said Oliver, placing the teapot and two mugs on the floor between the sofas. He sat down facing Seren. The cat immediately unfurled itself from the rug and leapt onto his knee. Oliver stroked its arching back and smiled at Seren. 'What would you like to know?'

Seren's mind was a blank.

'You told me Francesca is living with your father,' Oliver

119

prompted as he gently pushed the cat away and poured the tea through a strainer. 'It's such a relief to know that she's alright.' He passed Seren her mug. 'I haven't seen her for over three years. I had no idea where she was.'

'When did you split up?' asked Seren.

'Well, I don't know if you can really call it splitting up.'

'What do you mean?' Seren took a sip of tea.

'She disappeared.'

Seren's eyes widened 'You mean she walked out?'

'She vanished.'

'You had no idea where she'd gone?'

Oliver's face looked pale, Seren noticed that his hands shook slightly as he poured out his own tea. 'She left the house one day and simply didn't come back. I didn't even know where to start looking for her.'

'Did you tell the police?'

Oliver nodded. 'Of course. They did some checks to see if they could find her but she'd taken a bag of clothes, her purse, her phone, her passport. It seemed as though she'd gone quite willingly, so they weren't really interested.' He shrugged. 'Since then I've been trawling through the internet looking for signs of her, posting descriptions on missing persons' websites and asking around in chat rooms, just to see if anyone has met her or seen her in the last three years.

'How long had you been married?'

'Fifteen years.'

Seren wanted to put out her hand to touch him, he seemed so sad. Instead she took another sip of tea.

'The thing was, we'd always been so close. We had nothing in our lives we didn't share. Even this building.' He looked around him. 'This room was her studio; she'd paint in here every day. We rented a flat round the corner, a bed-sit really, but after she disappeared I couldn't bear to live there on my own.' He paused and the cat jumped onto the sofa again and settled down to lie against his thigh. 'I like living here. It makes me feel closer to Francesca.' Seren glanced around the sparse room again. There wasn't even a television. She pictured Oliver at night with only the cat for company, desperately looking through the internet for any sign of Frankie.

'It was a shock. We had ups and downs but I thought we were happy. I have never quite believed that she meant to leave permanently.'

'How awful it must have been for you.'

'It still is. Never an hour passes without me wondering where she is or what happened to her.' He started to stroke the cat under its chin and it let out a long low rumble. 'It's a relief to know she's well.'

They sat in silence for a while, then Oliver looked straight at Seren.

'Do you believe in love at first sight?'

Seren hesitated. 'Yes. I think I do.'

'You must believe in it, Seren, because I can tell you that it really does exist.' Oliver smiled. 'The first time I saw Francesca I fell in love with her. She was everything I'd ever wanted. I adored her.' He kept on smiling, his eyes were very bright. 'She was my angel. That's what I used to say to her, "you are my perfect angel girl".' His face fell, sadness swept across it like a cloud. 'But I lost my perfect angel and now all I can do is make angel sculptures over and over again. But they are never as perfect as Francesca.'

Seren wasn't quite sure what to say. All the questions she wanted to ask about Frankie somehow seemed inappropriate.

'Are you married?' Oliver suddenly asked.

Seren took another sip of tea. 'My husband's dead.' She bit her lip; the words sounded so blunt, so final.

Oliver leant forwards on this seat, 'Then you must know how it feels to lose someone.' He paused. 'Though for you, of course, it must be worse.'

Seren felt her mouth quiver. *Please don't cry.*

'It's alright,' said Oliver, and Seren found tears slipping down her cheeks, and words pouring out in a way they hadn't in the whole year since Tom had died.

Inexplicably she found herself telling him about the camping holiday in Scotland and Tom's determination to spend a day climbing Ben Nevis while Seren and Griff explored the hills and streams around their campsite. She told him of her growing realisation that Tom was later than he said he'd be, and the hours that passed while Seren decided when actually to tell someone she was worried, the long night waiting for news from the mountain-rescue team as she reassured Griff that everything would be alright. The dawn, the police car, the drive to the hospital to identify the body. The regret. If only she had reported him not coming back much sooner. The months and months and months of paralysing grief. Trying to stay strong for Griff. The support she'd had from Daniel and Nesta. And now Daniel had gone, had left them all for Frankie. As she said Frankie's name she stopped and picking up her bag found a packet of printed tissues that Griff had given her for Christmas. The red-nosed reindeers seemed ridiculously inappropriate.

'Sorry,' Seren blew her nose. 'I didn't mean to get so emotional.'

'You've had a terrible time.' Seren looked up at Oliver and saw kindness in his eyes, concern in his expression.

She wondered what sort of woman would walk out on this man. A thought struck her.

'Did you and…' She found herself unable to say her name again. '… did you have children?'

Oliver shook his head. He put down his mug and sat back. 'It makes sense that she'd search out a father figure.'

'What do you mean?'

'I mean that she's living with an older man.'

'Why?'

Oliver stared out into the courtyard. His fingers stroked the cat. The cat purred again, louder this time. Oliver turned back to

Seren.

'When she was eighteen she lost her entire family in a car crash.' He stood up and walked over to the book piles. From between a stack of Penguin Classics he pulled out a dog-eared photograph and handed it to Seren. She found herself looking at a faded family group. A smiling couple: the man had one hand on the shoulder of a skinny teenage boy, the woman had her arms around a girl who looked just like a younger version of herself. They were standing in a field of sunflowers. Behind them Seren could just make out a pale blue VW van. 'Francesca always said they were the perfect family.'

'That's very sad,' said Seren, handing the picture back to Oliver.

'Francesca wasn't with them when they crashed. She'd stayed at home that day. I think she suffers from a sort of...' He seemed to search the air around him for the word.

'Guilt,' said Seren.

'It made her prone to mood swings, depressions that could last for months. Paranoia.' He slipped the picture back between the books and ran his hands through his hair, and Seren noticed threads of silver running through the dusty brown. 'She needed support.'

Seren didn't say anything but in her head his words were ricocheting around as she wondered how much support her father was now going to have to give. Did he know what Frankie was like? Oliver suddenly looked at his watch.

'I'm afraid I have to go. I've arranged to meet a collector from America who's interested in one of my pieces.'

Seren stood up. 'Sorry to have taken up so much of your time.'

Oliver smiled at her. 'Don't be sorry.'

'Thank you for telling me about Francesca.'

'Thank you for telling me about what happened with your husband. I hope it hasn't upset you.'

Seren shook her head. 'I don't know why I went on so much.

I haven't really talked to anyone about it in that way.'

'Sometimes with a stranger it's easier?' Oliver suggested.

Seren nodded.

Oliver stood up and began to gather up the tea things from the floor. 'I feel like I've got a lot of questions I'd like to ask about Francesca; how she is now, what she's doing. I just wish I had more time today.'

'You could phone me,' suggested Seren.

'I could,' he paused. 'Or maybe we could meet up again? It's easier to discuss things face to face.'

'Here?'

'No, I'll come to see you. Save you coming all the way to London.' Oliver smiled. 'We could have lunch.'

'OK,' Seren smiled back. 'That sounds like a good plan.'

Nesta

Nesta waved at the computer screen and three boys in various states of undress waved back.

'Good night, Granny,' they shouted at the tops of their voices, and the grainy image jumped a bit before being replaced by Anni's flushed pink face. The boys appeared to be having a screaming competition behind her.

'They're driving me mad, Mum.' Anni turned around and shouted something at the boys that sounded like 'shut up'. 'Mike's been in charge all day while I was supposed to be putting my feet up. Now they're hyped up on too much TV and Pepsi Max – that's Mike's idea of childcare.' Nesta could hear Mike's voice in the background protesting. Anni turned around again and shouted something that also sounded like 'shut up'. Somewhere in the distance the baby started to cry.

'You poor thing,' said Nesta from the other side of the world. She shifted in her seat and wished that Anni would go back to phoning her instead of using Skype. It always made Nesta feel like an unwilling voyeur of her daughter's chaotic household.

'I can't see you, Mum. Remember the camera is at the top of your screen.'

Nesta didn't want to be seen. She'd been gardening since dawn, she had yet to brush her hair, and the old Breton T-shirt she was wearing was ripped from rose thorns and stained by lily pollen. She'd only come in to check the weather on the internet, hoping that there might be a bit of rain later for the plants.

Nesta straightened her back a bit.

'I can see you now,' said Anni. The baby was in her arms, squirming backwards and forwards, trying to reach the computer keyboard. 'Are you OK? You look a bit…'

125

'I haven't had a chance to get dressed properly yet,' Nesta interrupted before Anni had a chance to say what she looked like.

'Have you seen Dad lately?'

Nesta shook her head. 'Not since he came to discuss selling the house.'

'He's desperate to see Griff.'

'You've talked to him?'

'Yeah, he phoned me. Told me that Seren wouldn't let him take Griff for a picnic in the park. He was very upset.'

'She didn't tell me he wanted to do that.' The baby suddenly vomited down Anni's shirt. Anni dabbed at it with what appeared to be a pair of pants. 'Will you talk to her, Mum. Make her see sense. It's no good for Griff not to see his grandfather, especially after everything he's been through.'

'She's upset.'

'She's behaving as though she's more upset than you.'

'She's hurt and confused. Remember she's been through an awful lot already, with Tom dying the way he did.'

'I know, Mum, but we all have stuff we have to cope with…' Anni started on a well-worn rant about Seren's inability to leave home and properly grow up. Nesta slumped in the chair again. She'd heard it many times before. It wouldn't be long before Anni would switch to a long list of accusations against her brother. Nesta hadn't dared tell her he'd spilt up from Suki.

She picked up the red envelope that had been in the study since the day of the wedding anniversary. For the hundredth time she took out the tickets and looked at them, making sure to keep her hands well away from the computer camera. Only three weeks now until the flight. She closed her eyes. Could she? Couldn't she? Obviously she'd only need the one ticket. Maybe she could sell the other one on eBay.

'Are you asleep, Mum?'

Nesta opened her eyes. 'Look darling, I'm going to have to go. I'm helping Seren in the shop today, and as you can see I

126

need to smarten up a bit first.'

'But you will talk to her? About Dad seeing Griff? It really isn't fair on either of them. I remember when one of the couples at school…'

Mike started shouting in the background. Something about the boys having flooded the bathroom.

'Gotta go, Mum.'

The little study was suddenly peaceful again; the weather map returned to the screen. There would be no rain for her garden for days. Nesta did a search for Rome. 26 degrees, light rain showers. She thought of Leo. His pelargoniums would be doing very well.

Frankie

Frankie's arms ached. She'd done more lengths than she usually did. There was an energy inside her that needed to be expended.

She remembered Daniel's disappointed face after he'd received the text reply from Seren. A surge of anger bubbled up as her fingertips touched the wall of the pool. She twisted and pushed herself through the water again.

As her arms ploughed forward her brain whirred. How could Seren be so cruel? All Daniel wanted was a few hours with his grandson. If only Seren could understand how much Daniel missed Griff.

She imagined a conversation with Seren.

'Whatever you think of your father's relationship with me shouldn't matter. Griff is innocent in all of this. It's wrong to deny him access to his grandfather.'

'OK, you're right. Griff can see my father as often as he likes.'

In her mind she saw Daniel, so pleased, so grateful and Frankie felt a glow of happiness at being able to do something for Daniel, instead of Daniel constantly doing things for her.

She reached the deep end and stopped. She knew her thoughts were fantasies. Seren would never agree to talk to her, let alone be persuaded by anything she said.

Her hands held onto the metal bar and she let her legs float behind her, bobbing in the waves made by the other lunchtime swimmers.

Slowly a sense of peace descended on her as thoughts of Seren's unreasonable behaviour ebbed away. Maybe she'd go and visit Daniel at his office. Surprise him with a slice of cake from Tremond's.

She turned around so that the entire length of the pool

128

stretched out in front of her, undulating and blue. At the end she saw a dark-skinned man coming through the showers with a little girl. Even from a distance she recognised Arlow Laverne.

The little girl had one of those swimming costumes with an in-built ring of floats around it. She looked nervous, pulling back on Arlow Laverne's hand as though she didn't want to go in the water. Arlow crouched down and started talking to her, smoothing back her hair as though trying to reassure her.

Several of the swimmers in the shallow end had stopped and were staring at the actor. Frankie wondered what it must be like to be recognised everywhere you go with no chance ever of blending into the background. No chance of ever disappearing and starting your life again.

She was so engrossed in her thoughts that she almost didn't notice the man who walked in front of Arlow and his daughter. It was only the way he stopped and scanned the pool that made her focus on him, his self-assured stance, his folded arms. He looked as though he was searching for something. Or someone.

Frankie's whole body clenched. Fear flooded her limbs and her legs sunk down as though suddenly made of lead. The man slid into the pool, splashing water on his chest and shoulders before pushing away from the side and gliding straight in her direction.

For a few seconds Frankie was unable to make her body move. She tried to take a deep breath but could only manage a shallow gasp. Panic tore at her stomach. She could see the man's head coming nearer, his hair sleek against his skull, his arms propelling him powerfully towards her.

Finally she managed to take in one enormous breath and dived down under the water, as deep as she could possibly go.

She pushed herself forward. The only sound was her heartbeat; it hammered in her ears like a drum. She willed herself to keep swimming, not to come up to the surface however much she wanted air. For a moment the man's body was above her: Frankie kept on moving under the water, on and on until she thought her lungs might burst. At last she reached the shallow end, coming up desperately for air, wading the last few steps until she reached the side. Frankie daren't look back.

Maybe he was watching her from the deep end, maybe he was out of the water and already walking down the edge of the pool. She heaved herself out. How many steps till she reached the changing room? Five, ten, twenty? Her legs felt as though they were made of jelly.

The women's changing area was empty. Fumbling with the key on her wrist Frankie managed to open her locker and, grabbing her clothes, she almost fell into a changing room and locked the door.

Frankie threw the towel around her shoulders and sat dripping on the wooden bench trying to calm down. Maybe it hadn't been him. How could he possibly have found her? She closed her eyes, breathing slowly at last.

She heard someone and her eyes snapped open.

'Chez?'

His pet name for her. She recognised the voice. She pulled her feet up so they weren't visible underneath the cubicle's saloon style door.

'Chez?'

The voice was coming nearer. She heard a noise in the cubicle beside her. Frankie closed her eyes and pressed her face against her knees. *Please go away, please go away.* Surely it was a nightmare. She wanted to wake up. She wanted Daniel.

'Chez, don't be silly. Come out of there.'

Another noise in the cubicle next door. A bang. Frankie opened her eyes and saw a hand coming under the adjoining wall. She screamed.

'What's going on? Chez?' The man's voice much louder. 'Which one are you in?'

A child began to cry. A face appeared under Frankie's door, scanning the cubicle with large brown eyes. Frankie screamed again. The face hastily disappeared. The cubicle next door rattled, the hand vanished from Frankie's side and the man's voice said, 'It's alright, darling,' over and over again until the crying stopped. With a thumping heart Frankie realised that the hand had been small and brown and that the face, though familiar, definitely wasn't the one she had been expecting.

There was a gentle knock on Frankie's cubicle door.

'Are you alright in there? Sorry if we gave you a fright'.

Frankie stood up and tentatively opened the door.

Arlow Laverne held his daughter in his arms. She was clinging to him like a limpet, juddering tiny sobs into his shoulder.

'Sorry,' Arlow said again. 'Chez is scared of the water. We were just about to get into the pool when she turned around and ran in here.'

Frankie stared at him. Her heart was still beating much too fast.

'Are you sure you're OK? You look as though you've seen a ghost,' he said and the little girl turned around to look at Frankie for herself.

Frankie took a deep breath. 'I'm fine.' She repeated it three times more and then managed, 'I didn't mean to be so hysterical. It was just the changing room was empty and then I heard your voice and I thought a man was...'

'I know I shouldn't be in here,' Arlow interrupted. 'You won't tell the press, will you? They'd have a field day. "Actor found in ladies changing room – looking at women under the doors." I can just imagine the headlines.' He laughed and Frankie found herself laughing too.

The little girl looked from one to the other and said, 'What's funny?'

'Don't worry,' Frankie said. 'Your secret's safe with me.' She was still laughing, she couldn't stop herself. She tried but the laughter only increased. Tears started to trickle down her face.

'What's funny?' the child repeated. Arlow put her down

onto the floor, and squatting down to her level, smiled at her.

'You could have got your dad into trouble, Francesca Laverne.'

Now Francesca understood. 'My name's Francesca, too,' she wiped her eyes with the back of her hand feeling a little more composed. 'But everyone calls me Frankie.'

'Everyone calls me Chez,' said the little girl. They grinned at each other.

'I call her Francesca when she's cheeky or when she runs away from me in swimming pools.' Arlow lifted his daughter up again. 'Shall we give the pool another try?'

'No, no,' Chez buried her face in her father's neck. 'I don't like it.'

Arlow looked at Frankie and raised his eyebrows. 'Somehow my wife and I never got round to taking her swimming. This is the first time I've given it a go.'

Gently he lifted his daughter's face from his shoulder. 'And we've bought you a special swimming costume and everything, haven't we, Chez?'

Chez looked down at her stiffly padded swim suit. 'I don't like it,' she said.

Frankie laughed again. 'When I was little I didn't like swimming.' Chez turned her gaze back to Frankie. 'My mum and dad used to take me and my brother to France every year, and we always stayed on campsites where there was a pool. My brother would race in as soon as we arrived, but I'd always find an excuse to stay in our campervan. I'd say I had a headache or stomach ache or I'd offer to help my mum get the tea, or I'd hide my swimsuit in my pillow case. Once I said a lion had eaten it.'

Chez's eyes widened. 'Did it really?'

Frankie shook her head. 'No. I'd hidden the swimsuit in the bottom of a box of Rice Krispies.'

Chez giggled.

'But now,' Frankie went on, 'now I love swimming. I've

132

done thirty lengths today.'

'What made you change your mind?' asked Arlow.

'Chocolate croissants,' Frankie replied.

'Chocolate croissants?' Chez and Arlow said together.

'I discovered pain au chocolat in the campsite shop, and my father said I could have one for breakfast every day if I let him take me in the pool for half an hour first.'

'And that worked?' asked Arlow.

Frankie nodded. 'I just used to think about those delicious croissants waiting for me – still warm, oozing melted chocolate in the middle, the dusting of icing sugar on the top – and then I'd let my dad hold me while we walked up and down the shallow end. It wasn't long before I realised what fun the water was. I soon forgot about doing it for croissants and my parents had a terrible time persuading me to get out of the pool for long enough to eat any breakfast at all.'

Arlow looked at Chez. 'Would you go in the water for a chocolate croissant?'

Chez scrunched up her face as though thinking very hard, then she shook her head. 'I don't like them.'

'Is there anything you do like?' asked Frankie.

Chez thought again. 'Tutti frutti cupcakes.'

'Oh, I know, from the patisserie on the high street,' Arlow smiled.

'I'm going there now,' said Frankie. 'Shall I tell them to keep a Tutti frutti cupcake specially for you?'

Chez wriggled out of her father's arms. 'OK.' She took hold of Arlow's hand and pulled it. 'Come on, Dad, let's go swimming.'

'Wow,' Arlow looked at Frankie. 'That worked fast! Fancy coming back in and giving us some lessons? To tell you the truth I'm pretty poor at swimming myself.'

'No, sorry, I've got to go.' Her heart had started beating fast again and her head began to throb. *He* would probably still be in the pool. Looking for her. Waiting for her.

'Thank you for your help,' said Arlow. 'You seem to have done wonders.'

Frankie wasn't listening. She had to get out of the building as quickly as possible. With a polite goodbye she backed into her cubicle and locked the door.

Seren

Seren felt much too exposed. She wished she hadn't been seated in the window but it had been the only table left while the ladies' golf club was having its annual lunch. Hordes of well-coiffed, middle-aged women were busy getting tipsy on mojitos and salivating over the menu as though they hadn't eaten for weeks.

The waitress brought Seren's glass of sparkling water to the table.

'I like your dress,' the young girl said. 'Nice pattern.'

'Thank you,' Seren looked down at the swallows that were printed on the summer dress. She'd bought it from the expensive boutique on the high street the day before. Seren couldn't remember the last time she'd had new clothes. Her shoes were new too, from the same shop: red suede wedges. 'Very sexy,' the shop assistant had said and Seren had felt herself blush.

As she took a sip of water the charm bracelet on her arm jingled. Seren hadn't worn it since she, Anni and Ben had come to meet their father at the hotel weeks before. She wasn't sure why she'd put it on today, maybe in the hope that her father would come home as a result of what she might find out about Frankie.

The noise made by the golfing ladies began to rise and Seren wished she'd asked Oliver to meet her in the local café instead. The hotel now seemed much too ostentatious. He was an artist, probably much more at home somewhere less formal. She stared out of the window wondering why she'd got here so early. It wasn't as though she'd had far to come.

A man walked past holding the hand of a little girl. He stopped and bent down to do up the lace on one of the child's trainers. Seren opened the menu and held it up to her face in case he spotted her. After a minute she let the menu drop a little and peeped over the top.

Arlow Laverne was still there. The little girl seemed to be complaining about the way he'd tied her lace and he patiently crouched down to do it again. When he'd finished he said something that made the little girl laugh and she flung her arms around him in a hug. Rolled-up towels stuck out of an incongruous-looking Hello Kitty drawstring bag, hung over Arlow's shoulder in a way that made Seren smile.

She felt a lump rise in her throat and took another sip of water. She checked the time on her phone. Still five minutes before she'd arranged to meet Oliver. When she looked up again Arlow had gone.

'Hello.'

The voice made Seren jump. Oliver stood in front of her, much less dusty and a lot more smartly dressed than when she'd seen him a few days earlier. The hotel restaurant didn't seem too posh after all. 'Sorry. Did I give you a fright?'

'No,' Seren lied. 'You're nice and early.'

'Not as nice and early as you,' he smiled.

'I wanted to be sure we'd get a table, but I'm afraid this was the only one left. I hope you don't mind being on display to the entire high street.'

Oliver took off his linen jacket and slung it across the back of the chair opposite Seren. 'I don't mind if you don't.' He sat down and, casting his gaze across the busy dining room, asked in a stage whisper, 'Am I the only man in the entire restaurant?'

Seren nodded and whispered back, 'I think you might be.'

He raised his eyebrows. 'Well, at least I'm sitting with the most beautiful woman.'

Seren picked up the menu. 'The youngest woman anyway,' she mumbled.

The waitress appeared and asked Oliver what he'd like to drink. He glanced at Seren's water. 'Wouldn't you rather be drinking wine?'

'I have to go back to work in the shop this afternoon. I don't want to find myself getting my bridal bouquets muddled up.'

'Go on – live dangerously. Red or white?'

She paused. 'OK. White.'

He smiled at the waitress. 'A bottle of Chardonnay, please.'

The waitress smiled back and Seren noticed a slight shift in the young woman's posture, a tilt of her head, a brightness in her eyes. She finds him attractive, Seren thought.

'What do you recommend?' Oliver asked Seren.

The text on the menu swam in front of her and she had to focus hard to see the selection. 'Um, the duck is always delicious and the salmon is locally caught. But the pork is good too.'

'I think I'll let you choose for me.'

'I don't know what you like.'

'I'm pretty easy to please,' he grinned at her.

Seren put down the menu. 'Then I think we'll both have duck.'

'Great. Duck sounds fabulous. Now tell me more about your shop.'

'I thought you wanted to talk about Frankie, I mean Francesca.'

'I do, but first I want to know a little more about you and your life.'

Seren picked a tiny fleck of a fern leaf from the corner of her thumb. 'There's not much to tell. I live next door to my parents' converted windmill. I own a shop called Stems and I spend my days among flowers and foliage, and when I'm not doing that I'm looking after my son.'

The waitress appeared with their bottle of wine and two glasses. Seren could tell she was trying to catch Oliver's eye but he had his full attention turned to her.

'How's your mother taking everything? She must be very upset.'

Seren nodded. 'Dad wants a divorce and it looks as though they'll have to sell The Windmill. They've lived there for years, since before I was born. I can't imagine how she'll cope.'

Oliver poured the wine into her glass. 'Why can't he just let your mother stay in the house?'

'I don't know,' Seren shrugged and lifted up her glass to take a sip. 'I think he wants to buy a bigger house with Francesca. He probably wants to marry her.'

'She'd have to divorce me first.'

Seren stopped, wine glass midway between the table and her lips. 'I don't think my father knows that she was ever married, let alone *still* married.'

'Do you think he knows much about her at all?'

'I'm not sure. She seems quite secretive about her past. I saw her picture on the internet and she looks completely different now. Her hair is short and dyed blonde; she's very skinny and she calls herself Frankie, not Francesca.'

Oliver looked stunned. 'Really? That seems a bit extreme even for someone as unpredictable as Francesca.'

'Unpredictable?'

Oliver paused as the waitress appeared again for their order. He told her what they wanted and she reluctantly moved away.

'It was duck you said you'd chosen for us, wasn't it?' Oliver checked.

'Yes,' said Seren. 'But what do you mean by "unpredictable"?'

Oliver sighed and looked out of the window. It was at least half a minute till he turned back to Seren.

'She's just a little bit...' He paused, then said slowly, 'I think the word I'd use would be "unstable".'

'What do you mean?'

'I mean that she had a very traumatic experience in her past, and that sometimes makes her behave somewhat irrationally.'

'Irrationally how?'

Oliver sighed again. 'Look. Like I said I don't want to

prejudice you against her.'

'I'm already prejudiced against her. She's messed up my home, my family and my life!' Seren felt herself getting hot and gulped her wine, remembering too late that she hadn't eaten since the night before. The glass was empty almost at once. Oliver poured her another.

'OK,' he said, sitting back in his chair. 'But if I tell you some things about her it doesn't mean that she's still like that. For all I know she's undergone intensive counselling, or maybe she's happier now, not so prone to violent outbursts.'

'Violent?' repeated Seren.

Oliver looked at Seren with sad eyes. 'Sometimes, on her bad days, she was violent. But maybe I just brought out the worst in her.'

Seren's head was spinning from the wine. It took a few seconds to realise that she'd leant across the white damask table cloth, her hand only inches away from Oliver's, and that she was saying, 'I'm sure that's not true.'

She sprang back. 'It sounds like Francesca has issues.'

Oliver sighed. 'I think I need to warn you.'

'Warn me about what?'

'Duck for you, madam.' The waitress was back, two steaming plates in her hands. 'Careful sir, the plate is hot,' she said to Oliver, unnecessarily drawing out the last word.

Oliver started to eat immediately. 'I'm ravenous today.' He looked up at the waitress. 'It's delicious.' He looked across to Seren. 'Good choice.'

Nesta

Nesta sat in the café and watched as Daniel walked through the door. She still found him handsome. He'd kept his figure and his hair, though grey, had retained the slightly Byronesque dishevelment she'd found so appealing when she'd first seen him coming out of the V&A so many years before.

'Hello Nesta.' He looked down at her, his expression serious.

'Sit down,' Nesta gestured to the painted wooden chair opposite her. 'I'm told the soup of the day is carrot and coriander.'

'I don't want lunch.' He undid the buttons of his jacket and sat down. 'You said in your phone message that you wanted to talk about Griff.'

'At least have a coffee.'

'I have to get back to the office soon. Odette has arranged an urgent meeting with the planners about the tourist information centre. It seems they have problems with the proportions of the clock tower for the roof.'

'Typical! Two weeks away from retiring and you still can't slow down, even to talk about our grandson.'

'Nesta, did you ask me to meet you just so you could pick a fight?'

Nesta sighed. 'No Daniel, I didn't. I genuinely want to be civil about this, for Griff's sake.'

'Has Seren changed her mind about letting me see him?' His expression brightened.

Nesta shook her head. 'She seems determined to keep you away from him but, personally, I don't think she's doing the right thing.'

Daniel raised his eyebrows in surprise.

'I thought you would be agreeing with Seren. Do you know why she won't let me see him?'

'Anni Skyped this morning and said she thinks Seren wants to punish you,' she shrugged. 'But I'm not sure about that. I think she's just trying to protect Griff after everything else he's been through.' She reached across the table towards Daniel's hand but didn't touch it. 'He's still grieving for his father, they both are. This situation is a lot for them to take in on top of that.'

Daniel looked out of the café window. Nesta saw a look of astonishment pass over his face. She followed his gaze. A man and a little girl walked past hand in hand. The man's face looked familiar.

'Arlow Laverne,' Nesta said out loud.

Daniel picked up the menu. 'Maybe I'll have a coffee after all.'

'I wonder what he's doing back in town. Do you think that's his daughter?'

'I don't think it's him.'

'Of course it is. I'd recognise his face anywhere – I've seen it in enough magazines and TV trailers over the years. I wonder what Seren would think if she knew he was around.'

'That was all a long time ago.'

Nesta watched as Arlow and the little girl crossed the road and disappeared into a toy shop.

'I never understood why they broke up the way they did,' she said. 'It was so sudden, after they had been so close.'

'They were kids, Nesta. They were never going to stay together.' Daniel turned in his seat. 'How does one get served in here? Are all the staff on their lunch break? It's like the *Marie-Celeste*.'

'Sometimes I wonder if their break-up contributed towards her illness,' Nesta continued.

'Oh, for God's sake, don't bring all that up again. Seren wasn't ill, she just went through a bit of a bad patch after that

141

damned art-history course put so much pressure on her. She was absolutely fine after she met Tom – he was the best thing that could have happened to her, a perfect match – didn't we always say that?'

'Yes, Daniel,' Nesta muttered, but she was thinking of the day that Seren and Arlow had spilt up. Arlow had slammed the front door of The Windmill so hard that Nesta, baking biscuits in the kitchen, had feared the whole building might collapse around her.

Seren cried for days, but she refused to tell her mother why she and Arlow had fallen out. A week later Seren had seemed resigned to life without the boy she had spent every possible spare moment with for two years, and she had left for university, slightly nervous but positive about a new start. Three weeks after that Nesta and Daniel flew to Australia to meet their first grandchild, pleased that Seren seemed to have settled happily into student life in London. As far as Nesta knew Seren had never seen Arlow again.

A few months later, Nesta and Daniel had returned from their extended trip to find that Seren had given up her course and had been staying with her grandmother in Wales for most of their absence. They had brought Seren home and after a few weeks Nesta had driven to the run-down council house where Arlow and his mother had lived. She had hoped that Arlow might hold some clue as to why her daughter had become so sad and silent, locked into her darkened bedroom, a mere shadow of the feisty, passionate, beautiful girl that she'd once been.

The front garden of Arlow's grey house had been strung with rows of soggy washing and a wiry woman answered Nesta's knock. Shouting to be heard above the screaming of the baby on her hip, she told Nesta that Arlow and his mother were long gone; there had been a forwarding address but her dog had eaten the bit of paper it was written on.

'Dog's dead now', the woman had said. Nesta had the

impression she thought the bit of paper had contributed to his demise.

Not long after that Daniel had brought Tom home from work and Seren had slowly started to reappear from the shadows and become something a little more like the girl that she'd once been.

'Sorry for the delay.' A portly waiter appeared beside the table. 'Can I get you anything, sir?' He smiled at Daniel.

'I'll have an espresso.' Daniel said.

'Certainly.' The waiter glanced at the clock on the wall. 'Anything to eat? The soup today is…'

'Carrot and coriander, I know and I don't want it.' Daniel's voice was like a bark.

'Daniel, don't be so rude!' Nesta looked up at the waiter and smiled. 'Sorry, he's a little stressed.'

The waiter scowled at Daniel and moved away.

Daniel pressed his fingers against his eyes.

'I just want to see Griff so much.'

Nesta leant forward and this time touched his hand. 'Well, I have a plan.'

Frankie

Frankie closed the front door and let her swimming bag fall onto the hallway floor. In the kitchen she poured herself a glass of water and leant against the sink trying to steady her breathing. She'd had to fight the urge to run all the way home from the pool. Instead she had walked as fast as she could, checking behind every few steps.

She finished the glass and poured herself another, opening a drawer to search for Paracetamol for her aching head.

Dante jumped up beside her and rubbed himself against her bare arm. She stroked his back and looked through the kitchen window into the little garden. The sweet peas in the pot she'd planted were flowering in a lavish display of pastel colours crazily climbing the trellis that Daniel had put up for her against the red-brick wall.

Dante pushed his long nose against her cheek. 'I was just being silly,' Frankie said out loud. 'Now I think about it, I couldn't even see his face from the other end of the pool.'

Dante let out a gravelly cry.

'Do you need to go out?' Frankie picked up a pair of scissors from a drawer beside her. 'Come on. I'll pick some of those sweet peas for the kitchen table.'

She unlocked the back door and opened it. The smell of the flowers filled the warm air. Dante scooted between her legs and jumped onto the wall.

Frankie took a step onto the path and felt herself kick something with her foot. Looking down she saw that it was another mouse, dead on the flagstone, mauled and half chewed, one leg gone, its neck horribly twisted.

'Oh Dante, not again!' she looked up at the wall but the cat had disappeared. With a sigh she glanced back down, wondering whether she had the stomach to dispose of it. It was then that she noticed the trail of blood beside the body. Lines on the flagstones. Still wet in places, glinting in the sunlight. But the lines of blood weren't like a trail, they were too disjointed, too straight, too thick.

Frankie stared. It took a few moments to realise what it was. A letter, a capital letter. She squinted, trying to make it out and then she gasped,

F

Her letter. Her initial. Written on the path in blood, as if someone had taken the dead and bleeding mouse and squeezed it as though it were a tube of paint. She took a step back and closed her eyes tightly, willing the F to go away. Surely she was just imagining it.

She opened her eyes and it was still there. Something dripped onto the path. Another drip, and then another, and finally a large drip onto her sandal, splashing the brown leather, spraying her bare toes with tiny specks.

More blood.

Her own blood. She realised she'd been clutching the kitchen scissors so tightly that the tip had driven into her palm. She unclenched her fingers and let the scissors fall onto the ground. Her hand began to throb with pain. The wound looked like a stigmata. With one swift movement she kicked the mouse and scissors into the overgrown flowerbed. They disappeared into a froth of yellow Lady's Mantle but the letter F remained. She tried to rub it away with her foot but it was drying fast, baking into the hot flagstone.

F… F… F… It seemed to scream up at her from the path. Frankie turned and stumbled back into the house, locking the back door as fast as she could.

Seren

Oliver kept asking Seren questions. What books did she like? What films? What kind of music? Seren kept trying to steer the conversation back to Frankie but Oliver seemed unwilling to say any more.

After a while Seren found that she rather liked having someone taking so much interest in her. It had been a long time since anyone had asked her anything about herself, apart from how she was feeling or how was she coping, how was Griff coping, or did she ever think about letting Jesus into her heart? (This last question was asked on a weekly basis by one of the particularly pious mothers in the schoolyard. 'It will help you to understand that Tom is in a better place now.') Sometimes it seemed to Seren that she had completely lost her previous identity, and had simply become a grieving widow and mother to a grieving son.

As Seren sipped her third glass of wine, thoughts and opinions she didn't even know she had tumbled out of her mouth, filling her with an exhilaration she hadn't felt for years.

Oliver leaned forward, his cheek resting in his hand as he listened, occasionally throwing in a comment or asking another question. Seren liked the way his hair fell across one eye when he nodded in agreement, and the way his eyes crinkled at the sides when she made him laugh. She especially liked the slight undertone of his Yorkshire accent; his shortened vowels, the way he said glas instead of glass, every time he offered to top up her wine. But all the time Seren knew she should be asking more about Frankie. How had she been unstable? What did he mean about warning her?

'I like that,' Oliver nodded towards Seren's charm bracelet.

'A present from my father,' Seren said.

Oliver reached out and touched it, making it chime like silver bells on Seren's wrist. They both laughed and then the waitress was pushing a pudding menu in between them.

'The toffee tart is off,' she sniffed. 'Everything else is on.'

'This time I'll choose,' said Oliver with a smile.

'I don't like lemons,' Seren said, glancing down the menu.

Oliver's smile broadened and he looked up at the waitress who perked up and beamed back enthusiastically. 'Lemon and lime soufflé,' he said with confidence. 'Times two.'

'Two lemon and lime soufflés,' she repeated as she started to write in her notebook.

'No!' Seren shook her head. 'I really don't like lemons, and I especially hate limes.'

The waitress stopped mid-scrawl. She looked at Oliver, then Seren, then back to Oliver.

Oliver raised one eyebrow at Seren. 'When did you last eat a lime?'

Seren thought hard; she couldn't really remember a time, only the horrible, bitter taste. 'Years ago. Maybe when I was a child?'

'And a lemon?'

'Too much lemon cheesecake at my thirteenth birthday party.' Seren shuddered at the memory of how ill she'd been that night.

'There you are then,' Oliver sat back in his chair. 'It's about time you tried them again.'

'I'd really rather just have a cup of coffee; a cappuccino would be nice.'

Oliver looked up at the waitress, 'Two lemon and lime soufflés and another bottle of Chardonnay.'

Seren groaned. 'I'd have loved you forever if you'd ordered the chocolate fudge cake.'

Oliver laughed. 'I ate your duck. I'd never have ordered that myself after a very unpleasant experience in Chinatown as a student. But I didn't complain, did I?'

147

Seren reluctantly shook her head.

'I ate it and found that I rather liked it. I put myself at your mercy and you completely changed the way I feel about duck.'

'So you think you can do the same for me with lemons and limes?'

Oliver put the fingertips of both hands together and nodded.

Seren laughed. 'You look like a James Bond villain with an evil plan.'

Oliver feigned a Russian accent. 'I vill make you love zee lemons and zee limes.'

'And what about grapefruit? I really hate grapefruit,' she gave him a defiant look. He smiled at her but a change came over him. He picked up a dessert spoon and appeared to study it intensely. Seren noticed that his eyes seemed darker, the aqua blue had taken on a deeper tone.

Seren looked away from him to see the waitress sashaying towards them with another bottle of wine.

Suddenly she remembered Griff.

'What time is it?' she asked Oliver.

He glanced at his watch. 'Nearly three.'

Seren gasped, how could it possibly have become so late? Looking around the room she could see that only a few of the golfing ladies remained, lingering over teas and coffees, one or two still nursing large glasses of wine.

'I'll have to go. Griff comes out of school at ten past.'

'Sounds like a ploy to get out of eating the soufflé.'

Seren laughed and picked up her phone at the sound of an incoming text.

'It's from my mother. She says she's on her way to pick up Griff so that I can have a little longer to do the accounts.'

'Is that what she thinks you're doing this afternoon?'

'I couldn't think how to explain that I was meeting you.'

Oliver leaned back a little to let the waitress re-fill their glasses.

He looked at Seren with a small smile and resumed his

Russian accent. 'Vell, it looks as though you vill have to be subjected to zee soufflé after all.'

Frankie

The palm of her hand throbbed. Frankie had wrapped a bandage tightly round it to try to stop the blood but it still seeped through the clean, white gauze. She lay on the bed, trying to calm her spinning head, pressing her fingers to her temples.

A soft breeze blew through the open window and she began to relax as she listened to the birds in the garden and the distant drone of someone mowing their lawn. Dante had slipped back into the house through the window; he now lay curled up against Frankie's thigh, gently purring as she stroked his head.

She might have drifted off into sleep if she hadn't heard the rustling noise below the window. She sat up. Another noise, like the handle of the kitchen door being tried. Dante sprang off the bed and jumped onto the windowsill. Frankie swung her legs onto the floor and stood up. Then a thump, then a bang; it sounded like a kick. Frankie knew she should look out of the window, go into the kitchen to investigate, phone the police. Instead she picked up her sandals and without stopping to put them on ran down the stairs, through the front door and into the street, her bare feet stinging on the sunbaked pavement.

She almost ran into Odette who was clicking down the street in patent heels.

'Careful,' the little Frenchwoman cried out as Frankie slowed down to apologise. 'Oh, it is you.' She looked Frankie up and down. 'You have got no shoes on.'

'I'm going to see Daniel at the office,' Frankie said as though that explained her bare feet.

'He is not there,' Odette smiled. 'He went for lunch with Nesta.'

Frankie stared at her, 'Nesta?'

'He missed a very important meeting to go and see her,'

Odette watched Frankie's face. 'I have come to post these revised plans through the door for him to see on his return.'

Frankie looked behind her at the house then back to Odette. 'Do you know where they are having lunch?'

Odette laughed. 'You want to join them?'

'I, I just want…' Frankie stopped, she wasn't sure what she wanted. Daniel hadn't mentioned meeting Nesta. She wondered how often he had met her over the previous few weeks without telling her.

Frankie attempted to slip on one of her sandals but gave up when she nearly toppled over. 'I'll just go and see if I can catch him walking home. His car is at the garage having a scratch removed.'

Odette looked at the neat diamanté watch on her wrist. 'I believe he won't be home for a while. Next he is meeting his grandson at the park.'

'Griff?' Frankie tried not to sound as confused as she felt.

Odette nodded.

'Shall I give these plans to you?' Odette held out a brown envelope to Frankie. 'I presume you are going back into the house?'

Frankie looked back at the house again. In an upstairs window a curtain twitched. It could have just been Dante jumping off the sill but Frankie's heart was thudding.

'No,' she started to back away. 'I have shopping to do. And a library book to return. Please just post the plans through the front door.'

As she turned and started to walk quickly up the road she heard Odette calling after her.

'Don't forget your shoes. You don't want to cut yourself on anything sharp.'

Nesta

The bindweed was twisted in a tight spiral around the rose bush. Nesta knew she ought to go and look for her gardening gloves but instead she manoeuvred her bare hand through the prickles to pluck the weed away. The rose thanked her by ripping at her fingers with its thorns.

She stood back and sucked a tiny bead of blood from her thumb, tasting metal and remembering the way that Leo had once pulled a rose thorn out of her palm. She still hadn't made a decision about Italy.

The phone started to ring; a distant sound from within the thick brick walls of The Windmill. Nesta knew there was no point even trying to run to get to it.

She looked at her watch. Daniel and Griff would have been in the park for nearly an hour. They would have finished the marshmallow and Malteser muffins she had bought from Tremond's for them to share. Maybe they had borrowed a chess set from the park café to play on the concrete chess tables set out in front of the pond. Maybe they'd been feeding the ducks from the bag of crusts that Nesta had insisted Daniel put into his pocket; Griff had so loved feeding the ducks when he was a toddler.

She smiled at the memory of Griff's face when he had seen Daniel standing in front of the ornate Victorian gates.

'Grandad,' he had shouted and ran as fast as he could into Daniel's open arms, burying his face in Daniel's jacket and squeezing him so tight that Daniel had had to say, 'Steady on there, Griff, I'm finding it quite hard to breathe.'

Nesta had handed Daniel Griff's inhaler, just in case, and left them walking hand in hand into the park, Griff's face turned to Daniel's, Daniel's turned to Griff's. Neither of them were speaking, but even from a distance Nesta could see their smiles.

Nesta had arranged to pick up Griff at six o'clock. Daniel had wanted to drive him back to The Windmill but Nesta knew that Seren would be furious enough that Daniel had seen Griff. If she had to witness him bringing Griff home there would be an even bigger scene than the one that Nesta anticipated.

As a child Seren had had an admirable sense of justice. While Anwen and Ben would argue over petty personal grievances, Seren would fiercely argue for the larger issues: freedom for battery hens, the Iraq war, the right to wear trousers to school, standing up to playground bullies. But since her illness (in her mind Nesta always thought of it as Seren's illness) Seren had been calm and amiable, placid to the point of being almost serene. The fight had left her. Even when Tom had died, Seren never seemed to go through any stage of anger.

But now Seren was angry. She was furious with Daniel, especially since she'd found out he planned to sell The Windmill.

Nesta bent down and with a garden fork eased a clump of buttercups out of the flowerbed. Seren would probably be furious with her when she found out that she had let Daniel take Griff to the park. Nesta threw the weed towards a nearby trug; it missed and lay looking pathetically exposed on the grass. She thought of her own mother. Nesta would have been incensed if she thought her mother was meddling in her children's lives behind her back.

'It's the right thing for Griff,' she said out loud. Anyway, maybe it would be good for Seren to get angry with her for once. She knew she didn't deserve her daughter's unyielding loyalty but surely it would be impossible ever to explain to her why. She and Daniel had been experts at maintaining a veneer of happiness for the outside world. Even their friends thought of them as the perfect couple. Nesta sometimes thought she could have won an Oscar for her role as the loyal and loving wife.

She poked at the hole the buttercup had left in the soil and thought about Italy for the hundredth time. She shook her head; it would be madness. Maybe she should offer the tickets to Seren and Griff. Some time away from home might be just what Seren needed to put things in perspective.

The phone rang again. With a sigh Nesta stood up and began to walk towards the house, the garden fork still in her hand. The ringing stopped. Three seconds later it started again. This time Nesta dropped the fork and began to run.

Seren

They stood on the hotel steps.

'I'd offer you a lift to the station,' Seren said. 'But I think I've had a little bit too much wine,' she was conscious that she was swaying slightly.

'I shouldn't have kept topping up your glass,' said Oliver.

'I'm too drunk to drive home. I'll have to ask my mum to pick me up. I don't think I've had to do that since I was about eighteen.'

'I'm obviously a bad influence on you.'

Seren giggled. 'I'm sure there are rules about getting drunk with your father's mistress's estranged husband in the middle of the afternoon.'

Oliver laughed, 'I'll Google it when I get home and let you know the proper etiquette.'

Seren leant against a pillar to stop the swaying. 'I've had a nice time.'

Oliver stopped laughing, his face suddenly serious. 'I've had a nice time too.' His eyes held Seren's.

Seren tried to remember what it felt like to be sober. Did she ever feel as good as she did now? A warm breeze blew her hair across her face.

'Can I see you again?' Oliver asked.

She nodded, pushing her hair back from her cheek, the charm bracelet jingling musically in her ear.

'I'm flying to Amsterdam tonight,' Oliver said.

'You didn't say.'

He smiled. 'I think we had more interesting things to talk about.'

'I think I talked too much.'

'I enjoyed your company.'

Seren laughed. 'Why are you going to Amsterdam?'

I have an exhibition to arrange. Shall I phone you when I get back?'

'I'd like that.'

'We could go for lunch again?'

'OK.'

'I'd better go.'

Seren wondered if she should kiss him on the cheek, but she seemed to be unable to stand up straight. She noticed, rather sadly, that Oliver's hands were pushed deep in the pockets of his jacket and he remained at least a foot away from her.

'I really must catch my train.' He turned and walked down the steps. At the bottom he stopped and looked up at Seren. 'With all that hair you look a little like Rossetti's Beatrix.' He said something else but an ambulance was speeding down the high street and Oliver's words were absorbed into its siren scream.

'How long will you be in Amsterdam?' Seren called but he had vanished into post-school mothers and children and the ambling herds of summer tourists.

Seren stayed leaning against the pillar for quite some time.

A group of high-heeled golfing ladies clattered down the steps in front of her. Seren barely noticed. Rossetti's 'Beata Beatrix' – one of her favourite paintings. Elizabeth Siddal at her most dazzling, her father always said of the artist's red-haired model. Seren ran both hands through her own red hair and stared up at the higgledy rooftops of the high street, their terracotta tiles bright against the blue sky. Everything looked sharper, clearer, brighter; all around her the world took on a different hue.

The clock on the church struck four and Seren thought of Griff and felt guilty. She hoped he hadn't minded being picked up by his grandmother instead of her. She stood up straight and even though the ground began to shift and sway again she decided to go to Tremond's to get him something for an after supper treat. After that she'd phone her mother.

A wolf whistle greeted her as she crossed the threshold of the little patisserie.

'Well, look at you, all dolled up,' Trevor looked her up and down from behind the counter. 'New dress. And new shoes – oo là là! Trés chic!'

'How do you know they're new?' Seren asked.

Trevor laughed, 'Believe me, I know every garment that you own – I've seen you in them over and over for years!' He feigned a yawn.

'Are you trying to tell me that my clothes are boring?'

'I'm trying to tell you that it's been a long time since you've been shopping, and I know for a fact that that whole sexy little outfit is spick and span brand new!'

Edmond appeared, his 'Keep Calm and Carry On Making Muffins' apron covered in floury hand prints. 'Oh Seren, give us a twirl!'

Seren surprised herself by spinning around and immediately wishing she hadn't as she toppled inelegantly against the counter.

'Hey, Darcey Bussell. Mind my macaroons,' Edmond held onto a glass cake stand where a pyramid of pastel-coloured macaroons swayed and then collapsed across the top of the counter.

'I think she's a little tipsy,' Trevor whispered loudly in Edmond's ear.

'She is a little pink of cheek and bright of eye.' They exchanged a knowing look.

'New clothes, lunchtime drinking, uncoordinated and faintly distracted. I think she's been on a date.'

'No, I haven't!' protested Seren.

'It's all right, you can tell us,' said Edmond as he rearranged his macaroons. 'I think it's about time you had a little fun.'

157

'Is it your handsome TV PC ex?' asked Trevor, one eyebrow arched conspiratorially.

'No!'

'Have you joined match.com and found a chubby bald bloke who says he likes sky diving and romantic walks by the sea?' asked Edmond.

'No!'

'Or that "men in uniforms" site. I've always rather fancied having a look at that myself,' Trevor gave a little shudder of pleasure. 'I'm a sucker for anyone in a helmet.'

Edmond rolled his eyes, 'Remind me to enrol you in the local fire brigade.'

'I've always rather fancied being a nurse,' mused Trevor. 'I like those little upside-down watches and there's something quite sexy about the shapeless tops and matching trousers they all wear now – the thrill of something delicious hidden underneath all that functional fabric.'

Edmond shook his head sadly and turned his attention back to Seren. 'I know who it is. It's the man with the sticky-out teeth from the Cheese Emporium, isn't it?' He winked dramatically. 'I've seen him lingering around your lavender tubs on his lunch break.'

Seren was about to protest yet again when the sound of her phone ringing provided a welcome distraction. As she reached into her bag she briefly wondered if it could be Oliver calling to tell her again how much he'd enjoyed their lunch.

'Hi Mum,' Seren tried not to sound too disappointed. Then she heard the panic in Nesta's voice and suddenly felt very sober. 'OK, I'm on my way.'

'What's up, sweetie?' asked Trevor. 'You've gone quite pale.'

'I've got to go,' Seren fumbled in her bag and produced the keys to her van. 'Griff's had an accident. He's been taken to hospital. I need to get to him right now.'

Trevor rushed around from behind the counter. 'Lindsay

Lohan, put those keys away! You are in no state to drive. I'll take you to the hospital.' He looked at Edmond. 'You're in charge, Lone Ranger.' Edmond was already taking off his apron. 'No way. I'm coming with you. I'll hold Seren's hand while you drive. Besides, I'm not letting you loose with all those paramedics and male nurses about.' He stuffed a selection of chocolate brownies and cherry flapjacks into a paper bag. 'I often find a tray bake comes in handy in a crisis.'

Nesta

From the Trauma Room in A&E Nesta could see into the corridor outside. The long glass window had a frosted linear wave along the middle of it. Above the wave Nesta could see Daniel. His mouth was moving but she couldn't hear the words. He was speaking to a woman with short blonde hair and frightened eyes. Nesta watched intently, wondering what Daniel was saying. He looked exhausted, much older than he had earlier in the afternoon. The woman turned and stared through the glass straight at her. Nesta lowered her head so that her bob swung in front of her face, concealing it behind an iron grey curtain. She looked at Griff.

His face looked so pale against the white pillow, his hair so red. It stood up in clumps, the congealed blood visible around the part where they'd put the stitches. A thin rivulet of blood had dried on his neck; it disappeared under the Spiderman hospital gown the nurse had dressed him in after she had cut off his school polo shirt with a large pair of scissors.

Griff's eyes were closed and as Nesta watched the shadows around them seemed to be becoming darker. The doctor had said it would take twenty-four hours for the bruising to come out fully.

Nesta couldn't even bear to look at Griff's arm. It lay on top of the green blanket, swollen and oddly bent where it should have been straight. Later they would put it in plaster but for now they were going to put it in a splint to keep it stable.

The nurse had been a long time. Nesta wondered if she'd forgotten about the splint.

Nesta held Griff's other hand as tightly as she dared. After a little while he made a noise and his eyes flickered open.

'Where's Mum?'

'She's on her way.'

Griff's eyes closed again. Nesta felt sick at the thought of Seren arriving. She turned her gaze back to the window. Daniel was still talking to the woman. Nesta knew it was Frankie. He had his hands on her shoulders, his face very close to hers. At one point he stroked her cheek. Nesta turned away.

She still couldn't work out exactly what had happened. From the moment she'd run into the house to pick up the phone everything had seemed unreal. Daniel's shaking voice had told her to meet him at the hospital,

'Griff has had a fall.'

'What sort of fall?'

'A bad one.'

With a pounding heart Nesta had driven the ten miles to the hospital much too fast. As she ran into the A&E department she saw Arlow Laverne, and then strangely the woman who had bought a bunch of freesias in the shop a few weeks before. They were sitting side by side, a little girl playing at their feet. The woman stood up and tried to say something but Nesta rushed past her, through swing doors and down an endless corridor to a reception desk where a nurse escorted her to the glass-fronted room.

Daniel was standing beside the bed and it took Nesta a few moments to realise that the tiny, motionless figure under the covers was Griff. A ridiculously young doctor had appeared and started to explain about the broken arm and the head wound and then about concussion and how Griff had been very lucky. 'It could have been a lot worse having fallen from such a height.'

'Exactly what happened?' Nesta asked Daniel as they were ushered into the corridor by the nurse while the doctor stitched up the large gash across Griff's crown. Daniel rubbed his eyes and sighed.

'He wasn't expecting to see Frankie. I think he got a fright.'

'Frankie was at the park?' Nesta was incredulous.

'She came because she was frightened. She needed me.'

161

'So you told her to come to the park?'

'No, she just appeared.'

'And you introduced her to Griff?'

'No. He was on the climbing frame and he saw us…'

'Saw you what?'

'She was upset. I needed to comfort her.'

'And he saw you comforting her and got a shock and fell off?' Nesta was trying very hard to keep her voice calm.

'No, he… I… I can't remember exactly. He wanted to come down. I thought he needed help.'

'Why should he have needed help, Daniel?'

'He was upset. I thought he was going to have an asthma attack.'

'Seeing you comforting Frankie upset him?' Nesta kept her arms straight by her sides to stop herself from grabbing Daniel by the shoulders and shaking him.

'No… yes… I don't know. Yes, seeing me with Frankie upset him.'

Daniel sat down heavily in a nearby chair. He looked up at Nesta, his face ashen. 'I tried to climb up to him to give him his inhaler.'

'You were on the climbing frame?' Nesta's eyes widened at the thought of Daniel climbing up the spiderweb frame.

'Yes. But then Griff jumped off and ran over to the slide. The big one with the tower and the steep slide.'

'You know Seren doesn't let him go up there.'

'I know, but he started to climb up the tower. There was nothing I could do. I was calling to him to come down. Frankie was nearer. She went up to try and get him down.'

'And then?'

'He climbed right up to the top. I thought he was going to come down the slide but then he just seemed to slip over the railing or perhaps he climbed over it. Oh God, I don't know! It was all so quick. It's all so muddled.'

After a few moments Nesta sat down beside him. 'What on

earth is Seren going to say?'

Daniel dropped his head into his hands. 'She'll hate me even more now.'

Nesta wasn't sure why she felt the urge to put her arms around him, but she did, and then Frankie had appeared at the end of the corridor and Daniel had pulled himself away from Nesta and hurriedly walked away to meet her.

Seren

'You did what?'

'Could you keep your voice down please,' the nurse on the reception desk said icily.

Seren lowered her voice to a loud whisper. 'I can't believe you did that, Mum.'

Nesta touched her daughter's arm, 'I know, my love, and I'm sorry. I just didn't think it was good for Griff not to see his grandad.'

'And you think this is good for him?' Seren gestured through the glass to where Griff was lying, waiting to be transferred up to the children's ward.

'It was an accident. It could have happened when you were in the park with him last weekend, or when I was there with him on Monday after school.'

'No, Mum,' Seren's glare was fierce. 'It happened because he was with Dad and he saw him with that woman.' She turned to the window. 'Look at him! He could have broken his back, or his neck. He could have died! How would you have felt then?'

'Please Seren, don't be like this. I don't think you realise how much Griff was missing your dad. He lost Tom. I didn't think he should lose his grandad, too.'

'So you think you have a right to make decisions about my son, as if what I think doesn't matter at all?'

'Shhhh,' the nurse came out from behind her desk. 'If you can't talk quietly I'm going to have to ask you to go outside.'

'Sorry,' said Nesta to the nurse. 'Come on, Seren, why don't we go and get a cup of tea. Griff is sleeping now.' She touched Seren's arm again but Seren shrugged her off.

'No thanks. I'm going to sit with him in case he wakes up. He needs me.'

Seren sat down on the chair beside the bed and tried to steady her breathing. At least her father wasn't loitering in the corridor anymore. When she'd last seen him he'd been heading towards the waiting room, back to Frankie or Francesca or whatever she was calling herself. Seren had seen her sitting beside Arlow looking pale and anxious, as though the accident had happened to her child. Seren wound her hair into a tight bun and sat back on the uncomfortable chair. Arlow? For the first time Seren properly registered that Arlow had been sitting in the waiting room, too. What on earth was he doing at the hospital?

Everything seemed to be turning upside down. Nothing in her life seemed predictable: her father, her mother, even her first boyfriend. They all seemed to be doing things that Seren couldn't make sense of.

She took a long, deep breath and tried not to think about the expression on Daniel's face when she berated him for putting Griff's life at risk. Maybe she shouldn't have said then that she knew for a fact that Frankie was married and that she'd heard she had been unstable and violent in the past. At the time she wanted to hurt Daniel as much as he'd hurt Griff, her mother, her. Now she thought perhaps she had gone too far.

Then Seren looked down at Griff's poor bruised face and broken arm and she was glad she'd told him. Maybe Frankie had been so jealous of seeing Daniel giving his attention to his grandson that she had somehow made him fall. Daniel had said that Frankie had climbed up the tower after Griff. Could she have reached out and pushed him? Seren watched the second hand creep slowly round a clock on the wall. She should try not to jump to conclusions without more evidence. She hoped that Griff would be able to tell her what had happened at the top of the slide when he woke up.

Seren thought of Oliver. Should she phone him and tell him what had happened? Ask him if he thought Frankie would be capable of doing such a terrible thing as pushing a child off the top of a slide? He was probably on his way to the airport. She quickly tapped out a text.

Phone or text me when you can.

The door opened and Trevor and Edmond crept into the room. They perched delicately side-by-side on the bed.

'How's the bionic man?' Trevor whispered nodding at Griff. 'Can they re-build him?'

'He'll be OK,' Seren replied. 'The doctor says it's only mild concussion and hopefully his broken arm will heal quickly. But they're going to keep him under observation for tonight.'

'Will you stay with him?' asked Edmond. Seren nodded.

'Do you need us to pick up your jim-jams and a toothbrush?'

Seren smiled. 'I'll be fine in my clothes, but thanks for offering. And thank you for bringing me over here.'

'Well, we couldn't have you getting arrested for drunk driving could we!'

'I wasn't drunk!'

Trevor and Edmond exchanged a smirk. 'When are you going to tell us who got you tipsy in the first place?' asked Trevor.

'Don't say you were drinking on your own, darling.' Edmond shuddered.

Seren sighed. 'I can't say who I was with. It sounds too weird.'

'Now we're interested!' Both men leaned towards her.

'Mum,' Griff was suddenly struggling to sit up. 'I feel sick.'

In a flash Edmond picked up a cardboard bowl from the end of the bed and handed it to Seren. Seren held it for Griff. A marshmallow and Malteser muffin reappeared in an unappealingly altered state. Trevor looked dramatically away.

'Uh. Vomit – I can't bear it.'

'And you said you'd always fancied being a nurse?' hissed Edmond.

'Sorry Mum,' said Griff, flopping back onto the pillow.

'It's OK, love,' Seren stroked his forehead. 'The doctor said you might be sick. You must have quite a headache after falling from that slide.'

'What slide?' Griff's eyes searched the room, his expression confused.

He looked down at his immobilised arm. 'What's happened to my arm?'

'Don't you remember?' asked Seren, her heart beginning to sink.

Griff shook his head. 'I remember Granny picking me up from school and then…' He squeezed his eyes shut for a few seconds then opened them. 'I can't remember anything after that.'

'That will be the concussion,' Trevor said. 'I once hit my head on a low branch on Hampstead Heath – the next thing I knew I was having a civil partnership with Edmond at Islington Town Hall, followed by a disco boat on the Thames and a ten-day honeymoon in Marrakech.'

'Hey!' Edmond gave Trevor a mock slap across the face. 'You were the one who wanted the disco boat and buffet, I'd have settled for cava and cupcakes at home.'

'I think I'm going to be sick again,' Griff's complexion now matched the hospital blanket.

'Oh no!' Trevor groaned.

'Come on, Florence Nightingale, I'd better take you home,' Edmond, guided Trevor towards the door. He turned around to Seren. 'I'll tell the nurse that Griff's awake.'

Seren waved weakly as Griff retched into the bowl. She felt slightly nauseous herself and had an awful feeling that a post-lunch hangover was beginning to take hold.

Frankie

Everyone was silent in the car. Even Chez had stopped chattering away about the plastic tea set she'd been playing with in the hospital play area.

From the back seat Frankie could just make out the outline of Daniel's jaw and she could tell that he was tense by the way it jutted forward slightly. He hadn't wanted to accept Arlow's offer of a lift. In fact he'd been quite rude.

Frankie couldn't understand why Daniel would be so curt with someone who'd done so much to help. He should be grateful that Arlow had also been in the park, pushing Chez on the swings at the time of the accident; he had been calm and level headed in the face of Daniel and Frankie's incompetent panic.

It had been Arlow who ran over and felt the unconscious Griff's neck for a pulse; Arlow who stopped Daniel from scooping Griff up and running to the car with him; Arlow who had phoned for an ambulance; and then Arlow who had driven Frankie to the hospital while Daniel went with Griff in the ambulance. Arlow had sat patiently with Frankie while they waited for news of Griff's condition. He had calmed her nerves and listened to her as she repeatedly told him she wished she hadn't gone to look for Daniel in the park. He had waited while she sought out Daniel in the treatment rooms and, when she came back, he seemed to understand how awful it had been to see Daniel in his ex-wife's arms, and how guilty she had felt when Daniel had come to her leaving Nesta, looking so sad, on her own.

'Thank you,' she had said to Arlow as she accepted his second cup of hot sweet tea. 'I mean thank you for everything you've done.'

'No problem,' he'd replied, sitting back down beside her. 'I had no other plans today and Chez is as happy in the hospital playroom as anywhere else I could have taken her this afternoon. It's not like it's busy in here,' he waved his arm around the empty waiting room. 'Besides I owe you a favour for getting Chez to go in the pool earlier on.'

To Frankie their meeting at the swimming pool seemed a lifetime ago. Before she'd found the mouse, before the F drawn in blood, before she'd heard the noises, before she'd decided to go running off to look for Daniel in the park. Before she'd tried to explain everything to Daniel but found the words all choked up in her throat. 'A mouse, there was a mouse… and blood and my initial and… I think he's found me… and someone was trying to get into the house.'

Daniel had tried to get her to speak more slowly; he said he didn't have a clue what she was talking about. But he'd been kind and had taken her shaking body in his arms and kissed her forehead, and then he'd noticed Griff, motionless and staring at them on the climbing frame. Griff jumped off and was running to the slide and Daniel was running, and Frankie thought that she could help as the little boy started to climb up the tower. In her mind's eye she could still see Griff's skinny body toppling over the edge of the rail and hear the scream and then the thud. Frankie put her head into her hands.

'Hey,' Arlow squeezed her shoulder. 'Stop beating yourself up. You can't blame yourself for…' Frankie looked up as his voice trailed away. She saw his eyes following a woman in a pretty summer dress, a cascade of red hair swinging across her back as she rushed through the waiting room towards the treatment area. The woman turned around and stared straight at Frankie and her expression was furious. Frankie didn't recognise her at first: she'd never seen her in a dress or heels. But before Frankie could acknowledge her she had vanished through the double doors, leaving them swinging on their hinges as though a little bit of her rage remained. Arlow was staring after her, sitting forward on his seat as though he might jump up and follow.

'Hi,' two voices spoke in unison. Frankie looked up and saw the two men from the patisserie. They sat down beside Arlow even though there were lots of other empty chairs.

'Anyone for a tray-bake?' Edmond offered round a paper bag. Frankie and Arlow both declined but Chez came running from the play corner and took three brownies and all of the cherry flapjacks. Frankie waited for Arlow to tell his daughter not to take so many cakes, but he was still focused on the swing doors which were now completely still.

After a while the patisserie men began to probe Arlow for information about his filming schedule. His answers were short and vague so they began to ask about his celebrity friends: who was the most famous star he had ever worked with? what was the food like at the BAFTAs? had he and his wife ever appeared in *Hello*? Arlow shrugged their questions away along with Edmond's intermittent offering of the remaining brownies.

Then they all sat in a line of silence for a while. The only voice belonged to Chez who was smearing little bits of chocolate brownie across a moth-eaten teddy bear as she hosted a tea party in the play corner. 'You'll like this. I cooked it myself.'

Then Daniel had appeared, ashen-faced. 'We'd better go,' he'd said to Frankie without looking at her.

Arlow suddenly seemed to wake up from his trance. 'I'll give you a lift.'

'No thank you, we'll be fine with a taxi,' Daniel's voice had been brusque.

'I'm heading back to town now anyway,' said Arlow.

'No thank you, we don't need your help any more.'

Arlow stood up with a sigh. 'Come on. I'm willing to put the past behind us if you are.'

'I don't know what you're talking about.' Colour mounted in Daniel's previously grey face. 'And I've told you that I'd rather

170

arrange our own transport.'

Frankie didn't know what either of them was talking about but she was aware that the two men from the patisserie were listening to the exchange with wide, spectator eyes.

'Please Mr Saunders,' Arlow said. 'Water under bridges and all that. Just let me give you a lift.'

'It would be quicker than waiting for a taxi,' cut in Frankie. 'I feel a headache coming on. I think I need to get home as quickly as possible.'

Frankie put her head back against the BMW's leather headrest and watched the flower-filled verges speeding past. The evening light cast a pretty pink haze over the froth of cow parsley and foxgloves. Daisies bobbed on spindly stalks and wild roses bloomed in the hedges as though nothing bad could ever happen. Frankie stared out over a field of undulating green corn but quickly looked away when she saw a row of dead crows strung up along the cornfield's boundary fence.

She studied the wound on her palm. It had stopped bleeding and she'd unwound the bandage in the hospital toilet, but the cut from the scissors was deep and jagged. Daniel hadn't noticed it.

She wondered what Seren had said to Daniel after she'd arrived at the hospital. He seemed suddenly miles away: distant. Frankie closed her eyes. Perhaps this was where it all would end. But she couldn't bear to think of life without Daniel now.

Something warm and soft pressed against her fingers. Frankie looked down to see Chez's hand on top of hers. Chez's other hand was searching in the back pocket of her jeans. She took out something pale and flat and covered in little bits of fluff. She held it up to Frankie.

'Would you like a cherry flapjack?'

171

Nesta

The sky had turned from pink to lavender.

At the top of The Windmill, Nesta leaned against the balcony and looked up at the first star: Venus, named after the goddess of love. It seemed to be brighter than usual, glittering, or was it pulsing? Signalling through the light years, trying to tell her something? Nesta looked away; she didn't need a star to tell her about love.

At first, holding Daniel in her arms had been agony. Sitting under the bright striplights in the hospital corridor, Nesta had wanted to cry out with the pain. She had always loved him, that was why she had never left him. But as the pain subsided she had realised that, though she still loved him, it had changed. Now, in the warm night air, with all the memories swarming around her, she knew that in the hospital she had been letting him go. As he had pulled away from her to go to Frankie she had been sad but something about it had felt inevitable, as though that moment had been destined since they first met over forty years before.

Nesta looked down into the garden; through the gloom she could just make out the For Sale sign that had appeared on the boundary wall while she'd been out. She had been dreading it for days. It was evidence that their life together hadn't worked out. They had failed.

But suddenly Nesta didn't mind. The For Sale sign seemed like a key to freedom, to her future.

She looked back up at the star. 'I know what you're trying to tell me.'

Frankie

'Someone's washed it away,' Frankie spun round on the flagstone, searching for the letter F. 'It was written here, written with the mouse's blood.'

'Well, there's no sign of the writing or the mouse,' said Daniel.

'But I saw it. I saw my initial here, beside the mouse.' Frankie crouched down. 'I kicked the mouse under this plant. Look, the scissors are still here. I was going to pick some sweet peas. The mouse should be just beside them.' Frankie began desperately hunting through the flowerbed, tearing at the roots and leaves and flowers as she searched.

'Come on,' Daniel took her gently by the arm and pulled her upright. 'Let's go inside. It's too dark out here to see properly anyway.'

Frankie turned on him. 'You don't believe me do you?'

'Let's go in and get a drink. A nice cup of tea or maybe a glass of wine would do us good.'

'You think I imagined it. That I made it up.'

'No, of course I don't think that.'

'You think I imagined the banging noise as well, that I imagined someone was trying to kick down the kitchen door.'

'Everybody gets a little spooked sometimes. Especially if they're tired or haven't eaten properly. Have you eaten anything today?'

'Yes. No. I can't remember.'

'Well, there you go then. Lack of food can cause anyone to feel a little paranoid.'

'Paranoid?'

'Yes.'

Frankie shrugged his hand away from her arm. 'I think you

think I'm mad.' She said it very quietly.

'Frankie.' He tried to take her hand in his and she flinched with pain. He turned the hand over and for the first time he saw the deep wound in her palm. 'Did you do this?'

Frankie didn't speak.

'Did you do this?' Daniel repeated. 'Did you deliberately hurt yourself?'

'No!' Frankie pulled her hand away. 'It wasn't me. It was the scissors. They cut me, they dug into my hand...' She stopped, aware how crazy she was sounding. 'You do think I'm mad, don't you?'

Daniel sighed. 'It's just I realise I know very little about you. About your past. About your life before you met me.'

'I've tried to tell you but...' Frankie's voice seemed to lose all strength. In the darkness Daniel's face looked altered, hardened, colder. She couldn't speak.

'Frankie?'

'Yes.'

'I know about your husband.'

Seren

Time seemed oddly altered on the children's ward. Seren felt sure it was after midnight, but when she checked her phone it was only half past nine. She shuddered. The dimmed lighting and intermittent swish of curtains was too familiar. As the nurses carried out their night-time routine around her, it was as though the last twenty-three years had vanished and she was back in a small Welsh hospital trying to come to terms with the course her life had taken. Seren needed to get away from the memories, away from the ward.

Griff was asleep. The stronger painkillers they'd given him after supper seemed to have knocked him out. Seren went out into the corridor and found the room the nurse had described as the parents' lounge. In reality it was a cupboard with a small sofa wedged against one wall. A kettle and a selection of tea and coffee sachets sat on a shelf beside the sofa and some dog-eared women's magazines and Sunday supplements teetered in a perilous stack on the floor.

The only window was a skylight. Seren looked up at the dark square above her and tried to make out stars through the dirty glass. Looking up made her feel hungover again so she stopped and turned the kettle on. The sofa looked like a welcome alternative to the hard plastic chairs she'd been sitting on all evening, but when she sat down it sagged so much she was forced to perch on the edge to avoid being swallowed by it completely.

She checked her phone again, nine thirty-five and nothing from Oliver. She read a list of rules about keeping the parents' lounge tidy and picked up an ancient copy of *Closer* magazine.

A surge of rage washed over her. Picking up her phone she typed out a hasty text.

Keep away from my son or you will be sorry

'You have a visitor.'

Seren looked up with a start just as she'd pressed send. Three nurses were peering round the parents' lounge door. They were giggling and jostling with each other to be closest to the visitor as he walked through the door.

'Thank you,' Arlow edged his way into the room.

'Could I have your autograph?' the youngest of the nurses asked. 'For my mum. She loved *Island Beat*.'

'We all loved *Island Beat*,' said another nurse. 'You were fab in it.'

'Thank you,' Arlow said again and scribbled his name across the torn-off lid of a box of Quality Street.

'Can I have an autograph too?' One of the other nurses held out an official-looking form that was clearly not meant for autographs.

'And me?' This time it was the cover of a pamphlet about eczema.

'Oh, and another quick one on my arm.'

Arlow patiently obliged while Seren watched with eyebrows raised.

'I know. I know,' Arlow shrugged after the nurses had left. 'What can I do? It goes with the job. And anyway if they hadn't been fans they'd never have let me sneak in three hours after visiting time.'

'What are you doing here?'

'I came to see how Griff was doing.'

Seren's mind whirled. She wished she hadn't sent the text. Arlow seemed to be watching her face as though he could see her guilt. Then he smiled.

'Sorry, you look confused. Did your dad not tell you that I was in the park when he had his accident? I phoned for the ambulance. I brought your dad's...' Arlow hesitated. 'I brought your dad's partner to the hospital in my car.'

'Oh.' Once again nothing made sense. The kettle juddered

violently on the shelf, spurting steam and boiling water everywhere. Seren covered her head with *Closer* magazine to stop herself from getting scalded. Arlow turned it off and pointed to the fading yellow post-it note on the wall below the list of rules.

'Kettle does not turn off. Turn off manually.'

He picked the kettle up. 'Still a black-coffee-two-sugars girl?'

Seren nodded, though it was years since she'd taken her coffee without milk or had sugar in it.

Arlow divided the contents of the three Nescafé tubes and four sugar sachets between two plastic cups, added the water and handed one to Seren. She cradled it between her hands; the heat felt comforting. When she took a sip the sugar was comforting, too.

'Can I sit down?' Arlow indicated the sofa.

'You'll have to sit on the edge like me, otherwise it will eat you.'

'OK,' Arlow carefully perched himself beside her.

'Can you explain again what you're doing here?' Seren asked, peering at him over the top of her cup. 'It's been a long day and I'm just a little bit confused.'

Arlow started slowly. 'I was in the park with my daughter Chez. I saw your dad and a little boy, who I now know is Griff – your son.'

'OK, you can speed it up a bit, I'm not that confused!'

Arlow laughed. 'Alright, here goes with the quicker version. My daughter Chez was on the swings and I saw Griff fall from the top of the slide so I ran over as I have some first-aid experience and…'

'Stop! Did you actually see him fall?'

Arlow nodded. 'Yes.'

'Are you absolutely sure? Were you watching him just before, or did you only see him after he had fallen?'

'I saw him topple over the rail at the top of the slide. I was looking over at him because your dad was shouting his name and trying to get him to come down.'

'And what was my dad's, um… my dad's partner doing at that time?'

'She was at the bottom of the slide.'

'So she wasn't at the top?'

'No, like I said, she was at the bottom.'

'So there is no way she might have…' Seren stopped. She knew it sounded like a crazy thing to say but she had to say it. 'There's no way she could have pushed Griff off the slide?'

'What?' Arlow looked incredulous. 'Are you joking? You think that Frankie might have pushed your son off a thirty-foot-high slide?'

Seren pushed her fingers through her hair. 'I don't know what I think. But there's one thing I do know and it's that she's not who she seems to be.'

'She seems like a nice woman to me,' Arlow swirled the remains of his coffee round his cup and then finished it in one gulp. 'She reminds me a bit of my mum.'

'Oh,' Seren looked at Arlow, surprised. 'You know Frankie's not really blonde?'

'Did you think my mum was?'

Seren shrugged.

'She has that vulnerable look to her,' Arlow went on. 'Anxious, lost. Like my mum looked after all that time spent with that bastard who called himself my dad.'

Seren didn't want to hear about Arlow's mum. She'd spent years trying to put Arlow's mum out of her mind. 'I've been doing a bit of investigating into Frankie,' she said, trying to change the subject. 'In fact, I had lunch with her ex-husband today – well, legally he's still her husband – and he told me that she's unstable and she's violent.' She watched for Arlow's shocked reaction, but he simply shrugged again.

'My dad would probably have said that about my mum.'

'But, he said she…'

178

'Look Seren,' Arlow interrupted, 'we all go through down times in our lives. It doesn't make us mad.'

Seren looked into her coffee cup and tried not to think of all the dark days after she'd come home from Wales.

'But she walked out on her husband. She disappeared. Her husband didn't know where she was till I found out who he was through Google and got in touch with him. He thought she might be dead. My dad didn't even know that she's married.'

Arlow shook his head. 'So what? People are complicated; life is complicated. When I was younger I thought it was all black and white.' He laughed. 'I'm sure you remember that about me. I thought your dad was an even bigger bastard than mine, but now I see that he was just…'

'Don't.' Seren stood up.

'You believe me now though, don't you? About your dad…'

'I said *don't*. It was a long time ago.'

Arlow shook his head. 'Still have your dad up on that pedestal then?'

Seren scowled down at him. Had he really come just to gloat?

Arlow stood up. 'She's fine by the way. My mum. She's married to a boiler fitter in Dundee. They're very happy together.'

'Good.' Seren scrunched up her empty plastic cup in her hand. 'I'd better get back to Griff.'

'The nurses told me he's doing really well.'

Seren nodded. 'The doctor says he'll be fine.' They were both silent.

'I'd better go then,' Arlow said and headed for the door at the same time as Seren, they ended up doing a sort of dance, each one trying to let the other go first.

Once they were finally out in the corridor they stood facing each other. Seren was aware that the nurses were gathered round the reception desk, watching them. Arlow put his hands in the pockets of his jeans.

179

'Still wearing that bracelet your dad gave you?' he nodded towards the charm bracelet. She put her hand around it to stop it making a noise. 'I see you never added the charm I gave you.'

Seren looked at him. 'I don't remember you ever giving me a charm.'

'The little heart?'

Seren shook her head. 'You must have given that to some other girl.'

Arlow sighed. 'I don't know why you're still so angry.'

Seren pursed her lips and remained silent.

'I'd better be going home then,' Arlow said when he realised that he wouldn't get a response.

Seren thought about the waif-like Angellica Chadwick waiting for Arlow. She wondered if she minded him meeting up with an ex-girlfriend.

'I'll see you around.' Arlow took a step back. Seren could hear the nurses commenting on the loveliness of Arlow's bum. 'You know you still look just the same, Sez.'

Seren looked down at the floor. It had been years since anyone had called her Sez.

Arlow turned around and headed towards the exit doors, giving the nurses a friendly wave. Suddenly he stopped and walked back to Seren. Standing in front of her, he reached out, one hand nearly touching her shoulder. 'I just want to tell you to be careful.'

'What do you mean?'

'With your amateur sleuthing.'

'Amateur sleuthing?'

'Delving into Frankie's past and all that. I'm just saying don't get too involved.'

'I'm sure an *ex*-TV detective like you has vast amounts of advice to throw around about sleuthing,' Seren tried to keep her voice calm. The plastic cup, still in her hand, crinkled. 'But actually I don't think it's any of your business.' She turned around and headed back to Griff's ward, her high heels echoing along the corridor.

Griff mumbled something when Seren slipped through the curtains that surrounded his bed but when she bent down to ask him if he was OK she realised he was still asleep.

A camp bed had been set up for her alongside Griff's bed. She slipped off her shoes and lay down on it, too hot to pull up the blanket that the nurse had also supplied. In the half gloom she thought about her exchange with Arlow and wished that he'd go off and make a TV drama somewhere else. She threw an arm across her eyes to block out the light. Muddy memories swirled around her exhausted mind until she finally slept.

A vivid dream woke her, making her heart race; her dress felt clammy, her hair stuck to her face in damp tendrils. She sat up. Arlow had been pushing a big, old-fashioned pram. Seren had peered into the pram to admire the baby, but instead of a baby she found the gangly, bloodied body of a still-born lamb.

Seren rubbed her eyes and picked up her phone to check the time. The first thing that she saw was a text from Oliver.

Are you OK?

She lay back and studied the polystyrene ceiling tiles, trying to work out how to reply. A few hours earlier she would have told him about what had happened in the park but now she hesitated. Arlow had been very sure that Frankie hadn't been near Griff when he fell. To ask Oliver if his ex-wife would ever hurt a child seemed crazy. She'd hate him to think she might be paranoid. Instead she typed:

I'm fine thanks. Hope your time in Amsterdam goes well.

Frankie

Frankie had bought the bundle of old fabric in a charity shop. Most of it looked like scraps from someone who'd done a lot of dressmaking just after the War. Pretty floral prints, spots and stripes, a rather charming piece of cotton with a sketchy farmyard design. Some of it was from later decades: pink and purple paisleys, a big orange poppy pattern, some Liberty lawn, chintzy upholstery fabric, stretchy nylon, a big square of mustard-coloured corduroy.

Frankie sat in the middle of the living-room floor, carefully searching through and cutting the fabric into strips. She wanted to show them to her dementia group. The fabric might bring back memories of clothes they once wore, sofas they once sat on. Frankie thought they could then use the strips to weave a series of what she had decided to call *memory mats*. She'd created some small looms using wooden frames and string and also found some bits of lace and wool, even cuttings from old brushed-cotton sheets and blankets to add to their creations.

Frankie picked up a piece of printed fabric – a riot of geometric colour. It stirred her own memories of sunny mornings with her brother, pulling back the crazy 1970s patterned curtains and jumping on their parents' bed, trying to wake them up to take them to the beach. Her mother and father would pretend to be asleep and then suddenly catch one child each and tickle them until they couldn't breathe from so much laughter.

Frankie put the fabric to one side to keep. As she put it down she noticed that another piece of fabric had got caught underneath. She pulled the two pieces apart and found the splash of a yellow rose on a white cotton background. Immediately she was transported to a smokey London pub where she was wedged between two fellow art students, Sam Cooke playing on the juke box and the taste of lager and Marlboro Lights on her tongue. She had smoothed out her skirt to admire the vintage fabric of the 1950s rose-print dress she'd bought from Camden Market earlier that day. She'd found a string of plastic pearls to wear with it and a friend had lent her a wide golden ribbon that she'd tied around her freshly washed hair.

'Nice dress, Francesca', the handsome boy from the sculpture department had said, as he squeezed in beside her on the bench. Frankie couldn't believe he was actually talking to her. All the girls fancied him, some of the boys did too. She had been amazed that he had noticed her dress, even more amazed that he knew her name.

'You look like an angel,' he'd said in his gentle Northern accent before asking her if she'd like a drink. And that was the start.

'And that was the start,' she'd said to Daniel three evenings before. She'd been trying to answer his questions as truthfully as she could. Once she'd admitted she'd been married, was still married, had been married for fifteen years, there was so much he wanted to know. 'How did you meet? Where did you live? What is his name? Why did you leave?'

The questions came sporadically, as though it was taking Daniel time to process the information. He'd ask one question over breakfast, another while he stirred a stew at dinner time, another as they came out of the butchers, or as they put bottles in the recycling bin. Two nights before Daniel walked back into the bedroom in the middle of brushing his teeth, and asked, 'Why didn't you have children?'

That had been a hard one. Frankie could still feel the pain shooting through her stomach as she lay at the bottom of the stairs; wet warmth seeping between her legs, footsteps racing down the stairs. 'Oh my God, what's happened? Did you trip?'

'We didn't want children.'

183

Daniel seemed happy with Frankie's answer and disappeared to rinse the toothpaste from his mouth.

He wasn't so willing to settle for her answers when he asked her why she had left.

'I wasn't happy. I couldn't make him happy; he was a difficult man.'

In her mind Frankie begged Daniel not to ask any more.

'Did he ever hit you?' Daniel asked as they sat with Dante draped across both their laps, in front of the fire.

Frankie shook her head. 'No.'

A light push, a gentle shove. He was rather partial to a flick with his finger on her ear, a fork against her throat, a knife against her breast. 'No, he never hit me.'

Frankie stared into the flames. Or had she just imagined the pushes, the shoves, the flicks, the knife? Maybe Oliver was right: she was a fantasist, a storyteller. She'd invented a narrative about their relationship. She'd heard him telling the doctor that, heard them laughing together over it. 'Women have such fertile imaginations, don't they.'

Paranoid. She'd seen it written on her hospital notes. It was what the psychiatrist had suggested to her, in the nicest possible way, of course. Maybe he had been right.

'Are you alright?' Daniel's voice was concerned. Frankie nodded. Daniel put his arm around her shoulder and pulled her towards him.

'I love you.' He kissed the top of her head.

Frankie fought the urge to scream, 'You can't love me. You don't know what I did.'

Nesta

Papers lay scattered all over the floor, the writing-desk drawers gaped open and the files and folders had been rifled through time and time again.

'Where is my bloody passport?' Nesta said out loud, her knees aching from kneeling too long on the study floor. She'd been searching for hours, it was already dark outside. Daniel had always taken charge of holidays. Nesta picked up the phone to ask him where her passport was. She put it down.

Come on, woman. Where's your independence gone?

Anyway, she hadn't told him she was going to Italy. He might try to lay claim to the tickets – the holiday had been their anniversary present after all.

She hadn't even told Seren. Seren hadn't mentioned the holiday, though Anwen, in her usual brusque way, had Skyped her to ask what she was going to do with the tickets. 'Bung them onto eBay, Mum. There's no point in having a romantic holiday on your own.' That had made up Nesta's mind. She would have a holiday on her own and who was Anwen to say it wouldn't be romantic!

The only person she'd told was Ben. He'd spent the previous weekend with her at The Windmill. She'd been shocked to see how thin and tired he looked.

'What's happened to you?' Nesta had pulled at Ben's loose T-shirt as he walked in through the door. 'It looks like you've been shrinking.'

Ben looked down at his flat stomach as though he hadn't noticed before. 'Suki was such a fantastic cook. I suppose I haven't bothered with food much since she left.'

'Isn't there some way of working things out between you?'

Ben shook his head; he'd let a heavy beard grow and his

eyes were circled by dark shadows. Nesta wanted to scoop him onto her lap like she had done when he was a child. Instead she offered him coffee and a slice of homemade lemon meringue pie.

As he sat at the kitchen table pushing the pie round the plate, Nesta gently asked again. 'Couldn't you go to Ireland, try to patch things up with Suki? She's such a lovely girl.'

Ben let his spoon clatter onto the plate and sat back. 'What's the point, Mum?' He sighed. 'Suki wanted us to get married. Have kids – you know? But why bother if all that happens is you end up…' He couldn't seem to finish the sentence.

'If you end up like me and your father?' suggested Nesta.

Ben shrugged. 'Yeah, maybe.'

Nesta leaned across the table and took his hand in hers. 'You can't live your life not bothering to do the things that matter to you because they might not work out in the end. You and Suki aren't the same as me and your dad. Some people go the whole way together, others don't. If you love someone then what's wrong with giving it a go?'

'I thought you and dad loved each other.'

'We did. We still do. At least I still love him – I always will.'

'I thought you were so solid as a couple.'

'We had lots of rocky times. Don't you remember the rows we used to have when you and Anwen were little?'

Ben shook his head. Nesta felt relieved.

'All I'm saying is don't let this shape your future. Anything could happen. One of you could fall off a mountain, like poor Tom, long before you start to get fed up with each other.'

'How is Seren by the way?'

Nesta sighed. 'Still not really speaking to me. She'll be back from the hospital any minute. Griff's stitches have been taken out today and they had an appointment at the fracture clinic to see how his arm is getting on.'

'Poor Griffy. I've bought him a tablet with my new game

downloaded on it. I figured he'd be missing playing on Dad's phone.'

Nesta squeezed his hand. 'You know, you'd make such a lovely father.'

Ben wriggled his hand away from his mother's and changed the subject. 'So, Seren. Is she OK with this place being sold and everything?'

Nesta rested her head on her hand and looked sadly at her son. 'What do you think?'

The swivel chair rotated slowly. Nesta felt a little dizzy and stopped the chair from turning with her foot. She scanned the room, trying to think of new places to search for the passport. Maybe she wouldn't be able to go after all. Maybe this was a sign that it was a ridiculous thing to do. She looked at her reflection in the darkened window and made a face.

He probably doesn't even remember you.

She swivelled the chair once again and her eyes alighted on the blue spine of a book. She walked over to the bookcase and took it down. Sitting back down in the chair she gently traced the gilt lettering on the cover: *The Heavens And Their Story* by Annie S. D. Maunder.

It had been the afternoon of her thirtieth birthday when he handed it to her with muddy hands. It had been wrapped in brown paper, tied up with garden twine.

'I found it in the antique bookshop in town.' As Nesta unwrapped it, he added, 'It's all about the stars.' Nesta had stared at the beautiful first edition for a long time. Then she had reached up and kissed his cheek and ran inside to get the children's tea without looking back.

Thirty-two years later Nesta hugged the book close to her chest. As she released it a little square of paper slipped from its pages onto the floor and lay at her feet. Bending down she picked it up. It was cracked a little down the folds where it had, many times, been folded and unfolded, read over and over again. But now it was years since Nesta had looked at it, in fact she'd quite forgotten where it was.

She smiled as she started to read. It was written in her mother tongue in beautiful lyrical words: the way a Welsh gardener born to an Italian ice-cream seller might be inclined to write:

My Dearest Nesta,

I must apologise for my sudden departure. I didn't know what else to do. How can I, who can offer you so little, be responsible for taking away so much? I cannot bear to share you and yet I know it would be unfair to keep you for my own.

I love you. Please know that. I will always think of you. Remember that by day we will be amongst roses and by night we will be under the stars.

Leo.

Looking up Nesta saw her passport lying on the windowsill and realised it must have been there all along.

Seren

Seren checked her phone. Eight days had passed and Oliver hadn't been in touch. Seren was becoming increasingly desperate to speak to him: she had to find out more about Frankie's past.

Looking after Griff had been the one good way to keep her father and his mistress out of her mind. Griff had been off school for a week and Seren had stayed with him at all times, even setting up a camp bed in his bedroom so that she could check him throughout the night. She was constantly alert for the signs they'd told her to look out for at the hospital: dizziness; disorientation; deafness; drowsiness; blurred vision; vomiting.

'Mum, stop it!' Griff exclaimed, his mouth full of chocolate popcorn whoopie pie from a Tremond's selection box that Trevor had brought round earlier.

'Stop what?'

'Stop asking me if I feel alright all the time. I'm trying to watch the film.'

Seren hadn't even been aware she'd spoken as they sat side by side on the sofa watching a DVD. Asking Griff if he was OK was becoming as much a habit as checking her phone. She hugged him tightly.

'It's only because I love you so much.'

Griff pushed her away with his plaster-encased arm and took another bite of whoopie pie. 'I know that, Mum.'

Ben's visit had been another distraction though Seren had hardly had a chance to speak to him. He and Griff spent hours on the new tablet he'd brought, lost in Ben's latest fantasy kingdom, slaying dwarfs, trying to avoid being eaten by slime-oozing ogres.

'Are you sure it's age appropriate?' Seren asked her brother.

'Griff loves it,' he said, his head bent close to Griff's as Griff made euphoric noises; yet another dwarf had ended up with blood spurting from his severed head.

'I just think it might be a little gruesome for a nine-year-old.'

'Chill out, sis,' Ben mumbled.

'Yeah, chill out, Mum,' echoed Griff.

Seren sighed and leaned against the patio doors. It was hot, getting hotter every day. She watched one of Nesta's chickens that had wandered over to her patio; it pecked between the paving slabs at her shameful display of weeds and ruffled its feathers as though in disapproval.

Seren gazed out over Nesta's flowerbeds. They were a mass of summer colour now, though all Seren could focus on was the For Sale sign that poked its ugly head above the foliage.

Seren wondered what she'd be looking out on this time next year. Probably a high fence to separate herself from her new neighbours. She and Griff would be sleeping in earmuffs to block out their loud music and the sounds of lawnmowers, chainsaws and car engines revving first thing every morning. Strange children would be eternally poking their grimy faces over the fence, trying to climb over to play with Griff's toys. The smell of frying food and BBQs would waft into The Wheat House every evening. Their teenagers' parties would last all weekend and they'd probably set up a caravan park on her mother's lawn. Seren kicked at a dandelion with the toe of her sandal. Whoever they were, they'd be as unwelcome in Seren's life as the weeds she couldn't seem to summon up the energy to deal with.

Her father didn't seem to care that Frankie had been hiding her marriage from him. In fact he seemed more determined than ever to sell The Windmill and make a new life with her. Three potential buyers had been shown round by the estate agent already, maybe more. Seren suspected that Nesta didn't tell her about all the viewings.

She realised that she hadn't checked her phone for at least ten minutes. Taking it out of her pocket she drew in a sharp breath as, at last, she saw Oliver's name on the screen.

Ben and Griff turned around to look at her. 'You OK, sis?' Ben asked. 'You're not playing age-inappropriate games on your phone, are you?'

Seren laughed. 'I'm fine. I'll just go and get us all a nice cool drink from the kitchen.'

'Mine's a beer,' called Ben as she left the room.

'Mine's a beer too,' shouted Griff.

'OK,' replied Seren without thinking.

Once in the kitchen she sat down on a chair and opened Oliver's message.

Hi, how are you? Do you fancy meeting up on Tuesday? I have a meeting about a sculpture installation near Guildford. It's on your trainline. I could pick you up from Guildford station, 12.30?

Seren read it six times.

She thought of Griff. Monday would be his first day back at school; supposing he needed a rest on Tuesday? Supposing he felt ill and needed to be picked up from school? Supposing he collapsed with some hidden skull fracture or a brain clot? Seren had been very anxious when the doctor told her there was no need to do a scan. What if he had a brain haemorrhage, a stroke, a heart attack?

Chill out, Mum, she muttered and quickly tapped out an answer.

Sounds great. I'll see you outside the station on Tuesday.

Frankie

Frankie stared at the blank, white square in front of her. The brush in her hand dithered over it but refused to leave a mark. She turned away and went into the kitchen. It had been ridiculous to think she could just squeeze out some colours and start to paint.

She leant against the sink while she waited for the kettle to boil. Daniel would be disappointed. The night before he had come home with a selection of brushes, oil paints, an easel and several different sizes of canvas.

'Isn't it about time you started again?' he'd said.

Over the weekend she'd shown him images from her past exhibitions on the internet. It was part of her attempt to be more honest with him about her past. She'd also shown him a children's picture book for sale on Amazon that she'd done illustrations for.

'Those are brilliant drawings,' he'd said peering at the screen. 'Don't you have a copy of the book?' She shook her head; it had been too heavy. Everything she had taken had to fit into a small holdall she could carry with one hand. A few clothes, toiletries, some jewellery she hoped to sell, the one small painting she now kept on the mantelpiece and the details of the small trust fund she'd inherited when her parents died. She had wasted valuable time searching for the photograph of her family but it was nowhere to be found. Likewise with Rossetti, though she had called and called into the damp South London night, she couldn't find him. In the end it was only Dante who left with her, cowering in the wicker cat basket as she struggled to keep it steady with her other hand.

Daniel burst through the front door.

'Hello,' he sounded so cheerful. 'I've let myself out early, I'm easing myself into retirement. That's my excuse!' Frankie knew he would look in the living room first. 'Well, that's a start.' He was laughing as he came into the kitchen.

'I thought you'd be annoyed that I hadn't produced a masterpiece,' Frankie held out a cup of tea.

'The canvas is on the easel, there's paint on a palette. One step at a time, darling, one step at a time.' He put down his tea and wrapped his arms around her. She leaned against his chest and for the first time since Griff's accident she felt that everything might be alright.

'Oh, I nearly forgot,' said Daniel, unwrapping his arms and delving into the inside pocket of his linen jacket. 'This letter came to the office today. It's addressed to you and was hand delivered though Odette said she hadn't noticed anyone drop it off – a bit of a mystery.'

Frankie took the slim cream envelope from his hand. She looked at the address. It was typed out with an old-fashioned typewriter.

'I haven't seen proper type like that for years,' said Daniel.

Frankie slid her thumb along the flap. At first she thought the envelope was empty but then she saw a narrow strip of paper at the bottom. She pulled it out.

The words were in a single line, all lower case, typed out like the envelope but in red:

you should be ashamed of yourself

Bile rose in Frankie's throat and she had to swallow. She tried to hide the note from Daniel by scrunching it up in her hand but he'd already seen the expression on her face and gently took the ball of paper and unfolded it.

'Who do you think wrote this?' he asked her after he had read it. She shook her head – Seren, Nesta, some horrible town gossip? Or… she could hardly bear to form the name in her mind.

Nesta

A blanket of heat enveloped her, as comforting as a warm embrace. Nesta had never been one for sunbathing; much preferring to get on and do something in the garden rather than lie around in it. But today it was so hot she had felt compelled to stretch out along the garden bench after lunch. She placed a cushion behind her head, pulled up her skirt, extended her long legs and turned her face up to the sun.

She justified her uncharacteristic idleness with the rationale that she would need a bit more colour in Italy, or she'd stand out as a tourist straight away and be expected to pay twice as much for everything.

As Nesta's mind and body began to relax she thought about how well the white linen shirt she'd bought the day before would show off her brown arms and neck. She wondered if she should get some other new clothes. She'd already booked a cut and colour at the hairdressers, a few highlights, just to leaven the grey. And the beautician on the high street had a special summer offer on for manicures and facials – it seemed a shame not to take them up on it, even though she'd never bothered with either in her life before.

Nesta was relieved she would be away for Daniel's retirement party. She and Seren had started to discuss it secretly six months before. They'd envisioned a marquee on The Windmill lawn and a jazz band playing Daniel's favourite songs. Nesta would have spent the last few weeks organising the menu, ordering wine and outside fairy lights, asking the boys at Tremond's to make meringues and macaroons. Seren would have been in full swing, working out what flowers were needed to decorate the tables and would probably have made another cake.

Nesta had heard from the boys at Tremond's that the party was still going ahead but on a smaller scale and taking place on the Friday evening of the following week, the day that Nesta would be going away. It would be just a simple dinner at the hotel for Daniel's employees and his friends and associates around the town. Seren was invited but said she wasn't going. Ben was invited but said he had to work. The boys from Tremond's had also been invited but were in two minds whether to accept or not.

'You know how loyal we are to you, Nesta.'

'I don't mind. Why give up the chance of a good meal at Daniel's expense? Order the lobster and think of me!'

Trevor and Edmond had turned to each other, eyebrows raised.

'Oh, she's merciless,' gasped Edmond.

'Like Bette Davis in full sail,' said Trevor with admiration.

Nesta would be far away. By then she'd be ensconced in her Roman hotel room, poring over maps and her guidebook, familiarising herself with the route from Rome to Casperia. She already knew she'd need to take a train from Terni, then a connection to Rieti and then a bus. It was the next bit that worried her: would there be a taxi? She didn't want to find she had to walk and arrive at Leo's out of breath and sweating. What would have been the point of the highlights and the facial and the manicure then?

She wondered for the hundredth time if she should let him know that she was coming. What if he was out for the day? Away on a holiday himself? Lying in a hammock with some dark-eyed local woman? The magazine article mentioned he was widowed; maybe he'd have re-married by now.

Nesta must have drifted off because she was there, in Italy, panting up a dusty drive towards a sumptuous garden in the distance. She could see Leo. He lay entwined with a young Sophia Loren who wore an off-the-shoulder peasant top and a scarlet pelargonium in her hair. Sophia stood up and stared at

Nesta suspiciously, breasts like missiles, hands defiantly on her hips. The heat was intense and the drive seemed to be some sort of travelator going backwards so that, however hard she tried, Nesta never seemed able to reach Leo. He lay with his back to her and all she could see was his hair, copper bright in the sun. She called out to him and he turned but instead of Leo it was Daniel who looked back at her.

Nesta woke up. Her head felt thick and achey, the dream seemed much too real. She kept expecting Sophia Loren to walk around the corner, a red-haired Daniel suddenly to appear.

Nesta rubbed her throbbing temples. She'd spent too long lying in the sun. She peered at her watch. It must be nearly time to fetch Griff from school. At least Seren had entrusted her with that responsibility again, though strict instructions had been given to bring him straight back to The Windmill with no trips to the park, no meetings with Daniel. Nesta had felt about eight years old as Seren had issued her directives.

Nesta wondered where Seren was. She had only said, in her newly preoccupied way, that she was going to see a friend.

The day before Nesta had offered to help Seren in the shop and Seren, grudgingly, had agreed. They had been preparing flowers for a birthday party – sixteen vintage tea cups filled with lavender and old roses. The sweet smell filled the warm air around them as they worked and Nesta could feel Seren beginning to thaw.

They had just finished the last two arrangements when Seren had put down her scissors,

'There's a sale on at the new boutique. Shall we go?'

'It will be closed by the time we shut,' Nesta said, as she started carefully placing the cups into a plastic box for delivery.

'Let's go now. We can shut the shop for twenty minutes. It's too hot for many people to be about out this afternoon.'

Nesta had been surprised, but pleased that Seren had asked her to go with her and she had been thrilled to find the half-price linen shirt. Seren seemed determined to try on the whole shop, eventually buying a complete new outfit. Nesta didn't dare ask what had sparked this sudden shopping spree.

From The Windmill balcony Nesta had watched her leave that morning; hair loose and shining, a pretty floral skirt, a broderie anglaise blouse, a little pair of beaded flip flops that the boutique assistant had insisted were just perfect with the skirt.

As Seren's green van sped off down the drive Arlow had briefly popped into Nesta's mind, but then she remembered he had a wife. She knew that Seren was far too sensible to get involved with a married man.

Seren

The swans drifted in front of them, side by side.

'Did you know they mate for life?' Oliver asked.

Seren nodded, sipped her spritzer and watched the birds disappear around the bend of the river. She stretched out her legs and her new flip flops glittered in the midday sun. Oliver smiled at her.

'Very pretty,' he said.

She'd been nervous as she'd searched for Oliver at the busy station car park an hour earlier. Then she'd spotted him waving from a convertible Austin Healey. It seemed ridiculously glamorous. Oliver looked ridiculously glamorous himself in a white linen shirt, well cut jeans and sunglasses. Seren walked towards him wondering yet again what could possibly have made Frankie leave this man.

'You keep this car in Brixton?' she asked, admiring the silver paintwork and red leather seats.

Oliver opened the passenger door. 'No, I have a friend who owns a classic-car hire company. It was between this and a Morris Minor today. I thought this was a little more Guildford.'

Oliver drove them out of town. As they sped down country roads Seren started to enjoy the way the wind blew back her hair, the low growl of the engine and the feeling of the soft leather on her legs. She put on her sunglasses and began to feel ridiculously glamorous herself.

The pub was perfect too. Sitting on the riverside terrace Seren wondered if there could be a lovelier place to be on such a beautiful day.

'How's your drink?' Oliver asked.

'Weak,' smiled Seren. 'I have no intention of drinking too

much this time.'

'I don't mind,' Oliver grinned over his half pint. 'You were great company in a tipsy sort of way.'

'Thanks,' Seren laughed. 'Though I'm not sure if that's a compliment or not!'

'I have a present for you,' Oliver reached into the pocket of his shirt. 'I found it in an antiques market in Amsterdam.' He took out a small, square box and pushed it across the table.

Seren picked it up; it was light. She opened the lid. A tiny silver charm lay on a bed of white tissue. Seren held it up in front of her and saw it was a bee, wings outstretched in flight.

'A bee for Beatrix,' Oliver said.

Seren couldn't help her smile. 'Thank you.'

'You're not wearing your bracelet today.'

Seren looked down at her bare arm. 'No, it seemed too hot somehow.'

'Too hot for charms?' asked Oliver. Seren felt heat rise inexplicably in her cheeks.

'How was Amsterdam?' she asked.

'Good.'

They were silent for a moment or two while Seren wondered if Oliver was going to expand on good. She held the little bee between her thumb and forefinger, watching the sun glint back and forth on the delicate silverwork.

'I knew you'd like it,' Oliver said.

Seren closed her hand around the bee. 'Tell me about the piece of work you've been commissioned to make round here.'

Oliver took out his phone and showed her a series of photographs of a standing figure, modelled in clay, its face turned to the sky, wings stretched out on either side. 'It's to stand on top of a hill. A sort of Angel of the South East.'

'It looks amazing.'

'You have to imagine it ten times larger and cast in bronze.'

Seren's eyes widened.

'I'm hoping it will really make my name.'

'I thought you had a name for yourself already.'

Oliver leant back in his chair and looked at the sky. 'But I want a bigger name. I want a name as big as Henry Moore, Jacob Epstein...' He stretched out his arms in an imitation of his clay figure, 'Auguste Rodin.'

'Wow!' Seren said.

Oliver let his arms drop by his side and laughed. 'I'm only joking. Those men are geniuses.'

'And you're not?'

Oliver shook his head. 'Alas, no. I am merely an amateur chiseller compared to them.'

'But I think your work is amazing,' Seren said. 'You're so talented.'

Oliver smiled at her, 'That's what my mother used to say about the art work I'd bring home from primary school.'

'She must be very proud of you now.'

Oliver looked down at his hands. 'I'd like to think she would have been.'

Seren bit her lip. 'I'm sorry. How old were you when she died?'

'She didn't die. She disappeared the day after my eleventh birthday, same time as the man next door took off and left his wife and five kids. I never saw her again.'

'Oh, Oliver. That must have been terrible for you.'

Oliver shrugged. 'My dad wouldn't ever let me mention her name. I've no idea what happened to her. My father died when I was in my twenties. I don't know if he knew where she was. In the end he couldn't speak even if he'd wanted to tell me. The cancer ate away his throat before it killed him.'

'Your poor father.'

Oliver's face seemed to have become like stone.

'He was a weak man. He should have stopped my mother leaving. He should have seen it coming and stood up for himself. Instead he let her destroy him.'

'It must have brought back bad memories when Frankie

200

disappeared.'

Oliver looked away, still stony faced. Seren wished she could swallow her last sentence. She twisted the stem of her glass between her fingers,

'I'm sorry, that was insensitive,' she said.

Oliver suddenly smiled as a waitress appeared with their lunch. He rubbed his hands,

'Sandwiches. Just what we need.'

This time they had decided to choose for themselves from the extensive pub menu, and laughed when they ended up with exactly the same choice of smoked salmon sandwiches.

After lunch they drank coffee. Oliver didn't mention his mother or his father again but they talked about loss and grief and how it feels no longer to spend your life with the person you expected to be with forever.

'The days can seem so long,' Seren said with a sigh. 'Even mundane household tasks, like changing a duvet cover, can bring back memories that make me cry.'

'I think I've used my work to block out the pain,' Oliver stared down at his cup, absent-mindedly stirring the contents with his spoon. 'In the beginning I couldn't sleep so I'd spend all night in my studio, channelling my unhappiness into hunks of limestone, trying not to think about how much I missed her.' Seren reached out her hand and almost touched his arm. 'It was the not knowing where she was that felt so hard. I had no idea if she was well or happy. Safe or alive. I nearly went out of my mind with worry. Oliver looked up at Seren. 'At least I know where she is now.' Then he smiled and sat up straight in his chair. 'Enough of this sad stuff. Let's make a plan that will cheer us up.'

Seren laughed at his unexpected exuberance. 'OK.'

'Would you like to see a piece of my work *in situ*?'

'I'd love to.'

Oliver picked up his phone again. 'Let me just check the date. That piece you saw in my studio, the angel with the outstretched arms.'

'For the millionaire music mogul with the large hallway?'

'That's the one,' Oliver replied. 'The millionaire music mogul is having a champagne reception to show it off to all his music industry friends next Wednesday evening. I'm invited. Would you like to come as my guest?'

Seren hesitated.

'I'll need to think about it.'

'We might be able to do some celebrity-spotting together – there is talk of George Michael being there.'

'Much as I like George Michael, I'd need to get back to say goodnight to Griff.'

'It starts at six but I thought we might have dinner afterwards.'

Seren hadn't missed Griff's bedtime since Tom died.

'Don't worry,' Oliver said quickly. 'I understand that Griff needs you. It must be hard to lose your dad at his age.'

Seren took a sip of her coffee. 'Actually Griff's been through a bit of a hard time since I saw you last.'

'Really?' Oliver looked genuinely concerned.

Seren took a deep breath and recounted what had happened in the park.

When she had finished Oliver was quiet. He seemed on the verge of saying something, but stopped.

'This sounds awful,' Seren added. 'But I kept wondering if Frankie, I mean Francesca, could have pushed him. You'd said she could be violent; I was worried that she could have wanted to hurt Griff in some way.'

'No!' Oliver cried out. Several people turned around and he lowered his voice. 'No, Francesca would never do something like that – to a child. That would be unthinkable.'

'I know, I know,' Seren wished she hadn't mentioned it. 'Someone else in the park saw Griff fall. He told me Frankie wasn't anywhere near him at the time. I told you it was an awful thing to think. It was just after you had told me those

202

things about her mental health. I wasn't sure what she might be capable of.'

'You should have told me what had happened. Phoned me, texted.'

Seren shook her head. 'I don't know why I didn't. I feel bad now for thinking Frankie could have pushed him. Guilty.'

Oliver leant forward, 'I could have reassured you that Francesca would never hurt a child. She loves children. I often used to think that she was like a child herself. She has a kind of vulnerability, she needs to be looked after.'

'But you told me she was violent.'

'Yes, she was. She'd fly into rages, like a tantrum. She'd do things to try to hurt me but I don't think she'd be like that to someone else, especially not a child.'

'But what about someone else she's in a relationship with?'

Oliver was silent.

'Do you think she could be aggressive towards my dad?'

Oliver shook his head. 'It was probably just the effect I had on her. Maybe we weren't a good combination. We had very little money, we were struggling artists in our garret. I think she longed for something more luxurious: a house, holidays, a nice car, a comfortable lifestyle. She'd had an idyllic childhood, what I had to offer was far from that. She had a small trust fund she'd inherited. She painted when she was well enough and I worked day and night to gain a reputation, get commissions, sell my work. We didn't have much but I was happy with our life. She wasn't.' His mouth twisted into a grim smile. 'Now it's different. I have made money, lots of money. But it's too late, Frankie's gone.'

'And found a man who she thinks can offer her the materialistic things she craved?'

Oliver nodded.

'No wonder my father's so keen to sell The Windmill and buy Frankie a nice house. She must be pushing him to get the money.'

Oliver shrugged. 'Maybe.'

'Why didn't you have children?' Seren asked quietly. 'Was it because you couldn't afford to?'

'No. We tried for a while but when Frankie finally got pregnant she had a miscarriage.'

'That must have been heart-breaking for you.' said Seren.

'It didn't help Francesca's mental health. In fact the whole thing tipped her right over the edge. That was when she had to be sectioned.'

'Sectioned?'

'Hospitalised for her own safety.' Oliver paused. 'And mine.'

Seren gasped, she didn't know what to say. Oliver still held her hand. 'Hey.' He looked at her with his piercing eyes. 'It's OK. It doesn't mean she's crazy. It was just a bad time in her life.'

Seren thought about the months she'd spent shut up in her bedroom after coming back from Wales. She had thought she'd go crazy then, maybe she had gone crazy, whole days had vanished into black despair. But she'd never hurt anyone.

'I know it's hard for you,' Oliver continued. 'You're upset about your mum, your parents' house, Griff. But maybe it will all work out for the best. Your mum might find a whole new lease of life as a single woman, you might find yourself with wonderful new neighbours. Francesca and your dad might be blissfully happy together – I really hope they are.'

'You're very optimistic,' said Seren. 'And generous to wish Francesca well.'

'I spent a lot of time thinking in Amsterdam. Working out my feelings now I know Francesca's safe. What I came to realise was that she's not mine anymore. I just have to let her go.'

'That sounds positive,' Seren said, her eyes meeting his.

'It's time to move on.' Seren couldn't drag her gaze away. 'Maybe I would be happier with someone else.'

'Yes, you might,' Seren said quietly. She seemed to be in some sort of bubble; the noise of the pub and river had disappeared, the heat, the sun, the glare from the water, they had all diminished.

'And you might be ready to meet someone new,' Oliver said,

Seren's mouth felt dry, she reached out for her glass but saw that it was empty. 'I might.'

A noise startled her. Oliver's phone had started to ring. He picked it up. 'OK, I'll be there in half an hour.' He put the phone down. 'I'm so sorry, Seren. I had a meeting with the site developer at five but it's been brought forward to three. I need to go now or I'll miss the chance to discuss things with him before my proposal goes in front of the Arts Council.' Oliver started looking for his wallet to pay the bill. 'You probably need to get back to Griff anyway. It sounds like he needs his mum as much as possible at the moment.'

The bubble had burst, everything around seemed too loud and much too bright. Three men at the next table started to laugh at a joke the waitress was telling them and Seren noticed one of the beads on her sandals had come loose and was hanging by a thin white thread against her foot.

They hardly spoke as Oliver drove her back to Guildford to catch the train. He seemed distracted. Seren wondered if his mind was already with the site developer, thinking about his sculpture, his proposal to the Arts Council? Or were his thoughts full of Frankie? Was he as 'over' her as he made out?

At the station Oliver stopped the car in the fast drop-off bay, he didn't even turn the engine off.

'Thanks for lunch,' Seren eased herself out of the seat.

'It was a pleasure,' Oliver smiled at her as she climbed inelegantly out of the car. 'You're good company – even when you're sober.'

Seren laughed and Oliver started to reverse out of the

parking space. As he turned the car around he waved, and then he was gone.

Seren stood on the pavement for a long time. He hadn't mentioned the party again; she wondered if he had forgotten or had he thought she didn't want to go? Should she have been more enthusiastic? Should she have mentioned it again in the car?

Seren walked into the station. Maybe she should have agreed to go for dinner after the party? She walked across the bridge to the platform. Maybe she should text him and tell him that she'd love to have dinner? She was sure Griff wouldn't mind if she just missed one bedtime. A train stopped in front of her and she got on. It was sheer luck that it happened to be the one that would take her home.

Frankie

The heavy shopping bags pulled at her arms and Frankie wished that she were back in the cool water of the swimming pool instead of trudging home in the afternoon heat.

Today the pool had been completely empty, just Frankie swimming up and down, her anxieties ebbing away with every length. She had rolled onto her back, closed her eyes and let herself just float. As she lay, starfish like, in the water she couldn't imagine why she'd got into such a state. How could he possibly know where she was? And after all these years, why would he care?

By the time she got out of the pool Frankie felt so much better, lighter, happier. That was when she'd decided to make a special dinner. Daniel had cooked every night for weeks so tonight she wanted to surprise him.

As she dried her hair she planned the menu. Chicken and rosemary risotto with a green salad, strawberries with ice cream for pudding, white wine, Miles Davis on the CD player. She'd put the chairs out in the garden. It would be lovely in the warm evening air, even if they had to balance their plates on their laps.

On the way home she stopped at the wine merchants and bought a ridiculously expensive bottle of Sauvignon Blanc. At the Country Market she bought a free-range chicken, strawberries and locally produced vanilla ice cream. Then she stopped at the greengrocers for fresh herbs and salad leaves and lastly a crumbling wedge of parmesan from the Cheese Emporium.

As Frankie headed for home she noticed a pile of billowing meringues on display in the window of Tremond's. They would be perfect with the strawberries and ice cream. But as she approached the doorway she felt all the anxieties that the pool had washed away returning. Trevor and Edmond were Seren's friends. She'd been aware of their scrutinising gaze in the hospital waiting room. Could they have written the anonymous note? Had Seren written it, or had they all written it together? Frankie walked away, head down, suddenly wary of everyone she passed on the busy high street. With a sigh of relief she turned into the residential streets and slowed her pace.

She stopped under the shade of an overhanging fig tree and put down the heavy bags. She thought about Daniel's retirement dinner – only ten days away. Frankie wished she didn't have to go. Daniel had suggested a trip to London to buy her a new dress. 'Something to make you the belle of the ball.' It was the last thing she wanted to be.

She shuddered at the thought of having to make small talk with all his friends and colleagues, wondering what they thought, what gossip they had heard about her.

Looking up she could see the small, round beginnings of figs, yellow against the dark green leaves and bright blue sky – a patchwork canopy. She thought how lovely it would be to paint it. For a few moments Frankie lost herself in the colours and the patterns and felt the tension easing in her neck and back. She took a deep breath and determined that she would enjoy the retirement dinner. For Daniel's sake.

Picking up the bags again she walked briskly up the remaining few yards of the road. She would let Daniel take her to London that weekend, surely it wouldn't be that hard to find a suitable dress? Maybe she'd suggest that they see an exhibition or a play.

Approaching the house she could see Daniel's car parked outside. As he'd left for work that morning he'd told her he'd be home late. He had to see a client about one last job, an extension to a house that Daniel had designed years before.

Frankie's heart sank; her meal wouldn't be a surprise after all. As she opened the gate her heart lifted again. Maybe they'd be able to spend the afternoon together? Maybe they could go for a walk before she began to cook? She smiled – maybe they could go to bed?

She walked up the path and noticed that the rose that scrambled up a trellis beside the front door was flowering abundantly. Dozens of deep red flowers jostled for space on the wooden frame, stems shooting out in all directions. Frankie plucked a single scarlet bloom, put it behind her ear and went inside.

Daniel was standing in front of the kitchen table.

'You're home early,' Frankie smiled as she put the bags down on the floor. 'What a treat.'

Daniel didn't speak. Frankie noticed that he looked exhausted, his whole demeanour oddly stiff.

'Are you alright?' Frankie moved to give him a hug but he stepped back, and as he did so she saw what was on the kitchen table. Frankie froze.

'I found it in the shed,' he turned and touched a key on the old-fashioned typewriter. It made a clunking sound. 'The 'e' is slightly off-set.'

Frankie shook her head. 'I don't understand.'

Daniel turned back to her, 'I was hoping you might be able to explain it to me.'

Frankie felt as though her head was filling with icy water. 'You don't think…?'She stared at him. 'You think I put it there. You think I wrote that note myself.'

Daniel rubbed his beard and sighed. 'I just don't understand how an old typewriter, the same one used to write that horrible note to you, could suddenly appear in a locked shed in the garden.'

'Had the lock been smashed? Had someone broken in?'

Daniel shook his head. 'The key was hanging in the kitchen

as usual.'

'What were you doing in the shed?'

'I came home to look for my tape measure. I thought I might have left it in the shed after I put in the cat-flap for Dante. I opened the door and almost fell over the typewriter. It was on the floor.'

'But why would I have done that?' Frankie tried to keep her voice steady. 'Why would I have written the note to myself?'

Daniel shrugged. 'Why would someone else have written the note to you?'

'Because I had an affair with you, because you left your wife for me, because your lovely house is having to be sold, because your family has been torn apart – so many reasons I should feel ashamed.' A hot tear slipped down Frankie's cheek.

Daniel stepped forward and took her in his arms. 'I'm sorry, darling. It's just that you've seemed so tense lately. Jumpy. And that stuff about the dead mouse, and the cut on your hand, and finding out about your marriage. I just began to worry that maybe…'

Frankie looked up at his face. 'That maybe I'm crazy?'

'No,' he stroked her cheek. 'Of course not.' He held her tightly. They were silent for a few minutes before Daniel spoke again, 'I'm going to phone the police about this.'

'No! No, don't phone the police.' Frankie shook her head.

'Why not?'

'Because…' Frankie paused; her mind desperately searching for a way to stop him. She couldn't cope with talking to a policeman, with the fear that there might be something about her on some police file. She took a deep breath. 'Because… supposing Seren wrote the note.'

'Seren?' Daniel sounded incredulous. He dropped his arms down to his sides. 'You think Seren would do something like this?' He lifted one arm to point towards the typewriter.

Frankie was silent for a few moments. 'She sent a text last week. A threat.'

210

Daniel was shaking his head. 'No.'

'I didn't want to tell you.'

'She wouldn't even have your number.'

Frankie looked at the floor. 'I got her number from your phone after you told her about selling The Windmill. I just wanted to send her a message to say I understood why she was angry.'

'You did what?' Daniel stared at her. 'Why didn't you tell me you'd done that? What did she answer?'

'She didn't answer. Not then anyway. But she sent me a text the night of Griff's accident.'

'What did it say?'

'It said to keep away from her son or I'd be sorry.'

Daniel's mouth was open. For a few seconds he seemed unable to speak. When he did his voice was very quiet.

'Seren wouldn't do something so... so...' He couldn't seem to find the words.

'She's very upset,' Frankie said. 'I think she wants to hurt me, to frighten me away.'

Daniel looked at her, his face twisting, his eyes looked wet. 'I know my daughter,' his voice was a whisper now. 'She would never hurt anyone.'

'Daniel, I'm sorry.'

'I'm late for my client, I have to go.' He brushed past her. 'I don't know what time I'll be back.' The front door slammed, everything was silent.

Frankie sank down on to a chair. The typewriter stared at her from the table. It had a sheet of paper in it where Daniel had been testing it, looking for the off-set e; a jumble of letters typed with goodness knows what emotions going on in his head *aaae ghjke dcvbts eeeeeeeeeee*. It looked like some sort of code she couldn't decipher. Frankie turned her head away and something soft and red fell into her lap – the rose; she had forgotten that she had put it in her hair.

She looked down to see Dante at her feet. He started licking at a large white puddle seeping out from one of the shopping bags. Frankie let the rose fall from her fingers and wondered how long it would be before the sticky pool of ice cream reached the scarlet petals on the floor.

Nesta

Gloaming. The word ran through Nesta's mind as the garden grew dim in the evening light.

She'd always liked this time of day, an in-between time, before the dark and the moon and the stars. It reminded Nesta of haymaking on the farm. All day long she and her mother would run back and forth with jugs of beer and sandwiches for the men in the fields. As the sun set the men would start singing, working faster and faster to be sure to finish before dark. Nesta would sneak out of the farmhouse to join them in the gloom, turning the grass with her small hands, adding to the men's deep voices with her own, hoping her mother wouldn't come and find her too soon.

Nesta smiled at the memories and turned on the hose. She had been waiting for the *gloaming*, the best time to water plants. The air was warm, full of moths and bats and the scent of lilies.

Nesta glanced towards The Wheat House. Daniel had been there for over half an hour. She edged closer. The kitchen door was open but the voices were barely audible. Nesta turned off the hose but she still couldn't make out the words. She supposed Daniel and Seren were being quiet so as not to disturb Griff who would be in bed by now, or maybe they suspected she'd be outside trying to listen.

Nesta turned the hose back on and gazed at the darkening sky, searching out the first stars. She thought of Leo. He had arrived by night. 'I swept down on the Milky Way,' he'd said to the wide-eyed Anwen and Ben when they asked where he came from.

Nesta had seen his caravan as she looked out of the kitchen window first thing in the morning. 'What the hell is that?' she'd asked Daniel, who had been rushing around as usual looking for his shoes or wallet or briefcase.

'It's the bloke who's come to help you with the garden. Reggie Patterson recommended him, said he did wonders with their north-facing slope.'

'You never said he'd be camping on our drive?'

'I said we wouldn't mind. He travels round doing jobs all over the country; he describes himself as an itinerant gardener.' Daniel gulped down his coffee and kissed the top of Nesta's head. 'He's cheap, and anyway he's one of yours.'

'One of my what?' Nesta had to shout, Daniel was already half way out of the door.

'One of your tribe. He says he's from Aberystwyth.'

The door banged shut. Nesta had remained at the window studying the caravan. It was old and battered, the curtains were drawn, the door was tightly shut. It looked abandoned.

The front door opened again. 'Forgot the car keys,' Daniel started scrabbling around the work surfaces, pushing aside the children's toys and piles of dirty breakfast plates.

'Did you say Aberystwyth?' Nesta remained at the window.

'Yes, speaks your weird lingo and everything.' Daniel held up the keys like a trophy. 'What were they doing in the weighing scales?' Another kiss on Nesta's head. 'See you later.'

After the school run Nesta came home and washed up. The caravan was like an unopened box, its contents unknown and mysterious. Nesta made a Victoria sponge and watched out of the window for signs of life. As the cake baked she went outside and hacked ineffectively at the brambles around the base of The Windmill. By eleven o'clock she could bear it no longer and knocked at the caravan door with a cup of tea and slice of cake. The door opened and a whole new universe had seemed to open up.

'Hello Nesta.'

By now it had become so dark Nesta could only recognise

214

Daniel from his voice. He had appeared from nowhere and stood just a few inches away. Nesta thought she caught the faintest smell of whisky and she wondered if he'd been inside The Windmill sampling his collection.

'Is everything OK?' She aimed a stream of water at the murky outline of a buddleia bush, the moonlight caught the droplets and it looked like a diamond necklace arching across the flowerbeds.

'No,' Daniel's voice sounded husky.

'Want to talk about it?' Nesta turned to a patch of irises and changed the nozzle on the hose to mist. Daniel was silent for a few moments.

'Do you think Seren would be capable of sending someone an anonymous note?'

'Do you mean like hate mail?'

'Yes, threatening, hurtful.' Daniel repeated what the note had said. 'It was addressed to Frankie.'

Nesta laughed, 'Maybe you should be asking if I sent it.'

'It's not your style.'

'Do you mean I never sent hate mail to Lillian?'

'Nesta,' Daniel sounded annoyed. 'Let's not dredge up the past.'

Nesta bit her lip.

'What makes you think that it would be Seren's style?' she asked.

'Nothing. I mean, I'd never of dreamed that she would do something like that. She's told me herself she didn't send it.'

'Well, there you are then. Surely you believe her?'

In the darkness Daniel shrugged. 'I don't know. She's just admitted sending Frankie a text telling her to keep away from Griff.'

'Seren was very upset about the accident.'

'It wasn't Frankie's fault.'

Nesta didn't reply. They were silent again, the only sound the hissing of the hose.

'I feel awful,' Daniel said after a few minutes. Nesta concentrated on the plants in the borders, the smell of damp foliage and soil mingled with the smell of roses.

'Is it all worth it, Nesta?' he sighed.

Nesta turned off the hose.

'You're asking me?'

'Yes,' Daniel said.

Nesta laughed, 'You're asking me if it's worth it?'

'I'm asking if I'm doing the right thing?'

'Well, that's a first – I thought *you* always do the right thing – at least that's what you like to think.'

'Being facetious doesn't suit you, Nesta.'

'OK,' Nesta spoke slowly. 'Do you mean is it the right thing for you to leave me for a younger woman, petition for divorce, sell our home, force me to leave my garden to find a smaller house?'

'You make me feel awful when you say it all like that.'

'Not to mention the pain you've caused our children. Look how upset Seren is. And Ben has left Suki because he can't see the point in committing to her if all that happens is that you get divorced in the end.'

'I didn't know that,' Daniel's voice sounded small.

'Not to mention Griff.'

'OK, I get the picture…'

'And you want me to tell you if you're doing the right thing?'

'I'm sorry…'

'But I'll tell you what I think, Daniel.'

'It's OK. I shouldn't have asked.'

'I think yes, you are.'

'Yes?'

'Yes. You are doing the right thing because lately I realise I am so much happier without you.'

'You are?'

'I am.'

216

'Oh.'

'And I'll tell you something else. Next week I am going to fly to Italy and I'm going to enjoy it so much more than I would have if I'd had to spend the holiday with you.' Nesta dropped the hose on the grass and walked away.

'Nesta, please come back.'

Nesta ignored Daniel's pleas and headed towards The Windmill. The whole tower was illuminated in moonlight, like some floodlit ancient monument or church. Instead of heading for the front door Nesta went around to where the outside spiral steps began. She climbed them quickly, arriving at the balcony quite breathless. She leaned against the rail and inhaled several times; great gulps of air, like water for a thirsty man. She wasn't sure if it was the climb up the steps or what she had said to Daniel that made her heart beat so fast.

I'm happier without you. The words had replaced *gloaming* in her head, round and round. Was she?

She heard the sound of a car engine starting up, the crunch of wheels on gravel. Far below her, headlights moved slowly up the drive. Nesta felt a sudden aching in her chest. She wondered if she'd wanted him to follow her? Had she wanted him to say he'd come back home?

Nesta leant back against the railing, her head turned up towards the sky. A satellite moved steadily through the sea of stars. She thought about their marriage. A life of familiar routines and quiet emotions; pasts buried, passions quelled.

Had Daniel ever guessed? He never seemed to. He never questioned Leo's sudden departure or Nesta's behaviour that autumn when she seemed to drift through a mist of suppressed tears.

Sometimes Nesta longed to confide in him, to ask him to help her ease the agony of loss. But she would stop herself, give herself another day, until the days turned into weeks, then months, and then Seren came and everything became bearable again.

Nesta had visited a counsellor when depression enveloped her after her fortieth birthday. 'The secret must seem like something rotten at the heart of your marriage,' the earnest little woman had said when Nesta had finally confessed. Nesta had been horrified by the women's reaction. The secret had never felt like something *rotten*. In fact it glowed inside her like something precious, comforting. A star.

Seren

Seren leaned against the kitchen door and watched her mother. She could just make out her figure silhouetted in the moonlight.

Seren longed to call out as she would have when she was a child waking from a nightmare, but her mother wasn't even looking at her; she was looking in another direction, her face turned upwards to the stars.

The echo of her father's car engine still reverberated round Seren's head. She had watched the headlights until they disappeared, and now she watched her mother high above her on the tower. It was as though her parents were being sucked away from her in different directions and there was nothing she could do to keep them in her orbit.

Seren took a large gulp of wine from the mug she held in her hand. She hadn't had the energy to find a proper glass. Tom would have tutted at her laziness and gone and found her a long-stemmed wine glass or one of the little tumblers they had bought in Brittany. Seren wondered what Tom would have made of what was happening to her family. She suddenly had an overwhelming longing to speak to him; it seemed more impossible than ever that he wasn't there.

Tom, she whispered up into the sky.

The warm air around her hummed with silence. She wondered if she could call Ben, just to hear another voice, but he had his own demons to deal with. Anwen? Seren could just imagine how the conversation would go. *Quit moping around and get a life.*

Seren could hardly bear to think of the conversation she'd just had with her father. He'd shown her the note that Frankie had received, held it out and asked her if she had written it. Seren had denied it, of course, but she could see the doubt in his eyes. Then he asked about the text and when Seren had nodded she saw the doubt replaced with disappointment. Daniel had looked at her for a long time, silent and sad. Seren had longed to put her arms around him and tell him she was sorry, but her limbs were made of lead and she could neither lift her arms or take the single step towards her father that might have made a difference. Instead Daniel had turned around and walked out of her house without another word.

Seren studied the ceramic mug in her hands. A little house was painted on the front, beside it stood three stick figures, one tall, one with a head of long spirals for hair and another smaller figure with curly hair and huge goggle-like glasses. All were smiling and underneath them big wobbly letters spelled out 'Dad, Mum, Me'. On the back was the pepperpot shape of a windmill and two more grinning figures, with 'Granny and Grandad' written underneath. Griff had painted it at a pottery café on his sixth birthday. Seren remembered taking him to pick it up and how pleased he'd been when the mug was taken, still warm from the kiln and handed to him; the colours brighter, the glaze smooth and shiny.

Now it had all changed. The mug remained intact but the family were cracked and broken. Seren took another gulp of wine.

She'd been so desperate to glue as much of what was left of her family back together; to make her father see that Frankie wasn't right for him; to make him love her mother again. All that she had succeeded in doing was disappointing him and that was the one thing she'd spent her whole life trying not to do.

Seren buried her face in her hands. Maybe Daniel was happier with Frankie than he had been with Nesta. Maybe Frankie gave him a new lease of life and made him feel young again. Maybe she'd just have to accept that her father really did love Frankie and never would go back to Nesta.

An owl hooted in the distance. Seren sat up straight in her chair and drained the last of the wine from the mug. She felt light-headed and remembered she hadn't eaten anything since lunchtime. Daniel had brought a bag of Tremond's toffee & banoffee cookies for Griff. Seren reached across the table and took out a giant doughy disc. Ten minutes later, the bag was empty.

She felt sick and guilty, but most of all she felt alone.

Just leave them to it. Suddenly she could hear Tom's gentle voice.

'OK,' she whispered into the empty kitchen. 'You're right. It's none of my business. I'll just leave them to it.'

Her phone rang on the work surface behind her; frenzied vibrations propelling it close to the edge. In her slightly drunken daze she hoped it might be her father.

'Hello?'

'Hi, it's Oliver. I just wondered if you still want to come to the unveiling of my sculpture.'

Frankie

Daniel had his eyes closed but Frankie knew he wasn't asleep. Billie Holiday's voice filled the room and Daniel's fingers tapped out the melancholy rhythm on the arm of the sofa. The Sunday papers were strewn around him like a quilt and the afternoon sun poured through the linen curtains even though they were closed. Every now and then they billowed forward with the warm breeze from the open window.

Frankie sat on the floor and tried to concentrate on cutting out the stencils for her dementia-group fashion project. The memory mats had been such a success – bringing back a flood of recollections about clothes that had once been worn or longed for – that Frankie had decided to encourage the group to draw the outfits they used to wear. She was busy cutting out cardboard figures that they could draw around before painting or sticking the clothes on top. She had bought a selection of vintage magazines and paper sewing patterns to jog their memories and printed some images of 1940s, 1950s and 1960s dresses from the computer. Frankie had them neatly organised into piles according to the decade.

'Your pictures remind me that we still haven't found you a dress to wear to my leaving do on Friday.'

Frankie looked up startled by Daniel's voice. She wondered how long he had been watching her.

It had been three days since he had found the typewriter; since then he'd seemed remote and distracted. His plan to take Frankie to London had not been mentioned.

'We should have gone to London yesterday,' he continued as though he'd read her mind. 'It's just I can't seem to summon up the energy to do anything this weekend.'

Frankie got up off the floor and snuggled beside him on the

sofa. 'Are you alright? You're not ill, are you?'

Daniel kissed her and took her hand in his. 'No darling, it's just this bloody heat and all the little things I need to do at work before I finish and…' His voice trailed off into a sigh.

'And?' Frankie asked.

'And Seren.'

Frankie squeezed his hand.

'Why don't you go round and talk to her again.'

Daniel shook his head. 'It won't do any good. I think I've made it worse, accusing her of sending you that note.'

Frankie hesitated. 'But she said she did send the text.'

Daniel let go of her hand and rubbed his eyes. 'Yes. But she swears she didn't send the note.'

They were silent for a few moments.

'You're sure that the typewriter isn't yours?' Daniel blurted, turning his head to look at her.

'No!' Frankie met his gaze. 'I've told you, I've never seen it before.' The typewriter was still sitting on the kitchen table. Frankie didn't want to touch it and Daniel made no attempt to move it, as though he hoped the sight of it might jog Frankie's memory and she'd say, 'Oh yes, I remember that old typewriter now, and I remember writing myself that horrible message – silly me!' Neither of them talked about it, even though its presence seemed to fill the house.

'Maybe Nesta has the right idea,' Daniel said.

'What do you mean?'

'Getting away.'

Frankie concentrated on cutting out another cardboard figure.

'I should have asked for the tickets to Italy for us,' Daniel continued. 'It's a very nice hotel if I remember rightly.'

Frankie looked at him with raised eyebrows. 'I hope you're joking, Daniel.'

'Well, what about Morocco?'

'That sounds more appropriate,' Frankie settled back on the

sofa and smiled. 'A little hotel in Marrakech.'

Daniel put his arm around her, 'Or a Greek island: white sand, turquoise sea.'

'No!' Frankie pulled away from him and tried not to think about the white sand, blue sea and all the accusations and humiliations that had started on her honeymoon.

'What's the matter with Greece?'

'I just think Morocco sounds nicer.'

'OK, we'll book something next weekend, after my retirement dinner.'

Silence fell over them again. Billie Holiday had stopped singing; the only sound came from outside as a neighbour trimmed his hedge.

'I haven't asked you how your swim was this morning.' Daniel put his arm back around Frankie's shoulder and drew her to him. She relaxed and curled her feet up underneath her on the sofa.

'It was lovely. The pool was practically empty but then Arlow Laverne came with his little girl. She's so sweet. She loves the water now. She even jumped in from the side today.'

This time it was Daniel who stiffened. Frankie wanted to ask him what it was he held against Arlow but instead she decided to ignore his reaction and carried on cheerfully. 'Arlow told me his filming schedule is nearly over. Do you know, while we've been wafting around in our summer clothes they've been sweltering in woolly jumpers and hats and scarves acting out Christmas.'

Daniel made a huffing sound. 'So he'll be off back to London I suppose.'

'Actually he mentioned Hollywood.'

Daniel stood up.

'I think I'll get a cup of tea.' Frankie watched him leave the room. She wondered if his dislike of Arlow could have anything to do with the colour of Arlow's skin. She pushed the thought aside. Surely not? But then how well did she really know

Daniel? There was so much she didn't tell him about herself, maybe there were many things that Daniel hid about himself from her.

The curtain billowed again; a stronger breeze this time, it ruffled the newspapers and blew the pictures of clothes across the floor, mixing up Frankie's neat piles. A fly flew into the room and settled on the ceiling rose.

Frankie got up from the sofa and went to close the window. Afterwards she wondered how she'd noticed the envelope. It lay almost hidden by the bottom of the drapes, looking as though it might have blown in on the wind.

Frankie picked it up, a large pink envelope like the kind that would contain a luxurious birthday card. It felt slightly padded; soft, as though it had something more than just a card inside. She wondered if it was a surprise Daniel was trying to hide from her, a special gift. She was smiling as she turned it over, trying to decide whether to tell Daniel or put it back as though she hadn't found it, but her smile vanished in an instant as she saw her name typed neatly on the front. Her first impulse was to cry out for Daniel. But she stopped herself. Instead she sat down slowly on the arm of the chair, sickness rising in her throat as she saw the slightly off-set e.

Her fingers were trembling as she opened the flap. In her anxiety she dropped the envelope and as it hit the floor several red rose petals spilled out onto the carpet.

Frankie picked the envelope back up and forced herself to look inside. It was stuffed with rose petals – hundreds of them, crushed together in the small space. The smell was cloyingly sweet. Frankie's nausea intensified as she rushed into the hallway and opened the front door.

'Would you like a cup of Earl Grey, darling?' Daniel's voice called out from the kitchen. Frankie didn't answer him, she was stepping out onto the path, turning around to face the house, hoping with all her heart that it would look the same as when she'd come back from the swimming pool that morning. Flies were buzzing in her face, a terrible smell enveloped her. She made a noise – a cry, a scream – loud enough so that Daniel was rushing out to join her.

'What is it? What's the matter?' As Daniel followed her wide-eyed gaze, his voice dropped to a whisper. 'Oh, my God.'

The rose bush around the door had been stripped bare of its flowers. Every single rose was gone and in their place someone had tied the black and rotting carcass of a crow.

Nesta

Griff was laughing as Nesta failed to hit the tennis ball back over the washing line for the hundredth time. It bounced into the vegetable patch, frightening one of Nesta's chickens as it scratched around the dusty earth.

'Granny, you are hopeless!'

'Thank you for your encouraging words,' Nesta dropped the racquet and flopped down onto the grass. 'Shall we call it a draw?'

'A draw?' Griff sat down beside her. 'You hardly even touched the ball. I returned your serve every time and I was only playing with one hand!'

'OK, Andy Murray. You're the champ this time.'

'Every time, you mean.'

'I'm old.'

'I have asthma and a broken arm.'

This time it was Nesta who laughed. She propped herself up on her elbows and looked at her grandson's flushed face and gap-toothed grin.

'Your arm doesn't seem to stop you doing much and I haven't heard you wheeze all afternoon – despite your mum's careful instructions about not letting you exert yourself too much and making sure that your inhaler is in my pocket at all times.'

Griff sighed. 'She fusses too much.'

'She loves you.'

Griff changed the subject. 'Is that man going to buy your house?'

'What man?'

'The man I heard you telling Aunty Anni about on Skype. You said he looked round The Windmill yesterday.'

227

'Someone's ears are far too flappy for their own good. That was a private conversation.'

'Well, is he?'

Nesta lay back down and watched a single puff of cloud drift across the empty sky. The man had been charming, effusive, very handsome. 'My wife will love this house.' He'd said it over and over again.

'He wants to come back to look round with his wife.'

Griff made a face. 'If he buys it I'm going to be horrid to him every day.'

Nesta smiled. 'If he comes back I'll tell him that there's a particularly naughty little boy living next door, who eavesdrops on conversations and is especially fond of playing his trumpet very early in the morning.'

'And all night,' added Griff.

'That reminds me. We promised your mum you'd practise your poem for the end of term concert. Such a pity you won't be able to play your trumpet with one hand.'

'I hate that soppy poem my teacher chose.' Griff took a deep breath. 'Actually I do feel a bit wheezy now.'

'You sound very healthy to me.'

'Why has Mum had to go to London?' Griff changed the subject again.

'I think she said she was going to meet an old friend,' Nesta improvised as Seren had been rather vague about her sudden decision to disappear for the day.

Over the last few days Seren seemed to have become more distant that ever, disengaged from the world around her. Nesta had tried to talk to her but Seren simply didn't answer. Several times since Daniel's visit Nesta had looked up from her gardening to see Seren standing motionless at her kitchen window; the sadness of her expression made Nesta's heart ache. In the months following Tom's death she had been able to support Seren, hold her, keep her together, keep her whole. Now Nesta felt powerless and her daughter seemed to be slipping away from her, like fine sand between her fingers.

Maybe a day out in London would do her good. She seemed to have made an effort with her clothes again, had even smiled as she waved goodbye that morning.

Nesta was also pleased to be looking after Griff. The time spent with her grandson was a welcome distraction from thinking about the trip she was setting out on the following day. 'Your Grand Roman Escapade' the Tremond's Boys had called it when she'd gone in to buy a treat for Griff's tea.

'Maybe you'll meet a swarthy Italian bachelor with George Clooney eyes,' said Trevor.

'Maybe you'll meet George Clooney,' added Edmond wistfully. 'He has a house in Italy and such a lovely chin.'

'He's sold his house in Italy. And he's married now. To a woman,' Trevor nudged Edmond with his elbow. 'So you can take that dreamy look off your face.'

Nesta had laughed, picked up her box of chocolate brownies and headed for the door. At the threshold she stopped and turned back with a mischievous smile. 'Or maybe I'll meet a lovely Welshman with green fingers and stars for eyes.' She didn't mention Leo by name but it was the closest she'd come to telling anyone about her plan; it had made her stomach turn small somersaults.

'Oooo,' the boys had said in unison.

'Whatever floats your boat, signora!' called out Trevor as she closed the door.

'When will she be back?'

'Sorry?' Nesta realised she'd been miles away.

'Mum,' said Griff. 'When will she come home?'

Nesta improvised once more, 'Later.'

'Has she gone to London because she's sad?'

Nesta sat up. 'What do you mean?'

'She's sad all the time now.'

'She misses your dad.'

'And Grandad. She misses Grandad too.'

Nesta sighed. 'You don't need to worry about your mum.'

Griff's chin wobbled and his face suddenly seemed to crumple, tears ran down his freckles and he wiped his nose on his bare arm. Nesta pulled him towards her until he was sitting in her lap. She hugged him tightly and rocked him back and forth as he let out huge shaky sobs.

'*Mae'n iawn cariad*,' she whispered. 'Everything will be all right.'

Griff shook his head and words tumbled out of his mouth at triple speed. 'No it won't. It just gets worse all the time. First Dad died and now Grandad has gone and Mum has changed and you're not going to live here anymore and that horrible man is coming to live in The Windmill and I don't know the poem for the show and my arm itches all the time under the plaster and I can't play chess anymore and Grandad has a girlfriend and… and…'

Nesta kissed the top of his head. His springy red curls were damp and she realised she was crying, too.

She wondered if she should abandon her trip. A week was a long time for someone to be away when you were nine years old. Or was she looking for excuses not to go? The somersaults started in her stomach again.

Seren

Seren shifted and felt strong arms tighten around her. Fingertips began to lightly stroke her back. She'd forgotten how wonderful the feeling of another person's touch could be.

'Are you alright?' Oliver whispered.

Seren nodded. She kept waiting to feel guilty, waiting for Tom to appear in her mind, reproaching her with sad brown eyes.

Oliver kissed her neck and she stopped waiting for Tom to appear. After all she had made it very clear to Oliver that she didn't want things to progress too fast and she'd been especially clear about keeping all her clothes on even though they were lying on his double bed.

'You're beautiful,' Oliver propped himself up on one elbow so that he could look down at her. Sunlight poured through the skylight, illuminating the strands of her hair that he twisted in his fingers.

She felt beautiful.

'A bobby dazzler, as we'd say up North,' he added.

Seren looked up at him and laughed.

'Is that a compliment?'

'It certainly is.' Oliver traced the curve of her waist beneath her blouse with his thumb. 'It means you're the prettiest girl I've seen in a long time.'

'Thank you very much.'

'A very bonnie bewer my grandfather would have said, and he always had an eye for a good-looking lass.' He made his Yorkshire accent more pronounced. 'He might even have said you were a reight bridey popster.'

Seren laughed again,

'Now I think you're just making up these words.'

'You're a grand gradley champ, I reckon. A smasher masher. A smoot.'

Seren found she couldn't stop laughing until Oliver kissed her mouth and his hands pulled her blouse from her skirt, touching her skin with urgent fingers.

This time Seren didn't protest; instead she found herself undoing the buttons on his shirt, her hands exploring the scattering of blonde hair on his chest and the smooth muscles of his sculptor's shoulders.

It was then that Seren noticed it. A puckered scar just below his collarbone, almost silver where the skin had healed over what looked like a deep wound. Seren touched it and Oliver flinched.

'Does it hurt?' she asked.

'No. It's the memories that hurt. I don't like to be reminded of it.'

'Sorry.' Seren glanced at his face. His eyes had left her body and he looked through the skylight at the sky. Seren looked up too and saw an aeroplane high above them, slicing through the blue. He had become very quiet. She touched his hand in the hope that he might reach out to her. When he didn't she whispered 'sorry' again and wished she hadn't mentioned the scar.

It had been so perfect: the lunch that Oliver had laid out for her in his tiny courtyard; the cheese, the stuffed peppers, olives, wine. The conversation had been light; they laughed a lot. Seren had felt all the misery of the last few days dissolve away in Oliver's company. Her whole body relaxed and, for the first time, the image of Daniel's disappointed face didn't swim in front of her eyes.

'I'm not going to ask you any more questions about Francesca,' Seren told Oliver as, for pudding, they consumed half a giant Toblerone Oliver had bought at the duty free on his way back from Amsterdam. 'I've decided not to try to meddle in anyone else's lives anymore. What goes on in my mum and dad's relationship and Frankie and my dad's relationship is up to them.' She licked some melting chocolate from her finger. 'It's absolutely none of my business any more.'

'Good for you. Just leave them to it.' Oliver's words had echoed what Seren had imagined Tom would have said. Oliver's eyes met hers and with a smile he handed Seren another triangle of Toblerone. 'Maybe it's time you concentrated on your own love life.'

Seren looked away and hoped he couldn't see the blush mounting in her cheeks.

As Oliver made coffee Seren had started washing up the plates and glasses, asking Oliver about the reception that evening. Would there be many people there he knew? Would the skirt and blouse she was wearing be alright? Had he seen his sculpture *in situ* already?

'I'll do the dishes later,' Oliver had been suddenly beside her, taking her hands out of the warm water, gently drying them with a tea towel, pulling her closer towards him until her body had been just inches from his. It had been Seren who reached up and kissed him, freeing her hands from the tea towel, her fingers running through his hair and down his neck.

And now they were lying very still together, hardly touching. Seren could hear the ticking of a clock. She was aware that the afternoon was disappearing; soon it would be time to go to the reception and then it would be time for her to get the train. She searched desperately for something to say that would bring him back.

'Tell me a secret,' Oliver's voice made her jump.

He turned his face to hers. His eyes looked like deep blue pools, much darker than they'd been before. 'Tell me a secret about yourself that no one knows.'

Seren started to laugh then stopped. 'Why?'

'Because if you tell me yours I'll tell you mine.'

He picked up her hand and pressed her palm against the scar.

'About how you got this?' Seren asked.

Oliver nodded. 'But first you have to tell me a secret of your own.'

Seren rolled onto her back and stared up at the skylight again. It was a perfect bright blue square, no aeroplanes this time. She closed her eyes. Maybe it would be a relief to reveal her secret to someone else, even Tom had never known.

A dull thud heralded Rossetti's arrival on the bed. He purred and pushed himself at Seren's arm. She opened her eyes.

'If I tell you Rossetti will hear.'

Oliver sat up and began to stroke the cat.

'Don't worry. He's very discreet.'

Seren hesitated, was hers the sort of secret he had meant? Or was he only really looking for an 'I stole a Chapstick from Woolworths when I was twelve' sort of secret? Was hers too awful to tell? It was like looking down from a high diving-board, teetering on the edge. She took a deep breath and jumped.

'I have had two children.'

She kept looking at the blue square of sky but she felt Oliver turn his head to look at her.

'I thought you only had your son.'

Seren hesitated again; it wasn't too late to pretend she had been joking.

'I had a baby when I was eighteen. A little girl. They called her Rhiannon.'

'They?'

'The midwife, the doctors.' Seren shrugged. 'I don't know, but that's what they wrote on the forms.'

'What did you want to call her?'

'In my head I called her Sophie but I've never said her name out loud. Until now.'

'So your parents made you give her up for adoption?'

Seren let out a long sigh. The words seemed to clog in her throat, unable to come out.

After a few moments Oliver spoke again. 'Your parents wouldn't let you keep her?'

Seren turned to him. 'No. They have never known that she existed.'

Oliver studied her face with concern.

'Did they know you were pregnant?'

Seren shook her head. 'My sister, Anni, was having her first baby in Australia. My parents went over there to be with her and afterwards they spent some time in India and Thailand. They were gone for six months. They thought I was here, in London, studying at college.'

'But you weren't?'

'No. I was with my grandmother in Wales. My parents had arranged for me to stay with her that Christmas. It was obvious by then that I was expecting though I think I'd been in denial for months.'

'Did you just ignore it?'

'Sort of. My boyfriend and I had split up. Living away from home in London had been hard – when I discovered I was pregnant it just felt too much to cope with so I tried to pretend it wasn't true.'

'What did you think would happen?'

'I don't know.' Seren paused. 'Actually, I did get as far as going to a clinic for a termination but when I got there I couldn't go through with it. After that it was too late. I think I had prepared myself for life as a single mother. I think I'd even begun to get a little bit excited.'

Oliver didn't speak, though his hand was stroking Seren's shoulder. Rossetti let out little cries of protest as he tried to get Oliver's attention again.

After a few minutes Seren continued. 'If anyone mentioned my swelling stomach I blamed it on student food and lager. But when I arrived on the farm my grandmother wasn't so easily fooled. She knew my layers of baggy jumpers weren't just to keep out the cold Welsh weather.'

'What was her reaction?'

Seren's fingers plucked at the hem of her blouse. 'She had her own way of dealing with young women in trouble. At the time I didn't understand but now I'm pretty sure she knew what she was doing.'

Oliver stopped stroking her shoulder. 'What do you mean?'

'My grandmother had five hundred sheep. That year lambing started early. I arrived on Christmas Eve, the first lambs were born on Boxing Day. After that we were in and out of the lambing shed for over six weeks. We had a shift system going, one of us in with the ewes practically all the time, night and day.'

'Just you and your grandmother.'

Seren nodded. 'She usually hired a boy to help but she said that year I'd have to earn my keep.'

'But you must have been exhausted. That can't have been good for you or the baby?'

Seren shook her head. 'When I got ill I thought it was because I was so tired. My limbs and head ached, my throat felt raw. I developed a high fever; I remember hallucinating, a whole galaxy of stars was falling from the ceiling onto the bed, the whole quilt lit up, the stars were shimmering around me until I began to float on them, I floated up into the sky so that I was looking down at myself lying shivering under the quilt.'

'Did your grandmother not get a doctor?'

Seren shook her head. 'No, she said it was just a bad cold. It was years before I worked out what had really been wrong with me.'

'What was it?' Oliver asked.

'Chlamydiosis.'

'Chlamydi... what?'

'It's a disease you can catch from handling aborted or still-born lambs. Pregnant women are advised not to go anywhere near sheep at lambing time because of it. I was delivering lambs all day – that year was particularly bad for still births.'

'Were you alright?'

'I was only ill for a few days, but then I started my contractions eight weeks early. I was fifteen hours in labour. Terrified. Alone. My grandmother didn't come into the delivery room. She went home – all those lambs she'd seen being born and she wouldn't stay with me while I had my baby.'

'Was that because she disapproved of having an illegitimate grandchild?'

Seren paused, remembering her grandmother's words as she left her screaming through yet another contraction in the hospital corridor. 'It will all be for the best – in time you'll understand.' Seren had begged her not to leave but she had kept on walking towards the double doors.

'I think it was because she knew my baby was already dead.'

'Oh Seren,' Oliver sighed.

'She was so beautiful. Perfect hands. Even eyelashes. They let me hold her. I was so sure she was breathing.' Seren closed her eyes and remembered how the hefty midwife had prized Sophie roughly from her arms. 'That's enough now,' she had said and Seren had felt pain much worse than childbirth, as though everything inside her was shattering into a thousand shards.

She felt Oliver touch her cheek and opened her eyes. 'There.' She tried to smile. 'That's my secret. Now you tell me yours.'

Frankie

An air of lethargy hung around the policeman's bulky body as he pulled at the damp patches on his shirt, obviously uncomfortable in the early evening heat. Frankie could tell that he was finding it hard to focus as Daniel explained about the vandalized roses and the dead bird.

Frankie had begged Daniel not to phone the police; the thought of getting them involved frightened her far more than the roses and the bird. But Daniel had insisted and Frankie hadn't slept for two nights as they waited for the policeman's visit.

When he eventually arrived he held out a sweaty hand for Daniel and Frankie to shake and explained that he was a community officer whose main area was liaising with families and neighbours experiencing domestic disputes.

'But this isn't a family issue.' Daniel glanced at Frankie as though for affirmation. She nodded in agreement. 'And the neighbours all seem very nice.'

'Probably just teenagers. Bored on a Sunday afternoon.' The policeman scratched at his stubble with the biro he had produced from his shirt pocket, presumably to write down a statement. Frankie noticed a dark stain on the pocket where the pen must have leaked.

'But what about the envelope?' Daniel pointed to the floor where Frankie had found it. 'It was typed with the typewriter I told you about. It's been in our kitchen for over a week, we would have known if someone had come in and used it.'

The policeman shook his head.

'That's a mystery; it really is.' He scratched his chin again with the leaky pen; this time it left an inky smudge.

A long silence followed and the policeman looked from

Frankie to Daniel and back to Frankie again. Frankie felt her heart hammering.

'Well, Mr and Mrs Saunders, I don't know what to say.'

'Actually, we're not married,' Daniel interjected. The policeman looked at Frankie again.

'I'll need to take your name then, Miss.'

'Frankie Hyde,' she said.

'Miss Frankie Hyde,' the policeman repeated and wrote it down very slowly in the notebook. Then the policeman put his pen back in his pocket with a sigh, 'I'll go back to the station and log it on the computer, maybe do a bit of door-to-door with the neighbours tomorrow. If you have any more trouble give me a ring.' He handed Daniel a card. Frankie noticed a broad white band of skin on his wedding finger as if he'd recently taken off a ring. She wondered if his wife had left him or he had left her.

'I don't have much faith in our local Sherlock Holmes,' Daniel said as he came back into the living room after showing the policeman out. Frankie was sitting on the sofa, her fingers tapping against the arm as though to an imagined tune. Daniel sank down beside her. She waited for him to touch her but his hands stayed resting on his knees. He turned his head and studied her face. He didn't speak.

A car door slammed outside and Frankie jumped.

'Sorry,' she tried to laugh. 'It just makes me a bit jittery. All this stuff with the roses and the typewriter and the…' Her voice faded and they were silent again.

After a while Daniel got to his feet. 'I think I need a glass of whisky.'

'You think it's me, don't you?' Frankie said. Daniel stopped at the doorway. 'You think I'm doing all of this myself. I know you do, I can see it in your eyes.'

He came back and sat down beside her, taking her hand in his. Frankie's eyes traced the raised blue veins under his skin as she tried to ignore the silence in the room. After a few moments

239

Daniel spoke. 'I just can't understand why anyone would want to frighten us. It makes no sense.'

Nesta

Silly woman… silly woman… The words went round and round in Nesta's head in time to the rhythm of the train. She leaned back against the seat and wished she could sleep to pass the time. She closed her eyes, but they wouldn't stay shut, her legs ached with sitting still and her stomach churned. The journey to London seemed much longer than usual, the fields and hedges between the stations stretched out too far and the hands on her watch crept around so slowly that Nesta was sure the watch had broken.

In twelve hours she would be in Rome. How many days would she wait to travel to Casperia? How many days until she found the courage?

Over and over she had tried to write to Leo. She had found his website; a simple homepage describing the particular kind of lemon-scented pelargonium that he grew. The page had an address, phone number and a contact box for sending him a message. Nesta had stared at that box so many times that the white rectangle was now seared onto her brain. Once she started with a greeting in their native tongue, '*Annwyl Leo, sut wyt ti?*' Then she had deleted it and started, 'Hi, here's a blast from your past.' She'd deleted that as fast as possible.

'Dear Leo, I know it's been a long time since we last saw each other, but I just want you to know that I still think about you.' She had cringed and deleted that as well.

In the end she'd sent him nothing, determining what ever would be would be. *Que sera sera, que sera sera.* Doris Day's lyrics now took over from *silly woman* to accompany the sound of the train.

Nesta took *Country Living* magazine from her bag and tried to read an article about weaving with willow. The photograph of a pink-cheeked young woman making a willow basket danced in front of her eyes. She thought of Seren's flushed and eager face the night before.

'I've found out something, Mum.' Seren had rushed into The Wheat House just after Griff had fallen asleep.

Nesta put her fingers to her lips and pointed at his half-closed door.

Seren followed her mother into the kitchen and leaned against the Rayburn. 'When Dad hears about it I think he'll have to think twice about what he's doing.'

'Hears about what?' Nesta wondered if Seren had been drinking. She didn't seem herself at all and hadn't even asked if Griff had minded going to sleep without saying goodnight to her.

'Hears about what I've found out.' Seren picked up the kettle and started pouring water into it. 'Let's have a cup of tea and I'll tell you.'

'Darling, I can't. I'm leaving for Rome tomorrow. I have to catch the seven-twenty train and I'm only half packed.'

Seren opened the window above the sink. 'It's *so* hot tonight.' Water sloshed from the kettle in her hand onto her thin silk blouse, she didn't seem to notice. 'Anyway, it's probably best you don't know yet. You just go and have a lovely holiday.' She turned and looked at her mother, her face was very serious. 'I think you'll find that when you get back things will be different with Dad.'

Nesta wasn't really listening. She was looking at the purple and pink striped pelargonium on the windowsill. She hadn't seen it before. 'That's a pretty one,' she said to Seren.

Seren glanced at the pelargonium. 'Oh yes, they came in yesterday. They smell of lemons.' She reached out and pulled off one of the soft green leaves and handed it to Nesta. 'But I don't want you to worry about Dad. Don't worry about anything. I won't let her hurt Dad. It's all going to be alright.'

Nesta sniffed the sharply citrus-scented leaf. Seren kept

repeating that everything would be alright, but all Nesta's thoughts had been with the honey-coloured hilltop village and the pelargonium nursery and Leo.

Now, restlessly thumbing through *Country Living* on the train, Nesta began to go over Seren's words in her head. What had she meant, 'I won't let her hurt Dad'?

Nesta looked out of the window and noticed grey clouds bubbling up against the previously bright blue sky. She checked her watch. Eight o'clock. Would it be too early to phone? Seren would be getting ready to take Griff to school, probably rushing around making sandwiches and looking for bits of uniform and reading books. Nesta picked up her phone, she needed to catch her daughter before she left the house. She thought about the way Seren had kept repeating that everything would be alright, and something about the expression on Seren's face reminded her of Seren as a little girl – straight mouthed and serious. On a mission to right a wrong.

The phone rang and rang until it went to the answer machine. Nesta didn't leave a message. The rhythm of the train turned back to *silly woman... silly woman...* The train went through a tunnel and something began to gnaw in Nesta's stomach that had nothing to do with her trip to Italy.

Seren

The bank of cloud seemed to be building up from the east. Seren watched the dark grey line thickening above the rooftops, slowly covering the bright blue sky, heading for the sun. The heat seemed to intensify with the cloud and the air was thick with dust from the diggers and drills.

The new roadworks held up everything. Seren tapped her fingers impatiently on the steering wheel as the traffic crept slowly up the high street. She inched passed Stems and was relieved to see that Rose, a friend of Trevor and Edmond's, had remembered to put the new geraniums on the display stand outside. Damp patches on the pavement indicated the hanging baskets had been watered. Seren silently thanked Trevor and Edmond for coming up with Rose at the last minute. Without Nesta around it was hard to run the shop and do the things she needed to do to finally mend her parents' marriage. The traffic moved on and at last Seren was able to turn the van into the car park.

She checked the time on her phone and saw that her mother had been trying to call. Slipping the phone into her bag she stepped out of the van into a blast of hot air. She didn't have time to phone her mother back, it was vital that she got to her father's office as soon as possible.

'Hey, Sez, what's the rush?'

Seren had almost run straight into Arlow.

'Sorry,' she kept on walking. 'I've got to see my dad about something really important.'

Arlow fell into step beside her. 'I was hoping to bump into you.' He laughed. 'Well, not literally, but I was hoping to see you. I went to your shop but the woman serving said you weren't in today.'

Seren glanced at him and repeated, 'I've got to see my dad.' She swerved around a horde of old ladies spilling out of a coach on the edge of the car park, and momentarily Arlow was lost in the throng. Seren heard a murmuring of 'Oh there's that Arlow Laverne. Oh yes, off of that detective thingy. I like Arlow Laverne.' Then he was back beside her, a little out of breath.

'Please, Sez. Could we talk?'

Seren didn't answer but turned onto the high street, her eyes focused on the red and black swinging sign of the architecture practice across the road.

The pedestrian crossing forced them both to stop.

'Are you free for lunch?'

Seren turned to him. He grinned back. 'Or coffee? Tea? Glass of wine?'

'I can't. I'm meeting someone for lunch,' Seren replied, pressing the button on the crossing, willing it to turn green.

'Oh,' Arlow stopped grinning. 'It was just that I wanted to…' The sound of the green man beeping drowned out his words.

Seren crossed the road. When she got to the other side she turned and saw that Arlow hadn't followed. He remained on the other side watching her. A lorry stopped between them and Seren remembered the second secret she'd told Oliver. The secret about Arlow's mother and her father. The secret that Arlow had uncovered all those years before and that Seren had furiously refused to believe at the time. The lorry moved on with a blast of hot exhaust fumes.

'Arlow,' Seren called across the road. But when she looked back at the spot where Arlow had been he had vanished.

She turned away and started walking, trying to focus on what she was going to tell her father, trying not to think that Arlow could have been right.

In the coolness of the air-conditioned office Odette sat behind the reception desk looking chic. Her black linen dress seemed to crumple in all the right places and the bright red lipstick on her mouth was perfectly applied. She was typing briskly on a keyboard in front of her.

'Is my father here?' Seren asked.

Odette stopped typing, looked up, shook her head and spoke in her slight French accent. 'No, he has telephoned in and said that his…' She lowered her eyes as though checking something written down. 'He said that Frankie has a migraine and he must look after her today.'

'But it's his last day.' Seren couldn't believe her father would miss his last day at work before retirement.

Odette shrugged. 'Let us hope that she is better for his retirement meal tonight.'

Seren had forgotten about the meal. She wondered if she should wait until the next day to tell him; but she and Oliver had discussed it and decided that Daniel must know everything immediately.

'You're going?' asked Odette.

'Going where?' Seren already had her hand on the door.

'To the meal in the hotel.'

'No,' Seren pushed open the door; hot air hovered on the other side. 'I don't think so.'

'You should come,' Odette laughed briefly. 'It will be fun, I think.'

Seren stopped and turned around, wondering if she'd ever heard Odette laugh before. 'I have to go and tell my dad something. I'll have to go to his house.'

'And I will go and collect the cake from Tremond's,' Odette continued, with a smile; her teeth were very white between her scarlet lips. 'It will be a big surprise. Dark chocolate and strawberries. Your father's favourite.'

'Oh,' said Seren, the door fully open now. 'Well, I hope you have a good time tonight.'

'I will.' Odette turned back to the computer and Seren walked back into the baking heat with the sound of the keyboard rattling at full speed behind her.

Frankie

The air in the bedroom seemed to be pressing down on her aching head. The closed curtains hung limply against the open window. Frankie longed for a breeze to move the air and to dry the sweat that prickled along her hairline and trickled down her face. Dante lay stretched out beside her, basking in a slit of sunlight coming through the curtains.

Frankie was trying very hard not to think about the dress. She pressed her fingers to her forehead as another wave of nausea crashed over her. She wondered what the time was. How long before the meal was supposed to start? She'd never make it, the migraine held her in its grip; she and Daniel were hardly speaking and what could she wear now anyway?

Daniel had returned home the previous evening with a gold and black shopping bag swinging from his hand. Inside the bag a beautiful tissue-wrapped package looked crisp and untouched, golden discs secured each end.

'It's something special for you to wear tomorrow night. I bought it from that fancy shop on the high street at lunchtime.' Daniel had kissed her and with a huge grin on his face he had shooed her up the stairs to try it on. It was the first time she had seen him smile for days.

In the bedroom Frankie carefully unwrapped the parcel to find a neatly folded square of pale green silk. She unfolded it and it became a gorgeous dress. She lifted it up to hold against herself, anticipating the gentle swish of silk against her bare legs and the way the bias-cut fabric would fall from her shoulders. She was smiling when she turned to face the long wardrobe mirror but in a second she dropped the dress on the floor as though it had burned her fingers. Slowly she lifted it back up, holding it at arm's length this time, hoping that she had imagined what she'd seen.

BITCH. The single word was scrawled in thick black marker pen across the bodice of the dress.

'Can I come up and see what it looks like?' Daniel's voice called from the bottom of the stairs.

'Hang on,' Frankie rushed into the bathroom. 'I'll come down in a minute.' She began scrubbing desperately at the writing but her attempts did little more than make the pen lines bleed into the expensive fabric.

'Ready yet? It can't take that long to slip on a frock,' Daniel was laughing as he came up the stairs. Frankie's scrubbing became more fervent, the lines smudged further, the silk turning a horrible grey but the letters were still big and bold and black. She heard the bathroom door open and felt the dress being pulled out of her hands, water droplets bouncing up onto her face. She watched the dirty water swirl around the sink and disappear, not daring to look up at Daniel.

A minute passed, maybe several.

'What? How?' Daniel's voice was a whisper. Frankie looked up and his face was as grey as the smudges on the dress.

'I don't know,' she said.

A long silence followed. The bathroom pipes creaked.

Daniel cleared his throat, his eyes were staring straight into her own. 'Frankie, I have to ask you,' he paused. 'Did you do it?'

Frankie couldn't speak. The dull thudding in her head began and she retched into the sink.

Hours had passed, an evening, a night, half a morning. Daniel had come and gone with tablets, water, dry toast, a cold flannel for her forehead. They didn't talk about the dress. He slept downstairs.

Frankie heard the doorbell ringing, long and urgent. She heard the gentle pad of Daniel walking into the hall, Daniel picking up the post from the mat and putting it on the table, the

249

doorbell again, the bolt being drawn back.

'Seren!'

Frankie pressed her face into the pillow and tried to sleep.

After a while she heard Seren's voice, quiet at first, snatched words coming through the open window from the garden.

'Apparently… treatment… paranoid.'

Frankie raised her head from the pillow and strained to hear more.

'She stabbed him, Dad. She stabbed him just below the shoulder with a kitchen knife. On the left hand side. Inches lower and it would have been his heart.' Frankie sat up. She couldn't breathe.

'No. I can't believe Frankie would do that.'

'It's true, Dad. Oliver told me. I saw the scar.'

Oliver. Frankie swung her legs out of the bed at the sound of his name.

'She had already been sectioned once.'

'Sectioned? Why?'

'Psychotic. That's how Oliver described her. She lost all sense of reality. Thought that people were out to get her – things happened, letters, hate mail. She imagined things, imagined Oliver was doing things to her. She threw herself down the stairs when she was five months pregnant. The baby died as a result and Oliver said that sectioning her was the only way to stop her killing herself.'

No! Frankie gasped out loud. *No. It hadn't been like that at all. She never wanted to kill herself or hurt her unborn child.* She stood up, her legs were weak, like melting chocolate.

'I'd like you to meet him, Dad. He's offered to come here to see you. This afternoon.'

Frankie clung onto the chest of drawers and began to search for clothes. The room spun in circles. Somehow she managed to pull out pants, T-shirts, cardigans, jeans.

'He's a lovely man, Dad. He's really kind. How he put up with her behaviour for so long I don't know.'

250

'I don't understand, Seren. Are you saying she actually stabbed her husband?'

'Yes, and then she left him for dead and ran away. He couldn't find her, not even the police could find her.'

'She's wanted by the police?'

'No, he didn't want to press charges. He managed to get himself to hospital, said it was an accident, said he fell onto a bit of metal in his sculpture workshop. All he wanted was to find her to get her help again. That's how much he loved her. He said he would have forgiven her anything.'

No, no, no. Frankie dragged her suitcase from under the bed. *No. That wasn't love, he'd never loved her. He tormented her, hurt her in a thousand humiliating ways. The physical pain had been just one part of it. Sometimes he had damaged her paintings: a scratch, a splash, barely visible. Or he smudged the wet paint as he walked past. Once he'd squeezed a tube of oil paint into her hair, a joke, he'd said at the time. One morning she had woken up to find him urinating on her face.*

Frankie heaved the suitcase onto the bed and began flinging the clothes into it.

'Are you really sure that Frankie is the same person as this man's wife,' Daniel sounded bewildered.

Frankie stopped. *But she had stabbed him.*

'Yes, I've seen pictures of them together. Dad, I'm really worried. You've got to tell me, has Frankie ever seemed paranoid or done anything disturbing while she's been with you?'

A pause. Frankie could hear the bees buzzing, a low rumble in the distance, the clock on St Peter's Church chimed.

'Well, actually, there have been some rather odd things going on lately. I didn't want to believe it could have been Frankie doing them herself but now...' Daniel's words trailed off.

'But now you can see what she's really like?' Seren said so quietly that Frankie almost couldn't hear.

'I don't know,' Frankie could imagine Daniel's expression as he tried to take in his daughter's words. 'I don't know what to think.'

'She stabbed him, Dad. She stabbed him and left him for dead.'

He'd slashed her paintings for the exhibition with a knife.

Frankie rubbed her eyes at the memory of the devastating scene. But it was true. She had stabbed Oliver. She had left him for dead and run away. Frantically she pulled on some clothes, finished putting the others into the suitcase and went into the bathroom to grab her toothbrush.

Back in the bedroom she slipped on her shoes. Dante was still stretched out on the bed, he opened one eye and looked at her. The cat basket was in the shed, she couldn't possibly get it. Dante would have to stay. She slung her handbag over her shoulder and picked up her suitcase. Very quietly she crept down the stairs. At the bottom she turned around. Dante had followed her. He wound himself around her legs and purred. With one arm she scooped him up and with as little noise as possible left the house.

Nesta

London smelled of tar and petrol fumes. The people and the traffic and the humidity had driven Nesta into a coffee shop beside the station. She was still trying to make sense of the phone call.

The phone had rung as soon as Nesta had stepped off the train. The estate agent had sounded exited.

'Good news! We've had an offer at the asking price.'

Trundling her suitcase down the noisy platform Nesta struggled to take in the man's words.

'An offer? From whom?'

'The man who viewed it earlier in the week. He's coming back with his wife today but he is so sure she'll love it that he wanted to make the offer just in case someone else snaps it up.' The estate agent laughed delightedly. 'I can't get hold of your husband to tell him but I've left a message on his phone.'

Nesta's heart was sinking. It was too fast, too quick. She couldn't think properly.

'I'll take him round again with his wife this afternoon but he's one hundred percent sure The Windmill is the house of their dreams.'

In the coffee shop Nesta ordered a latte from a girl with a half-shaved head and a grinning skull tattooed on her forearm. Nesta poured in milk and stirred it with the wooden stick provided. She sat down in a window seat, took a sip of piping coffee and thought about her garden and her chickens and her beautiful daughter and grandson. What on earth would happen to them all?

She wondered why she had ever thought she could go to Rome, let alone find Leo after all these years. *Silly woman… silly woman…* It still ricocheted around her head.

Nesta took out her phone and dialled Seren's number. It rang and rang and went to answer machine again. She tried the shop but Rose said she didn't know where Seren was, only that she'd told her something unexpected had come up. Again Nesta remembered her daughter's determined expression the night before.

An over-sized clock hung on the wall above the counter. Nesta looked up at it. The trains were every hour, she had forty-five minutes before she could start back. She tried Seren's phone again. She needed to tell her she was coming home. Nesta had gone away and left her daughter when she needed her before. She wasn't going to make that mistake again.

Seren

Seren's heart raced as she drove, too fast, through the country lanes. The sky was overcast now but the heat was suffocating. Seren wound up the windows and turned on the air-conditioning in the car. She hoped it wouldn't rain so that they could sit outside at the riverside pub. She had told Oliver that she'd meet him at the train station but in the end her conversation with Daniel had gone on longer than she'd planned. When she got to the station the train had already gone and she'd had to drive, which was a shame as he'd promised that he'd hire a really special car this time. Maybe they could drive back to town in it to see Daniel later. There'd be lots of time; Griff was going to a birthday party after school.

She thought about the conversation with her father earlier. She hadn't expected him to be quite so disbelieving, to need to know the answers to so many questions. How had Seren met Oliver? How did she know she could trust him? He'd see, when he met him, that Oliver was a lovely man who Frankie had treated really badly.

A tractor suddenly appeared around a corner, hay bales towering on a trailer behind. Seren almost crashed straight into it. The high hedge scraped against her windows as she reversed to let it pass.

She tried to concentrate on the road; tried not to think about Oliver; the way his fingers had felt on her skin the day before, his lips on hers, the way he'd taken her face in his hands as she left him. 'I think I'm falling in love with you.' Seren ached with longing to see him again.

Daniel would like him, she knew he would. Seren was sure that Oliver would make Daniel understand about Frankie. Understand the kind of woman he was dealing with – unstable, violent, not worth giving up his marriage for. By the time her mother returned from Rome she was sure her father would be back at The Windmill, begging Nesta to forgive him, and their life together would resume again.

The text arrived just as she'd decided she was half way there. She stopped the car in a gateway to a field hoping it would be from Oliver to tell her that he'd got her message about meeting him at the pub instead of the train station.

Her heart plummeted when she saw it was from Griff's school.

'Griff has had an asthma attack practising for sports day. Don't worry he's recovered now but to be on the safe side could you pick him up.'

Briefly Seren thought of asking Nesta to pick him up but remembered that of course she couldn't. Daniel? No.

The sky was very dark now and large drops of rain began to splatter on the windscreen as she turned the car around. A sudden clap of thunder made Seren jump and then the rain began to pour.

Disappointment weighed her down, but she thought of Griff waiting for her in his classroom. He hated having attacks at school, all the other children staring, all the fuss. He'd want to be with her at home, safe, as soon as possible. She sighed; she'd simply have to tell Oliver she couldn't make it.

Frankie

Rain ran down the windscreen like tears as the car moved slowly up the congested high street. The temporary traffic lights glistened in the distance and the sky cracked intermittently with jagged lightning forks. People scuttled down the pavements searching for shelter. No one noticed the woman in the car.

The sound of the wipers was almost hypnotic, dulling Frankie's senses and making it increasingly hard to formulate a plan. For the umpteenth time she took off her seatbelt and inched her hand towards the door handle she knew she couldn't open.

His hand gently pulled the belt across her stomach and clicked it back into place.

Frankie couldn't look at him. She couldn't speak. Her migraine had subsided but the spinning hadn't stopped and she felt as though she might collapse at any time, although the thought of slipping into some sort of oblivion seemed like the best option. She closed her eyes and tried to take in everything that had happened since she had left the house an hour before.

As soon as she had turned out of her gate she had seen the police car. It had moved slowly up the street and parked in front of Daniel's Jaguar. Frankie lowered her head and started walking fast. At the top of the road she looked behind her and saw the broad back of the policeman enter the house. She turned the corner and took a short cut down a long cobbled alley that meant that she could cut out the high street completely.

The case was heavy; Dante struggled in her arms; and now the rain had started to fall.

She had desperately tried to work out when Daniel must have phoned the police. Had he texted the police station as

Seren told him everything she had found out? Had Seren called them before her visit and arranged for them to meet her at the house? What would they do? Arrest her? Have her sectioned again? She couldn't bear it; she couldn't go back to that awful hospital – the drugs, the psychiatrist, the other patients. Oliver had left her there for four months after she had lost the baby. It had been a living nightmare; no one had listened, no one had believed her.

'Why did you do it, Francesca?' She could still hear the psychiatrist's whispering voice. 'Why did you try to kill yourself and hurt the baby?'

When Oliver had finally collected her Frankie would have let him take her anywhere as long as she could leave the hospital.

The rain had grown heavy. Twice Dante had wriggled free but the alley was narrow and the walls on either side especially high. Frankie had managed to catch Dante and continue on. At the end of the alley she could see the long, low roof of the leisure centre and pool. Beyond that was the road to the station.

Frankie checked behind her and quickened her pace. Though the alley was deserted, she had a feeling she was being watched.

Thunder rumbled loudly overhead. Dante struggled again; he jumped out of her arms and slipped through a gap in a rotten door. Frankie called and called to him but he didn't come back. She peered under the door but all she could see was a backyard full of weeds and broken toys, no sign of Dante at all.

Her clothes were soaking now and water dripped from her hair into her eyes and made it hard to see. Frankie leant against the wall. She wanted to go home and see if Dante was there. She wanted Daniel. What was the point in running away from the man who had made her feel happy and safe? Hot tears mingled with the rain as she thought of never seeing Daniel again. Maybe it was time to be honest; if she told him everything surely he would understand? She brushed the tears away and took a deep breath. She couldn't leave him. Somehow she would make him see that she wasn't crazy. She picked up the suitcase and started walking back, retracing her steps, calling out for Dante in between the rolls of thunder.

As the rain become heavier Frankie lowered her head against it and began to walk faster. She didn't see the car until she was almost at the end of the alley. Her heart lifted at the sight of Daniel's Jaguar. He had come to find her and everything would be alright. She ran the last few yards and as the passenger door opened she slid in and turned to Daniel to apologise for running away.

'It's good to see you, Francesca.'

In an instant Frankie's hand was on the door handle, trying to open it and escape. He leant across and took her hand in his. 'Child locks are a wonderful invention. My friend who rents out these classic cars has to have them fitted on all his models.'

'Please let me go,' Frankie whispered.

The car pulled away from the kerb.

'I can't do that, Francesca. Not when I've organised such a lovely surprise.'

Nesta

The lightning lit up the sky on the horizon. Nesta peered through the rain-streaked window of the train and realised that the storm must be right over the town. The chickens would be terrified, but at least the garden would be getting a good soaking.

She sipped at her paper cup of coffee and wondered if she was making the right decision? Maybe she should go to Italy. There would still be time to catch the plane. She took the magazine with the article about Leo from her bag and let it lie unopened on her lap. She closed her eyes and thought of the new house she'd have to find and all the forms that needed to be filled in for the divorce. But most of all she thought of Seren. She put the magazine back in her bag and finished her coffee in one gulp. She was definitely going home, that was final; she couldn't spend the entire day going backwards and forwards on the train.

The tannoy announced that they would soon be approaching the station. Nesta picked up her phone. She'd just try Seren one more time before they arrived. As Nesta picked it up, it started to ring. She felt a surge of relief; at last Seren was answering her messages. But when Nesta held it to her ear it wasn't Seren's voice on the other end but Daniel's.

'I'm so sorry to call you,' his voice sounded shaky. 'I just don't know what to do.'

'What's wrong?' Nesta asked gathering up her empty coffee cup and its accompanying detritus and putting them into a bin bag that the conductor was holding out for rubbish. 'I presume you are delighted that The Windmill's sold so quickly.'

'What?' Daniel sounded confused. 'I don't know what you're talking about, Nesta.'

'Didn't the estate agent phone you?'

'I've seen that he's been trying but phoning him back has been the last thing on my mind.'

Nesta felt a wave of dread. 'Is it Seren? Has something happened to Seren? Or Griff?'

'No. It's Frankie. I can't find her.'

'What do you mean?'

'I mean she's gone, packed a bag and disappeared. I've been out looking for her and she seems to have just vanished into thin air.' His voice broke. 'Oh Nesta, I just don't know what to do.'

'So why are you phoning me? Do you think I've done her in and buried her under the azalea bush?' Nesta laughed. 'Or maybe you think we're running off to Italy together.'

'It's not funny, Nesta. It's my retirement meal tonight and Frankie is meant to be coming.'

'So you'd like me to accompany you instead?' Nesta was still smiling. 'Let me just check my diary and have a think about what I could possibly wear.'

'Nesta, please stop being flippant, this is serious.'

Nesta stood up and picked up her handbag as the train began to slow down. 'OK. Tell me what happened and I'll try not to refer to the list of reasons why your girlfriend running off is of no concern to me.'

'Just listen, please Nesta. I'm at my wit's end. I just need someone to talk to.'

Nesta eased herself down the aisle and tried to pull her suitcase away from the luggage rack. A young woman in front of her helped her get it down and Nesta thanked her before continuing, 'Alright Daniel, tell me from the beginning.'

'This morning Frankie was very ill in bed with a terrible migraine, she'd been ill since last night. Then a few hours ago Seren came round and told me things that she'd found out from Frankie's ex-husband, awful things about Frankie.'

'What sort of awful things?'

'That she had problems, some sort of mental illness, that she was violent, paranoid, delusional.'

'Do you think she's right?'

'There have been odd things happening – the note I told you about, a dead crow, someone stripped all the roses from around our door, my car was scratched, a dress I bought for Frankie was ruined. From what Seren told me it sounded like Frankie could be doing all these things herself.'

'Oh dear. It sounds like she needs professional help.' Nesta steadied herself as the train suddenly lurched to a halt just before the station.

'No. No, she doesn't.' Daniel took a deep breath. 'It wasn't her. I found out who was doing it. A policeman came round. He'd asked the neighbours if they'd seen anyone acting strangely near the house and the woman who lives next door said she saw someone cutting off all the rose heads.'

'Who was it?'

Daniel paused before he said very quietly. 'It was Odette.'

'Odette? Why would she do that?'

There was an even longer pause. Suddenly Nesta understood.

'Oh Daniel. How could you? I asked you if you were having an affair with her years ago and you told me that of course you weren't. You made me feel so awful for asking. If I remember rightly you told me she was uptight and difficult and that you pitied any man who got involved with her.' The women standing in front of Nesta turned around to look at her. She lowered her voice. 'You are unbelievable! Why I'm even talking to you I just don't know.'

'I'm sorry, Nesta. It wasn't a big deal. More of a brief fling, a one-night stand, well two nights, maybe three. Years ago. I had no idea she still had feelings for me. No idea she'd be so jealous about Frankie.'

'Honestly! My mother was right about you, she said you'd turn out to be a philandering fool.' The woman in front turned around again and Nesta turned to face the other way. 'I don't know why I didn't leave you years ago. And I don't know why Frankie wants to get involved with you at all. Maybe she's seen the light and realized she deserves someone who might at least be faithful to one woman.'

'Please Nesta, I know I treated you badly at times and I'm sorry, but I just want to find Frankie. I love her so much, Nesta, I really do.'

The train lurched forward again and slowly pulled up to the platform.

'OK,' Nesta sighed. 'I'm coming home anyway. Come round and I'll try my best to help.'

Seren

The kitchen lights flickered as another rumble of thunder drowned out the sound of the rain on the roof.

'Please can I go to Oscar's birthday party?' Griff looked up at Seren imploringly as she grated the cheese.

'Let's see how you are this afternoon.' Seren sprinkled the cheese over a slice of bread. 'Mrs Williams told me it was quite a bad asthma attack that you had.'

'I'm better now,' Griff took a deep breath. 'See, no wheezing.'

'Eat your sandwich, have a little rest and see how you feel at four o'clock.' Seren pressed the top slice of bread down and cut the sandwich into four triangles.

'Please Mum, I'm fine, it was just that stupid relay race we had to practise over and over and over again. I told Mrs Williams it hurt to run but she said it was my arm that was broken not my legs.'

A flash of lightning lit up the room. Seren peered through the window and saw her father's car moving slowly down the drive through the torrential downpour. It stopped outside The Windmill. She wiped her hands on a tea towel.

'Here's Grandad.'

Griff's face lit up. 'Will he play chess with me?'

'Maybe. Sit down and eat your sandwich and I'll put the kettle on. He's sure to want a cup of tea.'

Seren heard the car door slam and then she heard another door slam. He must have brought bags with him. She tried not to get her hopes up as she filled the kettle but she couldn't help the feeling of relief building inside her. Was her father coming home?

Twenty minutes passed. Griff had finished his sandwich and was on to a bowl of strawberries. Seren emptied the teapot and put the kettle on to make a fresh pot.

'When's Grandad coming?' Griff asked.

'Soon, I expect. Maybe he's waiting for the rain to ease off before he comes over.' Seren peered through the window again. The lights in The Windmill went on one by one until the whole tower was illuminated. Another peal of thunder was followed by another flash of lightning and all the lights went out. Seren's kitchen was also plunged into gloom and the sound of the kettle stopped.

'Oh no,' groaned Griff. 'Now what am I going to do? I wanted to watch television.'

Seren ruffled his hair. 'There are plenty of things you can do without electricity.'

Ten more minutes passed. Seren and Griff sat at the table and played I Spy. The lights still hadn't come back on and there was no sign of Daniel.

Seren had been looking around for something beginning with F for quite some time.

'I give up,' she finally said.

'Flood,' Griff grinned. 'Look at the garden.' Seren looked up and saw that half the lawn was now under water, there was also a rapidly expanding puddle around her father's car on the drive.

'I think I'll just go over and check that Grandad is OK.' She stood up and took Tom's old Barbour jacket from a peg beside the door.

'But it's my turn to choose again,' Griff said.

'I think you're definitely the I-Spy champion of today.' Seren slipped into the jacket. It was much too big for her. 'Go and have a rest. Read your book.' She bent down and kissed Griff's cheek.

'That coat smells of Dad,' Griff said.

Smiling, Seren wrapped the coat tightly around herself and

stepped out into the rain.

Frankie

In the semi-darkness of the room Oliver's face looked like it
was carved in granite. Frankie tried to press herself against the
back of the chair to relieve the pressure of the tip of the knife
against her chest. Without moving the knife Oliver crouched
down in front of her.

Frankie shut her eyes and waited for the pain. She could feel
his breath on her cheek. She tried to free her wrists but he had
taped them to the arms of Nesta's wooden bedroom chair so
tightly that she couldn't move. She opened her eyes and saw
herself reflected in the dressing table mirror. She tried to make
herself look calm.

He pushed a fraction harder with the knife. Frankie could
hear her heart thumping.

'I could do exactly what you did to me, Francesca. I could
stab you. I could leave you in agony. Right here in this room.
Not caring if you live or die.'

The pressure of the knife increased.

'Please set me free,' Frankie whispered.

Oliver leant forward and briefly brushed her forehead with
his lips.

'I wouldn't have had to tape you to the chair if you hadn't
kept trying to run away.'

'I promise I won't run away if you'll just untie the tape.'

Oliver slowly shook his head. 'I know I can't trust you,
Francesca. However much I want to.' For a few moments he
was silent. He stared unblinking into her eyes. 'Do you
remember the blood? So much blood all over the floor. All over
us.'

'I was frightened,' Frankie said.

Oliver took the knife away from Frankie's chest and stroked

her cheek. 'Shhh.'

'You were going to hit me. You raised the mallet above my head. I thought that you were going to…'

'Shhh.' Oliver repeated, and pressed his fingers to her lips. 'I would never have hurt you.' He leaned forward and kissed her mouth. Frankie twisted away but Oliver held her face firmly between his hands. 'You'll learn how to love me again. You always had to learn. I was the only person that could help you when you got things wrong. I still love you, I can still help you.'

'I, I didn't do anything wrong. I, I never…' Frankie stuttered.

In an instant the knife was at her throat. 'Didn't do anything wrong? Don't you remember all the men, Francesca. All the men you looked at, flirted with? I know now that you must have been sleeping with them all.'

'I told you over and over, there were no men. I never looked at other men.'

The knifepoint pressed a little further. 'Don't you remember why I had to get the mallet?' Oliver narrowed his eyes. Frankie tried again to move her arms. 'Does the name Samuel Brookes ring any bells?'

Frankie didn't answer.

Oliver stood up, moving to stand behind her, staring at her reflection in the mirror. He ran the knife blade lightly up and down the back of her neck. 'Samuel Brookes,' he repeated. 'Owner of the Furness Gallery. The man you were planning to have an affair with. The man I found you in the studio with. The man you arranged to meet when you thought I would be out.'

'No,' Frankie shook her head. 'All he did was come round to see the paintings for the exhibition. He came a day early, otherwise I would have told you he was coming. You didn't need to slash my paintings, you didn't need to hurt me.'

Oliver tutted in disbelief. 'It was just like all the other times, all the other men. Just like the man who fathered your child.'

Frankie stared at his face in the mirror. 'Is that why you pushed me down the stairs? Because you didn't think the baby was yours?'

'Pushed you down the stairs?' Oliver took the knife away again. 'I would never have pushed you down the stairs. You were so wracked with guilt you threw yourself down them. After that I thought you'd change. I thought the doctors in the hospital would make you better.' He touched her hair. 'So short now. We should have cut it before. All that long hair – it made you look like a prostitute. We should have cut it all off years ago and maybe then the men would have stopped looking.' He ran his hand lightly over her head and then suddenly grabbed a clump of hair and pulled so hard that Frankie winced. 'Except they didn't stop looking, did they?' He twisted her head side to side. 'That's right, Francesca, even with all your hair cut off *Daniel* looked at you. *Daniel* wanted you.'

'Why have you brought me here, Oliver?'

Oliver seemed to relax and let go of her hair. He dropped his hand with the knife in it to his side and looked around the circular room. 'To The Windmill?' He smiled and seeing him in the mirror Frankie remembered how he'd looked when they first met, the smile that had made her glow inside, the smile she had loved. 'Because it's our new home. I've bought it for us with all the money I've made for us while you were away.' His smile turned into a grimace that Frankie also remembered all too well. 'You always wanted a nice house, Francesca. This is nice, isn't it?'

'But it's Daniel's house,' Frankie whispered.

Oliver smiled again.

'He doesn't need it any more. He is going to let us live here now.'

'Please Oliver, don't.'

'What? Don't you want to live here?' His eyes narrowed. 'Oh, I know what it is. You don't you want to be reminded of the family you tore apart? Because the truth is you didn't just

269

ruin my life, Francesca. You ruined Daniel's poor wife's life, his poor daughter's, his innocent little grandson's.'

Oliver suddenly yanked her head back so that she was looking up at him.

'That is what you do, Francesca. You ruin lives, Francesca. Right back to your parents and your brother. They never would have had a car crash if you hadn't been such a stroppy teenager. Refusing to come out with them for dinner, throwing a tantrum, telling them you hated them, upsetting them so that your father couldn't concentrate on the road.' Oliver made a sad face. He was holding up the knife again. 'Do you remember telling me how guilty you felt about it when we first met? How it haunted you. You had nightmares all the time.' He drew the knife lightly down her cheek. 'You hurt people, you always have. And now you're running away from Daniel, just because he's found out all about you. You could have stayed and had a proper adult discussion about it, tried to explain, made excuses. But no, true to form, you run away. Poor Daniel, he'll be hurting now, just like I was.' He pressed the tip of the blade just below her eye. 'But now we're back together, you'll soon learn. You can never run away from me. I'll always find you, Frankie Hyde. I love you far too much to let you go.'

Oliver suddenly pressed harder and Frankie gasped as the knife pierced her skin. In the mirror she could see a trickle of blood run down her cheek. 'Oh dear,' Oliver picked up a scarf hanging from Nesta's dressing table and began gently wiping Frankie's face. 'You seem to have cut yourself.'

Thunder crashed outside. Oliver walked over to the window and looked out.

'What a magnificent view. Even in a storm it looks fantastic. We're going to be very happy here for a long long time.'

Oliver came back to Frankie and gently lifted up her chin to examine the knife wound. He dabbed it with the scarf again. 'You need a plaster for that cut. Shall I go and search for a first-aid kit?' He moved towards the door. Lightning suddenly lit up the room and in the mirror Frankie saw the door open to reveal a figure on the other side, a woman with long wet hair and an oversized coat. For the briefest second Frankie thought that maybe Seren was there to assist Oliver, but lightning flashed again and in the bright whiteness Frankie could see the horror on Seren's face.

'What the hell are you doing here?' Oliver's voice was angry.

Seren didn't speak; she seemed to be frozen. Frankie thought that Oliver was going to push her so that she would fall back down the stairs. Instead he grabbed the baggy coat and pulled her into the room. He shoved her roughly onto the bed and waved the knife in her face.

'I thought you weren't going to nose around in other people's lives any more.'

After a few dazed moments, Seren seemed to find her voice. 'You're mad. I heard you, Oliver, I heard you through the door. You're absolutely mad. You've used me to get to Frankie. I can see how stupid I've been; I should never have got in touch with you.'

Oliver grinned. 'But I thought you'd rather enjoyed it. I thought you liked me,' he gently pushed a damp curl from her face with the tip of the knife. 'I liked you. But I couldn't let Francesca get away again. Not once I'd found her. You see Francesca is my angel, my muse. All my sculptures, they are all her.'

'I'm sorry, Frankie.' Frankie could see Seren's reflection in the mirror. 'I didn't realise what you'd been through. I had no idea what Oliver is like.'

'Shut up,' Oliver barked. He reached into his jacket pocket for the roll of tape and taking both Seren's wrists in his hand he tried to bind them together. She started to kick out at him, one foot hit him between the legs and he dropped her wrists and shouted out in rage. In a second Seren was at the door trying to open the latch but the sleeves of the coat were too long, falling

271

over her fumbling fingers slowing her down. Oliver pulled her back onto the bed and held her down, the knife at her throat this time.

'Let her go,' Frankie shouted and struggled once more to free her wrists. She began to rock the chair backwards and forwards, pushing at the dressing table with her feet to get more leverage. The chair fell backwards and Frankie twisted round to try to bite through the tape at her wrists.

'Oh no, you don't,' Oliver was across the room in a second, picking up the chair, pushing it into the dressing table so that the edge of the table dug into Frankie's stomach, pushing the knife hard against the back of her neck. In the mirror, Frankie saw Seren running for the door again.

'You leave this room and I will cut her.' Oliver's voice was very calm.

Seren reached for the latch. Oliver drew the blade across the side of Frankie's neck. She cried out as she felt pain and something wet and warm dripping down her back.

Oliver turned around to Seren. 'Sit back down on the bed or I will cut her again.' Seren hesitated.

He drew the knife across the back of Frankie's T-shirt, slashing through the fabric and pressing the tip of the knife just below her shoulder blade.

In the mirror Frankie watched Seren sit back down.

Nesta

The rain had eased to a steady drizzle and the leaden sky had lightened to a gloomy grey. The taxi driver dropped Nesta at the gate and she trudged up the drive dragging her suitcase; it seemed much heavier than when she'd left that morning. She saw Daniel's car sitting in a large puddle and her heart sunk further. Was this how it was going to be? Every time Daniel had a crisis he would run back to her for help. Demoted from wife to agony aunt. Anger started to rise inside her; it grew as she realised she'd have to wade through the large puddle to reach the front door. She took off her shoes. They were new, bought specially for Italy, removing them seemed to finalise her aborted journey. The fine gravel of the driveway hurt her feet.

Inside the kitchen she turned on the light switch. Nothing happened. She sighed and called out Daniel's name. He didn't answer. Nesta padded bare footed into the living room and peered across the soggy lawn at The Wheat House. It looked dark and empty but she could see Seren's little green van parked at the side. She assumed that Daniel must be in The Wheat House with their daughter and wondered how much he would tell her about Odette's vendetta. Would he tell Seren about their little fling?

'Fling!' Nesta said the word out loud and tried the living room light switch. *Fling, fling, fling* she muttered to herself. *Did you never think your bloody flings would come back to bite you, Daniel Saunders?*

She knew she ought to go over and see them. See Seren especially. Daniel would be sure to be telling her about the offer on the house. Nesta picked up her wellington boots, she'd need them to get across the flooded grass. Suddenly the effort of slipping her damp feet into the boots seemed too much. It was

273

all too late; too late to protect Seren and Griff, too late to help Daniel, too late to find Leo. She stood in the middle of the room, the boots still in her hand. Leo had been a fantasy, a pipe dream, a way of coping with her broken heart.

Her heart ached, her whole body ached. She let the boots fall to the floor, flopped down in an armchair and closed her eyes. She was in a bath, hot and scented, a cup of tea in her hands, music playing on an old wind-up gramophone. She lay back into the bubbles and she was nineteen again and very much in love with Daniel.

The crash woke her with a jolt. She sat up. The sound had come from above. There was another noise, a thump, then silence. She closed her eyes again. Maybe she had imagined it. Her feet were cold now. The dream came back to her.

'A dip in the bath is what you need, girl.' She said out loud the words her mother used to say after a long night lambing on the farm; though the farmhouse's rusty iron bath-tub and lukewarm inch of water were a long way from what Nesta had in mind.

She stood up and heard a car draw up outside. Opening the door Nesta was surprised to see an identical blue Jaguar parking just behind Daniel's car. She watched as Daniel got out of the second Jaguar and started walking around the first.

Nesta called to him. 'What's going on? I thought that was your car?

Daniel shrugged and came towards her. 'I assume it belongs to the chap who's made an offer on the house. The estate agent phoned and asked if he and his wife could look round earlier than arranged – the bloke had to get back to London this afternoon and the agent had a meeting so he couldn't come with him. I said it was OK to give them the key.' He gave a weak laugh. 'Funny him having a blue E-type too.'

Nesta folded her arms. 'You could have told me they were looking around. I heard noises upstairs; I had no idea that it was him. I was about to go up to have a bath.'

'Sorry,' Daniel mumbled.

Nesta noticed how exhausted he looked. 'You'd better come in.'

Daniel stepped inside. 'A cup of tea wouldn't go amiss.'

'You're out of luck. The lightning has taken out the electricity.'

'I think I'll get a glass of whisky then.' Daniel headed for the understairs cupboard where his whisky collection still lay neatly lined up on the shelves. 'I just don't know what to do about Frankie. She's nowhere to be found, she's not answering her phone. You don't think Odette had laid some trap for her before she was arrested? Do you think that I should phone the police?'

He opened the door and took out a bottle of Scotch.

'Honestly, Daniel,' Nesta had taken out a glass and was opening a bottle of wine. 'I don't see why you expect me to help you after everything that's happened. You haven't even asked me why I'm not on my way to Italy.'

'I know, I know, and I'm so grateful to you for seeing me.' Daniel took a glass from the dresser. 'Why aren't you on your way to Italy?'

Nesta sighed. 'I really can't be bothered to explain it to you now.'

Daniel sat down and put his head in his hands. 'I'm just demented with worry about Frankie. I need to explain to her about Odette. I think she thinks I thought she was doing all those things herself.'

Suddenly another loud thump came from upstairs. Daniel sat up and looked at Nesta. 'What the hell are they doing? Throwing the furniture around?'

Nesta peered up the circular staircase. 'Maybe we should go and check that they're OK.'

Daniel stood up. 'Come on then. I'll go first.'

Seren

Her face hurt. She tried to move her lips but it was no good, the tape across her mouth was very tight. Her eyes searched the circular room looking for some way of escape. She thought of Griff all by himself in The Wheat House. She hoped he remembered that his asthma pump was in the dresser drawer. She hoped more than anything that he wouldn't come and look for her.

Please help me, Tom. Seren closed her eyes and the words went through her mind over and over again. She could smell Tom on the jacket and with her eyes tight shut she could almost persuade herself that he was beside her on the bed, trying to free her wrists from the elaborate iron headboard. *Tom, Tom, Tom.* However hard she tried, her thoughts couldn't block out Oliver's voice.

'I'm going to have to teach you a lesson, Frankie. Just a little lesson to stop you leaving me again.'

Frankie's mouth had been taped too. He'd done it when Seren had thought she heard a car stop at the top of the drive and had started to shout. Frankie had started to shout as well and that was when he got the tape out again.

With both women bound and gagged he had gone outside to the telescope and peered down the drive. He came back inside.

'Your mother's home, Seren. Looks like her little holiday has been cut short.'

Seren tried desperately to wriggle free. Oliver sat down on the bed beside her and gently stroked her face. 'Lie still like a good girl while I think of a plan.' He got up and walked over to Frankie. 'Still bleeding, Francesca?' He wiped his fingers through the blood that oozed from the shallow cut across the back of her neck and then rubbed the blood into her cheeks like rouge.

'Whore,' he whispered, and bent to kiss one bloody cheek. Frankie flinched away. Oliver laughed. 'I love you.' He went back onto the balcony.

Seren and Frankie stared at each other through the mirror.

This time Oliver was away a long time. Frankie began to rock the chair. Seren watched the balcony doors. The sun was pushing through the grey clouds glinting on the brass on the telescope like Morse Code. There was no sign of Oliver. Frankie looked at Seren again and Seren nodded her head. Frankie's rocking became more violent, until the chair fell on its side with a crash that resonated around the room. In an instant Oliver was back. He righted the chair with a bang on the floor. Seren could see the vibration go through Frankie. He turned the chair so that Frankie was facing Seren and then the knife was in his hand again.

'You women must learn to behave,' he said, his voice was no longer calm. 'You're making me get cross.' With one swift movement he slashed Frankie's T-shirt down the front so that it gaped open, revealing her bra.

'And you're making me do these awful things.' Oliver's voice grew louder until he was shouting. 'I'm not a bad man. I'm not, I'm not. You make me bad when you don't do what I say. When you try to leave me.' He stopped shouting and when he next spoke his voice was just a whisper. 'Don't leave me here alone.' His voice trembled and he sat down on the bed, his whole body shook. 'Please don't leave me. Don't make me do bad things again.'

Seren saw his mouth twist and thought that he was going to cry. She tried to mumble reassuring sounds through the tape across her mouth. With a sudden roar Oliver turned and plunged the knife into the outsized Barbour jacket. It missed Seren and went through the waxed fabric and into the mattress below. Oliver left the knife in place and went back outside. Seren could see him looking through the telescope again.

277

Frankie was crying. Tears streaking the blood on her face, silent sobs shook her body.

Tom please help me. Seren closed her eyes.

At the rattling of the latch her eyes sprang open and she looked at the door, willing her mother not to open it.

It swung on its hinges and her father stood in the doorway, his eyes darting from Seren to Frankie. Her mother's face came into view behind him and then they both rushed into the room.

'My God! What's happened?' Daniel didn't seem to know which woman to go to first.

Nesta rushed to Seren, trying and failing to free her hands, 'Hold on, darling. I'm going to go and phone the police.'

In an instant Oliver was back in the room. Nesta and Daniel shrank back against the wall as he ripped the knife from Seren's coat with an explosion of feathers from the duvet and started jabbing it at both of them alternately, narrowly missing their faces.

'Sit on the floor,' Oliver bellowed.

Nesta sank down against the skirting but Daniel lunged towards him, attempting to grab his arm. The knife came down at lightning speed into Daniel's shoulder and Seren watched her father collapse in pain. It seemed that at exactly the same instant she saw Griff on the other side of the room. He was standing at the doorway to the balcony, white with fear, his hand against his mouth. She realised he must have come up the outside staircase. With wide eyes she shook her head and he vanished.

Daniel was groaning, slumped against Nesta. A dark stain growing on the sleeve of his shirt. Oliver had his arm around Frankie, holding her against him. He smiled.

'It's lovely to meet you, Mr and Mrs Saunders. This is my wife Francesca. I believe you've been informed about our offer on your beautiful house.'

Frankie

A shaft of sunlight illuminated Daniel and Nesta on the floor. It highlighted the dark red stain growing rapidly on Daniel's new linen shirt. His eyes were shut but Nesta's were on Frankie's. Daniel opened his eyes and looked straight at Frankie. She was aware of all the blood on her face and neck, her bound arms and the gaping T-shirt and exposed bra. She tried to tell Daniel how much she loved him with her eyes, how much he needed to hang on.

Oliver stood beside her, passing the knife between one hand and the other, occasionally using it to scratch abstract marks into the veneer on the dressing table. He seemed uncertain as to what to do next. His eyes were much too bright as they darted around the room with increasing speed; they seemed to have become too wide, unblinking, they'd taken on a frenzied look. His jaw twitched and every few seconds he made a hissing sound between his teeth.

'Seren and I know a good way to pass the time,' he said suddenly. 'We like to share our secrets. Deep, dark secrets no one knows about. It's fun, isn't it, Seren? Lots of interesting things come out.' He took a step away from Frankie's side towards the bed. Frankie seized the opportunity to lash out with her foot, aiming for Oliver's calf, hoping it might give Nesta a chance to get away and phone for help. But Oliver avoided her kick and turned the chair back to the dressing table, pushing it in again so that her legs were immobilised.

He turned to Daniel. 'I'm sorry about my wife.' He bent down and kissed the top of Frankie's head. 'She has a temper.' He gestured at Seren. 'Not like your daughter. She's always trying her best to please.' He laughed. 'Though underneath she's just a whore like Francesca here. A whore like my mother.

Double-crossing, double dealing. Hiding things from the people who love her most of all.'

'No,' groaned Daniel.

'What don't you like?' asked Oliver calmly. 'The way I talked about your daughter or the way I talked about my wife or the way I talked about my mother?'

'You are a lunatic,' Daniel's voice was stronger. 'The police will be here very soon to lock you up.'

Oliver shrugged. 'I'm sure you're right. I can see that I've been forced to go a little bit too far and I may have some explaining to do, but in the meantime I thought your daughter might like to tell you her secret, Daniel.' He glanced at Seren whose eyes were widening. 'I'll have to speak for her as she can't seem to get the words out for herself at the moment. You might discover that she has almost as many secrets as you, Daniel?' The last sentence was a question. Oliver shook his head slowly and smiled. 'But I doubt it.'

Frankie glanced at Seren. Seren's face had drained of colour. She was staring at a crack on the ceiling high above her as though trying to escape into it.

'Now, where to start? Arlow was it?' Oliver directed the question at Seren. When she didn't answer he shouted, 'Arlow Laverne,' very loudly. Frankie jumped, while Seren looked at Oliver with pleading eyes. Oliver's voice dropped. 'Yes, Arlow. He was the father of your baby, wasn't he, Seren? The baby that you never dared tell your parents about.'

Nesta let out a gasp.

Oliver's mouth turned down in mock sympathy. 'Poor Seren, giving birth on a cold winter's night in rural Wales. Abandoned by her boyfriend, her parents thousands of miles away. Only her God-fearing grandmother for support. A woman who had found the only way she could think of to make sure that baby was born *dead*.' Oliver paused to let the word sink in and then continued. 'Rhiannon they called her in the hospital, but you had wanted "Sophie" hadn't you, Seren? Sophie, how very fashionable. But no one listened, no one cared about the teenager who had found herself in trouble. A half black baby as well. Tut, tut. Who gave a damn what name you wanted on the grave?'

Frankie watched the mother and daughter staring at each other, pain working its way across Nesta's face as she listened to Oliver's words.

'Oh *cariad*,' Nesta whispered. 'My poor sweet *cariad*. Now I understand.'

Nesta

Now it all made sense.

'I wish I'd known.'

Nesta wanted to take Seren in her arms, hold her, give her daughter the comfort she should have given her so long before. But Daniel's weight against her was increasing; he seemed to be losing blood very fast. She shifted slightly and Daniel's head fell against her chest. He groaned and she stroked his hair. The blood was running down his arm, seeping over his watch, trickling down his hand and dripping from his fingers onto the carpet. Nesta looked around, trying to work out what to do. She heard a noise outside. A shuffle, a scrape. A shadow fell across the threshold of the balcony door and then was gone.

Oliver didn't seem to notice. Nesta wondered if the best thing was to keep Oliver talking, keep him distracted so that he didn't go outside.

'I could have done something to help Seren,' she continued, looking up at Oliver.

He crouched down in front of Nesta and scratched his head with the point of the knife. 'And what would you have done, Mrs Saunders?'

'I would have looked harder for Arlow for a start.' Nesta looked at Seren as she replied. 'He should have taken his share of the responsibility.'

'And do you think Daniel would have helped you find him?' Oliver sneered. 'Would he have encouraged the two love-birds to get back together again?' Oliver leant forward a little. Nesta could feel his breath on her face as he finished his last sentence slowly. 'To *sort things out*?'

Nesta tried to turn her head from Oliver. 'Of course. Whatever Seren and Arlow had argued about can't have been that bad. They were only young.'

Oliver got down on all fours and lowered his face to Daniel's, which had now slumped to Nesta's lap. 'But Arlow wasn't so young that he couldn't understand what he had witnessed, was he?' Oliver's face was almost touching Daniel's.

Seren twisted on the bed, the headboard banged against the wall. Oliver smiled. 'Oh dear, Seren is getting upset, Daniel. I don't think she wants to hear the truth. She told me what Arlow had accused you of all those years ago. She didn't believe it at the time, she still doesn't want to believe it now.'

'Stop, please stop.' Daniel's voice was very weak.

Oliver suddenly stood up. 'Stop what? I thought you had denied it. You told Seren that Arlow was making it up. You told her you'd heard he was taking drugs, stealing cars, that he had another girlfriend, that he was a no-good, lying layabout and a waste of space.'

'Did you say that about Arlow?' Nesta looked down at her husband. She stopped stroking his hair. 'Why? You were so fond of him. You used to give him lifts home, chat to him for ages in the car outside his house.'

Oliver started twirling the knife in his hand. 'I'm sure that Daniel was only too keen to take Arlow home.' Oliver shook his head. 'But not to sit chatting outside his house. He was keen to get into the house, keen to catch a glimpse of Arlow's mother. A pretty, blonde, single mother, in her little council house, vulnerable and all alone. I can imagine how tempting it must have been for you, Daniel. I can imagine how you battled in your head to walk away; your daughter's boyfriend's mother – such a risk.'

Daniel groaned.

'But you couldn't resist, could you, Daniel,' Oliver laughed. 'I imagine wonderful, wild, abandoned afternoons in bed while Arlow was at school. No intention of ever leaving Nesta, though you probably said you would. I expect you made all

283

sorts of promises you couldn't keep.'

Nesta felt Daniel shift beneath her, she moved her hand from his forehead and thought about Arlow's sweet young mother and how sorry she used to feel for her.

'But then disaster!' Oliver sat down on the bed beside Seren and looked at her. 'Arlow finds your father in his mother's bed.' He clapped his hand over his mouth. 'My goodness, what a shock. He rushes round to your house. What did he want? Comfort, condolence, sympathy? Who knows?' Oliver shrugged. 'But what did he get? Disbelief, rage, hysteria probably. You couldn't believe that your perfect father could do such a thing? Arlow must have got it wrong, he was making it up, he was crazy. What a row you must have had.' Oliver stood up and theatrically walked to the bedroom door. 'Arlow storms out.' Oliver slammed the door. 'You probably cry.' Oliver mimed tears. 'But after a few hours you begin to think it might be true.' Oliver walked to the balcony doors and peered down the drive. 'You wait for Daddy to come home.' He turned around to face the room. 'You ask to see him in his study. You tell him what Arlow has said. He denies it all and that is when he tells you the awful things he's found out about Arlow – the drugs, the numerous girlfriends. He's even found out that Arlow has been stealing cars. You should never have been with him, what a terrible mistake his little girl has made.' Oliver sat down on the bed again and stroked Seren's hair. 'But never mind, because you are off to college in London and Daddy's off to meet his grandchild in Australia, and Arlow and his mother can rot in hell for all Daniel cares.'

Nesta felt sick. She remembered how Daniel had persuaded her to make that trip longer, how he'd tempted her with romantic brochures about Fiji, Singapore and India. 'Let's make it the holiday of a lifetime,' he had said. 'Like a second honeymoon,' he had said. Anger swelled in her chest at his deceit.

She looked down and saw that blood was seeping into her

skirt. Daniel's head was very heavy now and, looking down, Nesta saw that he'd lost consciousness. She wondered if there was any way she could get to the balcony to shout for help. She looked over to the doorway. The shadow was there again. It moved and Nesta was certain that there was someone standing against the outside wall.

Seren

Please don't die, please don't die. Seren didn't want to think about the things he'd done, she just didn't want her father to die. *Tom, don't let him die.*

Maybe they would all die. Maybe Oliver would kill them one by one. Only twenty-four hours ago she had been in his arms. He had seemed so kind, so caring. She'd trusted him. How could she have been so wrong? *Sorry Tom, I'm so sorry.*

She thought of Griff's terrified face at the doorway. Where was he now? What was he doing? *Help him, Tom.*

She looked at her mother. Nesta's face was drawn and pale. She seemed to be staring intently at the balcony as though watching something, but when Seren looked in the same direction she saw nothing but the railing and the trees and the sky. The sky was blue now as though there had never been a storm. The colour of it seemed ridiculous – bright Walt-Disney blue, the blue of hope and cheerfulness and nothing bad ever happening in anyone's world.

There was a noise outside the bedroom door and suddenly Oliver was hacking through the tape on Frankie's arms with the knife. He looked at Nesta.

'Sorry, Mrs Saunders, but my wife and I are withdrawing our offer. We've gone right off circular rooms, much too difficult to furnish.' He pulled Frankie to her feet and pushed her forward, the knife at her back.

Seren watched her trying to hold her ripped T-shirt together, as if modesty really mattered now.

'We'll go out through the outside stairs, I think.' He shoved Frankie towards the balcony just as the bedroom door burst open with a bang.

'Stop. Police.'

Seren saw the flash of a warrant card, the barrel of a gun. 'Put the knife down or I'll shoot.'

Oliver turned, his face twisted with surprise, then shock, then something that looked like fear. He took hold of Frankie's arm and started to pull her through the door, the knife waving wildly in the air. The policeman was advancing towards him, the gun pointed at Oliver.

'Let her go or I will shoot you.'

Frankie put her hands out so that she was clinging to the door frame; Oliver tried to pull her harder.

'Let her go,' the policeman was shouting.

Oliver let go of Frankie's arm and ran out onto the balcony, leaving her behind. The policeman pushed past Frankie and was outside in an instant, his gun still pointed at Oliver.

Oliver was at the telescope now, he swung it so that it careered around, hitting the policeman in the side, stopping him in his tracks, sending him sprawling backwards. Oliver ran towards the steps. From the bed, Seren could no longer see him.

The policeman struggled to pick himself up from the ground, clutching his ribs, trying to pick up the gun which had skittered across the ground in front of him. For the first time Seren properly saw his face. Arlow!

Seren heard a siren far away and then a scream. Long and drawn out, fading downwards into nothing. She didn't need to have seen what had happened to know that Oliver had fallen down the steps.

Frankie

Daniel opened his eyes. The nurse smiled down at him. Daniel struggled to sit up.

'There, there, Mr Saunders. You lie down and rest.' She adjusted the cannula in his hand. 'You've lost a fair bit of blood but we're managing to top you up nicely.'

'Frankie?' Daniel murmured.

'I'm here,' Frankie took his other hand. 'I'm right beside you.'

'I'll leave you two alone,' the nurse pulled the curtain round the bed and her footsteps echoed down the ward.

'What happened? Where am I?' Daniel's voice was weak.

'It's alright, you're in the hospital. They've treated the knife wound and you're going to be OK.' Frankie stroked his hair back from his forehead. Her neck hurt as she moved her arm, the stitches the young doctor had put in felt tight.

'Are you OK?' Daniel looked up into her eyes.

Frankie nodded. Her neck hurt again.

'The note, the roses, the bird, the dress. I'm so sorry that I didn't believe you. It was Odette, I...'

'Shhh. I know. Nesta told me. It's alright.'

'And Oliver?'

'He fell down the steps. He broke both his legs but he's in police custody now.'

Daniel closed his eyes. 'Thank God,' he whispered. Then his eyes opened and he looked up at Frankie as though he'd suddenly remembered the things that had been revealed in the room. He gripped her hand. 'I've done awful things, Frankie. I've upset my daughter, upset my wife, my family. Upset those other women.' His head twisted on the pillow. 'I don't know why I did it. I was selfish, foolish... I wanted...' He searched for words. 'I wanted… I don't know what I wanted.'

Frankie tried to calm him. 'It doesn't matter now.'

'You know I'd never hurt you, Frankie,' his grip on her hand tightened. 'Say you know that, please.'

'I know.'

Daniel released her hand and closed his eyes again. Frankie watched his breathing slow and deepen until he slept.

She looked at the beautiful long fingers that she'd noticed the first time she'd met him on the train, his silver hair that always seemed to have a life of its own. She gently took his hand in hers again and thought about Odette and Arlow's mother and Nesta and Seren and all the lies he'd told.

Trust, the word sprang into her head and with it the image of her A-level history teacher from school, a quiet Scottish woman who always managed to get respect from her pupils.

'Trust is the glue that binds us together,' she had told her class. 'If you lose that glue things quickly begin to fall apart.'

Suddenly Daniel's eyes were open.

'I love you, Frankie,' he whispered.

Frankie lifted his hand to her lips and kissed it and then Daniel was asleep again. A lump formed in Frankie's throat, she swallowed, and felt the pain more sharply in her neck. She gently eased her hand away from Daniel's and wondered what she really wanted.

Twenty years spent in fear of Oliver; living with him and then running from him. Nearly the whole of her adult life shaped by one man.

Frankie let out a long sigh.

Earlier, as she had waited to be treated in A&E, a policewoman had taken a statement. Frankie lay on a hard mattress, shifting awkwardly on a long strip of paper towel, the wound on her neck throbbing underneath the dressing the ambulance men had put on. The policewoman had asked so many questions. How long had Frankie known Oliver? Did Oliver have a previous history of aggression? Had Frankie reported him to the police before? Frankie tried to answer; she'd spent so many years bottling it all up, it was hard to get the words to come out.

'I need to ask you one more question,' the policewoman said as the doctor hovered beside the bed and a nurse began to prepare a tray of implements.

Frankie prepared herself for the inevitable, 'Why did you stay with him?' She knew the young woman would never understand the hope she'd carried with her every day. The hope that the abuse would stop. The hope that the funny, kind and caring man she loved would learn to control the demons that kept changing him into the monster. The hope that she would learn how to help him. And, of course, the paralysing, incapacitating fear.

Instead the policewoman asked, 'Do you know why Oliver Williams would have been so violent during the course of your marriage? He'll need a psychiatric report before he goes to trial and it might help initially to have a bit of background.'

Frankie had looked up at the buzzing striplight on the ceiling, remembering Oliver's father; a man beaten down by life, trying to bring up his only son in a run-down towerblock in Leeds, his wife long vanished, his heart broken. Had Oliver learned to hate women there? High up in that flat that smelled of stale bacon fat and cigarette smoke and disappointment. Frankie had only met Oliver's father once, just days before he'd injected himself with an overdose of the drugs he'd been prescribed for his fast-advancing cancer. Oliver's behaviour had been so much worse after his father died.

Frankie looked up into the policewoman's kind eyes. 'I spent many years trying to work Oliver out, feeling sorry for him, making excuses for what he did, how he behaved. I never understood.' She shrugged. 'What makes any of us behave the way we behave? What made me stay with him for so long? What made me think I had to hide?'

The policewoman had touched Frankie's arm and smiled.

'You don't have to hide any more.'

As Frankie sat at Daniel's bedside she thought about the policewoman's words. She stood up and moved to the window of the ward; the sky was still blue though a dusky pink smudge on the horizon heralded the sunset. She remembered all the things she'd planned to do when she was growing up, all the places she'd wanted to see. Africa, Mexico, Thailand, Japan. She'd planned to go to India for a gap year before college, she'd been going to paint her way around the country. She'd been fearless then, never imagining the awful things that could happen in life to stop you in your tracks.

She looked back to Daniel and watched the rise and fall of his chest under the hospital blanket. He looked frail but his breathing was strong, the colour on his cheeks returning. A single salty tear slipped down her face and stung the knife wound just below her eye.

'I need to stop hiding,' she said quietly. 'I need to come out into the open and find out who I really am.'

Nesta

The suitcase lay where she had left it by the door, and the opened wine bottle still sat untouched on the worksurface.

Nesta filled her glass and looked at the clock on the wall. Nine o'clock. She should have been in Italy by now.

She toasted the clock. *To life – to what happens when you're busy making other plans.* She tried to remember who had said that originally, had it been one of The Beatles? The Devil's boys, her mother used to call them, 'I doubt they've ever sung a hymn in their lives.' Nesta took a large gulp of wine and tried not to think about her mother, the resentment she felt towards the long-dead woman was too much. The thought of Seren up on that bleak hill farm, pregnant, frightened, then grieving for her baby. It was almost unbearable for Nesta to think about. Another surge of anger hit her, this time at Daniel. She took a bigger gulp of wine. It tasted very warm, the colour of it matched the dark stain that Daniel's blood had left on her skirt. She thought about the bath she'd never had and topped up her glass.

There had been so much commotion earlier with the police cars screaming up the drive, the ambulances arriving in a screech of brakes on gravel. The police officers and paramedics had been like ants pouring all over The Windmill, radios crackling, shouting instructions at each other. Now they had all gone and, apart from the ticking of the clock, the house was silent. Nesta had never felt so lonely in her life.

At least Ben was on his way. He said he would be there by half ten. 'I'll belt it up the motorway.'

Nesta had smiled. 'Not too fast, we've had enough drama round here today without you crashing your car.' She'd tried to explain what had happened.

'Save it, Mum, you can tell us when we get to you. Don't worry about a thing.' Nesta wondered what Ben had meant by *us* and *we* as she Skyped her eldest daughter in Australia. Anni had been getting breakfast when Nesta had got through. Intermittent screams and jumping children erupted from behind Anni's shiny face on the computer screen.

'Oh God, Mum, this isn't a good time. The baby's nappy is full to bursting, Mike's off to Darwin for a two-day conference and the cat's been sick in his hold-all, and the boys are arguing over who plays Angry Birds on my phone.' Anni turned around and shouted, 'Put the phone down now before you bloody break it.' She turned back to Nesta. 'Can you call back round 8 a.m. your time?

'No darling, this is important. Your father is in hospital.'

'Oh God,' Anni's hand flew to her mouth. 'Was it his heart? That is so common when men retire. They just drop down dead from heart attacks almost immediately. I met this woman at a kids' party last week whose father-in-law…'

'No Anni, it's not a heart attack. He was stabbed.'

'Oh God. Stabbed? Was he mugged? Nowhere is safe now in Britain. I heard a programme on the radio last week about the rise of street crime across the globe, and the UK was…'

'He wasn't stabbed in the street. It was in The Windmill, in our bedroom actually.'

'Oh my God, you had intruders! You so need a burglar alarm, Mum. I'd be terrified without mine on at night. Anyway why was Dad in your bedroom? Don't tell me you're back together – why didn't you tell me?'

Nesta suddenly felt very tired. It all seemed much too complicated to explain.

'Actually, Anni, I think there's someone at the door, I'd better go. I'll phone you, like you said, at 8 a.m. my time tomorrow. Don't worry about your father. I phoned the hospital half an hour ago, he's going to be fine. And no, we're not back together. Frankie's with him at the hospital and Seren and Ben will go in in the morning, I expect.'

'You know I'd come over but like I said Mike has a conference, and even if he didn't I'd have to bring the kids as Mike can't cope with them on his own, and his mother's hit the bottle again so she can't help out, and the air fare for us all would cost a fortune, and if Dad's basically OK...'

'Don't worry, darling. I'm sure we'll all survive without you.'

Nesta drained her glass and looked out of the window to The Wheat House. She wondered what Seren and Arlow were talking about. They'd been on their own now for over an hour.

After the police had taken her statement Nesta had changed out of her blood-soaked skirt and had gone over to help Seren with Griff's tea. Amazingly Griff hadn't seemed at all shaken by what he'd witnessed, only excited by his part in it.

'When I saw that crazy knifeman stab Grandad, and I saw that Mum and Grandad's girlfriend were all tied up, I knew I had to phone the police. I went back down the steps and I ran across the garden quick as I could and I tried to dial 999 but the phone was broken because of the lightning. So I got Mum's mobile and worked out that the passcode was her birthday numbers, and then I phoned 999 on that and told the lady who answered what was happening and then, straightaway, there was that policeman at the door, and I told him about the knifeman and the policeman ran up onto the balcony to have a look, and then he came back down and got his police badge and gun from his unmarked police car and ran into the house. And then I heard all those other police cars coming and then I heard the knifeman scream when he fell down the steps.' Griff was almost jumping up and down on his chair with excitement as he told his mother and grandmother the story. The scrambled eggs Nesta had made for him were getting cold. 'Are you sure Grandad's going to be alright?' he suddenly asked.

Nesta and Seren reassured him and then he was off again

about how he'd told the lady on the phone it was very important that lots of policemen came and that there would need to be an ambulance as well.

Griff had just got into his pyjamas and was drinking hot chocolate at the kitchen table when Arlow had poked his head through the window.

He grinned. 'I think the police have finally decided to drop the charges against me for impersonating a policeman.'

Griff's eyes had widened. 'I thought you were a policeman.'

Arlow had laughed. 'Well, kind of, but let's just say I took early retirement.'

'Are you some kind of Superhero then? Like Batman?'

Seren ruffled Griff's hair. 'Come on, sweetheart, finish your hot chocolate. It's time for bed.'

'Any hot chocolate left for me?' Arlow asked and winked at Griff. 'It's what gives us superheroes extra strength.'

'Of course, come in,' Nesta opened the kitchen door and Arlow stepped into the room and looked at Seren. 'Are you OK?'

'I need to get Griff to bed,' Seren said without looking at Arlow. 'Then I think I'll go to bed. It's been a very long day.'

'Could we talk?' Arlow shifted awkwardly from one foot to the other. 'While I was on the balcony, trying to think what DCI Zac Jones would do in a hostage situation, I heard what Oliver was saying about what happened to you... What happened to us.'

It was at that point that Nesta had taken Griff by the hand and taken him to bed. When she had returned to the kitchen Seren and Arlow were sitting opposite each at the table in silence.

Nesta poured them both mugs of hot chocolate and remembered them as carefree teenagers who used to come home to her after school, hungry for her homemade biscuits and cocoa to dunk them in. Now they looked as though all the cares of the world were on their shoulders. She asked Arlow if his ribs were OK after being hit with the telescope by Oliver. He took a deep breath in and winced dramatically. Then he grinned.

'Actually they're not that bad, a bit tender but I'm sure I'll live. One of the paramedics took a look at them and said they were just bruised.'

'I have arnica,' said Seren getting up and going to the dresser drawer. 'It's very good for bruises. Do you want to try it?'.

'Thanks,' said Arlow. 'That would be great.' Nesta watched them smile at each other and discreetly made her excuses and returned to her house.

Now she wished she had stayed at The Wheat House, at least until Ben arrived. The house began to creak. Nesta still felt Oliver's presence within the thick circular walls. She'd never be able to sleep in her room that night, maybe never again.

Nesta's heart jumped at the sound of loud knocking at the door. It burst open.

Trevor and Edmond pushed their way simultaneously into the room, Edmond brandishing a tower of strawberry meringues and Trevor holding out a plate of chocolate éclairs and brownies.

'International Cake Rescue Services,' cried out Edmond dramatically.

'Here to assist you in your time of need, madam,' Trevor gave a little flourish of a bow.

'Less wine more cake,' Edmond said pushing aside Nesta's glass to make room for the plates. Nesta laughed.

Trevor sat down beside her. 'We heard what happened.'

'The whole town heard what happened.' Edmond put the kettle on.

'What a shock!' Trevor took Nesta's hand. 'Who'd have thought that Frankie would have such a pyscho ex-husband? *And*, OMG, Odette!'

'Never trusted her,' Edmond wrinkled up his nose. 'All scraped back hair and a mouth like a cat's bottom.'

296

'And she was far too snooty about our cakes,' said Trevor. He put on a French accent. '*In my home town in France our macaroons are twice that size.*'

'Apparently she was going to poison the cake we'd made for Daniel's retirement party,' said Edmond. 'The police found weedkiller in a syringe in her handbag!'

'Probably a staple ingredient in her home town in France,' sniffed Trevor. 'What did Daniel ever see in her? '

'And to think all the time she was a bunny burner,' said Edmond.

'Bunny boiler,' corrected Trevor.

'Whatever. We thought the news about Odette was enough excitement for us for one day – who'd have thought that a real life Midsomer plot was unfolding over here.' Edmond took down three mugs from the dresser. 'We'd just arrived at the hotel for Daniel's retirement meal when we heard the police cars go past.'

'And the ambulances,' added Trevor.

'He was all for following,' Edmond said with a tut of disapproval. 'Boys in uniform and all of that.'

'Don't start, darling,' Trevor scowled at him. 'Anyway, it sounds like the lovely Arlow saved the day.'

'He was given his police badge and the gun when *Island Beat* ended,' said Nesta through a mouthful of éclair. 'Luckily he had kept them in the glove box of his car and was able to fool Oliver into thinking they were real.'

'What a hero,' the two men sighed in unison.

Nesta laughed and licked cream from her fingers. 'Well, you two are my heroes now,' she took another large bite of éclair. 'Just what I needed.'

The door opened again and Ben appeared.

'You did drive too fast!' Nesta scolded, and then noticed another figure behind her son.

'Suki!' she exclaimed. 'What a lovely surprise.'

'Hello Nesta,' Suki's face was glowing with happiness. Ben

put his arm around her.

'Suki was over from Ireland, and she'd come round to get the last of her things from the flat tonight.'

'When Ben got your phone call I just had to come with him to make sure everything was alright.' Suki grinned. 'We've had a long chat in the car on the way here.'

Ben was grinning too. 'We're going to give it another try together.'

'Well, I think that is the best thing that's happened to this family for a very long time,' Nesta said, and got up to give them both a hug.

Seren

They had hardly touched the hot chocolate. The mugs sat between them, getting cold. Seren stood up and switched on the kitchen light.

'I'm so sorry you had to go through all of that alone, Sez.' Arlow watched her as she sat back down. 'If only I'd known you were pregnant.'

Seren sighed. 'What would we have done? We weren't ready for a baby. We were only kids ourselves.'

'Maybe it could have worked out; if everything else had been different, if your dad and my mum had managed to keep their hands off each other, if I hadn't found them together, if I hadn't been so angry…' His voice trailed away. A moth fluttered around the light bulb above them.

'If I'd believed you,' added Seren.

'You could have got in touch?' Arlow said quietly. 'I could have helped you. We could have gone through it all together.'

Seren looked up sharply. 'I didn't know where you were. You and your mum left pretty fast.'

'But I sent the letter? With our new address and phone number and the charm for your bracelet.'

'What letter? What charm?'

'The heart?'

Seren shook her head. 'I never got it.'

They both sighed.

'Daniel,' Arlow said.

'Dad,' echoed Seren.

They fell into silence again. The moth had stopped fluttering and everything was very quiet.

Seren picked up the mug in front of her; the hot chocolate had formed a wrinkled skin.

'I'm sorry that every time you've tried to talk to me I've been so…'

'Rude,' said Arlow.

Seren looked up at him indignantly. 'I was going to say dismissive.'

'No worries,' Arlow smiled across the table. 'It's nice you're being a little bit more civil now.'

Seren looked down at the mug again trying to hide her own small smile. 'Won't your wife be wondering where you are?'

'Ex-wife, you mean.'

Seren looked up. 'I thought you were still married.'

'Didn't you see it in the press? It was all over the newspapers at the time. TV detective's wife has affair with his TV sidekick Sergeant Bannock.'

Seren shook her head.

'Well, if you happened to be trawling through the gutter press last year you would have found out that my marriage ended in a very public altercation between me and Sergeant Bannock in a bar on Harris, which unfortunately took place in front of several paparazzi photographers. I think that was when the BBC decided to scrap *Island Beat*.' Arlow drummed his fingers against the side of his mug and Seren remembered how he used to do that when he was upset. He sighed. 'Now there's talk of an *Island Beat* spin-off called *Bannock's Beat* and my ex-wife and the said Sergeant are getting married next month in a castle on the Isle of Lewis. Which, ironically, is where my ex-wife and I first met.'

'Ouch!' Seren winced.

'At least Chez is happy. She's very excited about being a bridesmaid.'

'Chez?'

'My daughter. I'd love you to meet her. I'm sure she and Griff would get along. He's a great kid.'

Seren smiled. 'Thanks.' She twisted her mug in her hands. 'I'm sorry about your marriage. That must have been hard.'

300

'We were never right for each other. Angellica played my love interest in the early episodes of *Island Beat* and we just sort of got swept up in the roles. But you're right; it has been a hard year. I've lost my wife, my job, my home and I don't see Chez nearly enough.'

'Have you got another acting role lined up?'

Arlow peered into his mug as though he might be reading tea leaves.

'Nothing much. An offer of a role in a new detective drama set in a remote Cornish town,' he made a face. 'And a soap opera is apparently putting out feelers about me for a role as a policeman with marital problems.' Arlow rolled his eyes and Seren laughed. 'My agent wants me to try Hollywood. He says they love the British at the moment, but I just don't want to be away from Chez for too long.'

'So what will you do?'

Arlow shrugged. 'I thought I might just hang around here for a while. Keep renting the cottage for a few more months, catch up with old friends.'

'There's not many around. Most people we knew from school have moved away.'

Arlow grinned. 'Except you.'

Seren bowed her head, letting her hair fall round her face, hoping that Arlow wouldn't notice the tears that had been building up all evening and were now threatening to fall.

'It's alright to be upset,' he said. 'You must have been terrified. I know I was pretty scared myself.'

'I just can't believe I was so deceived by Oliver. He seemed so normal, so nice. I believed all the things he told me about Frankie. I even believed that he cared about me.' Seren shivered and the tears spilled down her face. 'I've been so stupid. I was so determined to prove that Frankie was bad, that she'd bewitched Dad. I never knew that Dad had had other women in the past, I never knew about the affairs. Even when you told me about your mum I didn't believe you could possibly be telling me the truth. I thought my parents were the perfect couple, with the perfect life.'

'I remember,' said Arlow quietly. 'You always had them on a pedestal, especially your dad.'

'When I realized I was pregnant I felt like I had let them down; they'd given me everything and I'd messed up. After I came home from Wales I couldn't leave.' Seren's voice fell to a whisper. 'I just wanted to be at home. I wanted to feel safe. I didn't want to mess things up again.'

Arlow reached across the table and touched her hand.

'You didn't mess things up,' he said.

Seren pushed the hair back from her face and wiped her eyes with her fingers. 'I think I married Tom because Dad liked him so much, he practically pushed us together. But I did love Tom. He was kind and dependable. I knew he wouldn't hurt me or betray me.' Her eyes flicked up to Arlow's face. 'That he would be faithful to me.'

'I was always faithful to you, Sez. Whatever your father told you.' Arlow laughed. 'And I never stole a car in my life.'

'And the drugs?' Seren asked.

Arlow shrugged, 'Maybe, but I never inhaled.' They both laughed and then were silent.

Seren looked out of the window towards the lights of The Windmill. She could see figures entering the kitchen, her mother standing up and hugging someone she realized must be Ben, and then her mother hugged a smaller figure that she couldn't quite see.

'Looks like my mum is having a party over there,' she said.

'Do you want to go?' Arlow asked.

'No. I really don't feel like facing other people tonight.' She bowed her head again. 'Why did my dad lie to me?'

'Because he was frightened that he'd lose you if he admitted the truth.'

Seren looked up at Arlow. 'But to lie about you – just so he could hide his seedy affair with your mum.'

302

'It wasn't seedy on my mum's part. She thought she'd found the love of her life. She adored him and he broke her heart. That's why we moved away so quickly. After I found them in bed that day your dad ended the relationship immediately, dropped her like a stone. My mum was devastated.'

Seren shook her head. 'I feel like I don't know my father at all. I always thought of him as kind and now I realize he doesn't care who he hurts to get what he wants.' She put her head in her hands. 'I don't know if I can face going to see him in the morning.'

'I could come with you,' Arlow said. 'Maybe not into the ward. It might give him a heart attack if he sees me coming, but I'll drive you to the hospital and wait till you come out.'

Seren smiled at him. 'You don't have to do that.'

'I want to,' he said quietly.

Seren looked down at Arlow's slender brown fingers that were now entwined with her own, as though their hands were twenty steps ahead of their emotions.

'What will you do?' Arlow asked.

'What do you mean?'

'Do you have any plans?'

'For now?'

'Forever?'

Seren sighed. 'Well, I won't be meddling in anyone else's life again for a start. Especially my father's.'

'Anything else?'

'I'm not sure.' Seren looked through the window again. A slice of moon hung above The Windmill like a question mark among the stars. Seren turned back to Arlow with a shrug. Arlow grinned at her.

'Maybe you're finally ready.'

Seren looked at him. 'Ready for what?'

'Ready to leave home.'

One Year Later

Frankie

For hours the train had inched its way through densely packed palm trees and giant creepers. Frankie concentrated on her pencil sketch of the wizened old man opposite her until the light changed and she realised the dense greenery had opened out into grassy open spaces interspersed with villages of sugar-coloured houses and corrugated iron churches. The aroma of late afternoon cooking wafted through the open doors and windows of the carriage – a mix of herbs and spices and cooking oil that reminded Frankie she hadn't eaten since lunchtime. She took a little parcel from her rucksack and unwrapped five slices of papaya that she'd saved from breakfast at the tiny hotel in Madurai. The sweet juice dribbled down her chin and the wizened man opposite grinned toothlessly at her as she tried to mop it with the sleeve of her shirt.

Later she craned her neck out of the window, enjoying the feel of the warm wind in her hair as she waited for her first glimpse of the ocean. Then it appeared, at first just a brief flash of turquoise through the trees and huts, but soon the train track began to run alongside a long white beach; huge rollers crashed onto the sparkling sand.

She waved at a group of children splashing in the water while their mothers banged their washing against wooden boards. The children waved back at her and tried to run alongside the train. Soon they gave up running but they kept waving until they were tiny smudges on the sand.

Frankie sat back in her seat. This was it. This was the end:

the most southerly point of India was only a few hours away. She flicked back through her sketchbook. It was thick with watercolour sketches, drawings, postcards, labels, fragments of fabric, even a piece of chipped paint that had drawn her eye on the pavement in Varanasi. The book was a visual diary, there were four more like it in her rucksack; three thousand miles of memories from a journey that had started in Kashmir and was nearing its end in Kerala. Frankie had zig-zagged her way across the country by train, by car, by boat and sometimes by foot. The experience had been a heady mix of smells and colour and sounds and people.

She had been welcomed by strangers, shared jokes with women who could not speak her language, had been taught cricket by their barefoot children and taken into homes and treated like a queen. She had been jostled by great crowds at stations, seen young men hanging on for their lives outside train windows, their shirt tails billowing in the wind. She had seen dead bodies by the tracks. She had gazed at tall glass buildings and gated driveways and she'd left her shoes outside crumbling temples and marvelled at the golden statues inside. She'd slept in shacks and hotels and guesthouses. Once she had spent a night under the stars with a group of Australian backpackers smoking joints and eating jalebi.

Frankie knew she would never be the same again. She even looked different. Her hair was long and thick and chestnut brown, only the tips were blonde now. Her body was golden from the sun, plump from good food. She hadn't had a headache since she had arrived in India.

'*Chai, garam chai,*' the tea seller pushed his trolley down the aisle. Frankie shook her head as he passed and thought about how much she missed an ordinary cup of English tea.

She looked out of the window again as the train moved slowly through another village. A group of men squatted in a circle on the dusty ground, smoking cigarettes and playing cards. They looked up to watch a group of girls walk past them; the girl's brightly coloured saris fluttered in the breeze like butterfly wings. Frankie quickly sketched the scene; it would make a good painting.

At Heathrow she had bumped into a gallery owner who used to exhibit her work long ago. When she explained where she was going he had asked to put on an exhibition of paintings inspired by her trip when she returned. Frankie had been hesitant at the time but now she could imagine the vibrant canvases depicting lively street scenes, snatches of life and colour and happiness.

The last time she'd contacted Daniel at an internet café he'd told her that the whole house was nearly finished.

'Dante and Rossetti love it,' he'd said via a shaky Skype link. 'Lots of sun coming through the windows for them to lie in.' Later he'd emailed her a picture of them, happily curled up together as though they'd never been apart. Frankie wondered if she and Daniel could be like that; could they go back to the way things had once been between them?

'Don't wait for me,' she'd told him at the airport.

'There's nothing else I can do,' he'd replied. 'I love you.'

Frankie had looked at him for a long time. 'You do know that I don't know when I'm coming back?'

As the train began to slow down for the station Frankie looked out of the window and saw that the sun was setting, a bright red sphere sinking into the ocean. The sky was streaked with pink and purple and the first star shone in the dusky sky. Another day in India was drawing to a close.

Soon decisions would have to be made.

The train drew into the little station. Frankie stood up. For the briefest second her heart lurched as she thought she recognised the tall blond man on the platform, then she relaxed as she realised it was just another European tourist. There was no longer any need to hide.

As she was jostled off the train by her fellow passengers she could see the beach stretched out in front of her. The waves were calmer here, the water gently lapping along the shore. Fishermen were tying their boats to a little wooden jetty, bringing in their catches. Frankie watched them as they jumped between the multi-coloured fishing vessels, hauling in their nets, taking down the huge, white, billowing sails. She decided that in the morning she would sketch them setting out to fish again and afterwards she would dive into the sea and swim.

Seren

The roses smelt of England. Seren pushed them one by one in between the eucalyptus leaves in the china teapot, and then she turned the pot around to make sure the display was even.

'I think you're meant to say something all the time,' Griff said.

'And be looking at the camera,' added Chez.

Seren looked up at the two children. Their milkshakes had left chocolate moustaches on their lips.

'I'll never get it right by tomorrow,' she sighed. 'Maybe I'm not cut out to be a TV presenter.'

'Have another go, Mum,' Griff said kindly. 'You were good at the beginning.'

Seren took the roses and eucalyptus leaves out of the teapot and started again.

'Hello.'

'Smile,' said Griff. Seren smiled as broadly as she could at her audience.

'My name is Seren and I'm here to show you how to make a beautiful and unusual display for the tea table.'

With one hand she picked up the empty teapot. 'What could be more quintessentially British than a vintage teapot.' She picked up a rose with her other hand. 'And old-fashioned roses.' The petals fell off the rose and onto the breakfast bar. 'Damn!' she exclaimed.

Griff shook his head, 'Mum! You can't swear on afternoon TV.'

Chez giggled.

'I give up,' said Seren. 'I'll phone up the producer of *Heart of the Home* and tell her my flower-arranging item was a terrible idea.'

'Hey Sez, don't give up. You're a natural.' Seren hadn't noticed Arlow standing in the doorway. He walked across the vast expanse of kitchen and put his arms around her.

Seren reached up to his cheek and kissed him. 'How was your day at the hospital, Dr Amery?'

'Exhausting. There was a terrible explosion at the local shopping mall. Multiple injuries, the emergency room was total carnage. I was just about to save the life of a boy who had been trapped underneath a vending machine when the director yelled Cut. They've decided to have a re-write and instead of a shopping mall explosion it's going to be a fire in a basketball stadium.'

Seren smiled. 'Do you need a glass of wine to recover?'

Arlow nodded. 'A big one, I think. I'll just go and get changed and maybe we could sit out by the pool together.' He walked around the work surface and put an arm round both of the children.

'How was school?'

'Fine,' they chimed in unison.

'Homework?'

They both shrugged.

'Go and get it done right now,' Arlow feigned a stern expression. 'When it's finished you can have a swim.'

'I need a cookie,' said Chez.

'I need a jelly sandwich,' said Griff.

'Cookie! Jelly!' Arlow laughed. 'You two have only lived here for a few months and you're already sounding like all-American kids. Let's go and get your books out to see what you're meant to be doing, then we'll talk snacks.'

He ushered the children out of the room with a backward grin at Seren. 'See you on a sun lounger in ten minutes.'

Seren heard Chez's voice as she went down the corridor, 'I've got Math to do.'

'Math?' Arlow sounded horrified. 'I'm assuming you mean Maths!'

Seren swept the soft pink rose petals into her hand from the work surface and sniffed them. She was immediately transported back to the garden at The Windmill. It seemed impossible that she was now so far away from the home she'd never thought she could leave.

Beverly Hills was like another planet – everything was so big and shiny and new – though the real estate agent had told them that their house was one of the older and smaller condominiums she had on her books. Seren still felt swamped by the size of the kitchen and the three ensuite bathrooms in the Spanish-style house in the quiet cul-de-sac where everyone worked in film or TV and drove enormous 4x4s.

Angellica, of course, lived in one of the newer, larger condos in Beverly Hills: two pools, a gym, a sauna and a hot tub. It had once belonged to Brad Pitt, a fact that Angellica took great delight in mentioning every time Seren and Arlow dropped Chez at the house. She also liked to name-drop the long list of celebrities she'd met at The Ivy, or at premieres she'd wangled her way into with her Ralph Lauren model boyfriend Jake, ten years Angellica's junior and as far as Seren could work out, completely monosyllabic.

Angellica Chadwick's marriage to Sergeant Bannock had failed almost as soon as the ceremony had finished. The wedding took place on the same day as the disastrous ratings for the pilot episode of *Bannock's Beat* were published. Within days of their return from honeymoon Angellica announced she was leaving the now ex-Sergeant Bannock and that she had accepted a role as an English journalist in *Cut and Paste*, a sitcom about a women's fashion magazine. Arlow had discovered via a Twitter posting that she was taking Chez with her.

It had seemed like a whirlwind at the time to Seren. One minute she and Arlow had been getting ready for Christmas with the children in a cold and drizzly England, and then, within weeks, they had all been uprooted and planted in the heat and sunshine of Los Angeles, where Arlow was lined up for the role of Dr Amery in popular daytime hospital drama *Stent*.

Seren looked through the patio doors at the turquoise pool glinting in the afternoon sun and the garden overflowing with plants and flowers. It looked like an oasis.

With a sigh she turned away to throw the rose petals in the bin and wondered for the hundredth time why she had ever agreed to present a weekly five-minute flower-arranging slot on *Heart of the Home*. She had met the show's producer Carmen Carvella standing beside her at a school baseball tournament. Somehow, in between wincing as Griff failed to catch the ball again, and marvelling at the beautifully straight teeth and ample cleavages around her, she had started chatting with Carmen.

Now she wished she'd never told Carmen about her flower arranging skills or Stems, 'Your cute little flower shop in Enga-land,' as Carmen liked to describe it.

She turned back to the idyllic scene outside and thought about the months to come. It didn't matter if she made a fool of herself on some daytime home-improvement show; it might be fun, or at least something to tell Nesta when she next spoke to her on the phone.

Arlow reappeared dressed in swimming trunks. He feigned an American drawl as he walked up behind Seren.

'Hey! Quit daydreaming. Where's my wine?'

Seren felt him put his arms around her.

'I'm sorry. I was so busy being happy that I forgot.'

'Don't worry,' Arlow murmured and nuzzled his face into her neck. 'You keep on being happy and I'll get the wine. What would you like? Orange juice?'

Seren nodded. Arlow kept hold of her, his hands gently caressing her waist. 'I thought maybe we could go out for dinner with the kids. Would you like that?'

Seren nodded again.

311

'Let's go to Spago and see if we can spot some stars.'

Seren laughed. 'We can send Chez back to Angellica with a few more famous names to impress her.'

Arlow laughed too and for a few moments they were silent. Arlow kept holding Seren, rocking her gently. He kissed her cheek.

'And I thought maybe we should tell the children tonight.'

Seren turned to face him.

'Don't you think it's too soon?'

Arlow smiled at her. 'I think it's the perfect time.'

'Do you think they'll be happy?'

'Oh yes.'

'I'll tell my mum next time I speak to her.'

'What about your father?'

Seren leant her face against the warmth of Arlow's naked chest. 'What would you like, a boy or girl?'

'Don't try to change the subject, Sez.' Arlow lifted her chin and looked at her. His expression was serious. 'That letter has been sitting, unopened, on the hall table for over a week.'

'I can't,' Seren twisted away so that she was leaning with her back against him. 'I just can't read what he has to say right now. But I will.'

'OK, I understand,' Arlow encircled her with his arms again and they stood silently for several minutes.

'Hey!' Arlow suddenly said. 'I've got a great idea for a place to visit when your mum comes over.'

'Disneyland? Hollywood Boulevard? Santa Monica Pier?'

'The Griffith Observatory.'

'That's a fantastic idea. She loves looking at the stars. And not just in an Angellica way.'

Arlow laughed. 'She'll certainly get a wonderful view of them from up there. She'll be amazed at how bright they look through that huge telescope.'

'It will be the highlight of her trip. And Griff and Chez will enjoy that too. They'll never believe those stars could be so far

312

away.'

Arlow held her tighter and kissed her cheek. 'Do you want to know something?'

'What?'

'I think the brightest star isn't very far away at all.'

'What do you mean?'

Arlow looked down and put his hand on Seren's stomach.

'I think, for us, the brightest star of all is here.'

Nesta

A lizard scurried across the warm paving slabs to escape the deluge as water arched over the flowerbeds, glittering amethyst against the setting sun. The smell of rosemary enveloped Nesta as she turned the hose on the urns that bordered the terrace. The pelargoniums bobbed under the droplets of water, sending up their own sweet citrus scent. Across the valley, the lights of the little bar and the houses came on one by one, transforming the hill-top village into a fairyland.

'I never tire of looking at this view.'

Nesta turned at the sound of the man's voice beside her. She smiled. 'I can imagine it would be very hard to tire of it; it's beautiful at every stage of the day, but especially at dusk.'

'I thought you might be ready for this,' he held out a glass of wine.

'Thank you, Leo,' Nesta leant forward and kissed his cheek. He took the hose from her hand and laid it down at the foot of a climbing rose; the water hissed softly into the soil. Leo put his arms around Nesta.

'Have you made your decision yet?'

'Shall we talk about it over dinner?'

'What is there to talk about? To my mind it's simple.'

Nesta looked at his kind smile, his bright eyes searching her own. Maybe it was simple, but she felt a twist of anxiety in her stomach. It should be simple but she couldn't give an answer about the future when the past still hung like a question between them.

Tomorrow, Nesta said it to herself every day. *We'll talk about it tomorrow.* But now it had been six months since Leo had miraculously arrived back into Nesta's life and tomorrow had still not come.

Nesta had been about to close the front door of The Windmill for the very last time. The removal van had taken the few bits of furniture and the chickens had been safely transported to the garden of the little flint-stone cottage she'd bought on the edge of town.

She had been the last to go. Her children were scattered across the globe: Seren in America, Anwen in Australia and Ben in Ireland with Suki. Even Daniel had left months ago for the seaside town where he had started to build a cliff-top house with which to lure Frankie back from India.

Nesta had stood at the open doorway, keys in her hand, looking out across the bleak winter garden; the frost hadn't thawed all day, everything was very still. The Wheat House stood looking blankly back at her; she let herself imagine Griff running up the garden to greet her. She ached to scoop him into her arms and hug him.

In the silence she became aware of the sound of footsteps on the gravel drive. She watched a man approaching, bundled up in a thick coat, hands in pockets, hunched against the bitter cold. His breath escaped in little puffs in the freezing air. She wondered if he was a friend of Cath and Claire, the lesbian couple who were buying The Windmill, one of their fathers, maybe an uncle? Nesta stiffened: images of Oliver flashed into her mind even though she knew he was in prison. The man came nearer. Nesta peered at him. There was something about his walk, the way his pale hair curled onto his collar, the weathered skin of his face, his smile as he approached. Nesta couldn't breathe.

He stopped in front of her.

'Hello Nesta.'

Nesta felt the ground shift beneath her. The next thing she knew she was sitting on the doorstep.

'I'm so sorry, I didn't mean to give you such a shock,' said Leo.

315

Some time later, when Nesta had recovered, she locked The Windmill's door and together she and Leo walked away, too submerged in conversation to look back.

She had taken him to her new house and among the packing cases, piled up gardening books and boxes overflowing with family photographs and mementoes, they had shared a bottle of wine and Leo had explained that he had seen an article about Arlow Laverne in a newspaper.

'*Island Beat* was a very popular programme in Italy, my late wife and I never missed it. The newspaper reported Arlow's daring role in a hostage drama, mentioning that it had taken place in a converted windmill. On a hunch I looked it up on the internet, I had a feeling it might have been your windmill, that it might have involved you.' He shook his head. 'But it was still a shock to see your name.'

Nesta looked at him.

'But that was months ago,' she said.

Leo shrugged. 'It's taken months to pluck up the courage. I never stopped thinking about you, Nesta, but I thought you might have forgotten me. I was nervous.' He reached across the packing case they were using as a table and took her hand in his. 'Though it seems ridiculous now I'm with you again.'

Nesta had smiled. 'I know.'

Within a week Nesta had rented out the flint-stone cottage to a newly married couple, who were keen to take on her flock of chickens as well, and moved to Italy.

Anwen thought her mother had gone crazy: 'You hardly know the man, Mum!'

'Go for it,' said Ben.

Seren simply told her mother it was up to her.

The first time Leo drove her up the bumpy track to his yellow farmhouse on the Italian hillside Nesta knew she had found paradise. Only one anxiety spoiled the exquisite happiness

316

she'd found.

They sat on the terrace to eat dinner. Leo had lit candles and placed them on the table and on the low stone wall around the terrace pond. The flames flickered in the warm air and fireflies began to dart and dance around the bushes. The stars were pinpricks in the wide, dark sky.

Leo placed plates of risotto in front of them and helped Nesta to salad from a terracotta bowl.

'OK, put me out of my misery,' he said, handing her a glass of Soave. 'Is it yes or no?'

Nesta took a sip of wine. 'I think life is lovely just the way it is.'

'You don't want more?'

She touched his hand. 'It's perfect. Let's not spoil it with formalities.' She paused. 'I need to talk to you about something else. It's…'

'But if you said yes,' he interrupted, 'we could be married in the town hall within a few weeks.' He pointed at the twinkling village on the hill. 'Just over there, not far to go. What about doing it the traditional way, arriving in that old horse-drawn cart of Angelo's. His wife always decorates the cart with such pretty flower garlands. We could have a party here afterwards. Get a band to play.'

'But what about the children? They wouldn't have time to come to a wedding.' Nesta lifted a forkful of risotto to her lips and put it down again. 'And I think we should…'

Leo took her hand in his. 'I'm sure they'd understand. And it's not as if I have any children to take into consideration.'

'Well, that's what I wanted to talk to you about.'

The next words felt reluctant in Nesta's mouth. Did she know for sure? After all, Daniel's mother had had red hair, one of his cousins too. She searched Leo's face as she had done so many times in the previous months; the green eyes were familiar, the determined chin, the easy smile, the good-natured disposition.

317

'We could go on a world tour next winter,' Leo continued, pouring out more wine. 'After the gardening season's over. I'd love to meet them. Anwen and Ben were only little when I last saw them. Seren wasn't even born.'

Nesta wondered if he ever did the maths.

'A world tour,' she finally said. 'It's a good idea.'

'By that time Ben and Suki's baby will be born.' Leo said through a mouthful of risotto.

Maybe there will be another baby too. Nesta was sure that Seren had something that she wanted to tell her.

'Wouldn't it be nice if we could meet your new grandchild as man and wife?'

Nesta sighed. 'You are very persuasive.'

'I could be a step-grandfather.'

She smiled, 'Oh Leo, you're wearing me down.'

He smiled back at her across the table. 'Good.'

They were silent for a while. Cicadas chirruped all around them and guitar music wafted from the village bar.

Nesta took another sip of wine. 'There's just this important thing we ought to talk about.'

'Look,' Leo suddenly pointed at the dark horizon. 'Venus is rising. She's very bright tonight. It's a sign, you'll have to marry me now.'

'You are an old Welsh fool,' Nesta laughed.

'I'm an old Welsh fool who loves you, Nesta. I was once a young Welsh fool who loved you and let you go. I'm not ever going to do that again, that's the most important thing.'

Nesta leaned across the table and kissed him. 'I love you too,' she whispered. The conversation could wait until tomorrow.

Leo looked up at the dark sky again and grinned. Nesta followed his gaze. The sky was streaked with shooting stars.

'I had it specially put on for you,' Leo said. 'It took some arranging, I can tell you.'

They watched as the bright meteors shot across the darkness

above them, over and over again.

'Are you making wishes?' Leo asked.

'Yes,' replied Nesta quietly.

When the meteor shower ended Leo reached out and took her hand again. 'I know what you want to talk about.'

'You do?'

Leo nodded. 'But you're wrong.'

Nesta looked into his eyes. 'Wrong?'

He nodded again. 'She's Daniel's daughter, Nesta.'

'But the dates. I think there's a strong chance that Seren is your daughter.'

Leo sighed. 'I told you my wife and I couldn't have children.'

'I thought your wife... I thought she must have been...' Nesta's voice trailed away.

'No. We had a lot of tests and the doctors told us it was me. I'm infertile.'

'Oh,' Nesta swallowed as she realised just how much she'd always wanted to believe that Leo was Seren's father.

Leo gave a small smile. 'It makes things simpler, don't you think?'

Nesta looked away. She couldn't look at Leo.

'I think I always wanted her to be...' Nesta blinked back unexpected tears.

'Hey,' Leo reached across and touched her cheek. 'Surely it's better that she's Daniel's daughter. From what you've told me it sounds like they are very close.'

Nesta looked back at Leo and shook her head. 'They're not so close these days.'

'Well, hopefully they'll rebuild their bridges.' He smiled at Nesta. 'Just think of the money some Beverly Hills psychiatrist would make if Seren had to come to terms with the fact that her father isn't her father and her real father is the man her mother has just married.'

Nesta took a deep breath. He was right. It made things

319

simpler. She didn't need him to be Seren's father and Seren definitely didn't need to have her life turned upside down more than it had been.

'The man her mother has just married? I didn't think I've actually said I'll marry you.'

'Shall I ask you again?'

Leo stood up and walked around the table to pull her up into his arms.

'Nesta, my beautiful Lady of the Night Sky. My Celtic cariad. My Garden Goddess.'

Nesta tried to push him away.

'Stop being so soft!'

Leo held her firmly in his embrace, he was laughing now too. 'Will you make me the happiest man in the universe and marry me?'

One more shooting star arched across the sky in front of them. Nesta wriggled out of Leo's arms and took his face in her hands.

'OK, you old Welsh fool. I will.'

Acknowledgements

I'd like to thank the wonderful team at Accent Press for publishing *Stargazing* and for all their help and enthusiasm. I would especially like to thank my lovely editor Rebecca Lloyd who has offered great wisdom, insight and guidance – not just with the manuscript! Thank you also to Teresa Chris, my agent, for her hard work, encouragement and support in all areas, both professional and personal. Many thanks are also due to my parents, Hugh and Biddy, who have always believed in my dreams of becoming a writer and are very good at reading through first drafts and correcting my terrible spelling and punctuation! I know that initially they were worried that this novel might have been about them and were greatly relieved to find that it is about other people entirely – I'll save their story for another time! I would also like to thank all my fantastic friends who keep me sane with laughter, tea, gin and copious amounts of camaraderie – I would be lost without you. Lastly a very big, very special thank you to my three wonderful children, Harry, Daisy and Tomos – they have been so patient with me, yet again, only asking *when will tea be ready* every ten minutes instead of five as I sit at my laptop, engrossed in writing, the smell of burning sausages filling the air! *Tea will be ready soon and I love you very much!*

Heartstones
Kate Glanville

Moving between contemporary Ireland and the 1940s, .in both past and present it seems that everybody has something to hide. When Phoebe's married lover dies in a car accident she dare not openly express her grief for fear of their affair being discovered. Heart broken she leaves England to search out the old boathouse bequeathed to her by her Irish grandmother. Amid the stunning scenery of the West Coast of Ireland she finds herself swept up by life in the nearby village of Carraigmore. When she discovers a collection of her grandmother's old diaries hidden beneath the boat house floorboards she becomes immersed in a story of family scandal, repressed sexuality and a passionate affair between her grandmother and a young Irish artist. As Phoebe tries to piece together the truth about her grandmother's past she begins to realise that the repercussions of what happened all those years before have shaped not only her own life but the lives of those in the small community around her. With many questions unanswered Phoebe sets out to find out more but it seems that no one in Carraigmore is quite telling her the truth.

A Perfect Home
Kate Glanville

This is the beautifully observed and poignant love story of a woman who has to find out if home really is where the heart is.

Claire appears to have it all - the kind of life you read about in magazines; a beautiful cottage, three gorgeous children, a handsome husband in William and her own flourishing vintage textile business.
But when an interiors magazine sends a good-looking photographer to take pictures of Claire's perfect home, he makes her wonder if the house means more to William than she does.

For more information about **Kate Glanville**

and other **Accent Press** titles

please visit

www.accentpress.co.uk